CRACKED
SURFACE

JOHN-MICHAEL LANDER

Copyright © 2020 John-Michael Lander
All rights reserved
First Edition

LucasLand Publishers
Kettering, Ohio

First originally published by LucasLand Publications 2020

Library of Congress Cataloging-in-Publication Data is available upon request.

Paperback: ISBN 978-0-578-68657-8
Hardback: ISBN 978-0-578-68658-5
E-book: ISBN 978-0-578-68659-2

Library of Congress Control Number: 2020907903

Available in hardcover, paperback, e-book, and audiobook

Printed in the United States of America

ALSO BY JOHN-MICHAEL LANDER

SURFACE TENSION (Surface Series)

SPANDAU BALLET (Series)

LIFE'S A BEACH

I would like to dedicate this work of art to Nathan, my soul mate and life partner. Thank you for keeping me grounded and showing me, I can follow my dreams.

Thank you to the following people for their encouragement, support, and reading many drafts: Nathan Webber, April Audia, Merle Yost, Stacy Emoff, Paulette Noxon, Cheryl Mellon, Charlie Chadwick, and Karen Boston Editing and Proofreading. Also, Thanks to Illa and M.T. Taylor, Mike and Judy Webber, The Pikas Family, Leland "Buddy" Goldston, Jr., Brent Cary, Corrie Johnson, Lisa Moser, Nanette O'Neal, John Antoni, and Kary Oberbrunner.

A Special thanks to Bella, Barkley, Bryn, and Bailey.

Thank you for your influence and encouragement: Patricia Nell Warren, Robin Reardon, and Leanna Renee Hiebert.

A Special Thank you to my mom, Sally Lander.

*Sometime you only
know after you get
back that you have
been on a long
journey.*

Merle Yost
merleyost.com

PROLOGUE

UNIVERSITY OF CALIFORNIA, IRVINE. 1982.

Am I dead?

My eyes blinked several times and spheres of green, brown, and blue with some yellow swirled and created new hues in a mosaic kaleidoscope.

I couldn't feel my hands or feet.

Focus.

My eyes throbbed as a blade of grass with a single dewdrop took shape in front of my nose. Other green blades appeared as my scope expanded and I determined I was in a yard or grassy area.

Where am I? How did I get here?

I mustered enough strength to roll onto my back. Electricity shot up my spine. Above me, a lamppost softly glowed as the night sky ceded to morning.

What time is it?

I forced myself to sit up, sending a new sensation of pain running from the depths of my stomach, down each leg, and vibrating in my toes. My temples pounded as I supported my back against the lamppost. Deep inside felt bruised.

Unusual wooziness accompanied my pounding head. I pulled myself up with the assistance of the lamppost, revealing how exhausted and dizzy my mind was. The immaculately mowed lawn seemed familiar, but still was an uncharted landscape.

Is my dorm in that direction, or over there? No, my dorm is over in that direction.

I stumbled forward and stopped. My feet seemed to have lost their ability to remember how to walk. I glanced down and saw my bare chest as the rising sun accented the deep scratches with dried blood running over my pecs and stomach. My legs wobbled and gave way under me, sending me to the ground again. There was hollowness inside and metallic taste in my mouth. I forced myself onto all fours and emptied my stomach onto the grass, like a cat ridding itself of a furball.

I pulled myself up, stood, and staggered in the direction I thought led to my dorm. Shadows masked everything as the sun inched higher in the east. I followed the paved walkway as it curved and straightened. I held my arms out to the side for balance, calculated and measured each step, as if I was walking in a bouncy house. The meticulousness of solving how to perform each step overrode the pain.

Just over the hill should be the dorms...

CHAPTER 1
RETURNING TO THERAPY

DR. ALTHEA WARNER'S OFFICE—
DAYTON, OHIO, 2018

Althea's voice rang from the waiting room. "So, you have come back to get fixed?" Her laughter snuck into the office.

"I guess you can say that. Or maybe get fixed better." I forced a laugh.

"Now, when were you here last?"

"It's been a while." The room felt different, with an air of uncertainty.

"If I remember correctly, the last time you were here, you shared that you went to the White House for the athletes' dinner, where President Carter announced the boycott of the 1980 Olympic Games in Moscow. You also said your brother was getting married to a classmate and you and Mark were going to try and see what was between you two. Is that about right?"

"Yes," I called back. The couch seemed to have gotten harder since the last time I was here. I shifted into a new position but decided to return to the original one.

"So, tell me. Did you and Mark get together?"

"Well, not exactly."

"Scheisse." The clamoring of china banging together rang from the waiting room. "Oh, I'm so sorry. I didn't hear you. I almost dropped my Earl Grey tea."

"No problem."

My mind flashed back to the White House after President Carter announced to the room full of athletes that the U.S.A. would not be participating in the 1980 Olympic Games in Moscow and Mark took me to the coat check room.

WASHINGTON D.C., MARCH 21, 1980

"Look at me." Mark lifted my chin. His blue eyes burned with excitement and the urgency to speak, yet he forced himself to remain calm. "I'm not sure how to say this. I've rehearsed a million and one times, but I never thought it would be this awkward."

"Just blurt it out," I encouraged him.

"You're right." He took a deep breath. "This is scarier than doing a front three-and-a-half from the ten-meter with your eyes glued shut." He took another deep breath. "I realize I'm a bit older than you."

"Only four years," I said.

Mark nodded. "I'm four years older than you, and I have to go back to Ohio State University to finish this year, while you go out to California. I wanted to address the friendship we have, and I keep thinking of the time in Tønsberg and how much I enjoyed being with you."

"Mark, what are you talking about?" My palms started sweating.

"You know, like the night you passed out next to my bed…"

"I didn't mean it. I was being so stupid. I don't know what I was thinking…" I pulled away.

He restrained me. "I hope you meant it, and it wasn't stupid."

"What?"

His eyes were filled with longing and care. He reached for my hand.

"Don't." I pulled it out of his reach. "Please don't make fun of me."

"I'm not intentionally trying to," Mark said. "It's just that it's been on my mind, and we've never talked about it."

"What's there to talk about?" I crossed my arms against my chest.

"It's just…" He paused and ran his hands through his thick, dark hair, accentuating the cowlick. "After the World Games, you went back to Aulden, and I went to Columbus. I thought we could meet up one weekend, I'd drive down to see you, but you went to dive with Dr. Don out in California. I hoped you would come to this dinner, and when Dr. Don told me you were, I knew I had to talk to you. It's been on my mind, and I think we need to straighten some things out. But every time I've tried to bring it up, other things always seemed to get in the way. Duh, the Olympic boycott." He forced a laugh.

"I said I was sorry. It didn't mean anything. I was being stupid." I looked past his shoulder to watch more athletes and coaches leave.

"You wanted to see me naked, didn't you?" Mark directly asked.

I wanted to run as hard and fast as I could. My forehead started sweating, and I could hear my heartbeat.

"That's why I went to bed naked," Mark said.

"What?"

"I noticed you looking at me when you came to OSU to practice platform."

"Please stop."

"I thought I was making it up. When you made the World Games Team, I was so excited. I noticed you looking over to me then as well."

"You're freakin' Mark Bradley, world and national champion. I was in awe of you."

"That was all? Just because I won some medals?" He looked hurt and defeated. "I was mad jealous when you hung out with Giovanni Pizzini."

3

"He's straight." I dropped my head in shame, realizing I'd admitted for the first time I was gay.

Mark lifted my chin with his fingers and looked deep into my eyes. "I don't care if you're orange, blue, or purple."

My eyes welled, and I tried to break away. He held tight to my elbow and placed his lips on mine.

DR. ALTHEA WARNER'S OFFICE— DAYTON, OHIO, JULY 2018

"Are you sure you don't want a cookie?" Althea walked in from the waiting room, carrying a teacup with a Milano cookie balancing on the edge of the saucer.

"No, I'm good." I shifted again on the couch so I could cross my legs.

"They're my favs." She gently placed the cup and saucer on the side table by her chair, spun around so her pleated shirt billowed, and sat down. "I know, I know. But sometimes I need to let myself enjoy such things as Milano cookies. I don't do it all the time. I can buy one bag and ration it out to last a whole week if I'm diligent." Althea nestled into the overstuffed chair and looked directly at me. "Well, did you and Mark make a go of it?"

I forced a grin. "No, not exactly."

Althea cocked her head. "But I thought things were all worked out?"

"It fizzled out as fast as it started. We were in different places. Mark was at Ohio State University, and I was in California. When we did meet up, it was always awkward as if it was the first time again."

"Sounds like a lot of excuses."

My shoulders shrugged. "I don't think I was ready for a relationship." A strange feeling flooded me, as if I misplaced something significant, lost it, or it was taken away. I felt empty. My hands seemed more massive than ever with deep crevasses cutting across my palms and leading nowhere specific.

"What do you mean?"

I followed the lifeline that arched around the fleshiness of my thumb and collided with the crease of my wrist, disappearing and no longer traceable. "When I moved to California, it put a wrench in our trying to get together. Of course, we talked on the phone and wrote letters, but the distance took its toll."

"Did he come to your high school graduation?" She placed the napkin on her lap.

"No."

She looked at me for a long time. "Did anyone come to your graduation?"

I only shook my head. "I got cards from Hal, my parents, and some benefactors. My parents couldn't afford to fly out to California for graduation. Hal had an important case to defend."

The ticking of the clock filled the room.

"So, explain some more about what you were describing over the phone about these dreams or memories?" She lifted the cup and saucer with the cookie balancing on the saucer's edge.

"I'm not sure. They seem to come and go."

"What do you mean?" She ceremoniously lifted the cookie, took a bite, and closed her eyes. "OMG, I have just entered heaven." She continued savoring the Milano cookie as she gently placed it back on the saucer and sipped her tea. "I don't know why I love these things so much, but they are *it* for me right now." Returning the cup, saucer, and cookie on to the side table, she dabbed her lips with a napkin and repositioned herself in the chair with her ledger and pen. "Now, what do you mean that these images come and go?"

"I'm not sure if they're memories or dreams that keep reoccurring."

Althea held up her hand to me. "Just a moment." She took another bite and savored the cookie as her head fell on the back of the overstuffed chair and her arms dangled over the armrests while balancing her ledger on her lap. "Doyouthinkitsrelevanttoyourrecovery?" She popped the remaining cookie into her mouth.

"I'm sorry, I didn't understand."

She must have felt me staring at her because she opened her eyes and sat erect, chewed, and swallowed. She held up her hand and took a quick sip of tea. "So good." She deeply inhaled and regained her professional attitude. "Do you think it's relevant to your recovery?" She licked her lips.

"I'm not sure."

"So, let me get this clear. You're not sure if these flashes are dreams or past realities?"

"Yes." I rested my elbows on my knees and leaned into her. "I have these clear moments, tiny details that flash into my head during the day or distinct smells will cause my mind to flash particular images. Sometimes I'm not sure what the images are because they're distorted or convoluted."

"Do you have any idea what these images or pictures are attached to?" Althea cocked her head.

"That's the problem. I don't know. They appear as snippets or flashes of frozen moments, like GIFs of a scene from a film that keeps playing over and over. They never go anywhere and keep repeating the same sequence."

"I'm not quite following." Althea's eyes squinted as if she'd developed a headache from the cookie's sugar. "Can you explain?"

"They're mere moments, slingshots or boomerangs. The visuals are constantly on a loop, playing the same thing over and over and over and over. Sometimes it's like a faceless image moving toward me, but it never gets to me. Other times, it's an image of a room with no artwork on the walls or the image of tan corduroy pants. The smell of chlorine will cause me to lose my breath like I'm suffocating. And then it'll stop and repeat all over again." My voice quivered.

"Do you see anything different ever? I mean, does a color seem different or an object you didn't notice the first time?"

I took a moment. "I never thought about that." A flash of me wincing in pain with my eyes scrunched and mouth tense rapidly repeated several times.

"David? David, are you all right?"

The image vanished as quickly as it appeared. I nodded.

"How often do these *repeating moments* occur?" She scribbled down some notes.

"Randomly."

"Randomly." she wrote it down.

"But recently more often," I quickly said.

"More often." She paused. "Can you elaborate?"

"Oh, I don't know." I shifted my weight on the couch and crossed my legs. "A smell or sound or when I'm exhausted are when they fling to the surface."

"I see." Althea lifted the teacup and sipped while carefully watching me. "Are you sure you wouldn't like some tea."

"I'm good."

Althea froze with the teacup resting against her lower lip and her eyes peering over the top of her readers. "What do you think set these images off? Was there anything or anyone from the past that jarred them?"

I thought for a moment. "It's funny you say that. I got this call from an actress friend of mine, April Audia. We were inseparable while I was living in LA. We reconnected through Facebook. She started sending me all these pictures of when we hung out together. She took me to Las Vegas, and we joked about getting married. We were only twenty-one or something. When we got to Sin City, we stopped off at the Flamingo for a drink, and she started asking all these tough questions. I couldn't remember if I answered." I chuckled at an image of April and me sitting at a bar, with fishbowl glasses filled with frozen blue liquid in front of us. "April has a mind like a steel trap and said she remembers everything like it was yesterday. I can't. I have these blank spaces. She said I needed to write about the time we were together in Hollywood."

"April represents a happy memory, then?" Althea jotted down more notes.

"For the most part."

"What do you mean by that?"

"April is extremely beautiful and strong. I could never really be able to be myself because I was spending all my energy containing or managing the past in my head."

"And she wasn't supportive?"

"Oh, quite the contrary. She was completely supportive."

"So, why did it end?"

"I don't know. It felt like we were together for a lifetime, but it was merely months, a year maybe, but we were so intensely connected. We did everything together."

"And from this reconnection is when these images start appearing again?"

I nodded. "Yeah, I guess, sort of. But the visions have always been there."

"Are these images subtle or intense?"

"Depends."

She stopped writing. "On what?"

I looked down at my hands, which were interlaced and clutching, causing my knuckles to whiten. "Depends on what's happening around me, like I said, when I'm tired, stressed, or worried."

"So, they become more intense when you're tired?"

"Yes."

"I see." Althea held up her hands as if by doing so she could pause time. "After the World Games, you relocated to California to continue practicing diving. Did you go to the Olympics in LA?"

Confusion riddled my mind. I felt like we were getting close to a breakthrough, and just as I was about to open Pandora's box she threw a curveball. I could only shake my head and tried to remind myself of Althea's unorthodox approach to therapy.

"No, I didn't, not as an athlete. I did attend some of the diving events." I paused. "I didn't even compete in the Olympic Trials. After the World Games, I moved to California to dive full time with Dr. Don and finish up high school. After graduation, I went to the university and focused on preparing for the '84 Olympics."

An image of a faceless man wearing an unbuttoned white oxford shirt with a red emblem over the right pocket flashed in my mind. I shook my head to rid myself of this unwanted memory.

"David, did you just have another image flash in your mind?"

"No," I quickly said.

The scratch of the pen against the paper echoed throughout the room and everything else fell silent.

Althea broke the silence. "Why didn't you go to the trials?"

"I'm not sure." I paused as my stomach flipped and twisted.

"What university did you attend?"

"The University of California, Irvine."

Althea started jotting information down again. "On a diving scholarship?"

"And academic scholarship."

"What was your major?"

"Pre-med." My voice faded as I remembered the grassy area where I found myself alone and scared.

Althea's voice changed. "Did something happen at school to make you want to stop diving?"

I looked up, and Althea intently looked at me. My arms wrapped around my chest, and I was crunched over. I took a deep breath and leaned back on the couch and crossed my legs. "Going to the University of California, Irvine was my chance to reinvent myself. I was excited to be on my own and try to figure out what I wanted to become. I no longer had to be the diver, the World Champ, and I could be anything I wanted to be. What did I want to be, was the big question. When I moved into the dorms, I met this microbiology major, Sue Fiffle."

UCI, MESA VERDE DORMS. 1981

"This is awful." I swallowed another gulp of the rose wine Sue drained from a box.

"It may be awful, but it's affordable on a student's budget, and it does the trick." Sue plopped down next to me on her twin bed, causing the stuffed animals to fall off the side. I went to retrieve them when she demanded, "Leave them. If they want to be on the floor, let them."

As I nodded and repositioned myself, I had to stabilize myself with a hand on the mattress. "Wow, my head's spinning."

"That's because this is cheap medicine." Sue shook her head full of curly brown hair, which always looked like it was wind-blown no matter the time of the day. Her smile occupied most of her thin face, and her brown eyes sparkled under her thick brows. She held up her coffee cup, which was filled with the pinkish liquid. "To our truth serum."

I clinked the lip of my plastic glass with her cup. "To truth."

"And to always telling the truth to each other." She paused and her face became serious. "I don't give a fuck about what others outside this room say or do or think. I don't care about anything, as long as we're always honest with each other." She played with her puka shell necklace as if it had the power to cast a truth spell. "We have to promise always to be truthful."

"To truthfulness." I raised my glass.

"I'm serious.

I composed my serious face. "Me too."

Noise seeped under the closed door as a group of students shouted and banged down the hallway. "Because those mother-fuckers couldn't care less about us, the importance of life, or the progression of humanity. All they care about is how many points they got and who won the game."

"Sue, how did you end up in the athletes' dorm?"

"Fate. It's was fate, my friend." She got up, went to the door, and opened it. "Shut the shit up; I'm trying to study in here."

The noise ceased.

"Thank you. Maybe you should try to study occasionally too, so you can keep your athletic scholarships." She shrugged her shoulders, slammed the door, and returned to her spot on the bed.

"I have an athletic scholarship too," I sheepishly admitted.

"You're different."

"I am?"

"Yes, you're also on an academic scholarship and in pre-med. God blessed you with brains and brawn." She lifted her cup. "To truthfulness."

"Oh, we're back to that now, are we?" I lifted my glass. "To truth."

We clicked our drinks.

"I wish we had goblets, old fashioned goblets with rhinestones."

"Very medieval."

"Oh, yes. And when I'd get fed up with the stupidity of dumb jocks, I'd feed them to my pet dragon, Chrysophylax."

My eyes narrowed. "Chrysophylax?"

Sue's eyes widened. "Why, of course. Chrysophylax is one of the fiercest fire-breathing dragons ever to grace this plane of existence." She looked in my glass. "Down it."

I gulped the remaining liquid.

She grabbed my glass and went to the wine box that resided on her desk. She filled both vessels and brought them back to the bed. "So, tell me a secret about yourself, something I don't know." She handed me my glass.

"Hmmm. Something you don't know about me." My mind raced through all my secrets I kept hidden in files in my mind. I flipped through them to determine what I felt comfortable sharing. Then I came upon a safe bet. "This isn't that big of a secret, but it's something that I don't share with a lot of people."

"Is it juicy?" Sue perched herself next to me.

I hemmed and hawed and shrugged my shoulders. "Not juicy in that way." I paused for dramatic tension.

"Tell me!"

"I won the World Games Diving Championships on springboard when I was sixteen years old," I admitted.

"No fucking way!"

"Yep."

"Oh, my God. I knew you were special."

"When I called home from Norway to tell my folks I won, granted there was a six-hour time difference, my dad answered the phone. When I told him I won, he said, 'This is the worst joke anyone has ever pulled. My son would never win the World Games' and hung up."

Sue's mouth flew open. "No fucking way."

"Way."

"That's fucked up."

"But you got to understand it was early here in the States."

"That's no excuse. If I won, I'd shout that shit from the rooftops."

"It was just something that happened."

Sue looked hard at me. "That shit doesn't just happen."

"It did. I wasn't supposed to win. I barely made the team. The U.S. was trying to kick me off so they could move the next guy up who had international experience. The IOC stated I had to go even though I hadn't even won a state title yet. My first international meet was the World Games. It was just not the other guys' day. Like they say, 'A different day, a different winner.'"

"That's bullshit, and you know it. Alright, I get that it may not have been everyone's day. But for the love of God, it was your day, and you need to start owning that shit." She stared into my eyes. "Do you hear me?"

I nodded.

"No! Do you hear me?" She tapped her finger on my forehead. "You have to own that. Hear me?"

"Okay"

She tapped her finger harder. "Hear me. Or else I'm going to beat the shit out of you until you do."

"Okay!" I pulled away and rubbed my forehead.

Sue kept staring at me. Then out of nowhere, she suddenly stood and twirled. "You won the World Games at sixteen! You had a gold medal placed around your neck, and they played the National Anthem in your honor. How many people can say that happened to them?"

I shrugged. "Your turn. Tell me a secret."

"Oh, forget it. I can't top that. Nothing like that has ever happened to me."

"You have to share. You made me."

Sue paced the room, and then abruptly stopped. "This goes no further than these four walls."

"I swear."

"Pinky swear!" She rushed toward me with her pinky finger extended.

We wrapped pinky fingers.

She squeezed her finger and her eyes filled with liquid. "My parents were murdered during a home invasion."

My stomach dropped. "I'm so sorry."

She freed her pinky and started pacing again. "No, no. No. We're not feeling sorry for ourselves. And you can't feel sorry for me either." Silence filled the room as she continued pacing. She then walked up to me and held up her cup. "To truthfulness."

"To the truth."

My glass kissed the rim of her coffee cup.

DR. ALTHEA WARNER'S OFFICE— DAYTON, OHIO, 2018

"Sue and I became close friends. She was intelligent and beautiful in a more Earthy way. I loved talking to her and exploring our concepts of life and how things worked. It was the first time I felt special and powerful. She drove me to Los Angeles when I was cast to do an extra part on *General Hospital*. But things intervened and splintered our friendship. I also met this other girl, Jennifer Luff, who was Miss Sorority with a huge smile and was overly peppy all the time. Her family was wealthy and came from La Cañada, a rich-suburb located in the Crescenta Valley, just northwest of Pasadena. We met in the library and started talking. She was auditioning for the fall play and wanted to know if I'd help her out and be her partner. I refused at first, but she was very persuasive. So, I agreed. She was the perfect girl to be seen with in public. You know what I mean?"

"I'm not sure," Althea said with strangeness in her voice.

"Now, when I look back at the whole situation, I was pretty shallow. Jennifer was wealthy, popular, and flashy. Sue was plain, a nerd, and grounded. I know, I know how it sounds."

"How would you know what it sounds like to me?" Althea asked.

"By your expression."

"My expression?" Her eyes widened.

"Yes, your expression showed disappointment," I said.

"So what?"

"So, I can tell you're disappointed in me."

"Well, you're wrong. But even if I was disappointed, you have no right to make my decision for me. Let me voice my disappointment. And for your information, I was thinking back to a time when I wanted to be seen with a certain person I thought would make me more popular. And I felt disappointment within myself."

"I didn't know."

"How could you? I never told you. So, tell me more about Jennifer." Althea prepared to take more notes.

"Well, we met every day after diving practice and classes to rehearse and prepare for her audition. The day came, and we appeared in front of the theatre department head, the director for *The Visit of the Old Lady*, and two other men in suits. I had no idea really what the play was about, but I relied on the acting skills I picked up from Norma Sharkey, who ran a modeling and acting agency in Dayton. I would drive to Dayton once a week to take classes before the World Games. I thought it would help me with the media in Tønsberg, but secretly, I was hoping to be the next John Schneider on the *Dukes of Hazard*."

NORMA SHARKEY MODELING AND ACTING AGENCY SCHOOL, 1979

"Alright students, calm down." A woman in her late forties clapped her hands. Hair piled high on her head and sprayed stiff with hairspray framed her face, which was painted with deep rouge, dark blue eye shadow, thick mascara, and red lips. "Here we go."

Nine of us, ranging from eight to eighteen and all were female except for myself, were waiting patiently in a small annex off the side of the stage in the Biltmore Hotel, in downtown Dayton. I was more excited than any of them. The four little girls were too focused on the frilly dresses they wore to take this graduation seriously, and the four older girls were rehearsing their best Cheryl Tiegs pout. I needed to perform.

"Models, it is time. I wish you the best of luck." Norma gracefully exited through the curtain to the center of the classroom's makeshift stage.

I peeked through the curtain and watched as the great Norma Sharkey posed with her feet in the proper model "T" formation with the right foot turned to the side and the left foot's heel placed against the arch of the right. She elongated her spine and swiveled her hips to give a slimmer look. Norma inhaled and ran her hands over the silk scarf tied around her neck and down her jacket and multicolored wool skirt.

She spoke in a low register and over articulated her words. "I am Norma Sharkey and welcome to the Norma Sharkey Modeling and Acting Agency School. Today parents, you are here to watch your child demonstrate the qualities that will make them a star." Norma dramatically paused and held her hands up to the audience. "I cannot promise that your child will become a star, because that is out of my hands. But what I can promise is that your child will demonstrate to you the best they are today." Norma shook her head, as if a wind machine was accentuating the moment.

"Each child has faced enormous challenges to reach this level, and depending on their performance today, it will determine if they will proceed to the advanced classes. The graduates of the advanced classes are then represented by the Norma Sharkey Modeling and Talent Agency and will be vying for professionally paid assignments. Graduates have been in Elder Beerman's Catalogues, local and even state commercials, and several, like my twin daughters, Gigi and Gena Sharkey, are in NYC, modeling professionally. The students have explored runway, makeup, posing for the camera, commercial auditions, and even scenes from film and television. This showcase is being professionally videotaped by Aim High Films and copies may be ordered at the front desk afterward, so please, no taking of pictures or filming during the presentation. First, we would like to demonstrate the runway walk."

"Hey, you guys. We're starting." I ushered the four youngest girls to get in line.

Norma gave a forced laugh. "We will start with our youngest model. Tammy is eight years old and comes from Middletown."

The showcase flew by, and I loved every minute. I felt like I belonged. It felt natural and fresh. I wanted to be like the male models I studied, whose pictures I tore out of magazines to create my class portfolio. I wanted to be their friend and remove myself from Aulden, Ohio, and reinvent myself. I knew deep inside if I could get away from Aulden, I could forget about having to go to the arranged dinners, I could make some real money on my own and help the family. I wouldn't need *benefactors*. I could be self-sufficient. Modeling and acting gave me a sense of freedom and belonging, I'd only felt when I was diving. I knew this was my next adventure. I didn't know how I was going to make it happen, but I was going to go to New York, LA, Paris, or London.

The audience's energy and Norma Sharkey's admiration engulfed me as I stepped out on stage and performed the "T" pattern and presented my best runway and catalog poses. The only other time I felt this confident was when I was in seventh grade petitioning and changing the rules that boys could try out for cheerleading, in an eighth grade class debate standing up for women's rights, and whenever I was diving. Before I realized it, the showcase was over, and I was rushing to pack up all my things up.

"David, I didn't see your parents here."

I looked up, and Norma smiled down at me.

"No, they couldn't make it today. They had other commitments," I said.

"That's too bad. I would have liked to have met your parents to tell them what a wonderful job you did and encourage you to do the advanced classes." Her painted red lips creeped across her made-up face.

"Really?" I stood, inhaling her musk perfume, resisting the urge to hug her.

"You radiated and were in full control." Norma placed a caring hand on my arm. "I'm sorry, do you not like to be touched?'

"Excuse me?"

"When I touched your arm, you flinched." Her brown eyes behind the thick blue eye shadow and mascara were filled with care.

"I did?" I glanced at my arm where she'd touched it, and then back to her. "I didn't mean to."

"It's all right. I don't like being touched or hugged either." Norma produced a deep laugh.

I nervously nodded, forced a smile, and hesitantly asked, "How much are the classes?"

"Let me discuss that with your parents."

My eyebrows flickered up, and I looked away.

"Wait a minute." Norma guided my chin back. "Your parents know you're here and taking classes, right?" Her eyes widened, and she leaned in. "Right?"

My lips clamped up.

Norma sighed deeply. "Who signed for the permission?"

MOTEL 6, AULDEN, OHIO, 1979

I sat on the edge of the bed, holding my underwear in my hands. A coughing fit echoed from the bathroom, reminding me I wasn't alone in this Motel 6 room with its twin bed, dresser, and a broken television. The closet-sized bathroom's door was open, and Dr. Malcolm Schultz was cleaning up.

His reflection in the mirror grinned at me with rosy red corpuscles pushing against his fat cheeks' paper-thin skin—all the results of his taste for Dewar's, Camels, and the hope that the sun would keep him young looking. His body was an overstuffed sausage with a hard, protruding belly and flabby man breasts. His hairless and varicose-veined legs seemed too skinny and weak to support his torso. His cologne was an attempt to mask his overpowering body odor.

Staleness reeked from my mouth as the taste of his bitter tongue lingered behind. I could still hear his guttural grunts of pleasure and the repeated words, "Oh, yeah. You're so sweet. You're so pretty." I wanted to vomit as burning liquid rushed up and ambushed the back of my throat.

A sticky matter clumped at the base of my stomach. I grabbed the moth-eaten sheet and tried to wipe it off. I rubbed harder, unsure if the mess was his, mine, or a mixture. I wanted it off me.

"How you doing, baby? Dr. Schultz asked as he came back into the room, holding a wet washcloth. "Let me." He gently pushed aside my hands and laid the warm cloth on my lap. He struggled to bend over, willing his joints to function, and started to wipe the area. "You're such a beautiful boy."

What do I say?

He ran his tongue along the length of my neck as he cleaned me. When he finished he sat back on his heels, leaving his palms on my thighs, and looked at me for a long time. "I want to remember this moment. How beautiful you look with the light coming in from the window behind you. How sweet you've been to me." He giggled like a girl and used the edge of the bed to aid in standing. "My joints don't work like they used to." He staggered to his jacket, resting on the back of a chair, and pulled out something. He slowly turned and extended his arm toward me.

I immediately closed my eyes, wondering if I'd feel any pain.

"Here," he softly said.

I slowly opened my eyes, expecting to come face-to-face with a revolver. Dad's voice rang through my head, reminding me I was going to hell. To my relief, Dr. Schultz held out an envelope.

I didn't reach for it.

He cocked his head and offered it to me again.

I remained still.

He grinned. "You're truly something. Hal said you were special, but I thought he was trying to sell me. But he was right on all accounts. I want you to have this." He offered it to me again, then quickly pulled it away. "But you have to promise me something." He waited for me to respond.

A siren's wail filled the space as an ambulance sped by.

I finally broke my silence. "What?"

"This is for you. This isn't for your mother. Hal informed me that you give everything to your mother. Promise me you'll not let her know I gave this to you. I'll make sure everyone in your family has their examinations and whatever medical treatments are needed. I promise I'll continue working with Magdalyn's chin, but I want to know you'll keep this as a secret for yourself. Promise?"

"What is it?" I asked.

"You got to promise me first."

"All right, I promise," I said flatly.

"Good." He handed me the envelope.

I looked inside and found four fifty-dollar bills.

"Happy Sweet Sixteen, young man."

NORMA SHARKEY MODELING AND ACTING AGENCY SCHOOL, 1979

"David. Who signed the permission?" Norma asked.

I looked up and saw the concern in her eyes. "I did."

Norma slowly nodded her head and stepped away.

I couldn't stop the words. "I'm so sorry. I didn't mean to lie. It's just that I wanted to take the classes so bad and I knew my parents wouldn't let me."

Norma's spine lengthened. "Where did you get the money?"

"It was a birthday gift."

Still with her back to me, she nodded her head. "A birthday gift? You spent your birthday gift on taking my modeling classes."

"Yes, ma'am."

"Interesting. Where do you tell your parents you are every Wednesday night during class?"

"At diving practice."

Norma chuckled and faced me with one arched eyebrow high on her forehead. "You have talent. You have guts driving yourself into Downtown Dayton, but I don't condone lying. I will need to talk to your parents because you are not eighteen yet."

"I understand. But when are the classes starting?"

"The next session starts next month."

"Is there a chance I could start back after the nationals are over?"

Norma pouted her red lips. "Normally, the students move through the classes as a group. You would have to wait until the advance classes are offered again. But, let's first make sure we talk to your parents." She started to place a heavy hand on my shoulder, and then decided not to. "I am proud of you."

"Thank you." I grabbed my bag.

"But for now, I'm throwing you out. It's getting late, and I am ready to go home. Got everything?"

I flung the strap of the bag over my shoulder, headed for the door, and halted. "Thank you for everything. I enjoyed the classes."

"I know you did. Now get so that I can go."

I nodded and rushed out the door, down the marble staircase and out onto the Dayton sidewalk, bypassing homeless people, dodging businesspeople rushing home, and pausing in front of the Victoria Theatre. A large poster announcing the upcoming ballet performance of *Romeo and Juliet* with two dancers embracing sent me on an emotional rollercoaster.

The female dancer was stunning as her long curling hair framed her innocent face and cascaded down her shoulders and back. But it was the male dancer who was the most alluring. His short, tight, curly blond hair accentuated his angular cheekbones and added a golden glow to his skin. His sleek masculine physique indicated his agility and strength of a young colt. For some strange reason, I knew deep within in me I was someday going to dance on stage somewhere. The thrill of this discovery, plus the adrenaline rush from performing in the showcase, lifted me off the ground and carried me toward a magical and fantastical vision of an unlimited future.

DR. ALTHEA WARNER'S OFFICE, 2018

Althea rubbed her chin and clasped her hands together. She appeared in a meditative state of contemplation until she cracked a smile. "These flashes seem to contain unpleasant thoughts, while there may be many happy moments as well. You remember when you were here last and I had you work on *The Artist Way?*"

I nodded, trying to figure out what she was planning.

"Do you still have the journal?"

"I nodded."

"Do you still write in it?"

My back elongated, and I inhaled deeply. I reached into my satchel and pulled out the leather-bound journal she gave to me the last time I sat on this couch. I held the spine of the worn journal in my left hand. The bottom corner curled, the yellow ribbon dangled a little more than halfway through, and it was stuffed with scraps of papers I shoved into it. The journal's weight seemed like a ton, yet I waved it in the air like it weighed nothing. "I keep it with me everywhere I go."

"That's nice. Are you still writing in it?" She leaned in with her elbows resting on her thighs.

I looked at the journal, which housed some intimate realizations and revealing discoveries, as if it were an old friend with whom I'd lost touch; my best friend who probably knew me better than anyone in the world. And yet I felt distant from it. It betrayed me. With as much raw and honest emotions recorded, some lies lived with the other memories. And what was extremely sad, I wasn't even sure which entries were lies or truths.

The journal became even more cumbersome, and I couldn't keep it elevated. It landed on the couch next to me in a thump. It took on a persona of its own, like an unexpected person from my past who embarrassed and ashamed me.

I regarded the journal with disdain. "No, I haven't written in it for a while. I keep it with me, hoping to be inspired to jot things down. But I seem to have hit a block."

"Why do you think that is?"

My shoulders shrugged. "I'm struggling with trying to figure out if the memories are authentic or if I made them up in my head." I ran my hands through my hair, as if I was trying to scan through all the possible stories or memories I've written in the journal — worried I couldn't exactly remember what I've transcribed. The journal sneered at me because it was privy to secrets I've shared on its pages and not with anyone else.

"Does it matter?"

My eyes darted to her. "What do you mean?"

"Whatever you've written is whatever you wanted to write." Althea pointed to the journal.

I glanced over to the journal which grew one hundred times its size.

"And what you wanted to write, even if it's made up, maybe keys for you to uncover the truth. Everything you've placed in that journal has some amount of truth. So, it's a safe place for you to express your inner thoughts."

"What good is it if it's filled with lies or made-up stories?" My palms opened to the side.

"What if they're not lies or made-up stories? What if there are stories that are covering up the truth you're trying to understand? Sometimes we develop stories to allow us to deal with situations when we can't deal with reality." She jotted a note on her clipboard.

I slumped back onto the couch as all the air left my lungs. I felt like I reverted to where I was when I first came to see Dr. Warner. The amount of stress and anxiety seemed to have doubled in intensity.

"Let's go back and revisit *The Artist Way* and start up your morning pages. Just for a short time. Write down anything that comes to you. I want you to include any flashes and try to describe the images in as much detail as you can. But most importantly,

I want to start focusing on happier times. I want you to revisit all the accomplishments you encountered and write them out. Express how you were feeling at the time and how you were able to become successful. Maybe we can find out why you feel you have to remain connected to these negative things. But first, I want you to write about the audition and about..." She glanced down at her notes. "About Jennifer, Sue, and especially April. Don't judge. Let whatever emerge." She encouragingly smiled.

The clock outside chimed and I grabbed my checkbook and filled it out.

Althea went to her desk and opened her calendar. "Same time next week?"

"Yes, sounds good." I tore out the check and handed it to her, then gathered my satchel and headed out of the office.

"Be kind to yourself," Althea said as the door closed.

CHAPTER 2
FRESHMAN YEAR

UNIVERSITY OF CALIFORNIA, IRVINE, 1981

"Thank you. We have your information, and we will be in touch. The cast list will be posted by five p.m. tonight," the stage manager said as she sat at a long table next to Professor Blankenburg with an assistant director, two men in business suits, and another woman.

Jennifer smiled brightly. "Thank you for seeing us." She grabbed my hand and led to me the side of the room where we had discarded our book bags. "We did it. That was terrific." She wrapped her arms around my neck.

I stiffened and mechanically placed a hand on her back. "You think so?"

"Let's go celebrate." She kissed my cheek, grabbed her bag, and headed for the exit.

"David."

"Yes." One of the men in suits towered above me, and I quickly stood and slid the book bag's straps over my shoulders.

"I'm Mike Shapiro and I'm producing a TV Movie of the Week entitled *Single Parents.*" He offered his hand.

"Nice to meet you." I discovered he had a firm grip.

"Professor Blankenburg allowed me, us, to sit in on these auditions since we're looking to cast a couple roles. Would you be interested?"

"Sure, I guess." I pulled away my hand away, and rubbed my palm on my jeans.

"Great. Let me introduce you to Roland, our director, and Liz, his assistant." He guided me to the table where everyone stood, stretching their legs and spines. "Roland and Liz, this is David. David, Roland, and Liz."

"Hello." I respectfully reached over the table and shook hands with each one of them.

Professor Blankenburg and his stage manager moved to the far end of the table so they could discuss casting options for the fall play.

"Are you interested in our little project?" Roland asked. His eyes were magnified by the thick lens of his black-framed glasses which sat heavily on the bridge of his blunt nose.

"Sure."

Roland pushed the glasses up and looked at Mike. "I think he'd be a perfect choice for Greg."

"I agree," Mike said.

"Then let's do it. Liz, do you have his contact information?" Roland asked.

"I'll get it from Stacy." Liz made a note on a pad of paper. "David, what's your last name?"

"Matthew."

"Got it." Liz walked over the Stacy and Professor Blankenburg.

"What kind of character is it?" I asked as I adjusted the book bag straps on my shoulders.

"Greg is a very popular high school football player from a wealthy family. Since the parents are getting a divorce, Greg can't understand why he can't get what he wants," Roland said.

I nodded.

"Do you think you can do it?" Roland asked.

"Sure, I guess. I mean, yes!" I enthusiastically said.

"Then it's settled. We better get you out of here so Dr. Blankenburg can get back to auditioning for his play." Mike indicated for me to leave. "We'll be in touch."

I started for the door. "Thank you. All of you," I said, pushing open the door.

Jennifer leaned against the pillar as the afternoon sun stretched long shadows across the quad. "What took you so long?" she asked.

I looked back as the door closed. "I had to tie my shoe." I don't know why I lied. Maybe I thought I was sparing her feelings that they wanted to talk to me and not to her. Besides, it was her audition since she asked me to go in with her.

Jennifer slid her hand under my arm and smiled. "I'm so excited we did that. I don't care what happens. I mean I'd be super excited to get a part, even if it's a small role, but if it doesn't happen for some reason, I'm okay with that. We faced our fears, and we did it. Come on!" She pulled me down the marble steps and made me skip into Aldrich Park.

*****

The next day, Jennifer came bounding up to me in the cafeteria. "Congratulations." She nudged her shoulder against mine as we filled our plates from the salad bar.

"On what?" I carried our trays to a circular table, dodging students rushing to get lunch in before their next class.

"Don't tell me you don't know." She sat in the seat next to me.

"I really don't."

"The audition, duh." Her smile and lavender eyes reminded me of Vivian Leigh, from *Gone with the Wind*.

"I know. I'm sorry. I should have told you then."

"Tell me what?" She bit into a carrot.

"The reason it took me so long to get out of the audition room."

"Yeah, what was that about? You said something lame like you were tying your shoe?" She mocked surprise.

"Mr. Shapiro asked to speak with me." I felt this dread of being caught between a lie and coming clean. *Will she be upset with me for not telling her yesterday?*

Jennifer's face became expressionless. "Okay. Why so mysterious?" She put the remainder of the carrot on her tray.

"He offered me a role in *Single Parents*."

Jennifer slapped my shoulder. "Get out of town! Seriously?"

I nodded sheepishly.

"What role? You know they're shooting that here on campus." She reached into her book bag and pulled out a thin magazine.

"It's the role of the quarterback kid. He doesn't understand why he can't have what he wants, even though his parents are getting divorced. Something like that."

"That's awesome. That's one of the leads." She held up the magazine, entitled, *Dramalogue*. She opened it to the featured article, "MOW shooting on UCI Campus."

I took the magazine and looked closer. Under the title was a picture of Mike Shapiro and Roland Lockhart.

"It said they're going to use the Multimedia Sound Stage for interiors and shoot exteriors around campus. Look here." Jennifer flattened the magazine on the table and pointed to a paragraph:

In Single Parents, The Carter family experiences complications brought on by a divorce. The only child, a gifted high school student/athlete, comes to terms that his life has changed because of his parents' separation. He learns that the only thing he can count on is love.

"Isn't that neat?" She turned toward the back of the magazine. "And here are lists of auditions for film, television, plays, commercials, and print work." She guided her finger down the columns of audition descriptions. "Below each breakdown is the address where to mail headshots and resumes. You'll want to look out for this, if it has SAG or AFTRA, like this one." She pointed to one in the middle of the page:

ABC General Hospital, AFTRA-SAG, looking for extras to play Saudi Arabians for upcoming episodes.

"That means you need to be a member of the American Federation of Television and Radio Artists and/or Screen Actors Guild. They're the unions actors want to belong to as soon as possible. That's where the money is, and the union has bylaws to protect the actor. It's not easy to get into. Wait a minute." She looked at me with excitement in her eyes. "I think *Single Parent* is an AFTRA contract, you should check to see, because if it is you could be Taft-Hartley, which means you'll get your AFTRA card for doing the film. Make sure you ask. Otherwise, if the audition notice doesn't indicate AFTRA or SAG, like these." Jennifer turned the page and pointed to the more extensive list of projects. "These are usually non-union projects, and they can pay you nothing if they want. People do these to get more experience and build their resume."

"What if you mail a headshot and resumes to one of the notices that's SAG or AFTRA?" I asked.

"It probably will end up in the trash. But you never know. There's no rhyme or reason. But it's frowned upon to waste casting directors' time."

I nodded as I flipped back to the article about the Movie of the Week. "May I look at this for a bit?"

"Take it. I already went through it several times. It's so cool that you got in the movie. Remember to ask about the Taft-Hartley. But that wasn't what I was congratulating you on."

I looked at her, trying to follow her ever changing subjects and ideas. "What are you talking about?"

She held her breath, and then exploded. "You got in!"

"In what?"

"The play, you silly. You got in the play we auditioned for."

"I did?"

"Yes!"

"Did you?"

"No, but it's all good." Her smile never wavered. Was she generally happy for me? "Hey, I was thinking, and I was wondering if you'd be interested in, I know it isn't until next month, but the sorority I'm rushing has an annual semi-formal Halloween party, and I had this great idea that we could go as Scarlet O'Hara and Rhett Butler from *Gone with The Wind*." She sat tall with her hands folded on the edge of the table like she was praying.

"Seriously?"

Jennifer nodded.

"You looked like Vivian Leigh."

"That's so sweet. I've been told that before. I've this amazing dress that would be perfect. And we could spray your hair dark and draw a moustache. We'll look fantastic." Jennifer bounced in the chair and clapped her hands.

DR. ALTHEA WARNER'S OFFICE—DAYTON, OHIO, 2018

I recounted the books on the shelves behind Althea's desk as she scanned through my journal.

How many self-help books are there? How many psychology books? How many books about dogs are there?

There was a comfort in counting and asking myself questions. Whenever I felt uncomfortable or anxious, if I could count something, it seemed to sooth everything. Sometimes I'd even count the number of steps while walking.

"Wait a minute!" Althea's sudden outburst caused me to jump. She peered over her glasses and rolled her shoulders. "Back up a second." Althea held the pen in her hand and shook it at me. "You were going to UC Irvine for pre-med, met Jennifer, auditioned for a play, ended up getting a part, and the lead in a Movie of the Week?"

I simply nodded like it was no big deal.

"What about the Taft-Hartley situation?"

"I was given my AFTRA card at the end of shoot. Mike worked it out that my dues were included in my contract negotiations, so the production company paid."

"That's fantastic." Althea lifted both hands in the air.

"Yeah, I guess."

"You guess? It sounds like everything was falling into place."

"Well, it was more complicated than that. It didn't feel like I actually did anything. It was like I was just in the right place at the right time. I'd show up, and it happened. I can't explain it."

"Or why should you?" She narrowed her eyes. "Has it ever occurred to you that you may be talented?"

I slowly shook my head.

"You mean to tell me you can sit there and not have one iota of an inkling that you maybe just a little bit talented?"

I shook my head again.

"That's crazy. I'm here to tell you—please don't take offense at this—but you're a whack-a-doodle if you think you have no talent. Things like this," she indicated back to the journal, "don't happen to everybody." She waved the journal in the air. "Why do you think these things, amazing things, like winning a gold medal, getting cast in the Movie of the Week, and a part in the play, happened if you didn't have some small amount of talent?"

"I don't know."

She dropped the journal on her lap. "What do you mean you don't know?"

My body flushed with a rush of heat, causing my cheeks to blush and my hands to tingle. "I don't know."

Althea looked at me with the saddest expression I've ever seen.

My voice was low and slow. "It never really seemed to be me. I mean, I was there, I know that. But it was like it was all happening to someone else, and I was watching it happen. Just like my journal. I know I wrote it, but I can't remember what I wrote, or if I wrote it. I mean, I remember sitting down and writing, but not actually what I wrote. Sometimes I go back and read what I wrote, and it's as if a stranger wrote it. I sound so crazy."

"No, not at all. It's perfectly normal. Especially for a person who's experienced what you have."

"That's just it. I don't want to be that person who went through something. I don't want to have to keep paying this price of always feeling like I feel inside," my voice was laced with anger.

An image flashed of me being pinned down, water splashing, and struggling to get free.

Althea sat back as if to provide more space between us. "How do you feel?"

"Like a liar." Tears streamed down my face. I tried to wipe them, but I wasn't quick enough. "My life feels like a complete lie. If I didn't have the gold medal in a box at my house, I would have sworn I made the whole thing up. I remember feeling the weight of the medal as they placed the ribbon around my neck. I remember standing there, listening to the national anthem, and watching the American flag. But it seems as if I borrowed these memories from someone who deserved them." I grabbed tissues from the box on the side table and dried my eyes.

Althea was quiet. She was supportive, but she sat there studying me. Finally, she said, "I'm so sorry you feel this way."

I bit my lower lip. "I'm so angry." My fist clenched in tight balls.

"It's okay to feel angry."

"I don't know what to do with all this anger." My jaw locked.

"That's why you're here. We'll figure it out together. When I said this was normal, it's normal for someone who's experienced the things you've gone through. That's not bunching you into a label or stereotype. What I think has happened is that you discovered ways to deal with things, all things, good or bad, the best you could at the time. When we experience something that violates our psyche, it causes short-term and even long-term changes to the brain that may affect our behavior. This study is known as neurobiology. When the behaviors aren't consistent with society's, or even our own expectations, in your case, you start questioning your integrity. I just read an article about this."

31

She got up and went to her desk, leafing through piles of folders and papers.

I checked the time on my cell phone and noticed I had several unanswered messages. I fought against the desire to read them or run as fast as I could from this office.

"There are four chemicals that act simultaneously on parts of the brain, and when all four are present, it triggers our flight-or-fight response." Her voice was distant as she continued to rummage through the piles. "It was just here."

I replaced my phone into the side pocket of my satchel and watched Althea frantically looking to find the article. "If you can't find…"

"No, I know it's right here. I had it this morning. It talked about when there are repeated experiences and the person may not be able to comprehend or encode the information. Oh, here it is." Althea picked up the article and scanned the contents. "Here. 'The person experiencing a form of depersonalization may not able to encode the information in the correct context or sequence but has intense sensory fragments that can reappear periodically in nightmares or from specific sounds or smells.' In your case, it could result in fleeting images. So you see, you naturally found a way to defend and protect yourself." She held out the article as if I could read it from across the room. "Maybe this is why you always feel you're outside yourself, watching your life like it belongs to someone else."

"Are you saying I may have depersonalized or dissociated myself from these experiences?" The possibility of this reality was a bit overwhelming, and at the same time it filled me with the excitement of possibly being a solution.

"Yes, in an odd way. You've become so accustomed to removing yourself from the experiences that you've done it with every aspect of your life. It's something like watching a movie." Althea returned to her chair.

"So, am I borrowing other people's emotions and feelings, since I've detached from my own?"

"That'll be something we'll have to figure out." She handed me the article.

As I glanced at the print, the words swam over the paper. I looked back at Althea and decided not to tell her. "There's always seemed to be so many other things involved." My voice shook.

"Like what?"

"I'm not sure how to put it in words."

"Try." Althea lowered herself onto her chair.

"I felt there were always other reasons why things happened to me. Good or bad. It didn't matter. There always seemed to be some ulterior motive behind why people gave me opportunities. Yes, I got to do many things like travel the world as a teenager and dive in Norway, Canada, Mexico, Denmark, Sweden, Great Britain, Germany, and France. But no matter how good or talented I was, I couldn't have gotten to do those things if it wasn't for the people who helped me get there. And there was always a price. So, when something happened that was good, I kept waiting for the time when I'd have to pay the price."

"What happened when the bounty wasn't asked to be paid in trade?" Althea intently looked at me.

Was Althea speaking Greek?

"What?" I asked.

"What would you do if the person who gave you something didn't want sex in return?"

Bile attacked and burned the back of my throat, as the idea that I was a mere tool for other people's sexual pleasures brought shame, remorse, utter disgust, guilt, and anger from the depths of my gut.

My mind replayed the moment my face was pressed against the wet floor by a Jacuzzi while someone pressed against me and panted in my ear. I counted the tiles. *Sixteen, seventeen, eighteen...*

"David. Is everything all right?"

Nineteen, twenty, twenty-one...

"David?" Althea came back into focus. She was leaning toward me.

I nodded. "Yes, everything's fine." I forced a smile. "What was I saying?"

"You were responding to how you react to someone who does something nice for you." Concern wrinkled Althea's forehead as she scribbled on her notepad.

"Oh, yes. I didn't know what to do, I guess, especially, if these people didn't want something in return."

My mind filled with another flashing image of someone's fingers wrapped around mine, and his weight pressed against my back. I felt no pain. *Twenty-two, twenty-three, twenty-four...* He grabbed a handful hair and pressed my face harder onto the floor's tiles. Bubbles popped in the water surrounding my nostrils. *Twenty-five, twenty-six, twenty-seven...*

"Did you have another image flash?" Althea asked.

I took a deep breath and let it out extremely slow, biding time for the image to dissipate. "No. No. I was trying to think about how I felt when someone gave me something without any expectations." I ran my hands through my hair, hoping the images would stay at bay. "You're always expected to give something for something. My father used to say, 'Nothin's for free.' And I think he was right. The price I paid for going to the World Games was pretty high and has haunted me every day since."

"Okay, but not everything is paid with the price of your body."

"But the mental expectation and the anxiety of waiting for the demands to come were always exhausting. Never knowing when these people were going to come and collect. And there must be something wrong if there's no expected payback. What did I do wrong? Do they not like me? Am I not good enough for them? I carry these feelings with me today."

"Is that all you feel you're worth?"

"It was all I had to give. I didn't have money or other material things. So, I just assumed that was what people wanted. And if they didn't want it, I thought there was something wrong with me."

"You never thought it was because you had any talent?"

"I thought that was my talent. That was all I was good for. I was told as a kid that I wasn't going to amount to anything, and I needed to have people take care of me. I was constantly told I had no common sense and I'd have to rely on someone to save me. Dad kept telling me I was going to hell because of lying with a man." I paused. "Somewhere along the way, I accepted that I was worthless and doomed and figured it didn't matter anymore. I began to believe what everyone told me, I was too pretty to be a boy, and girls wouldn't want to be with me. So…"

"All right." Althea wrote down a few more things and set her clipboard to the side. "I want to try something. I want you to tell me some more about the time you spent at U.C.I."

"Now?"

"Sure."

"I'm not sure I know what to talk about." I rubbed my palms on my thighs. I wasn't quite sure where Althea was going with this little exercise.

"Talk about the Movie of the Week."

IRVINE, CALIFORNIA, 1981: FILMING SINGLE PARENT MOVIE OF THE WEEK

"Can you toss the football in the air while your mother is telling you that you can't have the latest Nike shoes?" asked Roland.

I nodded and practiced tossing the ball up with a spiral and catching it in one hand.

"That's nice." Roland glanced down at the scripts. "Now Carol, I need you to try a different approach in telling your son he can't have the shoes, even though he's gotten everything he's ever wanted from you and your husband. But since the separation and pending divorce, you can't afford these niceties."

"I'm not sure I understand. I'm delivering it the way you asked me. I don't get want you want," Carol retorted.

"I don't care what you do, but do something different. What you're doing isn't working. I want to see something else." He walked away from the actress before she could rebut. "Okay people, let's reset to one and do a take." Roland walked off the set and sat in a chair by the middle camera.

"Lights," bellowed Liz's baritone voice, the stage manager, as she positioned herself next to Roland.

The lights flooded the set with a bright whiteness. Carol covered her eyes and said, "Thanks for the warning."

"All right, let's have quiet on the set. Reset to one. David, you're off the set, so you can enter through the door. Carol will start on the phone this time," Liz said. Carol tried to interject, but the husky stage manager ignored her. "Places."

The business of the room quieted down.

I went to the mark off the side of the set, and watched Carol trying to find a position that would make her look the best for the camera.

"Settle on the set," Liz barked.

"Slow fade in on Carol on the phone," Roland said to the cameraman.

"In three, two, and rolling," Liz announced.

"Action," Roland called .

Carol froze. She stared off with an expressionless face. The whole studio was silent, everyone holding their breath and waiting for her to start the dialogue. The silence and tension suffocated the room like a wool blanket. I peeked around the partition supporting the fake front door and saw her bathed in the flood of white light, searching her mind for the first words. I tried to send the lines mentally to her by mouthing them.

Finally, she found the words, which she spoke in a stilted and monotone delivery. "Grant, why cannot you understand and be on my side with this? I only need some help until the alimony check clears."

That was my cue. I came through the door, took off my varsity letterman's jacket, threw it over the back of the kitchen chair, and pulled open the refrigerator. "What's for dinner?"

"I am trying to be patient, Grant, but you have to help me here." Carol stared into the middle camera.

"Mom, what's for dinner?" I hung on the open refrigerator door.

"Greg, close the fridge." She went back to the phone. "Grant, I cannot do this alone; you said the check would be here last week."

I slammed the refrigerator door and tossed the ball in the air. I sat on the back of the couch next to her head and kept throwing the ball.

"We agreed to this arrangement. What? Now, I was not the one who shacked up with a college intern."

I caught the ball with a loud thump in my palm and looked at her.

She looked up at me and pulled the phone to her chest. "Do you mind?"

"Whatever." I spun off the couch and went back to the refrigerator, whipped the door open, grabbed the carton of milk, and drank.

"Greg, use a glass. No, I am not talking to you, Grant. Can you please send the money? When? Like hell." She stood and slammed the phone's receiver into its cradle. "Use a damn glass and close the refrigerator door."

I glanced over and watched her pace in front of the couch. I took one more swig of milk before placing it back on the refrigerator's shelf and slowly closed the door. I tossed the football a couple more times and said, "I need money for the uniform. Coach said he left you a message yesterday."

"Not now, Greg." Carol rubbed her eyes.

"But Coach said if I didn't have the money in by today, I can't play."

"I get it, Greg." She turned toward on me and yelled unexpectedly, causing the boom operator to pull back the microphone. "What the hell do you think I was talking to your father about? Money! It's always about money!" The actress started improvising the script, and I had no idea my next cue.

Liz frantically flipped pages to try and find where Carol jumped.

Out of the corner of my eye, I saw the assistant director stand, but Roland held him at bay and intently watched.

Carol continued her awkward dialogue. "Why cannot anyone ever hear what I need? It is all about what you need and when you need it." She did a rather poor imitation of me as a whiny and spoiled teenager. "Coach said I need the uniform money, and I need my graduation gown money, and I need to pay for prom." She paused and shook her head and stood erect. "Well, guess what? If things don't change, and change fast, you aren't going to prom, or play ball this year, or have a gown for graduation." She dramatically threw herself on the couch as if she was slapped during a 1940s crime film. "I can't do this anymore." She sobbed into the couch cushion.

Carol's impromptu tirade seemed over, and yet she hadn't followed the script, so I thought I'd throw something in to see what would happen.

"I wish I was with Dad."

"What?" She twisted on the couch and glared at me. "What did you just say?"

I glared back. "I said, 'I wish I were with Dad.'"

She shook her head, trying to figure out what to say next. "What do you mean?"

I softened my expression, slowly walked to the couch, and sat next to her. I took her hand and looked deeply into her shocked eyes. "You're rather stressed and still trying to get a grasp on the separation. I feel you don't want me here, or that I'm a constant reminder of Dad. You even say I look and talk like him. I'm not my dad. I don't want to be my dad. I would never hurt a woman like he did. But maybe it'd be easier for you if I went and stayed with him for a while. That way, you can figure out what's best for you."

Carol's face softened, and a spark flashed in her eyes. "I'm at a loss for words." She pulled her hand away and wiped her face. "Why would I not want you here? You're my life, and the only thing I have left."

I shook my head. "No, you have you."

Tears filled her eyes as she reached and touched my face. "You're so beautiful, kind, and considerate. I've been a bitch ever since your father decided he wanted a younger model and left me in this huge place I can't afford." She leaned in so close I thought she was going to kiss me.

I pulled back and turned my head. "We'll figure something out. I'll tell Coach he'll get his money soon. Who cares about prom? I didn't want to wear a stupid gown for graduation. To hell with it all."

She laughed. "Watch your language."

I lifted my brows, rolled my eyes, and joined her laugh. "Whatever."

Carol laid her head on my shoulder, and I wrapped my arm around her. We held this pose for a time.

Roland shouted, "Cut."

Liz suddenly said, "Stay in place while we check the cameras' gates."

Carol held her head against my chest and whispered, "I'm sorry. I'm not sure what happened. I lost it."

"It was good. I just went with you."

"Camera one?" Liz called.

"Clear," the camera one operator said.

"Camera two?"

The camera two operator said, "Clear."

"Three?"

"Clear."

"All clear," Liz's voice rang through the studio. "Lights." The studio lights dimmed, and the fluorescent lights provided a softer hue.

Carol broke away from me and slumped on the couch, as if she just finished a marathon.

Roland approached us with his hand rubbing his chin, contemplating if we needed to reshoot the scene, which would make sense since we completely rewrote the script. He halted in front of us. He looked over at Liz, who rushed to his side. Then he looked back to Carol. "What the hell was that?"

"I'm so sorry, I just…"

Roland cut Carol off. "I don't give a damn. You need to thank the kid for saving your ass." He looked at the script Liz held. "How far off were we?"

"They were completely off," Liz said.

"Is there anything important we missed?" Roland's voice was terse and edgy.

"They completely bypassed the Nike shoe issue."

"Is that extremely important?"

"Nike is a sponsor, so yes, it's the utmost important." Liz closed the script.

Roland mumbled under his breath, looked at his watch, stepped off the set, and called over his shoulder, "Liz and Max, a word, please."

Like obedient, trained golden retrievers, both Liz and Max hurried to Roland's side.

Carol went to the couch where she kept her script hidden underneath and opened it to review her lines.

I listened to the impromptu meeting.

"What are we going to do?" Roland disgruntledly asked. "We don't have time to reshoot this whole scene tonight. And shooting it tomorrow will put us behind schedule."

Max volunteered, "What if we splice and insert the lines about the Nike shoes? We could shoot it first thing in the morning. It should only take a moment if we leave the set as it is."

"Are you suggesting not reshooting the whole scene?" Roland asked.

"It could work if we shoot the kid and voiceover the mom. We just need to lift the two lines from previous takes, and get reaction shot from the son."

"Liz, is this doable?" Roland asked.

"It sounds like the easiest solution. We can even do it without the mom. I'd hate to have to reshoot the whole scene since we're never sure what Carol is going to say or do," Liz hoarsely whispered.

"Agree. I like the way the kid took over the scene and put a twist on the whole dynamic of the situation. I don't want to lose that. It deepens his character and gives him vulnerability."

Max said, "That's why we focus on him with a close-up and just have the mom voiced over."

"Let's do it." Roland walked away. "Max." They disappeared into the shadows.

Liz turned to the set and crew. "All right people, that's a wrap for the day. We'll resume in the morning and start with this scene. Make sure to sign out, and be here on time."

Carol stood. "Liz, may I have a word?"

"Not now." Liz walked away.

"But-"

Liz stopped her in tracks and without looking said, "Carol, you're not scheduled for tomorrow. Enjoy your day off."

Carol cocked her head. "I thought we were starting with this scene in the morning?"

"We are. Without you." Liz turned to me. "See you bright and early."

I looked at Carol and then back to Liz. "Yes, I'll be here."

"Good."

"But Liz, I'm in this scene as well." Carol's voice was desperate.

"We got all we need from you." Liz looked at her clipboard. "You're not called tomorrow. Enjoy the day off." She slapped her clipboard against her thigh and walked off the set.

"But Liz, that makes no sense. Liz. Liz." Carol focused on me. "That doesn't make sense, does it?"

"You're talking to the wrong person. I don't know how this stuff works. I show up when I'm told." I glanced at my watch. "I have to go. Sorry, I've a meet. And if I hurry, I might make this one on time." I darted off toward the dressing room, leaving Carol floundering on the set like a fish out of water.

I barged through the dressing room door, grabbed my back-pack hanging on the back of a chair, zig-zagged around cast and crew members, and rushed out the exit into the bright southern Californian sun.

UNIVERSITY OF CALIFORNIA, IRVINE, OUTDOOR POOL, 1981

I ran across campus, hoping that I got to the pool before the diving event started. My mind throbbed with all the anxiety of trying to fit in all the pieces of my life: pre-med classes, studying, diving practices, competitions, rehearsals for the play, memorizing the scripts, shooting the Movie of the Week, eating, and trying to find time to sleep. Sweat beaded my forehead as my eyes pulsed with the pumping of my blood. I pushed through the gate to the pool.

Coach Schrober, the head Aquatic Director asked, "Cutting it close, aren't you?"

"But I made it." I threw my backpack on the ground and pulled off my shoes.

"Barely. Hurry, you might get to jump off the board before the meet starts. I'll let the officials know you're here." Coach Schrober walked to the score table.

I pulled my shirt and pants off, throwing them on top of the backpack. My heart raced as I fumbled with tying the drawstring to my Speedo.

"David," a voice called.

I scanned the crowd but didn't see from where the voice came. Sue and several people surrounded me, reaching over the iron railing to slap my hand. I felt someone grab my hand and shove something in my palm, but I couldn't tell who did.

"Give 'em hell, David," Sue shouted and blew a kiss.

I pretended to catch it.

"Go Anteaters!" another crowd member shouted.

I automatically waved back and bumped into Kimo, my dorm roommate. Kimo was from Hawaii and promised to deliver as a butterfly specialist on the swim team. He was stacked with biceps and pecs and had the personality of a beagle.

"It's about time you showed up. I was about to put out an A.P.B.!" Kimo laughed.

"Sorry, dude."

"No, prob. Let's see you kick some butt today." Kimo rushed off to the warm-up pool.

I nodded. Something was still crumbled in my hand. It was a note. I opened it:

I WANT YOU NOW!

I looked back into the crowd. No one caught my attention. I shoved the note into my bag and hurried to the diving board.

"Ladies and gentlemen, the score after the first half of the meet is...U.C.I. seventy-two, and Fullerton seventy-four. The next event will be the men's one-meter," the loudspeaker bellowed.

I hopped up on the springboard and adjusted the fulcrum. With a shallow breath, I took three steps, hurdled, and waited for the recoil from the springboard to fling me into the air. I reached above my head, brought my toes to my fingertips, unfolded, and sliced through the surface of the water. The noise silenced as the water swallowed me, and I zoomed through the pool's depth. I lingered on the bottom, and glanced up, witnessing the dance of light refracting against the rippling water. For a moment, everything paused as I felt my arms float weightlessly to sides. I didn't want to move. Returning to the surface would mean returning to all the things that were pressing down on me. I quickly realized I only had a few seconds before needing to resurface for oxygen. I shoved off the bottom, and streamlined to the surface.

"The first diver will be Parker Wallace from Fullerton. He will be doing a front two-and-a-half somersault in the pike position," the announcer said.

I swam to the edge of the pool and pulled myself out.

"Glad you could join us today," Jenny Chandler said in her sweet Alabama accent. Jenny was the 1976 Olympic Champion and appointed by Dr. Don, the Olympic and World Coach who helped me win my gold medal last year at the World Games in Tønsberg, Norway, and brought me out to California to train for the 1984 Olympics. She pressed her arms against her chest.

"I know. I'm sorry."

43

The diver entered the water, and the crowd reacted with hoots, shouts, and clapping.

"Focus on what's happening now," Jenny said.

I nodded.

"Awards. 7, 7.5, 7, 6.5, 7, 7." The scoreboard flashed the numbers and total for Parker. "Next from U.C.I. is David Matthew. David will be performing a front one-and-a-half with two twists."

"David." Jenny stopped me by grabbing my shoulder. "You have to report to the academic counselor right after the meet."

"What?"

Without a word, Jenny patted my shoulder and walked away.

I don't remember diving in the meet. I must have done enough to win, but I can't recall a single dive.

University of California, Irvine, Academic Advisor's Office, 1981

I knocked on Mr. Anderson's door.

"Come in." He motioned for me.

"Thank you, Mr. Anderson."

"Call me Sean." He shuffled some files on his desk.

"I was told you wanted to see me."

"Yes." Sean was in his early thirties, ruffled brown hair, and black horn-rimmed glasses that had difficulty balancing on the bridge of his long, thin nose. He absentmindedly and constantly adjusted the glasses, leaving fingerprints on the lens. "Have a seat. Your last name is Matthew, correct?"

"Yes." I sat on the chair in front of his messy desk, piled with papers and files.

He rummaged through another pile and pulled one out from the bottom.

I watched his hazel eyes strain through the smudged lens and rove over the papers. I appreciated how attractive he was and yet still looked like a nerd.

"Oh, yes." He pushed the glasses back up. "So, you're a premed major on an athletic and academic scholarship."

"Yes."

"But you've been missing a lot of classes." He looked up at me.

"Yes." I felt the weight of the room press down on my shoulders.

"Do you care to explain?" The right side of his mouth pulled back into a crooked smile.

"Sure." Nerves took over, and I was having difficulty forming words.

"And your explanation?"

I took a deep breath and nodded. "I've been cast in a play and I'm also doing a Movie of the Week."

"And this is causing you to miss your pre-med classes?"

"Yes."

He sat back in his chair and crossed his arms. "You do realize how difficult it is to get into the pre-med program?"

"Yes, sir."

"Please, call me Sean."

"Yes, Sean."

"UC Irvine is very diligent with the demands it places on pre-med students. Even missing one class puts you at a disadvantage." He looked at the papers. "And you've missed almost a full week."

I nodded.

"This isn't good. There's no way you'll be able to recover from missing so much. And now you're in jeopardy of losing your scholarships."

Any air left in my lungs rushed out. "I didn't think about that."

"What do you think we should do?" Sean encouragingly asked.

"I don't know."

"I want to help you. I really do" He paused a moment and then grabbed the phone and dialed an extension. "Yes, is Professor Blankenburg in? It's Sean Anderson, from the guidance office." Sean covered the receiver. "I have an idea."

I couldn't imagine what he was talking about. I feared he was going to inform Professor Blankenburg that I was failing my classes and request I be replaced in the play, the Movie of the Week, or both.

"Professor Blankenburg, it's Sean Anderson, from the guidance office. How are you today? Good. I'm sitting with David Matthew, and he said he's in the play. I see. Yes, he mentioned the Movie of the Week as well. It's incredible. I see. Well, we're facing a situation where David may lose his scholarships due to his absences in his major classes. Pre-med. Yes, that's exactly what I was thinking. Would it be a problem? Okay. Okay. Yes. I will. Thank you, Professor Blankenburg." Sean hung up the phone and folded his hands in front of his chin. "I think I may have a solution. I hope you're going to like it. To save your scholarships, you're going to have to transfer to the theatre department."

"You mean drop out of the pre-med program?" There was a sense of relief and fear of disappointing my parents, Hal, and the benefactors.

"It's your choice. But if you try and stay in the pre-med program, I'm afraid you're too far behind and won't be ready for the pre-quarter tests that start on Monday."

"The pre-quarters start on Monday?" Another wave of fear compounded on the first, as I realized that I hadn't even started studying.

"And if you get a 'D,' you'll be automatically removed from the program and lose your scholarships."

"What other choice do I have?" I wondered how Harold Hall and the other benefactors would react to such a change since they paid for the books, dorm, and additional miscellaneous costs.

"I'm glad you asked. Professor Blankenburg wants you to go immediately to his office. He wants you to transfer to the theatre program. Since you're already cast in the play and doing the Movie of the Week, he's willing to grant you Life Experience grades to cover the beginning of the quarter."

"But what about the academic scholarship? Wasn't that for pre-med?" I held my breath.

Sean flipped some forms in my file and scanned down a page. "Your academic scholarship is a general award, which means it can be applied to the major of your choosing. So, we would need to do some paperwork and have the funds transferred to the theatre department." Sean's smile was encouraging. "What do you think?"

"Sure, I guess. But I've never really studied theatre before."

"Well, all I can say is that they must see something in you. UCI is one of the top-notch theatre programs, and you've been cast in the play and Movie of the Week. That says a lot. So, are you sure about this transfer?"

"Yes, I'm sure." The heaviness in the room and my chest evaporated, leaving me feeling as though I could breathe freely again.

"Great." Sean handed me a few papers to fill out. "Do you have any plans for the weekend?"

I paused a moment to think. "I think I'm going to go to the beach and just veg."

Sean stood. "Sounds like a plan. But first, go see Professor Blankenburg. He's expecting you."

"I will. Thank you for everything." I offered my hand.

"My pleasure."

IRVINE, CALIFORNIA, ORANGE COUNTY TRANSIT ASSOCIATION BUS RIDE TO NEWPORT BEACH, 1981

The OCTA bus hissed as it came to a halt and the door squeaked open. The driver rested his fleshy elbow on the large black steering wheel and stared down at me.

"Are you going to Newport Beach?" I don't know why I asked this every time, even though the bus was labeled 'Newport Beach.' I guess there was this little fear that it might not have been the right bus, and I'd end up in a completely different area.

I discovered line number 79 would pick me up just outside of Crawford Hall, travel west on University Drive to Eastbluff Drive, turn right on Jamboree, left on San Joaquin Hills Road, right on Santa Cruz Drive, another right on Newport Center Drive, and drop me off on Pacific Coast Highway, where I'd trek for about a mile to get to this secluded beach that was adorned with craggy cliffs and the softest sand in the world. If I caught the 10:37 a.m. bus, I could get to Newport by 11:37 a.m. and be on my towel, soaking up the rays by noon. I usually went on this adventure on my own to get away from the dorm, campus, diving, everything, and have some 'me' time.

"Yes, this goes to Newport Beach." The driver's eyebrows lifted above the rim of his reflective sunglasses.

"Great." I climbed the steps and glanced toward the back to see if 'my stranger' was on board. I've figured out if I took this particular bus at this specific time, he'd usually be seated in the fourth row on the left and reading the newspaper.

The stranger appeared to be a couple years older than me, great taste in clothes, and would always get off at the Newport Center stop. Maybe he worked retail at one of the many shops in the mall, or he was a paralegal, or had some other corporate job.

I looked forward to nodding to him as I passed; hoping he'd glance up with his deep blue eyes and acknowledge me. As the bus took its route, I'd sneak glances at him and be enamored by the way his trimmed sideburns accentuated his jawline and the dark shadow of whiskers beneath his olive skin.

I'd fantasize we were on a luxury yacht, heading to a remote island in Fiji. We'd pretend we were strangers and not acknowledge or speak to the other. Even during the transported to the hotel, we would silently sit side-by-side, shoulders, hips, and knees bumping and rubbing each other as the Jeep drove over the uneven terrain. We remained silent as the eager bellhop led us to the suite that was prepared and waiting for us. Once alone behind the closed doors, our familiarity took over, and we were no longer strangers, but masters of one another. We'd only venture out of the room to take long walks on the beach as the sun streaked the fading sky with crimson, lavender, tangerine, and rose. When the unwelcome departure came, we packed, said goodbye, and he always left first.

As I watched him exit the bus, I prayed that he'd look back at me. If he did, I knew I was going to have a great and magical day. He always left the newspaper. I'd quickly move up to occupy his seat and read *his* paper

As I emptied my quarters into the machine to pay for my ride, I discovered the stranger was not riding today. Maybe he missed the bus or had the day off. When the machine beeped, I'd maneuver down the thin aisle toward the back. Since my stranger wasn't here, today, I'd have to look for someone new to focus my attention. The new person had to be fit, dark hair, light-colored eyes, and hairy legs were a plus. If I spotted a prospect, I'd find a seat that would allow me the best possible view without calling attention to my stalking. It was innocent fun, and for the hour ride, I was able to create amazing and romantic stories. But today, for some reason, the bus was empty — an older woman with a scarf tied around her head sat behind the driver.

Feeling a bit rejected, I made my way toward the back, counting my steps. *One, two, three, four, five.* There on the seat in the fourth row on the left was a newspaper, neatly folded. I plopped down and wondered if my stranger caught an earlier bus and left this behind for me. I retrieved the paper and leaned against the window. The headline grabbed my attention:

Rare Cancer Seen In 41 Homosexuals

A cement boulder punched me in the stomach.

Doctors in New York and California have diagnosed among homosexual men 41 cases of a rare and often rapidly fatal form of cancer. Eight of the victims died less than 24 months after the diagnosis.

The cause of the outbreak is unknown, and there is as yet no evidence of contagion. But the doctors who have made the diagnoses, mostly in New York City and the San Francisco Bay area, are alerting other physicians who treat large numbers of homosexual men to the problem in an effort to help identify more cases and to reduce the delay in offering chemotherapy treatment.

I scanned the article, and words jumped out like *Kaposi's Sarcoma, outbreak, spots, lumps, swollen lymph glands, kills, young men, death*. I read another section.

> *Many of the patients have also been treated for viral infections such as herpes, cytomegalovirus and hepatitis B, and parasitic infections such as amebiasis and giardiasis. Many patients also reported that they had used drugs such as amyl nitrite and LSD to heighten sexual pleasure.*

> *Cancer is not believed to be contagious, but conditions that might precipitate it, such as particular viruses or environmental factors, might account for an outbreak among a single group.*

The newsprint fell to my lap as I stared out at the changing landscape, counting the telephone poles; *six, seven, eight, nine…. could this be the hell Dad was talking about? Thirteen, fourteen, fifteen… Thou shall not lie with a man like a woman; it is an abomination. Am I an abomination? Am I diseased? Am I going to die?*

Guilt swam through my veins and clouded my vision as tears streamed down my cheeks. In a zombie-like state, I folded the newspaper, shoved it into my backpack, and zipped it closed. I pressed my forehead against the vibrating window and watched two seagulls soar, dive, and chase each other.

UCI MESA VERDE DORMS, 1981

The fluorescent marker squeaked across the page, highlighting lines for memorization for Monday's movie shoot. I should have been studying the cell's structure and function terms for the next day's test, but my mind was spinning with many unrelated ideas. Even though I'd transferred to the theatre department, I was encouraged to keep my anatomy class to fill my general education requirement.

I emptied my book bag's contents onto the bed next to me and my anatomy textbook. The *Dramalogue Magazine*, dog-eared and rumpled, fell out. I'd carried it everywhere since Jennifer let me keep it, studying it and rereading the audition notices. I even went as far as to send pictures and resumes to five AFTRA/SAG projects with cover letters explaining I was recently Taft-Hartley while shooting *Single Parent* and so excited to start my new career. I just knew all of them would be contacting me any day now. I felt confident I'd found something I was good at and could potentially replace the diving when I needed to move on.

A pen, two dimes, four quarters, one penny, small scraps of paper, and a folded newspaper landed on top of the magazine. I unfolded the paper that I found on the Newport Beach bus, and the article about the "gay disease" stared up at me, daring and threatening me.

What if I'm infected? How would I know?

I imagined a single microscopic virus incubating deep within me, so minute that it would take the most reliable microscope even to see it. The toxic protein would adhere one of its suction-like appendages to one of my healthy cells. The invader would infiltrate the cell's membrane, dump its viral poison, and begin to replicate and integrate by transforming this once healthy cell into a host for a vile cocktail. The concoction would replicate into long, snake-like chains and worm out of the healthy cell's membrane, escape and repeat the process until engulfing my entire body.

My dorm room door barged open. I yelped and quickly folded the newspaper.

"Why are we so jumpy?" Sue asked with a devilish grin as she hung on the door.

"Because people don't knock around here."

"Were you doing something?"

"Obviously not, or you would have seen it." I placed the article under my pillow.

With a banshee yell, "Weeeeee!," Sue flung the door closed, vaulted into the air, and landed on the edge of the twin bed, sending the textbook, *Dramalogue*, pen, scraps of paper, and coins into the air.

The coins rattled on the hardwood floor. The pen landed on the mattress, bounced back up into the air, and flipped onto Kimo's bed. The textbook and magazine returned to the same spots, while the scraps of paper fluttered down like snow.

"Make yourself comfortable," I sarcastically said.

"What's ya doing?" Sue spoke in a sing-song manner. Her unwashed, thick brown hair was pulled back in a ponytail, and she wore an oversized ripped T-shirt and grungy basketball shorts that made her look like a child in her father's clothes.

"Nothing much."

"Looks like it." She grabbed the script that I was highlighting and started mimicking me. "Mom, the coach needs the money."

"I don't sound like that," I said.

"You're right; it's more like this." She coughed. "Ma, the co-och nids the monay," she said in an exaggerated southern accent.

"I don't have an accent."

"Ah, but you do. It may be more of a midwestern flair, but you have a twang of some kind."

"You're the one with an accent."

"No, I don't. I'm from Anaheim. We don't have accents." She tossed the script back at me, rolled on her back, and lifted her legs into the air. "So, Gomer, would you like to share a pizza?"

"Well, I do declare, I was hopin' for some grits and opossum stew with some tatters and okra," I responded with a long, drawn-out southern accent.

Sue rolled onto her stomach and supported her chin with her hands. "Sorry Gomer, we are out of such delicacies, but would an old-fashioned pepperoni pizza suffice for tonight? I'll get some crawdads for you tomorrow. Yeehaw!"

I shook my head. "That's so stereotypical and wrong on so many levels." I tried not to laugh.

"I just can't help my little ole self sometimes. Oh, wait a minute." She reached into the pocket of her shorts. "This was left on the table by the RA's room." She handed me a note.

My stomach bottomed out when I recognized the handwriting on the white envelope. The sharp and defiant letters were superbly measured and spaced, like my father's meticulous architecture handwriting. I ripped open one end and pulled out the paper.

HEY BEAUTIFUL,

CONGRATS ON WINNING THE SECTIONALS. I LOOK FORWARD TO YOU WINNING THE CONFERENCE. "THEY KISSED EACH OTHER AND FORMED A FRIENDSHIP" (GILGAMESH). I'LL HAVE YOU, SOON!

XXOO

"Who's it from?" Sue tried to lean in and look at the letter.

"I'm not sure." I hesitantly showed her.

She took the letter and turned it over and found nothing else. She picked up the envelope from the bed and examined it. "I don't understand."

"Neither do I."

"Are you sure? You're as pale as a ghost."

I stared off into space.

"Do you have any idea who it could be from?" Sue's tone changed as she examined the letter again. "Could it be a team-mate playing a joke?"

"I don't know." My voice felt distant.

"It's a sick joke."

I just nodded.

"What does, 'I'll have you soon,' mean?"

I looked at her and couldn't speak.

"You're freaked out." She folded the letter and slid it back into the envelope. "It's someone that follows your diving and knows that you won the sectionals. Wait, what if he was at the sectionals?"

"Why do you assume it's a male?" I asked.

"It doesn't seem to be a method a girl would take. And the word 'beautiful' is throwing a wrench in the female equation for me. I don't know many girls that call a guy 'beautiful.' She wants to be the one called beautiful. Call me old fashioned."

"You actually think it's a guy sending me these notes?"

Sue stopped and looked at me. "Wait a minute. This isn't the first note you have gotten, is it?"

I pictured Sue putting on a deerstalker hat and placing a pipe in her mouth, looking like Sherlock Holmes.

"How many have you gotten?" she continued investigating.

"A few."

"What do you mean, 'a few?'"

"I've gotten a couple of notes."

"When?"

"Different times."

"Where?"

"Different places."

"How?"

"I found one left on my book bag at the library, one on my desk before anatomy class, another slipped into my hand right before a meet, and a couple of more shoved into my community mailbox..."

"Back up. Someone slipped a note into your hand before the meet and you didn't see who gave it to you?"

"I was shaking hands and high-fiving everyone. I remember all those people reaching out over the railing, and I felt someone shove something into my hand. But there were too many people; it could have been anyone." I reached under the twin bed and pulled out a shoebox, shimmied off the lid, and revealed more than a dozen or so notes written on different sizes of notebook and scrap paper. The only thing similar was the handwriting.

Sue grabbed the box. "Shit, this is a lot." She pulled notes out. "Why didn't you tell anyone?"

"I didn't think anything of it."

"You didn't think anything was strange that you were getting notes from the same person?"

"How do you know they are from the same person?"
"Just look at the handwriting."

HEY BEAUTIFUL,
LOOKING HOT!
WE'RE JUST LIKE DAVID AND JONATHAN.

"Definitely from a guy." Sue unfolded another note.

WISH WE COULD BE ALONE.
"YOUR LOVE TO ME WAS WONDERFUL, PASSING
THE LOVE OF WOMEN" (II SAMUEL 1:26).

She pulled out another note.

YOU HAVE THE HOTTEST ASS! CAN'T WAIT TO
OWN IT!

"David these are not good."

HEPHAESTION: I'M GOING TO BEND YOU OVER
AND MAKE YOU SQUEAL.
LOVE, ALEXANDRE THE GREAT.

"These are threats," Sue said.
I pulled all the notes away from her and shoved them into
the box. "They mean nothing." I got up and put the box into
the closet.
Sue's eyes never left me. "Then why are you keeping them?"
I turned and felt a wave of anger that I had been trying to
keep hidden. "I don't know." My body raged.
Sue slowly stood up. "It's okay."
"No, it's not. It's not okay. I don't know what to do. I feel
helpless, and I don't have any idea when another note will appear,
or where. I feel hunted, and I have no clue who the hunter is. At
first, I was okay with it. It was a harmless note, and I was flattered.

55

But when they started showing up in class, here at the dorm, and at the pool, I started getting nervous. I'm always looking over my shoulder everywhere I go."

Sue rushed to me and took hold of my trembling hands. "Okay, okay. Breathe."

I shook my head. "And now you said it could be a guy and that just…"

"Breathe, it'll be okay."

I broke away from her and backed up against the closet door. "How can it be okay? I feel like I have no control over when or where the next note is going to appear or what it's going to say. Are these just harmless jokes? Is this person watching me? Is this person just sitting there behind the bushes and waiting to see my reaction? How far will this go? I was okay being called beautiful and such. But I don't know how I feel when called a 'dirty slut boy.'"

"You got a note that called you a 'dirty slut boy?'"

"Among other colorful names." I buried my face.

Sue gently took ahold of my hands and pulled them away from my face. "Look at me."

I squeezed my eyes tighter.

"Come on, David, look at me." She placed her hands on the sides of my face.

I opened my eyes and noticed that her thin frame was taller than me. I had to look up to see the golden flecks in her brown irises. Her pale skin was accented with tiny tan freckles, and her lips looked thin and tense.

"We'll figure this out together."

Something changed in her eyes. Something different made her eyes darker. Her face morphed as well.

I felt strangeness in my stomach.

"But…"

"Don't." She leaned in and softly placed her lips on mine.

I froze, and my shoulders stiffened as she drew my body against hers.

There was a knock on the door as it opened and Jennifer stuck in her head. "Hello."

I pulled back from Sue's lips and banged into the closet door.

Jennifer came into the room. "What are you two doing in the corner?" Her extra-large smile was accented by her black linen halter-top pantsuit, multi-colored Hermes scarf wrapped around her shoulders, and a gold knotted necklace and matching earrings. Her make-up was evidence of ample time and practice, with the pastel colors blending perfectly and properly accenting her best features. "Hello, Sue."

"Jenn," Sue said.

"It's Jennifer."

I maneuvered around Sue and approached Jennifer. "What are you doing here?"

"We have plans, remember?" Jennifer's eyes danced between Sue and me. "Did you forget?"

"I have been so busy."

"I always have to write notes for this one or else he never remembers." Jennifer directed it to Sue, followed with a chuckle. "I don't know what I'm going to do with him."

"Throw him away and start all over, I guess," Sue sarcastically responded.

Jennifer forced a laugh and then looked at me. "We're meeting my parents for dinner in Newport, you silly."

"That's tonight?" I questioned.

Jennifer nodded.

Silence filled the room.

The phone rang, and I rushed to it. "Hello?"

"David?" the voice on the other end seemed rushed. "David Matthew?"

"Yes."

"This is Skitch Hendricks from *General Hospital* at ABC."

I waved to make sure everyone was quiet and mouthed, *It's General Hospital.* "Yes."

"You sent in a picture and resume, and we'd like to have you as an extra on the show. Would you be interested?"

I contained my excitement. "Yes."

"Great. Would next Thursday work for you?"

"Yes." I didn't even think about my schedule or how I was going to get to Los Angeles.

"I'll have an assistant follow up on Monday with details. Have a great weekend."

"You, too. Thank you so much."

The other end clicked off. I replaced the receiver in the cradle. "I just got on *General Hospital*."

"That's fantastic," Jennifer gloated.

"Awesome," Sue said.

A strange silence filled the room.

Sue grabbed my anatomy book. "Here we go." She held it up and shook it. "I promise I'll get this back to you as soon as possible." She stopped in front of Jennifer. "I'm doing some research on cell mitosis, and I left my book at my boyfriends. David said I could borrow his."

"I didn't know you two were in the same anatomy class," Jennifer's smile grew.

"We're not. It's for my psychology class. I don't feel like going all the way over to the library when all I need is a basic understanding of how the duplicated chromosomes attach themselves to the spindle fibers that set up genetically identical daughter nuclei." Sue opened the door and looked over her shoulder. "Thanks. Have a good evening, you two." She slipped behind the door.

Jennifer looked at me and cocked her head. "You're not wearing that, are you?"

"I guess not."

"Then chop chop. Time's a wasting." Jennifer placed herself on the edge of the bed.

I opened my closet door.

DR. ALTHEA WARNER'S OFFICE— DAYTON, OHIO, 2018

Althea leaned back in her chair and scratched her chin. "We've been working together for how long now, and I'm just beginning to hear about all this?" She dropped her ledger on the floor beside her chair, stood, and went to her desk. "Why have you not shared any of this before?" She lifted her hands into the air and lowered herself on to the desk's chair.

"It's not a big deal." I reached for my checkbook in my satchel.

"You are kidding, right?

I shrugged my shoulders.

She patted her forehead. "You win the World Games at sixteen years old, you move to California and are accepted into the pre-med program at UCI. On a fluke, you meet a beautiful girl and help her with an audition which leads to you getting not only a part in the play, but a lead in a Movie of the Week. And then you escaped from flunking out of pre-med by the skin of your teeth and are transferred to the theatre department, which allowed you to keep your academic and athletic scholarships. All this doesn't sound extraordinary to you?"

"Not really." I felt the need to defend myself. "It's just the way things went."

"You are either the humblest person I've ever met or the most disillusioned." Althea looked at her calendar. "Same time next week?"

I signed my check and handed it to her. "Sure."

She scribbled the next appointment on a business card and held it up for me. "I want you to continue journaling about your time at college. Maybe we can help you get a perspective of what you accomplished, and we can find out what these flashes of images are."

"Okay." I headed to the door as the church steeple's bells rang. "See you next week."

As I exited the small office, the hallway shrank and closed in on me. Anxiousness filled me as I worried if I was going to be able to squeeze through the hall, get down the stairs, and out of the building before the walls crushed and suffocated me. I stumbled down the stairs and encountered another long hall before I could reach the exit. I contemplated if I should crawl to avoid the shrinking ceiling. I decided against crawling and just went for it. I ricocheted off the walls as I made my way to the glass exit door and pushed through to the parking lot. I leaned against the car to calm my beating heart. I glanced up to the second floor, and Althea stood in the window, watching me.

CHAPTER 3

THE ENTERTAINMENT BUSINESS

HOLLYWOOD, CALIFORNIA, 1981—
SET OF GENERAL HOSPITAL

"Go on," Sue said.

"What are you going to do?" I asked with hesitation, although I was excited about what I was going to find behind the guarded gate that protected the *General Hospital* sounds stages from the rest of the world.

"I'll drive around and find a place to have lunch and do homework." Sue forced a smile.

"I feel so bad that you can't come in." Sue and I left U.C.I.'s campus at six a.m. and traveled a little less than two hours to make the eight o'clock call time. Traffic was unbelievably congested.

"I understand."

"Come on; you have to move your car. You're blocking the entrance." A man in a tan guard suit shouted through the driver's window while clutching to a clipboard with the list of names approved to be on the lot.

"All right, all right." Sue looked at me. "Hurry up and get your ass out. I'll meet you here at about five-thirty. Now go." She shoved my shoulder.

I gathered my book bag and opened the door. "Hey, thanks for giving me a ride."

"Not a prob. Just remember me when you become rich and famous."

"How can I forget? You're the best."

"Let's go, move the car." The guard pounded on the car's roof.

"All right." Sue let off the brake, and the car inched forward. I shut the door. "See you later."

I watched as the guard directed Sue to arc around and out of the studio's main entrance. She turned right on Prospect Avenue and disappeared.

"You want to go to that door there." The guard pointed to a glass entrance. "Go in there, and they'll direct you to where you need to be." He motioned for the next car to stop and walked to the driver's side.

"Thank you," I nervously said.

The guard just waved me off and focused on his list to see if the name the driver gave was on it.

I walked across the heated pavement to the glass door. As soon as I opened the door, a gust of coolness from the powerful air conditioners greeted me.

"May I help you?" A voice came from behind the desk.

"Yes. I'm here to do some extra work. It's my first time and…"

The heavyset black lady didn't care. She tapped her manicured finger with bright red nail polish on a clipboard without looking at me. "Find your name and sign beside it. Then you'll go down the hall to the room marked 'Extras.'"

"Okay, I just wanted to know…"

"Down that hall, and you'll find the door on the left." She busied herself with opening mail, pulling headshots out, and placing them in specific piles.

"The bathroom?" I asked.

"What?" She stopped and looked at me for a moment. "This is your first time, sweetie, isn't it?"

I nodded.

"I should've known by the way you walked in here." She nodded her head, and her red painted lips spread into a friendly smile. "The men's room is right next to the Extras' room. You can't miss it."

"Thank you."

"And you're polite too? Will miracles never cease? Go on, honey; you don't want to be late." She waved me toward the hallway.

I smiled and made my way down the hall with glamorous pictures of the show's stars adorning both walls. My chest pumped with excitement with every step I took. I pushed open the men's room door and was relieved to find it empty. I went to the sink and ran the cold water, cupped a hand full, and splashed my face. I didn't recognize the reflection in front of me as the water dripped from my nose and chin. I took a moment and studied the image. The eyes were red and blurred with tears. There was a distance in the eyes, a veil that seemed to mask the pupils and hide something. It was a look that I wasn't able to put into words, but there was a secret. Was the secret growing, or was I managing it? *How much longer will I be able to keep it under control?*

The door flung open. "Yeah, yeah, yeah. I'll be right there. I need a moment."

I grabbed some paper towels and dried my face.

Famous golden curls filled the mirror next to me as I shared the sink with Tony Geary. He turned on the faucet and rubbed his hands under the running water. He peeked over at me and elongated his spine. "You're new?"

I couldn't speak. I just nodded.

Tony refocused on his hands under the running water, turned the faucet off, flicked his fingers, and used the remaining water to control flyaway hairs. "No matter how much they spray my hair, it still seems to have a mind of its own. How do I look?" He turned to me and posed, with his arms out to the side.

"Good. You look good."

"Thanks." He went to the door, pulled it open, and glanced over his shoulder. "See you on set." Then he was gone.

That was Luke. I just met Luke Spencer. I gathered my backpack and went to the room marked "Extras."

Only four people were sitting around on couches; an older couple that seemed to know each other and two twenty-somethings that sat on opposite sides of the sofa. They all stared at me as I made my way into the center of the room, which looked like a doctor's waiting room. Sparse. White. Up in the corner was a monitor projecting the activities taking place in the Kelly's Diner interior set. I put my book bag next to a chair and sat down, entirely unnerved by the silence in the room.

The door opened, and a rather stout man with wild white hair and bifocals came in holding a clipboard. *Is everything run by clipboards here?* His foot held the door open, and his urgent breathing indicated that he was under some time crunch. "I'm Skitch Hendricks, head of Extra Casting here at *General Hospital,* and I want to check everyone in quickly. When I call your name, let me know that you're here. Miles Carson?"

The older man responded, "Here."

Skitch check off the name on the clipboard. "Skylar Edwards?"

"That's me." A pretty blonde raised her hand.

"Good," Skitch said. He squinted his eyes. "Sybil Galginhiemer, you're back to grace us with your presence, I see."

"Hello, Skitch," said the older woman who was impeccably dressed.

"Cynthia Holmes?" Skitch continued down the list.

There was no answer. We all looked at each other, but there was only the other young man and me. "Cynthia?" Skitch looked up and saw that no one was responding. "So, Cynthia is a no-show?" He looked at his wristwatch and notated something on the clipboard.

Skylar leaned to me and whispered, "That's the end of her on this show."

I just nodded.

"David Matthew?"

"Here." I raised my hand.

Skitch looked over his bifocals at me for an extended period. "You're the new kid. Good. Real good." He went back to the list. "And that leaves Steven Wilson?"

Steven had perfectly coiffed hair with feathered bangs and looked like one of the models I had in my Norma Sharkey portfolio.

"Yes, that's me."

Skitch made a last checkmark on the list. "All right, everyone has been here before, except David, so you all know the routine. Here's the situation. All of you will be in Kelly's Diner today. It's a long scene, and it's going to be a long day. So, I need you to make sure you're awake and listen to what the director has to say. I'm not sure where everyone's going to be, but you're going to be coupled." He looked back at the clipboard. "Of course, Miles and Sybil, you're a couple, as usual. Skylar and Steven is a couple. And that leaves David." He looked thoughtfully at me. "Don't worry; we'll figure something out." He wrote something on the clipboard as he continued speaking. "Make sure that you fill out your paperwork, which is located next to the coffee." He indicated to the table under the monitor. "Give them to Tonya at the front desk as you leave. Make sure you fill them out if you want to get paid. Now, let me see what you're wearing."

Everyone stood up as Skitch went around and looked them over. I felt like I was on display and judged on my clothes. I didn't know that I had to bring options. He stopped in front of Miles and Sybil and nodded. "Nice." He walked to Skylar. "Do you have a sweater?"

"Yes," she said and blushed.

"What color?"

"Pink."

"Wear it." Skitch stopped in front of Steven. "Change the shirt. That pattern will cause the camera to bleed."

"I have solid blue."

"Wear it." He stopped next to me and studied my clothes. He nodded. "Keep it."

I felt a sigh of relief.

"Okay. Now we're going to be heading to the set. I'll need you to remain completely silent and don't get in the way. If the director asks you to move, don't say anything, but move. My assistant, Tim, or I'll come over and make sure you understand. For some reason, they're having a tough time with this shoot's set-up, so we need to remain as flexible and focused as possible. Understand? We'll first walk the set, so you can get some sense of it. Then Tim or I'll place you in certain positions. We'll rehearse with the stand-ins and then shoot with the stars. Remember, don't talk to the actors unless they speak to you. We're not here to distract them; we're here to enhance them. Understand?"

Everyone mumbled in agreement.

"What are stand-ins?" I asked Skylar.

"Those are the people who stand in for the stars to make sure the lighting is right. That way, they can save time and not have to wait for the actual actors to finish makeup and hair."

A smaller man opened the door. "They're ready."

"Great. Everyone, this is Tim, make sure you pay attention to him or me. Let's go." Skitch ushered everyone out of the room.

Tim stopped the group. "A lot of adjustments are happening on set right now. Watch out for cables, and don't touch the props on the table unless you're asked. Whatever you do, don't touch the lights or cameras. I hate to say this but remember, you're living props or stage dressing. Now, before you go in, you're enjoying a wonderful time at Kelly's. I want you engaging in conversation with your date. But don't say anything. The mics will pick up every sound, and we'll have to start all over." Tim stopped and cocked his head to listen to the earpiece that was attached to a walkie-talkie. "This scene is being difficult to light, so be extra alert." He unclipped the walkie-talkie from his belt, brought it close to his mouth, and pressed a button. "We're coming now." He clipped the walkie-talkie back onto his belt. "Follow me."

I felt like I was back in kindergarten and we were going to the gym, art, or music class, and the teacher told us that we had to be extra quiet and stay in line. Our small caravan snaked down the hall and turned left, traveled through a more extended passage, and stopped at the door with a sign above that when lit would say, "On Air." We were greeted with a gust of cooler air as we walked into the darkened barn-like structure.

This massive structure was divided and quartered into spaces about 25 x 20 square feet and completely furnished and designed to look like different rooms and locations. The ceiling was constructed with metal bars with various sizes of the lights and filters dangling above each set and with a number to identify the playing area. The Quartermain's living room, a hospital room, Jeff Webber's Office, a bedroom, a hotel room, and a kitchen were in shadows as we passed.

Lights flooded an area just ahead as we heard the sounds of things being moved and metal bars pulled into place. Our group came to a stop at the edge of Kelly's Diner as the crew continued to fix lights, dress the set, and prepare the monitor for the stage manager and assistants. The room looked smaller than it did on television. Two people were sitting like statues at a table near the center of the space as a crew member took a light reading against their faces with an object that looked like it came out of *Star Wars*.

"She's at seven-point-four," the man with the light reader said as he placed the contraption next to the woman's cheek. He moved to the man's cheek and looked off into the darkness. "He's still at six-point-eight."

"Let's try this," a voice echoed from the darkness. With a click, the light filtering the woman's face altered ever so slightly. The crewman repositioned the contraption next to her right cheek. "Closer. It's at seven-point-two. But wait." He moved the tool to her left cheek. "She's too hot on this side now."

"I understand, let me make some adjustments," the voice called back.

The two actors remained frozen, and the crewman made his way to the other side of the table. "Stan?"

"I'm working on it."

"No, but I think I may have something." The man replaced the tool next to the woman's left cheek, looked at the reading, and then looked over his right shoulder. "Stan, there's refraction bouncing off the lighting outside the window."

"Chuck, check the exterior lighting."

Running steps filled the space as the exterior lights outside the window shook. "Stan, is the window in the shot?"

"Hold on, let me check. That's a negative, Chuck."

"Hold it," the crewman shouted next to the actors. "Whatever you just did, worked, she's at seven-point-zero." He reached over to the man's cheek. "He's now at six-point-nine."

Stan called back, "Lock it in, Chuck."

"Done."

A voice came over the loudspeaker, "Can we clear the set?"

The crewman with the light reading tool took a couple of more quick readings and rushed into the shadowed sideline.

"Please place the extras," the speaker filled the barnlike structure.

Skitch quickly waved for us to walk onto the Kelly's Diner set. The temperature rose some degrees under the lights. He quickly motioned for Miles and Sybil to sit at a round table in the corner. He placed Skylar and Steven at another table. He motioned for me to sit at the bar.

As I sat on the stool and swung my legs around, someone handed me a menu and whispered, "Pretend you're deciding on what you want to order."

I nodded.

"Check the cameras," the voice bellowed loudly. "Camera One, you'll pan up the menu and establish Kelly's and then pan over the patron's right shoulder at the bar to the discover Luke and Laura at the focused table. Camera Two, be ready for Laura's close-up. Camera Three, I need you to lock in on Luke. Let's do a walkthrough. People—we're working. Quiet on the set."

All the noise dissipated.

"Camera One, pull back a bit on the menu, we want a seamless pan over the patron's shoulder to focus on Luke and Laura's table. That's better. Pan back slowly. No, Camera Two, stay with Laura. Camera One, I need a clear two-shot of Luke and Laura. Three, too tight, pan back. That's great. Hold. One, there are some jerky motions as you panned up the menu. Can you smooth it out?"

"Affirmative," a voice rang out from behind camera one.

"Let's walk through that again."

Silence filled the space as someone positioned the salt and pepper shakers closer to me on the bar counter.

"That's it, One. Two, make sure you're level with Laura's eyes, I don't want you looking up her nose. Let's walk through it again. From the top."

I was intrigued by the menu's description. It literally made no sense. "Hot Peanut Butter Jumbo Lia: a smooth lasjing ehakaskjc rthosdjpadc thopdaksf." I chuckled.

"Let's bring in the actors."

I heard the chairs scrape against the floor as the stand-ins walked offset. The hubbub and commotion filled the space. I dared not move. I was able to see the action in the mirror that was behind the bottles. A group of about three people trailed Genie Francis as she gleefully walked on set and waved to everyone before sitting at the table. She was immediately surrounded by hair and makeup as they made final touches.

An announcement came over the speakers. "Anthony Geary, please report to the Kelly Diner set."

"I'm here." Anthony rushed to the chair opposite Genie. He looked around and spotted me. "Hey, newbie."

My spine stiffened, I diverted my eyes back to the menu, and I didn't respond.

"Clear the set."

I peeked over the menu and saw the hair and makeup teams scamper off. Anthony and Genie became Luke and Laura as they took each other's hands.

"Rehearsal for cameras in one, two…One, pan over the shoulder to a two-shot. Pick up on Two. Go Three. Back to Two. That's when your first line comes in, Luke."

"Got it," Anthony said. "Laura, you can't believe everything you hear."

"Go Two, on Laura's reaction," the director said.

"It seemed so real, Luke," said Genie.

69

"Great and then we'll remain here going between Two and Three, until Luke's line, 'It hurt that you would believe him over me.' Hold everything. Gloria's coming down."

The set became tense. I had no idea what was happening. I just got a sense that it wasn't good to have this Gloria lady come on set. Still, I wasn't daring to move, so I peered over the menu into the mirror.

A short lady with her hair in curls, wearing a matching red skirt and jacket and white Converse tennis shoes marched on the set, followed by two assistants. She held a white Styrofoam cup of coffee, chewed gum, and beelined it to the table where Anthony and Genie were sitting. "Where are their plates of food and drinks? Come on people we don't have all day. The props should have been attended to already." She looked at one of the assistants. "Why's this not taken care of?"

A prop person rushed out carrying two plates with sandwiches and placed them in from of Anthony and Genie.

"What's this?" Gloria handed off her cup and picked up a plate. "This is dried out, look at how the bread's curled. Take this away." She shoved it off to the prop person. "Take that one as well." Gloria walked to the edge of the set and looked out into the shadow. "Gary, we're going to have to do something else. I can't have sandwiches like that served in Kelly's."

"Do you want me to come down?" Gary, the director, said over the P.A.

"No, reset everything, and give me a minute." Gloria waved. As she walked back to the table where Luke and Laura sat, she cased the set. She stopped and looked in my direction.

I quickly looked at the menu.

I heard her stop next to me. I felt her study me. "Who's this?" Gloria questioned loudly.

My body stiffened again.

Another set of footsteps rushed to my side. "He's an extra," Tim said.

"I know he's an extra. But why's he sitting at the bar? He doesn't look old enough to order a drink. Kelly's doesn't serve minors."

"You can't see his face with the menu," Tim said.

"But I see his reflection in that mirror when Camera Two is on." Gloria pointed to the mirror behind the bar. She huffed and turned to the shadowed area. "Come on, people, what are we doing today? This is sloppy. Let's get this together. Do I have to do everything?" She didn't wait for an answer and walked back to my side. "Look at me," she directed.

I slowly turned and looked at her.

"What's your name?"

"David."

"David, what?"

My heart raced. This tiny lady held such power and energy. She scared me. "Matthew."

"Well, David Matthew, welcome to G.H. Now will you get off that stool for me?"

"Yes, ma'am." I scooted off the stool and stood in front of her.

She rubbed her chin and looked back to the shadowed area. "Gary, David is going to be a waiter today. Have wardrobe pull a waiter's uniform. Now, we'll keep the same camera angles, and have David pick up the menus from the bar and walk them over to Luke and Laura. Give them the menus, and have camera One establish a three-shot. David will exit, and we'll resume with the rest as planned. Okay?"

"Sounds great," Gary's voice rang throughout the studio.

"Let's walk through this while wardrobe gets the clothes." Gloria marched back to me. "I want you to start at the edge of the bar, pick up the menus so the camera can establish Kelly's Diner, and then slowly turn and walk to the table next to Luke and hand them both a menu. Then exit in that direction." She pointed to the shadowed area. "Can you do that?"

"Yes, ma'am."

"Good. Show me."

I stood by the bar and followed the direction, picked up the menus, slowly turned, and walked to the table next to Luke.

"Stop." Gloria rushed up beside me. "Good, but I need you to be closer to Luke." She repositioned me so Luke's shoulder brushed against my crotch. He looked at where he made contact and smirked. Genie batted his hands. "Give them the menus."

Luke took it and said, "Thank you."

I started to walk away in the direction she directed.

"Wait a minute," Gloria said. She pointed back to Luke. "What do you say when he says, 'Thank you?'"

"You're welcome?" I said.

"Then do it."

I repositioned myself and handed Luke and Laura the menus.

"Thank you," Luke said.

"You're welcome." I smiled and nodded before walking to the edge of the set.

"And then we'll pick up the scene from here. Let's do this." Gloria marched off the set.

Skitch came rushing to my side. "You just got your first under-five."

"What is that?"

"It means you get paid more."

Before I knew it, wardrobe was presenting me with a uniform. I quickly changed right there. Makeup was rapidly applied.

"Go back to One," the director's voice announced.

THE UNIVERSITY OF CALIFORNIA, THE CLOSING OF THE VISIT OF THE OLD LADY, 1981.

"How do I look?" Jennifer asked nervously.

We stood in the late afternoon sun in front of Professor Blankenburg's front door to celebrate the closing of *The Visit of the Old Lady*. The high archway donned with twinkling white lights, and potted ferns majestically sat on both sides of an oak door. A sense of pride filled my chest, and anticipation ran through my veins of what lied behind the entrance. I had never attended a closing party, especially one where the play received such praise and positive reviews. Mike, Roland, and Liz were in the audience and met with me inside the stage door after the curtain.

*****

"David, you're a natural on stage as well," Mark Shapiro said.

Roland added, "You were outstanding."

Our little gathering was soon encircled by the cast of the show, wanting me to introduce them to the creative team of the soon to be released Movie of the Week.

"All right, everyone. Let me introduce you. This is Roland Lockhart, the director; Mike Shapiro, the producer; and Liz Burke, the stage manager for *Single Parent*. This is the cast of *The Visit*," I stammered as my cheeks reddened.

A large hand reached over my shoulder and offered it to Mike. "I'm Brian Thompson, and it's a pleasure to meet you." His voice was deep and guttural.

Mike accepted the large mitt and shook it. "Nice to meet you."

Brian's gladiator muscles put stress on his shirt's seams as he made his way into the center of the crowd.

"Wow, you are fit," responded Mike as he tried to pull his hand away from Brian's grip.

Brian's laugh was deep.

Roland leaned and whispered into my ear. "I'm going to sneak out while I can. You did a swell job." He squeezed through the crowd before I could say goodbye.

Liz jumped to Mike's defense. "Thank you all for such a wonderful production. Unfortunately, I must get Mike back to the hotel; he has a flight to New York this evening." She guided Mike through the crowd, out the stage door, and disappeared.

Brian turned to me and wrapped his massive arms around me. "Thanks, man."

*****

"David? How do I look?" Jennifer's plea pulled me back to Professor Blankenburg's front door.

"Oh, you look swell."

Jennifer's face scrunched up. "Swell?"

"Great, you look great."

Her eyes narrowed.

"No, you look beautiful. Really beautiful."

"You think so?"

"Yes." I nodded my head as quickly as I could.

"Thank you. Now we can stay for only a few minutes. I want the faculty to see that I was here, and we're outie, okay? We must get over to the Kappa Kappa Gamma house for the potluck dinner." She turned and rapped on the door using the large iron knocker.

The door was opened by an elegant woman with grey hair framing her thin and tanned face. Her pink lips immediately smiled as she dramatically invited us in. "Hello, I'm Deloris Blankenburg, the professor's wife. Welcome to our modest abode." Behind her, guests mingled and talked in little groups.

Jennifer grabbed my hand, merged through the doorway and scanned the pods of guests.

"David." Deloris's voice, with a hint of a Southern accent, stopped me.

I let go of Jennifer's hand and the guests engulfed her.

"I don't want to keep you from your girlfriend." Deloris's heavily mascaraed eyes seductively blinked.

"Oh, no, we're not…it's okay." I glanced back to see if I could see Jennifer in the crowd.

"She's gorgeous, in a Vivian Leigh kind of way." Deloris closed the door and leaned against it.

I chuckled. "Jennifer would love to hear you say that. We went to Kappa Kappa Gamma's Halloween party as Scarlett O'Hara and Rhett Butler."

"I see." Deloris's face softened as her eyes scanned down my body and back to my face. She nodded her head. "You can do well in this business if you choose. You're not just pretty; you have something else going on." She reached out and lightly brushed my bangs to the side. She tilted her head as she gently brushed her fingertips over my brow, my cheekbone, and along my jawline. "You have beautiful bone structure, and your jaw could cut glass." Her eyes became intense, and she puckered as she grazed my lips with her manicured nails. She stepped closer and pressed her chest against me. "So young, so fresh, so raw."

Two massive arms wrapped around me and lifted me off the ground with ease and placed me to the side. Brian Thompson towered over Deloris. "This isn't the time to play Blanche DuBois, Deloris. We closed that show last year. You need to get another drink and cool off. The kid has not even gotten past the foyer yet."

For the first time, Deloris slurred her words, and her eyes glassed over. She teetered toward me and grabbed the nape of my neck. She stared at me for what seemed to be an eternity. "Young man!" She pulled me toward her. "Young man! Young, young, young man! Has anyone ever told you that you look like a Prince?"

I looked over to Brain, who was obviously enjoying the performance.

"Come here. I want to kiss you, just once, just softly and sweetly on your mouth!" She pressed her lips against mine before I was ready. She pushed me into Brian, who held me up. "Now run along, quickly! I have to be good." She started to exit but stopped and placed her hand on my chest. "It would be nice to keep you. No!" She withdrew her hand as if it burned. "I must keep my hands-off children." With that, she flitted into the crowd and disappeared.

Brian chuckled, nodded, and clapped. "That was awesome. She played Blanche in *Streetcar* in last year's spring performance, and she still hasn't let it go. She was truly fantastic. You should have seen your face."

"I didn't know what to do? My heart's still pounding." I tried to appear that I wasn't affected in the least.

"That was great."

The front door opened, and Theresa Larkin, the leading lady of the play, and her handsome boyfriend, Jeffrey Meeks, stood in the entrance. The way the sun backlit them added to the glamour and beauty this couple possessed. The crowd hushed, turned, and everyone applauded for the royal couple of the U.C. Irvine Theatre Department. The two waved to the masses and made their way toward the living room, bypassing Brian and me.

Another guy came up to Brian. "It's time to get out of here before we get stuck having to listen to her majesty recreate every moment she had on stage."

"All right. Can David come with us?" Brian asked.

"I don't care, but let's go!" he said as he rushed out the door and was followed by two others.

"We're going to Disneyland. Want to come? We do it after every production. It's like tradition." Brian's face was radiating with excitement.

Jennifer came rushing up, took my hand, and pulled me toward the door. "Okay, I did my loop, so let's get out of here."

"Wait a minute, Jennifer." I dug my heels into the floor.

"What?" She impatiently looked at Brian. "Oh, hello, Brian." She quickly looked back at me.

"How are you, Jenny?" needled Brian.

"It's Jennifer."

"Okay. Jennifer," Brian chuckled.

"David, we have to go." Jennifer pulled my hand.

I didn't budge. "I'm going to go hang out with Brian."

"What?"

"We're going to Disneyland and say hi to Mickey and Minnie," Brian said.

Jennifer leaned in close to me and whispered, "Seriously?"

I whispered back, "Why not? It could be fun."

"But I can't. You know that. I have to get to the sorority house."

"Why don't you go there, and I'll go see Donald Duck and Goofy."

Her face soured, and then she smiled. "Sure, that'll be great. You guys go have a good time and give my regards to Tinker Bell." She turned and left the house and didn't look back.

"I think she's pissed," I said.

"So, what? You two aren't married," Brian said.

"You're right. Let's go."

He wrapped his big paw around my neck and ushered me out.

DISNEYLAND, CALIFORNIA, 1981

"When the train rounds that bend, we rush up and jump on the back. You got it?" Brian busily poured two shots of rum into plastic glasses.

"Where'd John and Chris go?"

"They went to steal the apple from the Wicked Witch. Here." He handed me a glass. "Down it on three." He held his glass up and waited for me to hold mine up. "One, two, three!" He downed the contents. I followed and coughed from the burning path the liquid made down my throat.

The rails started shaking.

"It's coming. You know what to do?" Brian's excitement lit up his blue eyes, and he looked like a child, even though he was six-foot-four-inches of solid muscle.

I proudly replied, "When the train comes around the bend, we run up the embankment and jump on the back."

"Here she comes. Get ready." Brain put the bottle back into his backpack and squatted.

I mimicked him.

The whistle blew as the red train curved around the bend. "Now!"

Brian sped up the hill, and I followed. He leaped over the guard rail and hid behind a bush. I followed. We waited. My heart raced causing my eyesight to pulse and my body to vibrate with anticipation. The red train rattled past.

"Go!" shouted Brian.

He rushed from behind the bush and jumped onto the back of the train with ease. I followed, hesitate before leaping. Brain grabbed the back of my pants and started to pull me on board.

"Hold it there!" announced a Disney employee.

Brian released my pants, and I slipped off the train. He jumped with a banshee yell and ran past me.

"Hold it there!" the employee shouted as the train continued.

I ran after Brian down an embankment.

Brian leaped and cleared the guard railing.

I jumped, my foot clipped the metal, and I flew forward face-first into the cement sidewalk.

"Come on!" Brain called.

"Brian!" I yelled as I sprawled out on the concrete.

He ran back and helped me up. "Oh, shit."

"What? What is it?" I said, dazed. I felt no pain as blood gushed from my chin and down the front of my shirt. "Oh, no. What happened?"

Brian scooped me up in his massive arms and carried me to a bathroom.

"Take your shirt off." He rummaged through his backpack.

I pulled my shirt off, looked in the mirror, and saw a gash seeping blood under my chin.

Brian pulled out a tank top and a T-shirt from his bag and draped them over his right shoulder. "Ball up your shirt and press it against your chin to try and stop the bleeding." His large hands took my shirt from me, folded it up, and gently pressed it against my chin. The cotton shirt turned red.

"Is it bad?"

Brian pulled the shirt from my chin to look. "It's going to need stitches." He covered the cut and added more pressure.

"Oh, geez." My head felt woozy.

"It's not so bad, at least you didn't mess up your pretty face. Here hold this against your chin." Brian got some paper towels and soaked them with warm water. "Once I get you cleaned up, put on this tank top, and we'll go to the emergency." He carefully wiped the blood from my cheeks, nose, and chest. "Keep the pressure on your chin." Brian unbuttoned his shirt and shimmied his massive shoulders free, exposing the results of hours of pumping iron.

"Did I get blood on your shirt?"

"No, I don't think so." His developed pecs danced as he slid the T-shirt over this head, shoulders, and arms. "Security may be looking for us by the color of our shirts, but changing them may be just enough to give some doubt."

"Do you always have spare shirts in your backpack?"

"You never know when you're going to need to change." He laughed as he took the tank top from the counter. "Lift your left arm, but keep the pressure on your chin." Brian guided the tank top over my arm, and carefully pulled the shirt's neck over my head. "Let me hold your shirt against your chin, while you slip your left arm through the tank top." He got behind me, encasing me against his rock hard chest, and replaced my hand to keep the pressure on my chin. I slid my arm through, and the tank top's straps settled on my shoulders as the rest of the material swallowed my body.

"Look at us," Brian said as he smiled. "Are we two misfits, or what?"

Brian's six-foot-four-inch frame dwarfed my five-foot-nine-inches. I felt safe in his arms as they wrapped around my chest. He could've crushed me with the power his arm portrayed, but he was caring and gentle.

He spoke to my reflection in the mirror. "We're going to say we were over by Cinderella's Castle and you tripped on the curb of the sidewalk. That's how you fell and busted your chin. We'll promise not to sue the park."

"Okay." I wanted to remember us like this, the gentle giant and the elfish kid.

DR. ALTHEA WARNER'S OFFICE— DAYTON, OHIO, 2018

As Althea rubbed her chin and looked over my journal, I looked out at the church tower with the bell, encased in shiny ice crystals.

"Were you affected by the ice storm last night?" Althea asked as she skimmed.

"We had several large limbs fall in the back yard, but luckily none of them hit the house."

She glanced up over the edge of her glasses and arched an eyebrow. "A tree fell on the neighbor's house and took out the cable line."

I nodded and giggled. "The puppies weren't sure what to make of it. As we were outside, broken branches littered the yard, like a war zone. It was quite scary."

"Especially if a branch fell on one of them."

"One almost did. Barkley stopped to do her business when we heard a crack, ice fell, which scared her, and then a branch landed next to her. She scurried away and ran for the door."

Althea chuckled. "I would've, too." She stopped and looked at me with a stern expression. "Oh, that reminds me. I wanted to ask if you'd mind if I brought Glady in next week. She's my Golden Retriever, and she's having surgery to have some cysts removed, and I'd like to keep an eye on her. She's almost twelve."

My face lit up and smiled. "I'd love that."

Althea smiled back. "I thought you might. I sometimes bring her in, and the clients seem to enjoy her. It calms them."

"Dogs are the best."

The mood in the room shifted as Althea returned to my journal, scrunched her brows into one, and readjusted her glasses. She took a deep breath, leaned back, and seemed to be swallowed by the overstuffed chair. "Thank you for sharing these moments. How do you feel about them?"

I didn't need time to think about my response, or maybe I was still thinking about what it was going to be like to have a dog in the room during a session. "They seem to be random and all over the place."

"Would you like to talk about them?"

"Sure, I guess." I wondered if I could bring Bella or Barkley, my two Boston Terriers, or both to a session. Would Jake allow that?

"You don't sound too sure." Althea cocked her head.

I shifted my weight on the couch. "No, I do. I'm just afraid that I'm going to learn that it was all made up."

Althea took her glasses off and tapped her lower lip. "It's not so much the matter that it happened or not. What's important is what you've adopted as truth. Are you following me?"

"I think, but I can't remember any real details."

Althea slid her glasses back on and looked at her notes. "You mentioned the accident at Disneyland with…" She looked down at the journal. "Yes, Brian Thompson." She pulled her glasses off again and looked at me. "Is this the actor, Brian Thompson, from *Hire to Kill*?"

I was stunned that Althea would know his film. "Yes."

"You seem shocked?"

"You don't seem to be the type that would like that kind of film."

"Who said I liked it? But I did. I love to see women empowerment in spite of the misogynous prick your friend played." She ignored my reaction. "Were you attracted to Brian?"

"How do you mean?" My spine elongated, and my arms immediately crossed my chest.

She repositioned her glasses and looked at my journal. "You said that you felt safe in Brian's arms."

"He was like a big brother."

"That doesn't answer my question."

"Why does everything have to be sexualized?"

"Why are you so defensive?"

"I'm not."

She nodded, looked at me, and waited.

The silence in the room was deafening. I dared myself not to respond, but the silence was intimidating.

"Alright. Maybe. I'm not sure. I don't know." I ran my hands over my hair and down my face. "No." I took a deep breath. "He was kind and gentle, and I liked that. He looked at me differently than most people. But…"

"But what?" Althea's voice was caring.

I stared at her for a long time. "I don't know."

She nodded again and looked back at the journal. "You talked a little about some of these recovered memories or flashes of images that you have been having. And you aren't sure if you made these things up. Did you make up the stitches under your chin?"

"What?"

"Do you have a scar under your chin?" Her voice was clear and patient.

"Yes."

"Is the scar real?"

"Yes."

"Did you get the scar from falling and hitting your chin?"

"Yes."

"Did you fall and cut your chin while you were at Disneyland?"

"Yes."

"Were you with Brian Thompson at Disneyland when you fell and cut open your chin?"

"Yes."

Althea smiled. "So, that's real to you."

My eyes danced to different objects in the room. "Yes."

"Good. That's where we'll start." Althea closed the journal. "If we can string together these images, maybe we can create a better picture for you to look at and then determine if the situations took place, or if they were ways for you to cope at the time. You see, I don't believe we intentionally created a traumatic situation for the fun of it. It's always based on some truth. I do think that we can embellish or diminish the details to fit the schematics of our brain in order to function the best we can in society."

I felt pulled toward Althea. Maybe we can finally figure out why these images are flaring up now and maybe find a way to put an end to them once and for all.

Althea continued her clinical assessment. "Most people are reluctant to acknowledge sexual abuse of any type, even though they recognize abusive events."

I interrupted her. "But Brian never sexually abused me."

"I didn't say that he did. But he's a part of this track of your memory. He's important to your survival. You see, I believe that sexually abused people have this continuum scale. On one end of the scale are the predators and abusers, and on the other end are the allies and caretakers. A person who is constantly on guard and experiencing high-stress defensiveness, such as you were during this period, the elements of both extreme ends of the scale start flying together to provide a manageable medium. You see, taking qualities from this end of the scale and combining to the qualities from the other end provides the person a means to create a safe environment."

"I don't understand."

"Many people don't want to be associated as a victim or survivor. I think this may be an issue with you, because this stigma doesn't fit your self-image. Since your ego is refusing to accept this label, it may be causing a hindrance in recalling the events in specific details because you aren't able to classify the abuse in your mind. By negating an appropriate category in your subconscious, or even your conscious, your boundaries were blurred. You weren't able to decipher the difference between when someone truly cared for you from someone who wanted something. A sexually abused person can be successful for a period, repressing or refusing to remember the event or events. There'll always be a certain odor, a color, a trigger that'll reveal and bring more of the puzzle pieces to the surface. Sometimes these bits of memories may appear as flashes and make you feel they were imagined or made up. Most often, humans only acknowledge the memories that are safe, and as time passes, the events fade further into the past and puts distance between the person and the event."

Althea abruptly stood up and dashed to the bookshelf behind her desk. She ran her fingers over the spines of the books inhabiting the shelves. "I know it's here. I saw it the other day." She paused as if she was trying to remember what she was initially looking for. "When we're not able to understand or we refuse to understand an experience completely, we'll forget about the details because we don't want to think about, remember, or relive it. And by not thinking about it, we can trick the mind into not remembering those unwanted images and details. It isn't because we can't recall them; we subconsciously choose not to recall them. The human brain is remarkable at adapting, adopting, and protecting. Therefore, people forget traumatic events or experiences in their lives." She released a held breath. "I can't find it right now. I'll find it, and I'll show it to you next time." She threw up her hands and crept back to her chair.

I reached for my satchel to retrieve my checkbook.

"We still have ample time. Do you have to leave early?" Althea's voice was terse.

"No, I just thought our time was up." I replaced the checkbook into the satchel's outer pocket.

"So, do you recognize or acknowledge yourself as a victim?"

My chest and throat constricted. "The word victim's true definition is foreign to me. It can be spoken in French, Italian, Greek, Spanish, or even Latin and the tonality of the word would have the same restricted effect. I have a hard time considering myself a victim because there are so many factors that go into the deconstruction of the word. Just the way it's spelled provides me with this image of two males, Vic and Tim. These two males are at odds with each other. Vic is short for 'victorious,' which embellishes the masculine ideals, the alpha, and the physically overbearing macho man. Tim is short for 'timid,' who encases all the feminine qualities that are considered unworthy and emotionally unbalanced. The polarities of these two males are in a constant tug-of-war within me, where neither one appears superior. The word 'victim' also represents Vic as the abuser, while Tim is the abused. Could they both harmoniously reside within me and be cohorts?

"And then there's the image of Brian and me in the bathroom mirror at Disneyland that contradicts this ideology, because Brian, although he was the 'Vic' and I the 'Tim,' was an example of someone that's caring and compassionate. That's why I felt safe in his arms." I shook my head. "I don't know."

Althea spoke slowly and methodically. "It's funny how we as individuals determine the meaning and attachment of words into our lives. Many people brush off victimization based on the type and how many times the sexual abuse happened. Some people considered someone exposing themselves as a form of sexual abuse, while others have a way to ignore it. Some people will only consider themselves as victims if the sexual abuse happened numerous times, while others will refuse to adopt the word even after a violent rape. It's all in how we each process the terminology and how we attach it to our memories. But I do believe that these memories are stored somewhere in the corners of our minds and are just waiting to be revealed. That's why so many people don't recall childhood sexual abuse until later in life."

"What causes these memories or repressed memories to reveal themselves in later years?" My heart pounded as I treaded on thin ice, wanting to break through the barrier that has kept me a mediocre man.

Althea rubbed her brow. "Any number of triggers can bring the memories forward. You had mentioned teaching students who were your age when you experienced the issues with the coaches, doctors, and benefactors. Coming across an old letter or picture can trigger these unwanted memories to flash into your mind. Being overworked and tired can allow your defenses to be down and permitting these dark thoughts to emerge. You see it can be any number of things." She handed me back the journal. "Keep up the good work. Trust yourself not to judge what you write. We'll explore if it truly happened or you embellished it." She stood and made her way to her desk. "Same time next week?"

I slid the journal into my satchel. "Sure." I stood and walked to the exit. "Same time."

"Did you and Brian remain friends and stay in touch?" Althea asked as she wrote on her desk calendar.

"No." I reached for the door knob.

"Why not?"

The question seemed simple and innocent enough. Was she correct in that I may have been attracted to Brian and when nothing was expected I didn't know how to cultivate a true friendship? *How many people did I disregard in this way?* "We lost touch."

"Maybe that's something to think about as well. The way you described him, he was a true friend." Althea continued writing.

I left. I don't remember the walk down the stairs and out into the parking lot. I don't remember unlocking the car, opening the driver's side door, or climbing onto the seat. I found myself with the journal open and my pen scribbling.

CHAPTER 4
WINTER BREAK

DR. ALTHEA WARNER'S OFFICE— DAYTON, OHIO, 2018

While waiting in the little anteroom off Althea's office, I counted the number of New York Times Book Reviews that littered the round coffee table and surrounded a large ficus plant that needed some major pruning and water. *Four, five, six...* I paused and became interested in the dates of each booklet. They were weekly and dated back three months ago. *What would it be like to see my name on that impressive list? How would I feel?*

The other door leading out of the office closed, as the door next to where I sat cracked open. Althea whispered, "I hope you don't mind, but we have a guest with us today."

"A guest?"

"Glady."

My eyes widened.

Althea put a finger to her lips. "She's still a bit groggy from the anesthesia."

I grabbed my bag and thought that if I was extremely quiet, I wouldn't disturb the patient resting inside. I nodded.

Althea slowly opened the door.

There lying on the floor next to the couch was a beautiful Golden Retriever with her eyes closed and one paw resting over her muzzle.

My face reacted with my mouth wide open.

Althea motioned for me to enter.

I crept in and carefully stepped over the sleeping dog, to sit on the couch.

There were several areas on the animal's shoulders and hind-quarters that were shaved and covered in white gauze.

I slowly lowered myself onto the couch, when the dog snored. I covered my mouth to keep from laughing out loud.

"How is she?" I whispered.

"The vet said they think they got all the tumors, at least the ones that they were worried about. They said she'll always have them for the rest of her life. I want to make her as comfortable as possible."

"I hear that." I fought the urge to pet the sleeping dog.

"Glady?" Althea looked down at the sleeping pet.

I held up a hand and shook my head so as not to disturb her.

"She should get up and have some water. She's been asleep since we got here this morning after the surgery. Glady, we have company."

The dog lifted her head from under her paw and blinked several times.

"There she is. Who's my good little girl?" Althea spoke as though she was talking to a child.

I almost broke out laughing again, because this Golden was probably a hundred pounds of lean muscle.

Glady reared her head up, pushed with her shoulders, and whimpered, while her hind legs took longer to respond. She struggled to balance on all four legs but happily nudged her head against Althea's thigh.

"Glady, we have a visitor."

The beautiful blonde-haired dog understood. She looked over her shoulder with the gauze and looked at me. She took several small steps to rotate her large frame and sauntered over to me and placed her large head on my lap.

I looked up to Althea and smiled. "May I pet her?"

Althea nodded. "By all means."

I fought back from wanting to hug this beautiful brown-eyed creature smiling up at me. I gently placed my fingertips on her crown and lightly stroked.

MATTHEW HOME—KETTERING, OHIO, 1967

The summer was just heating up the suburban plat we lived in before moving to the farmhouse in Aulden. I lived for the freedom of running from house to house, playing in different families' backyards, seeing who could fit into the washers or dryers, and exploring the differences between boys' and girls' body parts behind the bushes by the front door. There was a constant energy of exploration.

On this day, Mom asked me to take Caine's medicine to him. He was at the Ford's house, playing in the sprinkler. The Ford family lived about six houses down from us. All the houses in this area looked alike, except maybe the wood trimming was painted different colors. Each house was brick, rectangle ranch style, with the picture window in the front right side, the front door in the center, and two smaller windows occupying the left side of the façade. Three bushes fanned the left side of the house, with two cement steps emerging from the small front porch, and a pathway led to the driveway.

I had just finished a cherry popsicle, and my lips were bright red. I pretended it was my lipstick like Mom used and said it was to brighten my face. I held Caine's two capsules in my tiny hand and was proud to be asked to perform this 'adult' task. I felt grownup, so to speak. I pushed out the screen door with my chest puffed up and my head held high. I remember feeling that I looked good, wearing Dad's T-shirt, which I cinched at the waist with a belt, and my favorite red terry-cloth shorts. I was barefoot, because my tennis shoes didn't match my outfit.

I marched down the steps and followed the cement path to the driveway, which led to the sidewalk. Since I was barefoot, I didn't want to step in the grass and potentially squash an earthworm between my toes. That'd be utterly disgusting and would take forever to clean. So, I remained on the warm concrete.

The summer breeze brushed through my buzzed-cut head, and it felt great. The robins sang, and the old stray black alley cat ran across the street ahead of me. The sun snuck around the trees' leaves and created strange shadows on Dad's white cotton T-shirt. I was meticulous not to step on any pebbles, rocks, or sticks that were scattered on the sidewalks. I passed one, two, and three houses. I heard the kids playing further down the road, squealing and laughing, which indicated that the sprinkler's water must be cold.

As I approached the Packtons' house, I noticed King, the German Shepherd, sitting in the front yard, unleashed. King and I were friends and would often play together.

"Hey, King," I said as I approached the driveway.

The dog lowered its head and hunched its shoulders. His eyes were glued on me.

The closer I got, the more I wanted to pet him. "Hey, boy." I turned up the Packtons' driveway and made my way toward the waiting dog in the yard.

King lowered his head further.

I lifted my hand, waved, and kept approaching.

King growled.

"Who are you growling at? It's me, David. You know me." I kept approaching.

King lowered his chest to the ground and bared his canines.

I kept closing in, with my hand extended to pet the dog.

King leapt.

I staggered back.

Its massive paws planted on my shoulders and forced me to the ground.

I yelled and closed my eyes.

His jaws clamped shut.

I yelled again.

Hot liquid covered my face.

In the distance came shouts and commotion.

King sprung off me. I opened my eyes and saw the leaves dancing in the afternoon sunlight.

Caine appeared above me. "Oh, shit." He guided me up.

Red stains soaked into the cotton T-shirt.

Caine wrapped his arm around my shoulders and guided me home.

"Caine, I have your medicine." I held up my open hand with the capsules nestled snug in my palm.

DR. ALTHEA WARNER'S OFFICE— DAYTON, OHIO, 2018

As I petted Glady's head between her velvety ears, I confessed, "I was bit by a German Shephard when I was around four."

"Where?" Althea asked as she nestled into her chair and placed her note pad on her lap.

"Above my left eye." I pointed to the scar, while the other hand kept scratching Glady's head.

"What happened?"

"As I passed a neighbor's house, their dog, King, jumped and bit me."

"Just out of nowhere?"

"Well, I actually walked into the neighbor's yard to pet the dog."

"Maybe it was protecting the house?"

"Maybe. But I never told anyone that. I told them that I was walking by, waved, said hello, and then got bit. I don't know why I lied. Maybe I was afraid I was going to get into trouble. I don't remember."

"Did the owners take responsibility?" Althea looked over the edge of her glasses at me, waiting for my response.

"No. Dad didn't press any charges. He was disappointed that the Packtons didn't really apologize. There was some strange unsettled tension between the Packtons and us from that point on. Soon after that, Dad moved us to Aulden, to the farmhouse."

"You seem to be okay with dogs now."

"It took me some time. When we got to the farmhouse, Dad got us a puppy that was a German Shepherd and Chocolate Lab mix. We named him Bear, and he was awkward, clumsy, and always tripping over his big paws. I slowly warmed up to him. How could I not? He was always kissing on me. And then while I was in Boston, shooting *All the Rage,* the host house had two Golden Retrievers, and I fell in love. They were so gentle. Now, I have Bella and Barkley, both Boston Terriers, and they're my best friends."

Glady placed her paw on my arm.

Althea reached over and patted Glady's haunch. "Dogs have a tendency to have a positive effect on people."

"You are so cute, Glady."

"Don't keep reminding her, she's completely aware of how adorable she is. Just ask her."

Glady turned, went to Althea and wagged her tail in my face.

Althea tried scribbling some notes down, but Glady's nose got in the way. "Lay down, Glady, I don't need your help writing." Althea pointed to the floor. Glady circled twice before lowering herself onto the floor with an exasperated moan.

"May I sit on the floor with her?"

"She'd love that."

"So would I."

I scooted off the couch and sat next to Glady. She lifted her large head and then used her back legs to inch herself closer to me, until she placed her head on my lap.

"Would you be interested in trying something?"

I glanced up at Althea, trying to figure out what she was planning.

"It's really not that bad." She leaned forward with her hands clasped together and her fingers extended, tapping her lips. She then pointed toward me. "I want you to sit there and pet Glady. Just focus on petting her. Let your mind go, and talk about what comes up for you. No filter. No judgment. No editing. Just a free-flowing stream of consciousness. Don't try to make any sense out of it. If it's jumbled and disconnected, let it be."

A flood of hesitation washed over me as nerves ignited and sent sparks racing to each fingertip, toes, and to pulse in my temples. "I guess."

"You don't have to do this," Althea said.

"Can I stay here with Glady?" I felt like I was five again.

"Most definitely. You must keep petting her and focus on her. Don't worry about what you think you should talk about or what you think I want to hear. Whatever comes to mind, I want you to share. But you must keep in contact with Glady. Understand?"

I nodded.

"Good." Althea sat back in the chair and picked up the pen to take notes. "Begin whenever you feel the urge."

I stroked the golden fur between Glady's ears. She lifted her head, and her brown eyes looked deep into mine. Her hot breath panted against me. Her long tongue hung slightly over her bottom teeth and to the side of her mouth. She licked my cheek and rested her head back on my thigh. The dog provided the most amazing comfort and encouragement.

"I felt free when I was living in Kettering. Whole. Together. Right. Unaltered. Pure like." I looked up at Althea for approval.

"Don't look to me. Keep focused on Glady. Pretend I'm not here." Althea nodded.

I looked back at the dog, whose eyes were looking up at me. I took a deep breath. "It's the only time I felt that I didn't care what people thought of me. I was me. I wore what I wanted, sang and danced when and wherever I wanted. My favorite outfit was wearing one of Dad's T-shirts with a belt around the waist. I played Barbie Dolls with the neighbor girls. I played tag and kickball with the neighbor boys. I was free to express and discover who I was." I paused and pictured the confident toe-headed boy, running around the house, jumping off the couch, and doing somersaults in the backyard. My face brightened. "I was notorious for running through sliding glass doors, storm doors, or screen doors. I can't remember how many I broke. I'd go running through the house like I was flying, and the next thing I knew, I was crashing through the glass. I'm surprised I never really injured myself. It became a regular occurrence, or something always happened. I remember this one time I was bouncing on the couch, lost my balance, flew into the air, and came down between the couch and the coffee table. I thought that I had ripped my ears off." I laughed to myself.

"Do you miss him? The boy you described?" Althea's voice was warm and encouraging.

I nodded.

"What do you miss most about him?"

My face changed. "I miss his innocence."

"What do you mean by that?"

"I miss his freedom to explore, experiment, and be a child."

"Tell me about this."

"There was this sense of anything was possible. Every day, I woke with this excitement of what the day was going to bring. I knew something new and special was waiting outside the room. I remember this one day, Mom and Dad called me into the kitchen and asked me if I wanted to be a boy or a girl. I think it had to do with me wearing Dad's T-shirts. I remember looking down at my creation and then back at them and said, 'I like being me.' I then turned and skipped out to join in the tag football game happening in the backyard. It wasn't anything I thought about—it wasn't a question or an issue. I was simply me."

"What happened to him?"

My heart raced, and my hands tingled. The room became extremely warm as sweat beaded on my forehead. "He disappeared."

"What do you mean?"

"The boy, me, the innocent me." I struggled to force the emotion back down into the depths of my stomach. I didn't want to let it show its ugly face. "Everything changed when we moved to the farmhouse."

"Change is always hard."

"When we moved, we became more isolated than ever before. We weren't near anyone. Dad kept telling us it was better for us to have the acres and woods to run and play. But I didn't feel that way." I looked up at Althea. "It was like a magnifying glass was held over me when we moved to the farmhouse. I was more under scrutiny than when I was running around the Kettering neighborhood in my T-shirt design. I was no longer allowed to wear Dad's T-shirts, play with dolls, and it was frowned upon to sing and dance. Which I did all in the privacy of my room, the basement, the barn, or where ever I could create a safe space."

"Focus on Glady."

I cupped Glady's ears and I lifted her head to kiss her wet black nose. I rubbed my forehead on hers and guided her head down on my thigh.

"Everything was different. For a while it was just Mom and me at the farmhouse, because Dad was at work and Caine was at school. I swear the old place was haunted, and it scared me all the time. I felt compressed and boxed in, and I started to withdraw within myself. When I did start school, I was so different than anyone else that I was instantly made fun of and bullied. No one wanted to be my friend. They joked that they didn't know if I was a boy or a girl. So, making friends was hard. I wasn't invited to overnights, and no one came to stay the night at our house." I halted. "Dad started spending more time away, while Mom started taking more diet pills and working odd jobs. I started diving, and Magdalyn was born, things seemed to become mayhem. As I started moving up the diving ranks, I was away from the farmhouse more and more, which made going to school harder and harder, since I never made any friends. No one understood diving or seemed to care, if it wasn't football it wasn't a real sport. Then when the abuse started…"

An image flashed of me sitting on the Motel 6 bed, holding my underwear. Another bright flash, and I was sitting in the eye exam chair with a hand sliding up my thigh. Flash. The image morphed to Coach Trevor pressing my head down and moaning

95

in pleasure. Flash. I was forced onto the tiled floor with my arms pinned behind me.

"What?" Althea asked.

My stomach twisted, and I bent over, burying my face in Glady's fur. I fought hard not to let the anger surface, but I wasn't able to keep it at bay. Anger shot up from the depths of my stomach, causing my face to burn, my ears to turn bright red, and my eyes to stream with hot tears. My words were filled with hatred. "I never got the chance to figure out if I was gay, straight, bi, pan, asexual, or whatever. I didn't get to discover it for myself. I didn't get to explore with other kids my age to find out what it felt like to be attracted to someone and nervous about the first kiss. That was all taken from me. It was decided for me.

Maybe I was going to be gay, but I didn't get to experiment and figure it out."

I paused for a moment. "Oh my God, when I was taken, I was taken as if I was an experience partner. I wasn't asked any questions or asked if I was okay. All that mattered was that the other person was able to get his rocks off. Even after it was over, they never asked if I was alright. I sat there completely numb, scared, and confused. All I remember thinking was, *Did that really just happen? What am I supposed to do now? How am I supposed to act or say?* I had no answers. I started pretending I was somewhere else. It was always different places that I wanted to go or somewhere I had been to before. It didn't matter as long as I wasn't present. If I focused hard enough, I knew I could get through it. I don't remember the actual act. Yes, I knew what happened, but I didn't know what to do with the information. It was so overwhelming. The older men were fine and proud. I wasn't. I was lost. I had no idea how to process what happened." My body shook, eyes streamed, and snot came out.

Glady sat up on her hind legs, placed a paw on one shoulder, and rested her chin on the other. I wrapped my arms around her and held her.

I cried.

AULDEN, OHIO, YMCA, 1981

I lowered my chest to my thighs while stretching out on the YMCA pool deck. This wasn't exactly what I had in mind for winter break. I wanted to get away from all the structure my life had become and let loose, eat whatever I wanted, gain weight, and experience some rest and relaxation. But Dad had other things in mind, like me winning Sectionals and NCAA. And then there was the importance of confessing why I was no longer a pre-med major looming in the back of my mind.

It had been a while since I had been back to the YMCA. The last time was when Cain picked me up after the World Games in 1979. The pool had not changed much, but the lifeguards were younger. The display with pictures of me diving at the World Games, my sweat suit, Speedo, and some of my medals was still visible in the main hallway trophy case between the men and women's locker room. There was a sign that stated, "Our own 1979 World Champion, David Matthew." *How long are they going to keep that there?* My world medal was not part of the exhibit; I wouldn't part with it, even though it had since resided in a wooden box someone made for me, nestled in a small space between the chest of drawers and window in my childhood bedroom.

It was odd to see Trevor's office being occupied by someone else. His essence lingered around every corner of this place. I kept expecting to see his smiling face charging out of his office at any moment. The need to gain his approval outweighed everything else. How strange it was that I felt such an emotional pull to please him. *Where is he? Last I heard, he was married and started a family.*

"I've something to show you." Dad lowered his six-foot-four-inch frame next to me on the towel and held a roll of paper, which I assumed contained his latest theory.

My chest tightened up as the memory of his President Carter, Hitler, Caesar, and the end of the world theory flared every nerve's end. *Don't show any emotions, and count. One, two, three, four, five...*

"I've been thinking, and I think I know how to help you with your inward two-and-a-half somersaults," he said with excitement and indicated to the tube of paper.

I took a deep breath and push aside my feelings that I really didn't want him coaching me today. Or ever. But there was no one else, and the pool's manager said I could only practice my competition list if I had someone with me on the deck. Conference finals were coming up fast, and Dr. Don didn't really want me to come home for the holidays. But I needed a break from school, diving practices, the Movie of the Week, the play, and all the other things that I wasn't able to explain.

Dad unrolled the paper and pointed to detailed drawings of the springboard in varying positions of being compressed, and lines indicating different parabola arcs into the air. "Now, if you compress the board to this angle, the board's recoil will propel your body in this direction. According to your weight and the gravitational force of the compressed board, you'll need to wait on the board until it returns to this angle. This angle will lift you into the air and give you the height needed to complete the rotations."

"You mean I'm not waiting on the board long enough?" He must have heard the challenge in my voice.

Dad nodded. "Well, I know it's not proven, but I think so." He started rolling the paper up.

"No, wait." I flattened the paper on the pool deck. "You actually think this can work?"

"According to my calculations, I can't see it not working."

"So, what do all these dashes mean?" I pointed to the drawing.

A small smile appeared as he leaned in next to me. "Well, if you leave the board when it's in this angle, the trajectory of your body will have this arc of flight. This is because the board is in a downward angle. But if you wait until the board springs to this angle, your flight will be increased by about one-point-seven-three feet."

"What if I wait until the highest angle of the board?"

He sat back on his knees and used his hands to demonstrate. "If you wait until the board reaches this angle, you'll have to be extra careful that you're not leaning over the board, or you'll be pulled into the board." He lifted his hand into the air and brought it back down on top of the hand that was flat and representing the board. "Bang! You don't want to do that."

"I really don't." I laughed, and he joined in.

His excitement was contagious. "Now, make sure that your body is at a seven-degree angle as the board is recoiling. This will place you in the correct position to be able to lift off and spin inward toward the board."

A huge smile crawled across his face, crinkling his eyebrows like the time he tied the laces to my brand new ice skates and helped me up to glide across the makeshift rink he created for me so many years ago. I saw it again briefly when he constructed the dry-land board by attaching a plank of wood to an old tractor tire. I thought I'd never again see his blue eyes sparkle beneath his dark brows and how his wrinkles made him more attractive. But here it was, again. The connection chased away the anger and resentment I harbored against him for not rescuing me from the men that drove up the driveway. I didn't want the moment to end.

"How will I know that I'm at the seven-degree angle?" I asked.

"I think it's more of a feeling than anything else. I imagine that you'll be able to determine it by the amount of pressure you place on your toes."

I jumped to my feet and pretended I was on the end of the diving board. I positioned my arms out to the side and rose up on my toes. "Like this?"

He stood next to me and placed the rolled paper under his arm. "I think that's too much of a degree." He placed his large hands on my shoulders, adjusted the weight pressure on my toes, and stepped back. "It's about right there."

I cocked my head to side. "That seems like the slightest adjustment."

There was that smile again. "Yes, that's exactly right."

I went through the motion of the inward press, making sure that the pressure remained the same on my toes as I swung my arms through, bent my knees, pressed through my legs, and sprung into the air.

"Yes, that's it." His voice rang with excitement. "Do it again, so you can remember the feeling."

I immediately obliged and reset the starting position. As my arms swung through, my weight shifted, ever so slightly.

"No, you fell off your axis. Did you feel it?"

"I think so." I repositioned myself and went through the motions again. I felt more balanced and controlled.

"Yes, that's it. That's what you want to do on the board." He nodded and clapped his hands together three times.

I couldn't help but smile and blush. His approval was like hot lava rushing through my blood vessels. "Let's try it."

"Yeah?" His eyes widened.

"Yes."

I pulled my sweatpants off and tossed them on the towel. I scaled the three-meter ladder, adjusted the fulcrum, walked to the end of the board, and bounced several times. With each bounce I was reintroducing myself to the old apparatus.

Dad looked at the drawing again. "Remember, it's an ever-slight adjustment with the weight on your toes. And make sure to wait for the board to lift you into the air." He quickly consulted his diagram. "Oh, I almost forgot. Your arms must come down straight and narrow in front. You don't want them wide because this will pull your shoulders into the board."

I nodded. "I'm just going to do an inward dive first."

"Yeah, yeah, that's a great idea. Do the dive first." He crossed his arms in front of his chest, carefully hugging the rolled paper. His face hardened with a serious concentration, like when he worked on *The Looper*, his invention to create an engine that ran on water instead of gasoline.

I positioned my toes on the end of the springboard with my arms out to the side. My arms swung as my knees bent to press the metal board down. I focused on the slight amount of weight on my toes as the board recoiled and flung my body higher into the air than I had ever been. I touched my toes well above the board. I extended my arms out to the side, reached over my head, fell to the surface of the water, and entered without a splash.

When I resurfaced, Dad smirked and nodded his head.

"Did you see that?" I asked.

"I saw it."

"You were right." I quickly pulled myself out of the water and rushed up the three-meter ladder again. I dried my shins with my chamois and went to the end of the board.

"You do it the same way. Don't change anything," Dad's voice echoed up to the rafters.

I took my position on the end of the board. The press was easier this time, and the pressure on my toes felt natural. I waited for the board to lift me into the air before I threw my arms narrow and down in front of me to start the two-and-a-half somersaults. The height was higher, and the rotation of the somersaults was faster than I expected. I misjudged the come-out and washed over on the end.

"That was it!" Dad jumped like a child. "That was what you wanted, but you missed the entry."

I pulled myself out of the water. "I was so high and spun so fast, I didn't know where I was. Let's do it again."

"Don't change the takeoff. Make sure you see the water. You're going to have to really come out strong to stop the rotation."

Before I knew it, I was pressing the board down again and sailing and spinning through the air. I saw the water once, and then twice. I kicked out hard stretching my arms over my ears. I ripped through the water with that familiar zipper sound and raced toward the bottom of the pool. I pushed off and torpedoed to the surface. Dad stood there with his hands over his head.

I swam to the side, where he stood. As I got out, he wrapped his arms around me and kissed me hard on the forehead. He cupped my face in his palms and looked down into my eyes. "That was fantastic. Easily the best inward two-and-a-half somersaults you have ever done." He pulled me into his chest again, harder.

"I'm getting you all wet."

"I don't care."

I didn't want him to let me go. I wanted to stay in his arms forever. I felt safe and wanted. I felt the warmth, I ached for. I felt a connection to another person that I forgot that I craved. I had Dad back to myself, even if it was just for a short time; this was my time with him. But it didn't last too long.

Dad broke the bear hug, turned me, guided me to the board, and said, "Do it again to make sure you really have it. That was really good."

I suddenly felt empty. Lonely. Cold. *Was I just an experiment that went right? What would've happened if his theory didn't work?*

I nodded. Without saying a word, I climbed the three-meter ladder.

MATTHEW HOME, DRIVING HOME; 1981

Dad sidled in behind the steering wheel of the Old Blue Plymouth. I swiveled my hips back into the passenger's seat and took a deep breath as I plotted how to bring up that I was no longer a pre-med major and a way to present the checks from *Single Parent* and *General Hospital* without appearing smug or elitist.

Dad pushed in the lighter on the console and positioned a cigarette between his lips. The lighter popped, he pulled it out of the receptacle, pressed the red glowing nichrome coil to the end of the cigarette, and inhaled deeply, causing the paper to sizzle. "You looked good today," he said as a stream of white smoke escaped his nostrils. He replaced the lighter, slipped the key in the ignition and turned over the engine.

"You really think so?" I meekly asked.

"I said it, didn't I?" He shifted into reverse and pulled out of the YMCA parking place.

"Thanks." I braced myself with one hand on the dashboard and the other on the door as Dad merged into traffic.

We drove in silence, and I watched the world whiz by outside, trying to muster enough courage to tell him about school.

"When are the NCAA championships?" He rested his elbow on the window sill and pinched the cigarette between his two fingers.

"Conference is first. If I place well, I should be able to go to NCAAs." The dreary gray clouds threatened to dump snow on the brown landscape of naked trees.

"You surely should qualify." There was a laugh in his voice.

"One can never be too sure."

"Why not? You're the world champion." He took a long drag on the cigarette and expelled a white cloud that got trapped against the windshield.

"Was! I never defended my title." A flood of embarrassment and resentment filled me.

"That peanut farmer is to blame. He's the one that boycotted the Olympics and your shot." Dad sped up and passed a truck hauling pigs. "If he wouldn't have intervened, everything would've been perfect. But no, he wanted to prove his power and stick it to the little man again."

"How did he stick it to the man?" I dreaded asking it as soon as it came out of my mouth.

He looked sharply at me. "He screwed your chances, David. He wiped away any Olympic dream you had. All for what? A political stance that had nothing to do with our country. He fucked you without using any spit."

My mouth flew open. I was speechless.

"Am I right, or am I right?"

My stomach tightened up, and a flair of fire raced through my intestines. I doubled over in excruciating pain.

"You know I'm right. If that weaselly, peanut loving farmer had left things alone, you'd be on the cover of Wheaties right now, wearing your Olympic gold medal."

Just as the pain eased, another flare of cramps twisted my intestines and stole my breath. Sweat sprouted on my forehead and chest. This time, the pain felt like a knife carving the length of my gut. I pulled my legs up to my chest to try and ease the pain.

"Well, things are only going to get worse before they get better." He glanced over to me. "You all right?" He reached over and placed his large hand on my forehead. "You're clammy. Are you coming down with something?"

"I don't know." I fought to say the words without whimpering.

The smell of the burning cigarette mixed with the twisting action of my gut, making me want to rid myself of any content in my stomach. I leaned my head against the cold window pane and watched as the pregnant clouds sprinkled the world with fragile white flakes. I counted them as they hit the window. *One, two, three, four, five...*

Dad took a last drag on the cigarette, rolled the window down, and allowed the crisp cold air to rush in and fill the car. The coldness sent a chill through me and provided a moment of reprieve from the onset of sickness. Dad flicked the half-smoked stick out and rolled the window back up. "I just need to stop off and get a bucket of chicken for dinner. Does the colonel sound good?" He patted my thigh.

The idea of eating Kentucky Fried Chicken sent another rancid bout of nausea racing up the back of my throat. It took every ounce of willpower to force it back down.

Dad took the next exit and pulled into the lot under the famous rotating red and white striped bucket sign. The smell of grease permeated through the old car's vents and caused my intestines to twist up even tighter. I thought I was going to have to rush inside to use the bathroom.

"This'll only take a minute." Dad parked and killed the engine. As he opened the door to get out, he asked, "Do you want anything?"

"No," I immediately said.

"Not even a 7-UP? It might help settle your stomach."

"Sure." I didn't care. I just wanted some time alone to see if I could ease this pain. As he slammed the door, I closed my eyes and focused on breathing as deeply as I could. I tried stretching my legs, but the cramping prevented it. I curled up in the fetal position, wondering if this was the onset of the "gay disease" that was randomly killing people all over the world. I managed to rid my mind of the disastrous thought as my pounding head recalled the last time that I was alone in the car with Dad.

MATTHEW'S HOME: DRIVING WITH DAD, AULDEN, OHIO, 1978

Dad's fingers strummed the steering wheel as the car idled in park.

I leaned against the darkened window, feeling the pane's coolness kiss my forehead. I wished I was home in my room, far away from here. I wasn't prepared to deal with this, so I counted the bare branches on the tree...*eight, nine, ten... What's tomorrow? Friday. What do I have to do tomorrow? Eleven, twelve, thirteen...*

"Sometimes I need to talk to someone. Candy listens," he confessed.

"Candy?" I speculatively looked at him.

Defiance tightened the corners of his eyes. "Yes, Candy's her name."

"How many times have you talked with this...Candy?"

"Watch your tone," he ordered.

I cowered closer to the door.

"It's not what you're thinking," he said.

"What am I thinking?"

He was taken aback for a moment. He squinted and clenched his fist.

This is it.

I prepared myself for the impact, maybe an openhanded slap or an uppercut with his closed fist. I tried to relax my neck so the blow wouldn't be too costly. I waited. It didn't come. Instead, he gently caressed my cheek with his rough knuckles and ran his fingers through my hair.

"Someday you'll understand."

He traced his large thumb roughly over my lower lip. I smelled the residue of burnt tobacco.

"You're something else, so sensitive, so emotional. You need to toughen up a bit. You need to be more of a man. I sometimes look at you, and I'm not sure who you are. Where'd you come from? Where'd that blond hair come from? How are you ever going to make it out there?" He dropped his head and looked at me from under his dark brows. "You're too pretty to be a boy. It's amazing how pretty you are. You have a pretty mouth."

I tried to move away without him noticing. I could smell the whiskey and cigarettes as he leaned in closer.

"What was God thinking when he made you?" He roughly pulled back the flesh on my cheek.

"Dad, we need to get going. Mom will be worrying." I tried to gently push his hand away.

"What's the rush? Can't I spend some time with my son?"

"Sure, but it's getting late. I've got homework, and I need to start a research paper."

He grabbed me behind my neck and pulled me to his mouth. His aggression surprised me. He pressed his mouth against mine, parted his lips, explored me, and bit my lower lip—hard. He withdrew and with disgust shoved me away. The door's handle jabbed me in the lower back.

He gripped the steering wheel and banged his head against it. "See what you made me do? The way you look at me." His voice was harsh and filled with disdain.

I huddled against the door's frame, shocked and stunned. I wanted to fling open the door, run into the woods, disappear behind all the bare branches, and cease to exist. I felt ashamed and responsible for some odd reason. But I didn't dare move as I tasted the blood from my swelling and bruised lip.

A strange, high-pitched, squeaking sound filled the car, like a wounded animal or a puppy whimpering. Dad hunched over with his arms wrapped around the steering wheel. I don't know why, but for some reason, I felt sorry for him. I placed a hesitant hand on his shaking shoulder.

"Dad, are you all right?" I spoke with a softness that even surprised me.

"I don't know what that was all about." His voice broke.

"It was nothing," I said.

"What the hell's happening with the world? Everything's going to hell in a handbasket." He shook my hand off his shoulder, propped his chin on the back of his hands, and stared out the windshield. "It's all going to end, you know, the world as we know it. All this running around is nonsense. Everyone's rushing around, going here, going there. You've got to be at a certain place at a certain time. Everything runs on a schedule that 'The Man' devised. Who does all this benefit? I'll tell you. It benefits the rich, the wealthy, the upper class—it's all about little people doing all the work for the big shots, but no one cares what happens to the little people, they're easily replaced."

The dashboard's light revealed his narrow eyes as he continued. "They're watching. They know what we're doing. They could be watching us right now." He stopped suddenly and looked up at the black sky. "They have informants, you know. For all I know, you could be one. You could be on their side." He looked at me accusingly.

"Dad, no. I'm not," I said.

"How do I know?" His eyes grew wide, like two silver dollars. "They're after me, son. I just know it. They don't want me to finish the Looper. If the Looper gets out there, there'll be hell to pay, because it'll cost the government a lot of money. The little people wouldn't have to pay such high gas prices. They'll probably want to kill me."

"Dad, no one's after you. We'll protect you."

"I don't know. I just don't know anymore."

I placed a hand on his shoulder again. He turned and collapsed in my arms, crying hysterically. I wasn't quite sure what to do. I wrapped my arms around his large back and rocked him.

MATTHEW'S HOME: DRIVING WITH DAD, AULDEN, OHIO, 1981

The driver's side door opened. Dad placed the bucket of chicken and the bag of fixings between us and handed me the 7UP.

Propping myself up in the seat, I sipped some soda through the straw, allowing the sugary liquid to race toward the inflamed area. The refreshing cooling chased the nausea away and I started to feel better. The car immediately filled with the aroma of the fried chicken which twisted my stomach again. I took another sip. The world outside the Old Blue Plymouth was dusted white as the snow starting to steadily come down.

Without a word, Dad turned over the engine, flipped on the wipers to remove the collection of snow on the windshield, and shifted into gear. Before I realized it, we were on the highway speeding toward home. Finally, he asked, "How are you feeling?"

I sipped more. "Better. I guess. I guess I just got overheated."

"When was the last time you ate?"

"Breakfast."

"You may not be eating enough; you look like you lost weight."

"Maybe." I pulled out my wallet. "Dad, I want to give you something."

His stern eyes and tense mouth caused a kaleidoscope of butterflies to swarm around in my stomach. I wasn't sure if it was my nerves or I was really fighting off some foreign virus that was causing me to feel sick. There was a sense of pride as I removed the *General Hospital* and *Single Parent* checks, but also dread as to how I was going to explain why I'd kept this a secret.

"I want to give these to you. I know I usually give these things to Mom, but I want to give them to you."

"Give me what?"

I paused for a moment. I wanted him to be proud of me. I wanted him to respond with such happiness and amazement. I wanted him to shower me with love and appreciation. "These checks."

"If it's money, you better give it to your mother." His intently focused on the road as the snow fell heavier.

The interior of the Old Blue Plymouth shrank as the outside world became enraged with the whipping and blowing snow. The heater struggled to put out adequate heat to keep us both from freezing. The wipers worked overtime, attempting to provide enough clearing for Dad to see the road ahead.

"I really would like to give them to you."

"Why?" His voice was curt.

"I just want to." My image of him praising me for bringing home such large amounts of money was quickly fading like the road.

"Can't you see I'm trying to drive?"

I nodded my head and muttered, "Yes, I can."

We drove the rest of the way in silence. Dad's hands were on the steering wheel and mine were holding the checks and the soda. Another wave of nausea enveloped me and this time it wouldn't subside with the assistance of the 7UP. I reclined, lowered my head on the seat rest, and watched the outside world turn white as it sped by. The motor's humming was like a lullaby. *One, two, three, four, five...* I wasn't counting anything in particular. I was just going through the motions.

"David. Wake up, we're here." Dad nudged my shoulder.

"What?" My eyes were heavy, and numbness occupied my body.

"We're home."

"What happened?"

"You fell asleep, like you always do. As soon as you get into the car, you're out. I wish I could do that."

As I sat up, I discovered the checks still in my one hand and the soda in the other. I was amazed that I didn't spill the 7UP all over my lap.

Dad started to gather the food.

"Dad, could you take these?"

"What are they?"

"Checks I wanted to give to you."

"Why?"

"I wanted you to see them before Mom." I handed the checks to him.

"I've got to get this chicken in before it turns to ice."

I remained steadfast with my arm extended, offering the checks.

"Your mom's the one that takes care of these things."

"Please."

He took them, held them up and looked at them, shifting back and forth between them. "What are these?"

I leaned over the bucket of chicken and pointed to the checks. "That one is for a movie of the week and that one is for *General Hospital*.

His mind was trying to calculate the total.

"It comes to $12, 562.69." I tried not to gloat about the amount; I had never earned anything close to that before.

"I don't understand."

"Remember when I called and told you and Mom that I met this girl, Jennifer, and she wanted me to audition with her for the play? Well, during the audition a production company was looking for people for a movie of the week. I got a part, actually one of the leads. I also sent my picture and resume in for *General Hospital* and I got an extra part on the show."

"Really." He remained transfixed on the checks. "You did all this while diving and taking classes?"

"Yes." My stomach knotted again as I decided not to inform him about almost failing out of school. I was praying that the total amount would soften the truth.

"How did you do all of it?"

"It wasn't easy."

"I can only imagine." He nodded his head and handed the checks back to me. "That's great."

"I want you to have them."

"Why?"

"Because I want to help with the family."

"I don't want them." He pushed them toward me.

"Why not?"

"It's your money."

"It's our money."

"I don't want to take your money." His voice became steely and cold.

"Please. I want to give back for all the things you and the family did for me." I fought back the tears. *Don't cry, not now. Stay calm, and show no emotions.*

"I can't take these."

"Why not?"

"Because it's your money."

"But I did it for us." Anger rushed to the frontline of my battlefield. *Why is my money not good enough?*

"You worked for it; you keep it." He tried to push them back to me.

I pulled away from him. "And I'm giving them to you." My voice sounded like a machine gun rapidly firing.

"I don't want them." His face flushed red.

"Why?" I wanted to shout out—*You had no problem taking the free doctor appointments and medication when I was the dessert. Why can't you take this money that came from honest employment?* But I found the strength to hold my tongue.

"I don't feel comfortable taking your money."

"First of all, it's our money. I did it to help the family."

"This is too much."

"It's money."

His neck flared red and his blue eyes turned black as he looked at me. His voice was low and steady, but it was holding back a barrage of emotions. "The father's supposed to provide for his family. Not the son."

"Just take them and pay some bills and let's have a fantastic Christmas. No one needs to know, especially Mom. You know once she knows, she'll be expecting more from where they came."

"That's why I can't take them."

"She doesn't have to know." I surprised myself at how assertive I was, and yet I feared for the repercussion.

His eyes burned into mine, staring at me to back down. When he realized that I was steadfast, his brows softened. He folded the checks and slipped them into his coat pocket. "Grab the bucket of chicken." He took the bag of fixings and climbed out of the car and headed toward the back door.

I sat there a moment, trying to calm my racing heart and settle my knotted stomach. The heavy, wet snow landed on the windshield and piled up, terminating my view with a blanket of whiteness. I retrieved my bag from the back and grabbed the bucket of chicken. The cold wind felt soothing against my feverish forehead, and I slid as I made my way to the back porch. Garbage bags were piled in the corner while assorted boxes, odds and ends, and other discarded items lined the other walls.

I pushed open the back door and was greeted by Bear, jumping up, placing his paws on my shoulders, and licking my face.

"Someone missed me?" I whispered as his tongue took another swipe up my cheek. I dropped my bag on the chair by the door. While cradling the bucket of chicken, I hugged Bear and nuzzled his big head.

"I'll take that." Dad took the chicken and placed it on the counter, removed the cardboard lid, dug through the bucket, retrieved a breast, and started eating.

"What's this?" Mom said.

"Those are from David. He wanted you to have them."

Shock rattled me as I realized that Dad gave Mom the checks.

"Where did you get these?" She laughed, with pleasant surprise.

I looked at Dad as he ignored me and continued devouring the chicken. A burning shot ploughed through my stomach and raced along the small intestines. "I got a part in a movie of the week and an extra role on *General Hospital*."

"Why didn't you tell us?" Mom mentally calculated the sum of both checks.

I pushed Bear off and stood, confronting both and fighting from doubling over in pain. "I wanted to surprise you."

"That's a lot of money." Mom kept looking from one check to the other.

"Surprise." I joked.

The phone screamed.

Mom reached over and answered in her most professional voice, "Matthews. Yes." She looked over at me. "He's right here." She covered the mouth piece and whispered, "A Skitch Henry or something."

I immediately reached for the phone. "This is David."

"David, Skitch here, I hope this isn't a bad time to call." Skitch's voice sounded distant.

"This is a great time to call," I said as Mom tried to offer me a piece of chicken. I shook my head. She pulled the skin off and ate it while trying to overhear the phone call.

"When are you coming back to California?"

"It'll be around the seventh."

"That's perfect. Would you be interested in some more work on the show?"

"Yes, I'd be honored."

"I'll get things ironed out here and have you back in the studio on the tenth."

"Great."

"Have a great holiday."

"You too." The phone went dead.

"Who was that?" Mom asked as she licked her lips.

I hung up the phone. "That was the casting director for *General Hospital*. They'd like me to come back when I return."

"Save a breast for Magdalyn. She'll be hungry when she gets home." Dad's voice was distant.

Mom slipped the checks behind her bra strap. "Oh, I almost forgot. Hal wants you to call him as soon as possible and have dinner with him. He said he wants you to meet some people while you're home."

A sharper pain attacked, forcing me to lean against the counter to remain standing. "I think I need to lie down for a while."

No one responded.

I staggered down the hallway and crawled up the stairs to the landing, where my room was. I removed some boxes in order to lie down. It took me a couple of minutes to find a comfortable position.

"What am I going to do with this money?" Mom's voice echoed up the stairs.

"Do whatever you do with the money. Pay some bills and let's have a wonderful Christmas." Dad walked into the living room and turn on the television.

The Family Feud's theme song played as I closed my eyes.

HUMBLER INN, AULDEN, OHIO 1981

"Good evening. My name is Ben, and I'll be serving you tonight." Ben unfolded the maroon swan-shaped dinner napkin that sat in front of Hal Hall and placed it on his lap and did the same for me while talking. "Our specials tonight are a succulent prime rib smothered in butter and accented with garlic mashed potatoes, or a Chilean Sea Bass accompanied with grilled asparagus and pineapple. You have a choice of a Caesar salad with fresh anchovies or a chopped green salad with endive, blueberries, arugula and raspberry vinaigrette." Ben stood erect, with his hands behind his back. "May I get you something to drink?"

Hal leaned in, clasped his hand before his mouth while the candle's light danced on his high forehead, and studied me. He smiled, and without looking away, he said, "I think we need something to celebrate. Bring us a bottle of Martini and Rossi Asti Spumante."

"Very nice, indeed," said Ben. "Would you like an appetizer while you're deciding on your entrée? We have a nice artichoke heart with a chipotle mayonnaise."

Still locked in on me, Hal puckered his lips. "Bring us each a shrimp cocktail and an order of calamari."

"Very well, indeed. Please excuse me and I'll put that in for you." Ben nodded and scampered away.

The ambiance of the dining room was warm from the glow of a single candle on each table and the soft piano music wafting in through the speakers. The interior of the room looked quite different from when Mom brought me here after the Jr. Olympics, and I was introduced to the man sitting across from me. Yet, there was an unsettling angst lingered in my being as I attempted to present the mature me. Ever since I went to California, I've been trying to reinvent myself, become more independent, and self-sufficient. I wanted Hal to see these changes in me, acknowledge them, and accept me as an adult and equal. I wasn't the boy who left Aulden.

No matter how hard I tried to act grownup, there was this gnawing and unsettling anger, extremely small and pushed way back into the recesses of my mind. This was the man that introduced me to the other benefactors that helped support my diving at a cost to my psyche. I wondered if I would have been as upset if it was only Harold Hall that ushered me into adulthood, but he never indulged. He passed me off to others. *Why was this mousy man sitting across from me never physical with me? Was I not good enough for him? Could I have been too special to him that he wanted to keep things separated? Was he even aware of what happened when he left me with the good doctor, lawyer, or businessmen for the week? Was he aware that I was passed around? Where would he go? Why didn't he stay to protect me?*

Hal excitedly said, "I want to hear all about school and California. How are classes and diving?" Hal resembled a kid with his eyes full of wonder and innocence.

The mature me slipped, and I reverted to the expectation of the polite kid. "Diving's okay." I played with the fork's prongs.

"Just okay?"

My voice was calculating. "You know, practice and dual meets. I won Sectionals and now I'm getting ready for Conference." As I pressed the prongs down the handle lifted, like a springboard. I tried to deter myself from the memories of being left with the "good" doctor in Columbus, the parties where I and several other older boys were displayed like a menu for the guest to peruse. The game of pretending that we weren't aware of what was happening, the coyness of wearing skimpy swimsuits the doctor got for us, and the frolicking in the pool as the guest trolled around, making silent bids on which boy they wanted. The game of who earned the highest bid would get a bonus from the good doctor.

"What are you holding back? I can tell there's something you're not telling me," Hal said in a joking manner.

"Well." I forced a smiled but hesitated in sharing what was truly on my mind.

"Tell me."

I was taken aback and enchanted by his enthusiasm and his ability to make me feel important. Giddiness rushed to the foreground and pushed the anger aside. "Well, I met this girl, Jennifer."

"A girl?" His eyes narrowed.

"Yes, and she wanted me to audition with her for the fall play. Well, while we were auditioning, there was also a production company there, and they were looking for people to cast for a Movie of the Week."

Hal's face was alive and listening to me.

I felt compelled to continue. "We auditioned, and I was asked to stay back, and they offered me a role in the movie and a part in the play. Jennifer wasn't."

Hal clapped and burst out with a hearty laugh. "Does she still talk to you?"

"We're good friends," I replied. "We went to her sorority Halloween party dressed as Frank Butler and Scarlett O'Hara from *Gone With The Wind* and won best costume."

"Good friends?" Hal asked in a suggestive tone.

"Just friends," I qualified.

He laughed. "Does she know that?"

"I hope so."

Hal feigned applause. "That's fantastic."

Ben returned with the bottle of champagne and showed the label to Hal.

"Show it to him," Hal said as he pointed to me. "He's the big star now."

Ben presented the bottle's label to me.

"Looks good to me."

Ben unwrapped the metal wire, undressed the foil covering, and used a white napkin to pop the cork. He poured some into my glass and stood back.

I looked at Ben, and then to Hal.

Hal fluttered his hands. "Taste it."

"Oh." I lifted the champagne glass, sniffed, and tasted it. "Good."

Ben poured more for me, a glass for Hal, and placed the bottle in an ice container next to the table and walked away.

Hal lifted his glass. "To you. I'm so proud of you."

I lifted my glass. "To you. None of this could've been possible without you."

We clinked the glasses and drank. The bubbly's sweetness went down very smoothly.

"So, what else?" Hal asked. "Oh, wait. Before I forget, Erik wanted me to tell you hello."

My stomach fluttered at the mere mention of his name. His Clark Kent-ish image filled my mind. "You talked to Erik?"

"Not only talked with him, but had dinner with him when I went to Colorado." Hal smiled. "He looks amazing and he's graduating this spring."

"Wow. That's great." I always wondered what happened to Erik, ever since he was shipped to Colorado for wanting to be my friend.

"Anyway, he's back here for the holidays and wants to see you."

"Me?"

"He always asks about you?"

"I don't know what to say. I tried writing, but I never heard from him."

"He got all your letters. He felt it was better not to respond."

What does that mean? He read my letters and decided it was best not to respond? Didn't he care how that affected me? Did he care? Why did he get to make the decision?

I nodded and sipped some champagne.

"So come on, what else? I want to know everything."

"Why do you think there's any more?" I snickered.

"By the way your eyes are sparkling and your smile," Hal said. "I'm a lawyer and it's my job to read people's body language."

"You're right." I took a deep breath, pushed Erik's memory aside and found that I was so excited to share with him. "I also did an extra part on *General Hospital*."

"The soap opera?" His eyes widened.

I simply shrugged like it wasn't a big deal.

He smiled. "Did you enjoy it?"

"I loved it." I couldn't hide my joy.

"I can tell. You're glowing."

Ben returned with the shrimp Cocktails, placed one in front of each of us, and positioned the calamari next to the candle. "Are we ready to order?" Ben asked politely.

"Sure. Bring us one of each of the specials," Hal said, without looking at Ben.

"Very well, indeed." Ben excused himself.

"If he says 'indeed' one more time, I'm not sure what I'm going to do," Hal joked. "I can't even look at him anymore."

I giggled. "These are huge." I held up a jumbo shrimp and imitated Ben, "'Indeed.'"

Hal laughed so hard, he almost knocked his shrimp cocktail over.

I giggled and dipped the prawn into to the cocktail sauce. Hal watched me as I slipped the crustacean between my lips. I thought he was waiting to see how they tasted. "Incredible. It's so good."

"You're incorrigible. So, how are studies going?" He dunked a shrimp into the red sauce and let it marinate for a while.

Silence engulfed our table. Murmuring from other tables added to the soft playing piano.

I discarded the shrimp tail on the plate under the cocktail glass. I tried to regain my adult persona. "Well, that depends on how you look at it."

"What do you mean?" He fished his shrimp out of the sauce and popped it in his mouth.

"Well, with diving, the play, the movie of the week, and *General Hospital*, I started missing classes, and one thing led to another and..."

Hal swallowed and remained quiet, with his full attention on me, listening, and waiting.

"So, I was called into the academic advisor's office and was informed that if I didn't do something...quickly..." I took a deep inhalation. "I was going to flunk out. He suggested that since I was spending so much time in rehearsals and shooting the movie that I should transfer to the theatre department. This was the only option to keep my academic and athletic scholarships."

"So, no more pre-med?"

I could only nod.

"Are you happy?"

This threw me for a loop; I wasn't sure how to respond. Was this some trick?

"I am. I really am. I like acting and performing. I don't think I was really cut out for medicine. I think I did it because I thought it looked good on paper and people wanted me to do something like that. It was expected." A sense of relief encompassed me as I felt this heaviness lift from my shoulder simply by telling someone. For an instant, I didn't care if Hal approved. I felt full and true to myself.

"I don't care what you do, as long as you're happy and you put your all into it. You're very special, and you need to feel special." He reached over and took my hand. "Promise me something."

I distinctly inched my hand out of range and looked around to see if anyone was looking at us.

Hal grabbed my hand and laced his fingers through mine. "No one cares." He caressed my fingers. "Promise me that you'll always do your best and not let any negative thoughts prevent you from following your dreams."

"That's easier said than done." I tried to gently pull my hand away, but he tightened his grip. I huffed as my fingers and shoulders tensed.

"Relax," he coaxed.

I couldn't release the rigidity in my entire body.

"Why do you say that it's easier said than done?" His brows creased, and there was a sense of concern narrowing his lips.

I whispered, "I'm not sure I can just forget all the things that have happened."

Hal cocked his head and let it sink in. "The past is the past. You have the future to look forward to. Everything's possible if you only believe it's possible."

I chuckled. "You sound like a greeting card."

"If there's one thing I can instill in you, it's that you must follow your dreams and never let them slip away, no matter what happens or what anyone says." He reached with his free hand into his coat pocket and pulled out an envelope. "I've been sharing your story with some people, and they want to meet you and help. They're extremely supportive. I want you have this and use it when you get back to California."

"Oh, Hal, I don't know." I refused to take the envelope.

"Be honest. Did you give the money you earned from acting to your mom?"

My lips tensed.

"You don't have to answer that." He leaned in closer. "Don't make a scene, and just take the envelope."

"But..."

"No buts." Hal's eyes narrowed and grew darker, while his bushy brows met above the bridge of his nose.

I leaned into him. My voiced wavered. "I appreciate everything that you've done for me. I really do. I want to try and figure things out on my own."

Hal grinned. "That's why I admire you so much. You're always trying to figure things out and aren't looking for a free handout. But would you deny your dear old friend from wanting to be a part of this exciting new life you're creating for yourself?" He inched the envelope closer to me.

"Hal, I..."

"Just take it." He squeezed my fingers.

"Alright. Alright." I took the envelope and looked inside. "Hal, this is too much."

He shook his head. "I don't have children, and I can't take it with me when I die. I've worked hard to create a comfortable life. So, let me have this opportunity to help someone that I admire and who I know will do amazing things with his life. Please."

A pang rippled through my heart, and I felt that he really cared for me and I was being seen and acknowledged. I nodded and slipped the envelope into my jacket pocket.

Hal squeezed his fingers tighter around mine, leaned back in his chair, and lifted the champagne glass again. "I want to make a toast."

I lifted my glass.

"I'm so proud of you and everything you've accomplished. May your future journey be paved with gold and all your dreams come true."

"Hal?" A tall and thin man made his way to our table. The candlelight reflected a chiseled face, framed with dark hair, and Clark Kent good looks.

"Erik." Hal released my hand. "What a pleasant surprise. We were just talking about you."

"All good, I hope." Erik burned his blue eyes into mine. "David."

"Erik." The word snuck out as a whisper. The past few years had benefited Erik, making him more attractive as he matured.

"Please join us," Hal said.

"I would love to. I'm with a couple of friends."

"The more, the merrier," replied Hal.

"Fantastic. You're still coming for New Year's Eve, right?" Erik waved for his friends to join.

"Of course, Erik. Maybe I can talk David into coming with me."

"You have to come, David. It's going to be the event of the year," Eric said.

"Will it be at Dr. Miller's?" I asked with hesitancy.

Erik looked at Hal and then back to me. "No, it's not at the Miller's estate. And he won't be there."

"Why not?" I knew I shouldn't push it.

Erik looked nervously at Hal.

Hal somberly said, "David, Dr. Miller got sick. He passed away several months ago."

"What happened?" I wasn't sure if I was happy, sad, or what to feel.

Hal nodded. "He developed a rare kind of cancer."

My mind raced to the article I read on the bus, about the strange cancer that was killing gay men.

The clinking and scraping of utensils against plates filled the air as the piano music subsided.

"Are we on for New Year's Eve?" Erik mischievously asked.

Hal nodded. "I'll make sure David will be there."

"Good." Erik made room for his friends. "Everyone, this is Walter."

Hal stood.

Walter gave Hal a hug, "Long time, no see, my dear friend."

"Too long," responded Hal.

The other friend watched patiently.

Hal broke the embrace, patted Walter on the shoulder, and turned to greet the other friend. Hal's eyes filled with familiarity when he saw the young man.

"Surprise," said Erik.

Hal blushed as he held his arms open, and whispered with such longing, "Kalvin."

Kalvin stepped in, and Hal wrapped his arms around him. The tenderness that emitted filled me with such empathy. From what I could gather from the embrace, Hal hadn't seen Kalvin for some time. Their body language indicated that this was something more than a friendly hug.

"How are you?" Hal asked.

"I've missed you so much," whispered Kalvin.

"Okay, okay, break it up. Grab a chair, and sit down." Erik moved a chair next to me and sat. Erik smiled while everyone settled and then leaned toward Hal. "What a surprise to run into you here tonight." His voice and demeanor revealed that it was planned. "We're going to go to Cincinnati, you must come. And we'll show David the ropes." He reached under the table and placed his hand on my thigh, sending electricity throughout my being. He squeezed the muscles and grinned at me. "We'll have a blast."

I looked at Hal, who was intimately talking with Kalvin, while Walter poured himself some champagne.

"Hal?" Erik called, louder.

"What?" Hal chuckled. "Let's do it. Are you okay with that, David?"

"Sure, I guess."

Erik turned and looked at me as his hand slid higher in my thigh. "There's so much I have to say to you."

"You never answer my letters. Why?" I asked.

"I wasn't allowed to."

"But why?"

"This isn't the time to talk about that. We're here now, and we can make this moment magical."

"Okay."

"Then it's settled. Let's get another bottle of champagne and get this party started," Erik said. His hand inched higher on my thigh as he turned to locate the waiter.

"David?" Hal called for my attention. "Get ready, you're going to have hardly any time to see your parents. I've booked everything for you from now until you get on the plane back to California." He lifted his glass again. "To the best holidays."

I slowly lifted my glass.

"To the holidays," Erik confirmed, and he smiled at me.

DR. ALTHEA WARNER'S OFFICE— DAYTON, OHIO, 2018

Glady licked my tear-stained cheek, which I was surprised that I let her.

"That's enough, Glady. I'm sure David doesn't want you slobbering all over his face."

Glady's tongue tickled my neck and it made me laugh. "I don't mind." She licked again, and I pulled back. "But maybe not in my mouth.

"Settle, Glady," Althea firmly stated.

The Golden Retriever sauntered over to Althea and placed her head heavily in her owner's lap and waited. Althea scratched her forehead and gently pushed her away. Glady returned and plopped down next to me, pressing against my side.

"It's not uncommon to feel anger when you speak about not getting to discover your orientation." Althea was meticulous in her delivery. "Boys and male teens that were sexually abused by older men may find themselves seeking out sexual encounters and situations in adulthood with an unconscious effort to comprehend, understand, or even resolve the guilt and shame that accompanied these encounters and memories. These questioning moments may lead to fetishes that the person doesn't consciously understand. And once these acts have been played out, the person is riddled with even more shame and confusion. But it doesn't necessarily mean they're gay. This is a social misconception that if a man has sex with another man, then he's a homosexual. It's not as cut-and-dried as that. What research today is teaching us is that there are many issues that come into play when dealing with abuse of any kind. Many men who have been abused as children or teens have been able to get married and have families because they discovered that their core orientation was heterosexual or bisexual. Even though they've figured out their sexual orientation, they may still find themselves in compromising situations or surroundings in which they are re-enacting the abuse in order to try and understand and figure out why it happened." She looked at me sternly and shook the pen toward me. "Does this make any sense?"

I smirked. "I guess so. It all sounds so clinical."

"It depends on the day." Althea lifted her chin with pride. "Somedays I'm a walking encyclopedia and other days I'm just a tree-hugging hippy." Althea lifted her eyebrow, chuckled, and looked down at her notes. "I want you to think about something, and I don't need you to respond to right now. But have you had any compulsions or attractions that you think may be out of the norm?"

"First of all, I'm not sure I know what 'the norm' is." Glady awkwardly stood and lifted her huge paw for me to take a hold. "Secondly, I'm not sure what you're talking about."

"Okay, fair enough. Let me try to be a little bit clearer. Do you ever find that you have placed yourself into a compromising situation, location, or encounter that you're not sure why you were there? Or have you done something that you're not sure why you did it? Afterwards, you completely berated yourself for doing it?"

As soon as she finished the question, a dam broke and unleashed a memory that flooded my mind with a swirling recall that I tried to forget.

DR. MILLER'S HOME—COLUMBUS, OHIO, 1979

Three college students and I waited patiently in Dr. Miller's sunken living room with plush white shag carpeting. We all wore skimpy cut-off shorts, jockstraps, or speedos and stood in a single file line. I wasn't sure how the order was arranged. *Why was I at the end? I wasn't the tallest or the oldest.* At first, there wasn't any rhyme or reason as to why we stood in this asymmetrical alignment. The more I studied the line; it became apparent that we were arranged by how long we had been considered a "Miller Boy."

The *Miller Ranch*, as this elaborate, expensive, and exclusive club became known around Columbus, was conceived and hosted by Dr. Charles Miller. It was a highly secret social men's club, like Yale's *Skull and Bones*, Harvard's *Porcelain Club*, or Cornell's *Quill and Dagger*. Potential members had to be professionals with a qualifying income of six figures and be nominated by one of the Founding Five. The nominees would go through an extensive background check of their character and business and had to provide a hefty and nonrefundable initiation fee for consideration.

The Founding Five would visit the nominee's home and business and determine to what extent and benefits the nominee and his business could bring to the other members of the Miller Ranch. The interview process was rumored to be extremely tedious since the members were invited into a community that served each other and had a gay mob-like mentality. Was the nominee trustworthy, willing, and able to keep the identity of all members secret and protect each member at any cost?

If the nominee passed the initial qualification, the next step would be the Nights of Five Dinners, where the nominee was expected to entertain the Founding Five at a predetermined and prestigious venue. The nominees hoped to impress the Founding Five by creating a unique dining experience at a location that was challenging to obtain. Each year, five new members could be tapped, pay the additional members' fee, became privy to and reap the benefits that the secret vows provided, and sit back and watch his business thrive and become more successful than ever before or could ever have been on its own.

While the five nominees were put through the initiation proceedings, the rest of the members faced the renewal process and the potential to be excommunicated without cause or warning. Secret ballots were submitted by all members to nominate the "Weak Link." If enough negative votes were received, one would find himself on the outside of this secret community, and his business would struggle and usually close within five months.

At the end of the Hell Month, the nominees that passed became full-fledged members, the returning members must renew, and each would be delivered a handbook through personal messenger. This handbook helped decode the secret locations and dates of the many exotic parties with the promise of enjoying fine cuisine, top-shelf liquor, and the exquisite company of the Miller Boys.

Intense strategy herded the corral of boys together. Often referred to as ponies (newbies) or colts (veterans), they were usually comprised of students attending The Ohio State University, who were in various stages of trying to pay for their educations.

Grooming led the boys into believing the "good doctor" was the only one that genuinely saw their potential and was willing to help each young man achieve his academic dreams. Many colts graduated with honors, obtained Masters and PhDs, and become successful professionals without the burden of student loan debts. Each pony or colt had to sign a legal non-disclosure agreement, and if he breached the document, he paid back every penny. Once a Miller Boy received his educational goals, he would donate back to the educational fund when he had achieved and established a successful business.

A young man could never go seeking this opportunity. Dr. Miller had to be the one to discover the student and recognize the potential of a working collaboration. Although Dr. Miller would consider outside suggestions, he rarely opened the barn door to just any young man. Many varying variables went into selecting the perfect ponies. The perks of becoming a Miller Boy outweighed the struggling student personae. There was the yearly travel to watch OSU in whatever football bowl they played, the New Year's Eve Gala at the Hyatt Regency, concerts, theatre performances, and the occasional ballet. There were the trips to New York, Los Angeles, Fiji, Europe, and Miami for spring break. The Miller Boys attended every sporting event imaginable. Athletes were highly regard on the Miller Ranch, especially since Dr. Miller was The OSU Buckeyes' official team doctor to fourteen varsity sports, including swimming, diving, wrestling, gymnastics, track & field, lacrosse, baseball, volleyball, water polo, fencing, field hockey, cross country, soccer, and of course football. He had firsthand knowledge of which athletes and students were perfect for the ranch. Other ponies were discovered at dance clubs and bars. These were considered "wild ones" and needed to be broken in and tamed with an iron fist, or they could cause havoc for the ranch. Every year, six young men were "lucky" enough to become Miller Boys and have their higher education ultimately paid.

Each pony had to be personally invited by Dr. Miller to participate in the parties and receive cash and prizes.

John was on the far end, the second tallest, and around twenty years old. He was the "bad boy," with messy brown hair and dark brown eyes that were half-mast from his enjoyment of marijuana. Since being red-shirted last year from the soccer team due to a torn Achilles tendon, John was constantly in some entanglement with the law, which usually accompanied a warrant. Dr. Miller bailed John out many times and promised to keep John supplied with the wacky weed if he remained a good boy and did what the good doctor wanted. But last week, John wrapped one of Dr. Miller's Mercedes around a tree while swerving on black ice to avoid careening into the back of a cement truck. Hal had the honor of representing the young man in court. The arresting officer found several blunts in the ashtray and a small plastic bag with Mary Jane residue under the passenger's seat. The judge dismissed the case when Dr. Miller agreed to donate heftily to the annual Police Academy Drive. Dr. Miller always put John in blue terry-cloth mini shorts, which barely covered his pubs in the front and advertised his round asset with a hint of crack showing. His legs were thin and speckled with brown fur.

Sam was next and stood about three inches shorter than John and was the temperamental one, with a thick carrot-colored mop and matching body hair, which he always preened and manscaped to keep his smooth go-go boy body appearance. The twenty-year-old always seemed antsy, fidgeting with his fingers, as if he was obsessed with maintaining dirt from residing under his nails. Dr. Miller found him dancing in a bar and offered to help him through school. But school was the last thing on Sam's mind; he lived for the moment and enjoyed life. He bragged about how many guys he bedded in one night and the different positions he accomplished. Sam didn't have time for my goody two-shoes appearance. He feared that I was moving in on his turf, so he always wore a jockstrap so he could easily display his assets.

Erik resembled Clark Kent, the tallest and most attractive one, with a wave of black hair hiding his dark blue eyes. He was the oldest at twenty-four and was considered a colt. He wanted to be an archeologist, excavate the Mayan temples, and learn the mysteries of life. He exemplified the worthiest candidate for an all-paid-for-education and came on the "good doctor's" radar when he needed a physical to attend a semester in Kenya to help build water huts. Dr. Miller always put Erik in a matching Hawaiian swimsuit and shirt, opened to display the black curls on his chest.

Since I was the athlete, the shortest, the youngest, and obviously a pony, I had to wear white Speedos that hardly hid anything. "I want your assets noticed," Dr. Miller would always whisper to me. I didn't fall into the usual selection protocol for consideration to be a Miller Boy, since I was still in high school and I was only here because Hal brought me to the "good doctor."

The fifth boy, Kalvin, was a no-show at the last minute. It was rumored that he had the flu and there was no time to replace him.

The four of us were instructed to stand, pose, and wait as the parade of guests came through the living room to get to the patio and pool. We were expected to be polite and engage in conversation.

Cordialness was always a challenge for John. Even though John was Dr. Miller's leading project and off-limits to the guests, he was still expected to be charming and involve a guest to the point that Dr. Miller would have to dramatically swoop in and pull John away from the interested party member.

An hour after the early birds sauntered through and we were still standing, waiting for the next wave of guests to arrive.

Erik leaned into me and whispered, "Where's Hal?"

His warm, minty breath caressed my ear. "I'm not sure."

"He just drops you off and disappears?" There was concern in Erik's voice.

"Seriously? You two are as subtle an earthquake. He drops him off so he can go see Kalvin," Sam disdainfully said.

"What do you mean?" I asked.

"This has been going on ever since I can remember," Sam said with authority. "Dr. Miller threw Kalvin out when Kalvin said he didn't want to go to school anymore. But what was happening was that Kalvin took a shine to Hal and they have been rendezvousing ever since. That's why you're here sweet cheeks. It's because Hal felt guilty about Kalvin, and you're the replacement."

"Shut the fuck up, all of you," grumbled John. His head swayed from side to side, and his lips were thick and dry. "Shut up before we all get our asses kicked."

A murmur of voices grew.

"This way." Dr. Miller, a short, round man, wiggled in front of his prestigious members. "We'll go through the living room to get to the patio and pool. Wayne's busy grilling up something delicious." Dr. Miller stopped at the top of the two steps that led down to the plush white shag carpet and directed his guests. "Now, now, no touchy, just looksy right now. We don't want to keep Wayne waiting."

The gaggle of men of varying shapes, sizes, ages, and professions streamlined past the four of us. The lead crone was a bitter, old CPA, with a taste for cigars that preceded him, and when he smiled, he looked like a Jack-o'-lantern with missing yellow teeth. He stopped in front of me, sneered, and said, "Call me when you decide to sprout some hair on your balls. If I wanted something that smooth, I'd sleep with my wife." He laughed hard at his joke.

"But you should see what he's packing under those Speedos," Erik said. "It'd make your mouth water."

"I don't mind lollipops, but I don't want sugar diabetes. He's too pretty to be a boy. Next." He bypassed Erik and looked at Sam. "Now, this is more like it. Smooth, but masculine. Bend over and spread them."

Sam puckered his mouth, suggestively turned, bent over, and pulled his butt cheeks apart.

"Now, that's what I call the dark hole of Calcutta. I might get sucked up in there and never find my way out." The man licked his finger and probed Sam, sliding his digit inside.

"I hope you have more than that," Sam said as he looked at the man from between his legs and swiveled his hips.

The man roughly pulled his finger out causing Sam to moan. "Maybe someday when I want it to burn when I piss, I'll come find you. Next!" He moved on to John. "Just what the doctor ordered and everything I ever wanted." He slid his hand down the front of John's terry cloth shorts and exclaimed, "And it's all-natural, which I crave."

Right on cue, Dr. Miller gently removed the man's hand from inside John's shorts and stated, "He's off-limits." He guided the accountant toward the sliding glass doors leading to the patio deck and pool. "I'm sure you'll find what you're looking for out here."

Erik grabbed my hand and tugged. "Come with me."

I followed him down the hall and into a small utility room. He quickly looked out the door before quietly closing it. In the dark, he reached for me. One of his hands found my chin, while the other wrapped around the back of my head. He ever so gently pulled me against his chest and placed his warm lips against mine. The kiss was sensual yet spiritual and tasted minty. His lips were soft, the day-old stubble gently pricked my flesh, and his sensuality encouraged my response.

"I've wanted to do that from the first time I saw you," Erik breathlessly said as he pressed his forehead against mine. The floral scent from his shampoo caused my head to spin.

"You've a funny way of showing it. You've hardly said two words to me." I leaned my head back.

"I wasn't sure you were going to stay around."

"What does that mean?"

"Sometimes, the good doctor brings in trials to see how well they respond to the surroundings. Most are never asked back. But you're different."

"How so?"

"You're special. Now, I didn't bring you in here to talk about what makes you different. I wanted to do this." He pressed his mouth against mine again.

I withdrew just enough so my lips brushed against his as I asked, "Is it everything you thought it would be?" I joked.

"More so." He tasted my lips again.

The door opened.

"Busted," said John. "Miller's looking for you two."

"We'll be right there," Erik said.

"You better, I can't hold him off forever." John closed the door.

"Are we in trouble?" I asked.

"Not you, but I am," Erik said.

I placed my palm on his chest and pushed away. "I'm so sorry."

He restrained me by wrapping his arms tighter. "It was worth it." He slowly leaned down, as they do in the movies, and confidently explored my mouth with his. The tip of his tongue traced the parameters of my lips. Something ignited deep within me; it was familiar yet foreign. It was a small flicker in the pit of my stomach, which sent a shudder throughout my body and left my toes and fingertips tingling. He withdrew and placed a palm on each side of my face, held my head still while the rest of me vibrated with small aftershocks. "Watching you dance last night was so hot. You know how to move."

"Really?"

He brushed my bangs from my forehead and kissed the bare skin. "There's something about you that's different from the rest of us. You've something that's innocent and pure, something real and unattainable. Whatever it is, don't lose it."

"If I don't know what it is, how can I lose it?" I tried to joke.

"You're such a nerd."

"Is that a compliment coming from the biggest nerd here?"

"Just shut up and kiss me again."

I chuckled and perched up on my toes to be eye level with Erik. I pressed my eager mouth against his.

The door cracked open. "Miller's coming," John whispered harshly before closing it.

"I'll tell Miller it's my fault. He won't do anything to me because of Hal," I suggested.

"You're sweet." He kissed me again. "We better go." He opened the door and held it for me to exit. As I walked out of the utility room and into the hall, Hal and Dr. Miller stood at the far end of the hallway.

"We have to head back," Hal said to me. "Meet me at the car." He left Dr. Miller standing there, with his arms crossed.

"Okay, let me get my things." I glanced at Erik and headed to the bedroom that I was assigned.

Dr. Miller called after me. "Leave the Speedo on the bed."

I ducked into the room.

Dr. Miller's voice echoed down the hall. "What the hell do you think you're doing?"

"Nothing," Erik said.

"This doesn't fucking look good for you to be hiding when we have a house full of guests. After all that I've done for you and this is how you treat me? Embarrassing me in my own home? If it wasn't for me, where would your sorry ass be? Is it too much to ask for some respect for all I do for you boys?" A solid slap rang throughout the hallway. "Get your sorry little ass out on the patio, now."

"Sorry, Dr. Miller," Erik's voice was strained as he hid his emotions.

"Just go. I don't want to see your two-timing face for a while." Dr. Miller graveled his voice.

Footsteps echoed, and then silence.

As I pulled the Speedo off and threw it onto the mattress, a strange feeling crept into the room, causing me to turn. Dr. Miller stood in the doorway, watching.

"Don't mind me." He stepped into the room.

I reached for my clothes that were on the bed.

"Not yet. I want to look at you." He took another step into the room.

I immediately covered myself with both hands.

He picked up the swimsuit from the bed, untwisted it, placed it back on the mattress, and flattened it with his palms. "The white Speedos don't do you justice." He waddled up to me, and his fat fingers took ahold of my hands. "I want to see." His puffy cheeks made his eyes look like slits.

I resisted and tightened my hands, protecting and hiding my private area.

He looked up at me with his bloodshot orbs and whispered, "Let me see."

I stared back at him, challenging and resisting.

"You owe me this much. Just a little peek," he said in a child-like manner.

"You've seen it before." My voice was filled with disdain.

He chuckled as his chubby paws gripped harder. "Make Papa proud."

"You're not my papa."

"No, I'm not, thank goodness, but at least I'm here for you, and that's more than I can say about your real father." He leaned his hard belly against me.

"You know nothing about my father." I backed up against the wall.

He pressed harder against me. "I know that I'm able to help you more than he is."

The words stung, and my grip eased.

The "good" doctor moved my hands to the side, exposing everything I was trying to hide. His eyes widened with pleasure. "I almost forgot the endowment you have been blessed with." He cupped me with his small, stubby hands. "Your balls are so soft and heavy. When was the last time you came?"

Numbness filled me. I felt myself leave my body and float to the corner of the room. My naked physical form was down below, with Dr. Miller pawing it. His heavy breathing and grunting ricocheted off the stucco ceiling and down the hallway. He awkwardly manipulated and caressed my body. I felt nothing. I felt nothing when he pushed me onto the bed and bent down to lick my inner thigh. I felt nothing when he wrapped his mouth around my swollenness. I felt nothing when I chose to end the session by climaxing. I felt nothing when he pressed on my thighs to help himself stand. I felt nothing when he tossed a wad of money onto my stomach and left the room.

"You may leave now. I'm finished with you," the good doctor called from down the hall.

My astral-projected essence returned to my body, and the feeling was a mixture of enormous shame and guilt. *Why didn't I say, "No?" Why did I let that happen? What is Erik going to think?*

I shoved the emotions aside, quickly dressed, and made my way down the hall. As I passed the living room, I saw Erik on the patio, talking with a couple of people.

"You need to leave, Hal's waiting for you," John said as he stepped in front of me.

"I wanted to say goodbye to Erik."

"That's not a good idea." John led me to the front door and opened it. At the bottom of the steps, Hal's car idled, with him in the driver's seat.

"But..."

John indicated for me to leave.

I stepped out the door as it closed behind me. I hopped down the stairs, pulled open the car door, slide onto the passenger's seat, and fastened the seatbelt.

"What took you so long?" Hal said as he shifted into drive.

"I wanted to say goodbye to Erik." I looked back at the door, hoping that by some chance Erik was looking out.

Hal pulled out of the circular driveway that had become a parking lot filled with different makes and models of expensive cars. "You seemed to have taken a shine to him."

"He's nice. He made me feel like I was something."

"How much do you like him?"

"A lot." My feelings surprised me.

Hal nodded as he merged onto State Route 75 South. "I could tell. I'll see what I can do."

I looked over to Hal. "What does that mean?"

Hal released a held breath. "Dr. Miller will do everything in his power to keep you two from getting to know each other any better."

"Why?"

"It messes up his parties." Hal pulled around a semi-truck. "He doesn't want the boys to fraternize with each other." Hal changed lanes so that he could be in front of the truck and not have to remain in the fast lane in case a police car was using radar to trap speeders. "Dr. Miller said he heard that Erik was talking about you last night at the club and was worried."

"Erik talked about me?"

"Yes. Didn't Erik take you and Sammy to the club to dance last night?"

"Yes."

"You see, Dr. Miller has eyes and ears everywhere. And he heard that Erik was saying how nice you are."

"With who?"

"I don't know, but it doesn't matter."

"Erik didn't even talk to me at all last night. He left me on the dance floor and disappeared. I started dancing with this guy who leaned in and said, 'I'm not interested in getting messed up with a 'Miller Boy' and left me. What did he mean?"

"Someone said that to you?"

"And who is Kalvin?"

Hal gripped the steering wheel until his knuckles turned white and squeezed his lips together. He remained that way as he drove in silence.

I finally settled back into the seat and stared out the window, watching the farmland whiz by and buzzards circling in the darkening sky. *One, two, three, four.* I resigned to the fact that nothing more was going to be discussed and Kalvin was a taboo subject.

Hal broke the silence. "Dr. Miller will not allow Erik to communicate with you. He's sending Erik to Colorado to finish school."

"Because of me?"

Hal nodded.

Anger and pity mixed with the shame and disgust made me speechless.

"I'll see what I can do," Hal said.

We drove the rest of the way in silence.

DR. ALTHEA WARNER'S OFFICE— DAYTON, OHIO, 2018

I chose not to share the recall with her, and I just shook my head.

"Are you sure you can't think of any time you found yourself in a situation where you weren't aware of how you got there?" Althea restated the question, "Or did something seem abnormal or out of the realm of possibility?"

My mind quickly filled up with other scenarios, like standing at a urinal in the fourth floor bathroom of the UCI library and someone exposing himself. Another time on a red-eye flight and the guy next to me was pressing his knee against mine while rubbing his crotch. Jogging through the woods, coming to a clearing, and witnessing someone pleasuring himself while smiling at me.

I realized that I've always been an observer, in almost every memory, even when I was forced against my will—I was still a watcher. I felt a sense of control with watching. Maybe this was my way of initiating some form of dominance? I used to believe I could control people with my mind. Make them do whatever I wanted.

I created a scale to earn points through my telepathic powers. If I concentrated hard enough and made someone glance at me as he walked past I got a point. If the same guy turned around to look at me again it was worth an extra point. I practiced this phenomenon and played this game every chance I got. I used to sit on the bus, in class, at church, anywhere, and focus on a guy sitting across from me. If I could get him to look at me, I earned one point; a smile received two points; touching his thigh earned three points; spreading his thighs earned four more points; touching his crotch was worth five points; rubbing his crotch was awarded ten points; and if he became hard, a whopping twenty points. If I could see the slightest twitch, I deemed myself successful.

For some reason, I never used these powers on females, maybe because I heard my father's voice reminding me that lying with a man was abomination and a path straight to Hell. I adopted the belief that I was never going to take a woman to Hades with me. Many times, in the presence of a female, I'd cast an invisibility spell on myself. This would make me passive and encase me in a protective force field. She would have to use extra-human powers to counter my spell, and it'd be her choosing to interact with me. Despite my desire to disappear, I subconsciously surrounded myself with women. This caused constant nervousness for me in their presence. But for some reason, I was nervous and guarded in front of women over the manipulation, confusion, and anger I felt toward men. My damaged soul struggled to interact with people, since I was battling between feeling foolish in front of women and a pleasure tool for men. My focus of casting spells was always toward men, even on myself.

"No, I can't think of anything," I responded.

"Just think about it. You may not remember anything right now, but don't judge or analyze them if they do come forth, just feel free to write about them in your journal, and we can look at them together. The important thing here is to figure out your true orientation and build from there. Many people who have experienced abuse have some degree of shame imprinting and attached false labels in order to make sense of the experience. If the person has repeated abusive experiences, these false labels can, and most often, become permanently embedded in their psyche. They begin to believe these lies and ultimately act out on them, leading to future bouts of confusion, anger, depression, and other issues."

"What do you mean by shame imprinting?"

Althea elongated her spine and gently shook her head, as if she were preparing to perform a front three-and-a-half somersault from the ten-meter platform. She began speaking rather slowly and in control. "As a developing teen, you were constantly put into situations or compromising positions and expected to perform in a certain way, even if it wasn't against your will or your natural orientation. With some men, this abuse is internalized and later can become an eroticized fantasy which the victim repeats in order to gain some type of understanding and an attempt to figure everything out. The person is basically unconscious as to why these events keep repeating and infused with repetitive questions, like 'Was there something about me that made him pick me?' 'Did I ask for it?' 'Did I want it?' 'Was there something that I did or said that made him interested in me?' 'Since my body responded, does this make me gay?'"

Althea pointed her pen at me. "You've become quite adept at compartmentalizing, which helps you bury or forget about certain impulses until you find yourself in situations in which you discover you're a part of it again. This creates more confusion, shame, and even anger."

She rose from the chair, walked to the bookshelf, took a quick breath, and rushed her words as if she didn't get them all out right then. "This shame imprint prevents you from talking about it with anyone. The anger and shame build up internally and have no way to be eased, like a volcano building pressure to explode. Since you've never had anyone explain these feelings or how to deal with them, you push them aside and try to forget. Yet there's this anger and embarrassment you feel; and you may not be sure from where it stems. It could be from the loss of your innocence or the fact that you didn't get the chance to experiment sexually with partners your own age and discover your orientation on your terms and in your own time. It can be helpful for you to understand that your sexuality was eclipsed by the selfish desires of your predators and resulting with you being sexually disoriented. Sure, you may have ended up gay anyway, but it was your gayness to discover, not someone else's gayness to be thrusted upon you." Althea leaned on the bookshelf.

I fought the impulse to applaud her performance. I was in such awe of what she said all I could do was sit there and stare at her. Finally, I found my voice and said, "So, you're saying that the abuse didn't orient me, but may have disoriented me."

"Exactly." She ran her fingers along the books' spines.

"This is more confusing."

"Why?"

"Then if I was disoriented, I've been living my entire adult life as a lie. How would I ever figure this out?"

She found the book she wanted and pulled it from the bookshelf. "You may not be truly following me." She made her way back to her chair, while Glady's tail thumped against the wooden floor. "What we want to make sure of is that you look at your anger and try to understand it. Your anger stems from not being able to explore and experiment with other children your age to figure out your sexual orientation. You were thrust into adult situations which you were not ready for, and a false orientation was thrust upon you. You were shamed imprinted to the point you adopted characteristics of a certain ideology, based on what you knew, learned, and how to survive. You may have equated that you could only experience the pleasure of climaxing with older men. You didn't have a healthy example of sex or sexuality. You tried to figure things out on your own. No one shared with you how to deal with the feelings you were experiencing before, during, and after the episode. So, you started to comprehend the best you could with your undeveloped mind."

"How would I even begin to decode or figure all this out?" I scratched Glady between her shoulder blades, and she pressed her head against my shoulder.

"Now, make sure you hear this. Your natural orientation may be homosexual. I'm not trying to say that you've been denying your natural sexual orientation and that you've been living a lie all these years." Althea's face flushed and she handed me a book. "I want you to read this. Don't study it, just read through it."

"*The Power of Now: A Guide to Spiritual Enlightenment* by Eckhart Tolle." I looked up at Althea. "What is this?"

"I want you to understand how humans attach meaning to words and situations, get caught up in mental thinking, and lose the importance of the present moment." She sat on her chair. "I had a reservation with some of the terminology at first, but once I started to realize it was my own doing and my own meanings I placed on the words, I started to understand the worth of Tolle's ideology."

I flipped the green and yellow book over and read, "To make the journey into the Power of Now, we will need to leave our analytical mind and its false creative self, the ego, behind." *Is this bullshit?* I looked out the window toward the clock tower and saw a mass of flies landing on the windowsill, and I started counting: *seven, eight, nine, ten, eleven...*

"Just read through it and bring it back next week. There's a section on disassociating from the body, which may help you with your anger." Althea skimmed through her notes. "Tell me more about Erik."

"How did you know about Erik?"

"You mentioned him."

"I did?"

"In one sentence." She pulled up the journal and flipped to the page.

"Are you sure?"

"Here it is." Althea adjusted her glasses. "There were only a few people that I allowed to truly enter into my sphere at this time; Mark, Erik, and April, and I sabotaged them all."

I leaned forward and cranked my head to see what she was reading. She turned the journal around and pointed to the passage that revealed more than I ever wanted.

"I don't remember writing that."

She closed the journal and handed it to me. "So, tell me about this list."

"You know about Mark; he was the diver I went with to the World Games in Tønsberg. April, I told you, was during my Hollywood years."

"What about Erik?"

I glanced at the clock on the church tower.

"We still have some time." Althea removed her glasses and set them on the side table. "It interests me that throughout your journal, you have mentioned Mark and April. But there's only this one line that mentions Erik. I'm just curious." She clasped her hands and placed them on top of the notepad resting on her thighs.

I squirmed in my seat.

"Okay, fair enough."

I glanced at the church tower again.

"What's the resistance to talk about Erik?"

141

I defiantly locked eyes with Althea.

"You don't have to talk about him." Her voice was calm and patient. "It's just that I sense there's a chunk of your story that's missing. You met Mark while diving, but nothing really transpired there because you were sent to California and he went back to Ohio State University. Then you went to U.C. Irvine and met Sue and Jennifer and switched majors. Then you've shared that you met April when you moved back to L.A."

I hoisted myself from the floor and sat on the couch. Golden hairs were on my lap from where Glady rested her head. *One, two, three, four, five…*

Althea closed her notepad and placed it and the pen on the floor next to her chair.

I tried not to talk, but the upsurge took me by surprise. "Erik saved me."

Althea cocked her head and remained silent.

My hands shook, and I tried to slowly speak. "I met Erik when Hal took me to Columbus to meet a doctor who wanted to help with my diving."

"What was the doctor's name?"

I hesitated. "Miller. Chuck Miller."

Althea nodded.

I continued. "Erik lived at the doctor's house while he was going to OSU. He was ten years older than me, so he was twenty-five or twenty-six. Hal would leave me with the doctor for the weekend or the entire week, depending on whatever was happening. Erik and I became close friends. He understood me and what was happening around us. He took me under his wing and made me feel safe, no matter what happened in the house. Even when we had to attend 'special' parties the doctor hosted and we were expected to follow the doctor's rules, I'd just have to look at Erik and I knew I'd be able to get through anything. He didn't judge me or place any expectations. We were surviving together, and in secret. The attraction grew between us, even though we both knew it was against the rules. One day, he pulled

me into the utilities closest during a party, and we were caught."
I paused. "OMG!"

"What?" Althea leaned forward.

"That's when Erik was sent to Colorado and I was sent to California." The weight of the discovery was overwhelming. "Dr. Miller sent Erik to Colorado to finish school, and Hal sent me to California. They wanted to separate us."

"Why?"

I looked at Althea. "I don't know."

"Did you keep in touch?" she asked.

"I wrote to him all the time, but he never responded. Later, I learned that Dr. Miller made Erik promise not to communicate with me, or Dr. Miller would stop paying for Erik's schooling. I saw him during the winter break of my freshman year. I never saw him after that."

"That must be hard to process."

I fought back tears and forced away the lump in my throat. "I think about him to this day. He was the first person, close to my age, that broke all the rules that I had created for myself."

There was a knock on the door leading to the waiting room.

"Our time's up. I want you to read the book and keep journaling."

CHAPTER 5
SPRING QUARTER

UNIVERSITY CALIFORNIA IRVINE,
RETURN TO CLASSES, 1982

"Welcome back, everyone. I hope you had a restful and recharging winter break," Dr. Blankenburg said as his fingers stroked the lapel of his tweed sport-coat.

Brian Thompson waved to me from across the room while sitting next to Theresa Larkin, Jeffrey Meeks, and other seniors. Jennifer laced her fingers through mine as she snuggled closer to me for Brian's benefit, which made me feel more like a prop than a person.

"I'm excited to get this quarter started, but before I send everyone off and prepared for classes to start tomorrow, I wanted to share some information and changes about this spring's productions. We've added a new show that will perform right here in our experimental theatre, and it is..." Dr. Blankenburg paused to create drama. "*The Judgement at Nuremburg* by Abby Mann, which will be directed by our own senior acting major, Jeffrey Meeks." The professor indicated in Jeff's direction.

A polite applause rang through the room as everyone cranked their necks to get a peek at the renowned Jeffery Meeks. Theresa gracefully bowed before him and blew him kisses.

Dr. Blankenburg continued. "This production has a large cast, and everyone is expected to audition."

"Oh goody, I can't wait," said Jennifer with excitement. "We should get prepping as soon as possible."

I pushed down the overwhelming feeling of adding another thing to my already over-loaded schedule. The conference meet was coming up, and I felt the expected pressure to dive well and qualify for NCAAs. I had to make sure all my academic and athletic scholarships were transferred to the theatre department. And I'd be playing catch-up on the classes that I still needed to complete in order to remove my incompletes from last quarter. I was mostly excited to return to *General Hospital.*

"Have a wonderful quarter, and remember you can't grow without trying. So, stretch yourselves and breakout of the box you have put yourself in." Dr. Blankenburg's voice echoed throughout the auditorium. "Change your thoughts, and change the world." He waved and walked off stage.

"What do you think?" Jennifer smiled and shook her head so her dark hair bounced around her face.

"Sure."

"What's wrong?" Her smile faded.

"Nothing." My belly churned and gurgled quite loudly.

"Is someone hungry?" Jennifer placed her hand on my stomach.

"Hey, kiddo. I hope that you'll be auditioning for the play." Jeffery Meeks towered above me, looking down with his hypnotic eyes and dazzling smile. "You have the perfect Aryan look."

"I'll make sure he's there," Brian Thompson added as he leaned next to Jeffrey.

"Good." Jeffery smiled.

"He's perfect," Theresa added her two cents before pulling Jeffrey away.

"How's the chin?" asked Brian.

"Yeah, the last time I saw you, you split open your chin at Disney Land," joked Chris as he draped his arm around Brian's broad shoulders.

I chuckled. "Good. Everything's good.

Brian offered his massive hand. My hand looked elfish in his, and with the slightest of pulls, I was standing.

Jennifer stood next to me and placed her chin on my shoulder. "I have to leave. I have a sorority meeting in ten minutes, and I just can't be late."

"No probs, man. We're going over to Chris's for some pizza and beer. You're welcome to come once you get rid of your ball and chain," Brian said.

Jennifer's temper rose. "I'll have you know, I'm no one's ball and chain."

"No, you just have him whipped," Chris interjected as he imitated whirling a whip over his head and snapping it in my direction.

Jennifer took ahold of my arm and started walking to the exit. "Whatever, you Neanderthals."

"Words hurt." Chris grabbed his chest.

"Catch you later, David," said Brian. "Chris, you're such a nimrod."

Jennifer pushed open the door and led me outside and down the stairs. "They can be children sometimes." She increased the pace.

I stopped. "I like them."

"What?"

"I like Brian and Chris."

"I know. Everyone likes Brian and Chris. Come on, I don't have much time."

"You go ahead. I have to go do something."

"What?"

"Something." I looked off in the distance.

Jennifer huffed. "I thought you were going to walk me?"

"I'll catch up with you later." I started to walk toward Aldrich Park.

"David." She stomped her foot.

I waved over my head and kept walking to the path leading into the wooded area.

"David!"

I walked faster.

"Whatever."

The slate sky was ceding to evening, and the lamps along the park's path were dimly glowing. I followed the curved pathway toward the dorms. My mind raced with the things that I had to get done and places I had to be, and I was uncertain how or if I could get everything accomplished.

"Keep walking, and don't look back."

"What…" I started to turn when I felt a hard shove against my back, and I stumbled to remain upright.

"I said, don't look."

I continued walking.

"It's nice to see you're back." The voice was deep and almost gravelly, like the owner was pressing down on his voicebox.

"Who are you?"

"You should know."

"How can I know if I can't look at you?" I turned my head.

Another blow connected to my back.

"Don't look. You just should know. How many notes have I left for you?"

My heart skipped a beat as I realized this must be the mystery person. "What do you want?"

"You know."

"Why are you doing this?" I asked.

"You'll soon know."

I saw the lighted area at the edge of the park that led to the dorms. A hand landed on my shoulder as a foot clipped mine, causing me to fall to the ground. As I pulled myself up and looked back, I saw a person wearing a black baseball hat, dark jacket, and tan corduroy pants walking in the opposite direction and shadowed by the trees. Adrenaline raced through my blood vessels.

"Why are you doing this?" I screamed.

The stranger never responded and disappeared in the depths of the wooded park.

I brushed myself off, and I jogged to the dorm.

The chill of the air conditioner greeted my feverish skin as I pushed through the door to the dorm's main entrance. On the table next to the mailboxes was a copy of *Newsweek*, with the cover's headliner, *Epidemic*, in bold white letters and a blood-filled test tube with a label inscription, "Caution." I turned the magazine slightly to see it better, so no one saw me reading it. The sub header stated, "The Mysterious and Deadly Disease... May Be the Public-Health Threat of the Century. How Did It Start? Can It Be Stopped?"

A familiar cough from the living room area pulled my attention away from the magazine. My mind needed a distraction from the ramifications of the rare disease and the possible connection to Dr. Miller. Sue was just what I needed.

Sue sat on the couch with a book as if she never left the spot to go on Winter Break. Curled up with her legs tucked under her, hair pulled back in a ponytail, and no make-up.

"Sue." I made my way around the table and partition to the seating area.

"David," she coldly responded.

"How was break?"

She nodded her head as if she was trying to contemplate an answer. "Nothing to write about. And you?"

"Probably about the same." I sat on the edge of the couch next to her.

"What's this?" She pulled a piece of paper from my back and read.

DO SO TO ME, AND MORE ALSO!

I grabbed the paper out of her hand as all the blood drained out of my face.

"That's from the weirdo, isn't it?" She scooted to the edge and looked at the paper in my hand. "I recognize the handwriting. David, you're shaking."

"No, I'm not."

"Like hell. Look at me." She turned my chin. "What the hell's going on? Is this starting all over again?"

My intestines knotted up, causing me to double over in pain.

"David?"

I held up a hand for her to give me a minute as I grimaced from the intestinal attack. "I'm fine."

"I can tell. What is it?"

I took a deep breath, the twisting in my gut eased, and I sat up. "Nothing. It's nothing." I got up and started to go to my room.

Sue grabbed my hand. "I'm here for you."

I fought against my initial reaction to pull my hand away. I focused on her thin hand tightly holding mine. "I just need some time to figure things out." I wanted to run and hide and not let her see my eyes water.

"But wait a minute." She held me from moving. "Let me in."

"I'm trying." I couldn't look into her eyes, so I stared at the length of her thin fingers.

"You're shutting me out, again."

"I'm not trying to."

"But you are." Sue lifted my chin with her other hand and looked into my eyes. "What are you hiding?"

Everything shut down inside me. A defensive wall materialized and enclosed my emotions and froze my blood stream. A calculating iciness emerged as I dissociated from the moment. "Nothing. Really, I'm fine. I have to go to the library." I smiled and nodded to convince her.

"It's Sunday, classes don't start until tomorrow."

"I have to find an audition piece and study for that anatomy makeup test."

She withdrew her hand as if the ice burned her. "All right, whatever."

I started for my room but stopped. "Maybe we can do a pizza later?"

A smile grew on her face. "I'd like that. I really would."

"Then it's a date."

"Don't let Jennifer know that." Sue forced a laugh.

I ran to my room and pulled a shoebox out from under my bed. I removed the lid and deposited the note among an assortment of other notes that I had received from the unknown stalker. Notes he left on my bag during diving practice, outside my classrooms, and on my dorm room door. Sue was wrong; this wasn't starting up all over again because it never stopped.

UNIVERSITY OF CALIFORNIA, IRVINE, LIBRARY, 1982

As I walked past the book shelves on my way to the restroom in the back corner on the library's fourth floor, I noticed someone sitting on a lounge chair with a black UCI Anteater baseball cap shadowing his face. He nodded to me. I nervously kept walking, went into the men's room, and stopped at the urinal.

I mentally reviewed the different muscles for my upcoming anatomy make-up test. I pictured the major anterior muscles: *Sternocleidomastoid is in the neck. Deltoid is the upper shoulder. Teres major is the upper portion of the pectoralis. Pectoralis major is the pecs, Latissimus dorsi is...*

"Do you always mumble while you pee?"

"What?"

The guy from the lounge chair was standing at the next urinal. "It's cute."

"Oh, no." My face heated up, and I quickly focused on the chrome of the urinal's piping and saw his reflection. The black UCI Anteater baseball cap was strategically lowered to hide his eyes. His lips were reddish-pink and surrounded by dark stubble peeking through his olive skin. "Sorry, I was just trying to memorize for a test tomorrow."

"Tomorrow? On the first day back?" he asked with an accusatory tone.

"It's a makeup test."

"I see. What are you studying?" He looked down at me.

I tried to hide myself. "The muscles."

"Looks to me like you're handling it just fine." He leaned back and exposed himself. I refused to look. He laughed, shook himself, and zipped up. He took out an index card and whispered in my ear. "You're cute. Come by tonight, and I'll help you study." He slipped the card in my back pocket and patted my butt. "I better see you tonight, if you know what's good for you."

The bathroom door opened, he slithered around another student, and exited. When I left the restroom, the lounge chair was empty. I reached for the card in my back pocket and discovered a map. There was no address, name, or telephone number. There was a box with an "X" labeled "library," arrows leading to another box with a "£," and the inscriptions "first floor, first door on right, 8:00 pm, don't be late."

UNIVERSITY OF CALIFORNIA, IRVINE, CAMPUS VILLAGE GRAD HOUSING, 1982

A door opened, and a dark-haired man greeted me with a huge smile. "You came."

"Yes." I scanned his toned, tanned body donning a white oxford button-down neatly tucked into tan corduroy pants, emphasizing a 32" waist.

"I didn't really think you would come." There was surprise in his voice.

"Why not?"

"Don't get me wrong, I'm glad. I'm just pleasantly surprised."

"I don't understand." A flutter of nerves sprouted in my stomach.

The man's olive cheeks crimsoned, and he puckered his lips. "You're not easy to get near. Never mind. Where are my manners? Please." He opened the door wider and invited me into the darkened room, aglow with candles on the coffee table. The room was sparse, with no pictures or artwork on the white walls, and there was a strong scent of patchouli or herbal cigarettes.

"It's not much, but welcome to my modest abode," the faceless man said.

I stepped further in.

The door closed and locked.

"How about something to drink?"

"Sure, I guess."

"Great. Make yourself comfortable." He looked around the room and joked. "Or as comfortable as you can." He stared at me for a long time. "Wow, you're really here."

I nodded. "Yep, I'm here." I held up the index card he slipped into my back pocket in the library bathroom."

He took the card, rushed to his desk, and placed it into a drawer. "I know. It was a drastic measure. I didn't think it'd work. Anyway. It did You're here." He rushed back to me and took a long inhale.

"Did you just sniff me?" I bewilderedly asked.

He nodded. "I did. It's a quirk of mine."

I nervously looked around the room. "I see."

"It's nice. The way you smell."

"I'm glad, I guess. I hope I don't reek of chlorine."

His smile grew. "No, it's not chlorine." He deeply inhaled again. "Sensory stimuli from smells connect neural mechanism to the behavior centers in our brains. Certain smells activate the hypothalamus, which releases hormones that regulate the body's temperature, appetite, thirst, sleep, moods, and sex drive."

"Wow, impressive."

"Not really. It's really kind of boring."

"What do I smell like?" I asked.

He took a moment and leaned in closer. "You have sweetness, like a mixture of ginger and almonds, with a hint of basil."

"Sounds like ingredients to a recipe." My joke fell flat.

We remained close. Since he was taller, my nose was near his chin. He emitted an earthly scent with a hint of vanilla.

He whispered, "I better get the drinks." He slid past me and disappeared into the other room.

I was left alone with the smell of melting wax overtaking the herbal aroma as the candles' glow danced on the ceiling. A black UCI Anteater baseball hat hung on a hook by the door. A beat-up leather couch occupied most of the room even though it was pushed against the wall and a coffee table sat before it. There was no television, but in the far corner, sitting on an upside-down plastic milk crate, was a portable record player, like the one I used to play the Carpenters on and danced with my sister, Magdalyn. A stack of albums piled up next to the makeshift table displayed *Madame Butterfly* on top. In the other corner was a small writing desk with a pad of paper similar to the notes left on my diving bag and dorm room door.

"Here you go."

I turned to find a plastic glass of wine held before me.

"Thanks. I usually don't drink," I said. I took the offering to be polite.

"You'll like it. It's white zinfandel."

The faceless person must have smiled and made me feel more comfortable, even though my nerves were on edge.

"Wait." He held up his hand. "Always smell the wine before drinking. It prepares your brain in the best way possible, so you'll enjoy it better."

I chuckled and lifted the glass to my nose.

"Nice and slow, like this." He took a long, slow inhale.

I mimic him. The wine's bouquet filled my head with a rush from the sweetness.

"Now sip," he instructed.

I drank the wine like it was water.

"You like it?"

"It's sweet." My glass was refilled, higher this time.

"Sit."

"Okay." I made my way around the coffee table and sat on the couch, causing a leathery odor to release into the air.

He sat next to me. "To a wonderful evening."

A glass was held before me, waiting for me to clink it with mine. I did and drank. The sweetness was inviting.

"I'm glad you came."

"Yeah?" I giggled.

"Yeah. I have been watching you."

"You have?"

"Drink up." The glass was guided to my mouth and tilted so I had to drink.

After another mouthful I pulled away, and the wine dribbled from the corners of my mouth. "Sorry." I wiped my chin with the back of my hand.

"You spilled on your shirt." His hand pressed against my chest. "And on your pants." The same hand moved and pressed my thigh near my hip.

"Sorry, I'm so clumsy." I studied his forearm sprouting out from under the rolled-up sleeve and followed the veins running under the tanned skin and dark hairs to each of his long, thin fingers and well-manicured nails.

"No problem." The glass was refilled.

"That's enough, thank you."

"I'll let you know when you've had enough. You're safe with me. Relax." His hand lifted from my thigh and touched the side of my face, tracing my jawline. "You're pretty." He pressed his lips against mine.

I tasted a smoky residue, nervously pulled away, and giggled.

"You like that?" he asked.

All I could do was grin, because my lips tingled with numbness. The background colors completely disappeared into the darkened room. Objects melted into pools on the floor. Woodenness filled my cheeks, my hands became useless, and my arms weighed a ton. It was becoming difficult to hold my head up.

"Let's go to the Jacuzzi."

A hand guided me up, but my feet were glued to the floor.

"Here, let me help you."

The buttons on my shirt were undone, revealing my naked chest. Fingernails scraped down the length of my torso, leaving long red marks that periled with red droplets. There was no pain.

"You have a really hot body." His lips scaled and nipped my neck.

The faceless man took hold of my belt and tugged me around the coffee table, lugging me to a screened-in porch where the Jacuzzi was bubbling and sending white steam throughout the room.

"You have a Jacuzzi in your apartment?" My words were slurred.

"It was the only perk in renting the place." The faceless man removed his white oxford shirt with a red insignia over the right pocket, exposing a diamond patch of dark hair between firm pecs.

The Jacuzzi's chemicals filled my lungs as my belt was unbuckled, pulled through the pant loops, and tossed into a corner. The baggy jeans slid down my hips, revealing the elastic band of my underwear.

"Briefs. I suspected. I go commando myself. I hate having the boys constricted." He pulled my jeans to the floor.

An unsurmountable wave of heat washed through my head, causing my temples to pulsate.

The faceless man guided me to the edge of the Jacuzzi, and I stepped down on a step as the bubbling waters swallowed my feet. The warmth sped through my veins, causing my armpits and forehead to bead with sweat.

"Wait a minute." He took our glasses, placed them on a small table next to the hot tub, quickly reached around from behind me, grabbed my Fruit of the Loom's fly, and ripped the material from my body. The cotton material tore easily, leaving the elastic band hugging my waist.

"Oh, my goodness." I covered my nakedness up with my hands, while the heat of the water and the embarrassment reddened my cheeks.

"No, no, no, no." He spun me around to face him and gently removed my hands. "Stunning. How in the hell have you been able to hide that?"

I covered up again.

He forced my hands to the side. "No, you never need to cover up, you're perfect." He took several steps back. "I want to take this all in." He stood there like a painter, analyzing the model he was about to immortalize with his brush strokes. "The way the light is hitting you and the steam from the Jacuzzi are creating this ethereal effect. You're an angel. A perfect angel. My perfect angel."

He left me alone and rushed into the other room. After a couple of clicks, soothing music filled the speakers. His voice blended in with the recorded female's voice for a few bars, stopped, and enthusiastically announced, "I just love this aria, *Un bel di vedremo*. Do you know what opera it's from?" He called to me. "David?"

"What?" I called back. I was trying to figure out how to get my pants.

"Do you know this opera's title?" He asked in such a way, it sounded like we were longtime friends.

"No, I'm sorry."

"It's Puccini's *Madam Butterfly*," he said with disappointment. "I thought for sure you'd have known that." He returned with a Polaroid Instant Camera in hand and snapped a picture.

"Please, don't." I hunched over and hid myself.

The high pitch of the picture squeaking out from the bottom filled the small area. The faceless man held the film and flagged it in the air. "I just want to show you what I see. I promise, it's just for us tonight." He watched the image appear like magic, and his smile grew larger.

"I just don't feel comfortable." I felt small and insignificant, like one of Magdalyn's Barbie dolls I used to play with.

MATTHEW HOME—AULDEN, OHIO, 1979

"Does anyone need to use the bathroom?" I announced.

I walked into the living room to find Magdalyn curled up on the pull-out couch and watching television. She was cocooned beneath the comforter with only her huge eyes and forehead peeking out from under the blanket, which was pulled up to cover her chin. Her glazed eyes didn't register me coming into the room; they only glistened with the life of the images from the television dancing across her irises.

Caine was listening to Van Halen or Aerosmith upstairs in his room, composing another one of his infamous love song/poems for his secret girlfriend.

I hesitated as I heard the familiar swirling of a spoon against the sides of the coffee cup in the kitchen, reminding me that Dad was working on the plans to his invention, the Looper. I contemplated not bothering him with my announcement of occupying the only bathroom in this old farmhouse, but something warned me against it. The last time I snuck into the smallest room without so much as an utterance, I was constantly interrupted by a parade of people needing to use the facilities. I thought that if I announced it tonight, it would assure me of some privacy. I wanted to make it quick and not get caught up in one of Dad's teaching moments. I took a deep breath and raced through the kitchen, heading directly to the other hallway leading to the bathroom.

"Dad, I'm going to be taking a bath, okay?" I quietly uttered, intentionally mumbling my words.

He waved me off with a flip of his hand, which sent mixed feelings of relief and the constant "I don't matter" mantra. I fought the urge to glance back at him and went into the bathroom, closed the door, and leaned against it whishing there was a lock or a least a latch to keep everyone out.

The house rules rang through my mind: *The bathroom is the one room that must always be accessible to everyone —especially if someone was in dire need; they're permitted to come right on in.*

I took stock of the materials I had wrapped up in a towel, neatly exhibiting them on the floor next to the bathtub: two Ken dolls, a G.I. Joe, a roll of toilet paper.

Where is the pencil?

I shifted through the items again and couldn't find the new yellow #2 pencil with the good eraser.

Did I drop it?

I froze for a moment, realizing that if I broke the seal to the door, my time of solitude could be invaded with someone realizing that they needed to use the bathroom. I spread the towel out, no pencil. I glanced around the small cubicle.

Where could it have gone? I know I had it. The pencil was the first thing I grabbed, then the dolls.

I scanned the room.

There.

On the floor, next to the clothes hamper was the pencil.

I retrieved the pencil and placed it on the towel with the other items. I started the water and poured in an ample amount of bubble bath. I devised this method to hide myself in case someone had to use the room while I was in the tub. I ruled out taking a shower a while ago, since the shower curtain was clear. I also learned to move the clothes hamper next to the tub for added protection to hide behind, since the wall opposite the toilet was mirrored.

Last month, I was in the tub without bubbles or the hamper next to me. I was on my knees rinsing my hair under the faucet, when I felt a rush of cold air as someone came busting in. I knock my head against the spouting faucet while trying to cover up. Soap and water went everywhere. I leaned halfway out of the tub to grab a towel and rid my eyes of the stinging soap. Mom's reflection was in the mirror, sitting on the toilet, watching me.

"You're growing up so fast," she said and smiled. "It just seems like yesterday that I was bathing you myself."

I cowered back down into the water pulling my knees to my chest. "Mom, please!"

"What? When can't a mother look at her child?"

"When he's almost sixteen years old!"

"Oh please. You don't have anything I haven't seen before?" She reached for the toilet paper.

I pushed to the far back end of the tub, pulling the towel over my face as if by hiding she'd disappear and this humiliation would be over.

A flush sounded, and the water swirled down the toilet.

I squeezed my eyes tighter.

The bathwater agitated next to my thigh, and I realized she was washing her hands.

I clamped my hands over my ears.

Tomorrow is Friday, I have a test in religious studies and I have practice after school.

The towel was tugged away from my clutched fists.

I squeezed my eyes even tighter.

Oh my God, I'm completely exposed.

"You sure have grown up into a nice looking young man," Mom said. "Just the other day, Sharon was saying how you get more handsome the older you get."

I peeked out of the corner of my eye, and she was standing there, looking at me and drying her hands on my towel. I shut my eyes and hid my face in the palms of my hands.

"Don't be so bashful, there's no need to hide from your mother. Come on."

I peeked through my fingers again.

Mom stood there holding the towel with her arms stretched out wide. When I was a little boy, I'd enthusiastically climb out of the tub and couldn't wait for her to wrap me up within the towel like a burrito.

"Mom," I said with hesitation and dismay. I hugged my knees closer to my chest.

"Come on, let's go. You've been in there too long. You'll shrivel up like a prune."

"But mom…"

"No buts, come on."

"I don't want…"

"Stop wasting time." There was a harsh undertone to her voice.

My mind started racing with different options. I could continue to hesitate, and maybe she'd grow tired of this game and leave. Then she'd be angry, and I'd have to deal with that later. I could comply, get it over with, and somehow pretend that it never happened. I froze.

"What are you waiting for?"

"Mom?"

"Let's go!" she said with finality.

I realized she wasn't going to give up. She was planted there and would outwait me. I took a deep breath and I stood, trying to cover my private parts. I kept my eyes shut.

"Lift your arms."

I started to resist but knew that it was useless. I obliged. I lifted my arms above my shoulders.

"That's my good boy." She dried my shoulders and chest, and then wrapped the towel around me. She placed her palms on each side of my face. "Keep the water, Maggie needs to take a bath." She kissed me lightly on the lips, as if this was something normal between every mother and son in the world.

Maybe I was the one who had become skittish and made this awkward.

Since then, I started to improvise ways to hide myself while in the bathtub. I discovered that the clothes hamper could camouflage a good third of the tub if I positioned it near the faucet—this would also impede the reflection in the mirror.

I needed to create a reason for why the hamper was placed there. That was when I decided I could conduct diving meets with the Ken and G.I. Joe dolls and use the hamper as the platform. I immediately realized that if I pulled the shower curtain up next to the hamper, it created an isolated area, and I could use the excuse that the curtain was to protect the floor from any splashing from the dolls.

This game became my ruse, my protection, and I could spend up to an hour in the tub. I justified this as creative visualization, in which the diving coach instructed me to practice. I figured that I appeared to be taking this exercise seriously, and to another level.

I positioned the dolls on the edge of the hamper and announced the dive that they were to perform. "David, of the USA, will be performing a front dive in the layout position." I imagined myself as the doll and envisioned the perfect dive in my mind, and then toss the doll from the hamper. The doll arched through the air and dove into the tub's sudsy water. I even scored the dive by determining the angle of entry and the amount of splash the doll created.

I was always the blond Ken doll. The dark-haired Ken doll was Klaus Dibiasi from Italy, and the G.I. Joe was Alexai Alexandre from Russia. Although I was partial to the USA winning all the time, I was always a fair judge.

Although this was the initial occupation with the dolls, this within itself became a rouse. I had discovered another game. I found myself becoming preoccupied with something I wasn't quite understanding. It seemed to come from somewhere that I wasn't aware of, as if it belonged to someone else. I wasn't conducting diving competitions any longer; only if someone interrupted to use the facilities.

In this revised game, the dolls weren't allowed to get wet until I was fully immersed beneath the bubbles and water. My hands had to remain dry. I took the pencil to the dolls, and one by one, I drew body hair on their chest, under their arms, and on their legs.

Each doll would have a variation in the amount of hair and how dark. If I was not satisfied with the creation, I would erase the markings and start all over.

This game developed as most games do. There were rules that needed to be followed. The dolls had to have swim trunks; they couldn't be completely naked. Toilet paper was molded and stuffed into the swimsuits to create the desired bulges. Each doll had a certain "size," depending on who the doll was representing.

Each doll represented different people at different times in my life: the blond Ken doll was always me, the dark-haired Ken would alternate between a schoolteacher and a doctor, and G.I. Joe was an optometrist or a lawyer.

Once the dolls were prepared, they reenacted different scenarios and the clothes hamper became the stage. The dolls took on a life of their own and I was the audience.

Blond Ken would be in school. Why he was wearing a Speedo in a classroom, I would never know, but he'd be in religious studies and the teacher, portrayed by the dark-haired Ken, would be lecturing.

"The twelve disciples were dedicated in spreading Jesus's message. They were devoted in trying to lead the life that they were being taught, to become examples of the spiritualism that man desired. They followed Jesus wherever he went. They listened to him lecture and retell parables, because they believed that every time they heard them, they would learn something new," orated the dark-haired Ken. He walked up next to Blond Ken.

Blond Ken didn't say anything but looked at the teacher.

"Why do you undermine my instructions?" asked the teacher.

"Excuse me, sir?" Blond Ken asked.

"Do not play dumb with me. You failed to turn in your assignment."

"I did turn it in."

"Not to my liking. You'll spend time in detention and redo the assignment."

"Yes, sir."

"Today!" The teacher walked away. "Now, when Jesus asked his disciples to do something for him, they immediately complied without hesitation." The bell rang, and the other students got up to leave, but Blond Ken remained. "Class, remember that your persuasive paper on, *Was the Water Really Turned into Wine?* is due tomorrow."

The teacher walked over to Blond Ken. "Please stand."

Blond Ken stood, and the teacher looked him up and down.

"Now you know why you're here in detention, don't you?"

"I didn't do my assignment correctly," Blond Ken answered.

"Your assignment is fine...more than fine...in fact, it's beyond fine."

"Then why am I here?"

"You know why." The teacher stepped closer to Blond Ken.

"No, sir, I don't."

"Maybe this will jog your memory," the teacher said. He placed his hand on Blond Ken's Speedo, leaned in, and kissed him.

The scene usually stopped at this point.

The next scene was at a doctor's or optometrist's appointment.

Blond Ken sat in a chair with a metal contraption that looked like huge glasses, and Dr. G.I. Joe would adjust the lens to find the proper prescription.

"Is the machine at a comfortable height?" Dr. G.I. Joe asked.

"I believe so," Blond Ken responded.

Dr. G.I. Joe positioned himself closer. "Tell me which one is better… number one…" Several clicks as the lenses were adjusted. "Or number two?"

Blond Ken took a moment. "I'm not sure."

Dr. G.I. Joe moved in closer, switching the lens. "One or…" He changed the lens back. "Two?"

"Two. I think."

"Number two…" More clicks, "Or three?"

"They're almost the same."

Dr. G.I. Joe placed his hand on Blond Ken's thigh. "Just relax and think about it. Two or three?" His hand inched up the inner side of Blond Ken's thigh.

"It's too hard, they look the same."

Dr. G.I. Joe slid his hand behind Blond Ken's speedo.

Once the anecdotes were played out, I submerged the dolls into the water. I made sure that their arms were extended above their heads and they were completely covered with suds. I leaned my back against the far end of the tub, extend my legs out to the sides, sometimes resting my right leg on the lip of the tub as I rested the left on the soap dish. I agitated the water, causing small ripples, closed my eyes and waited, anticipating which doll would float up against me. The anticipation was exhilarating, exciting, and thrilling. The waiting sent electrical waves throughout my body, causing my lower stomach to constrict, and tingle with pressure. The fantasy of which found me irresistible, and the first to touch me was intoxicating.

As soon as it was over, I was always filled with shame and disgust. I'd quickly wash the dolls clean from the pencil markings, rid them of their man-made bulges, throw them out of the tub with disgust, and promise I'd never allow myself to play the game again. Then I submerged myself under the tepid water, remain still, and pray for forgiveness.

UNIVERSITY OF CALIFORNIA, IRVINE, CAMPUS VILLAGE GRAD HOUSING. 1982

The faceless man held the Polaroid up for me to look at.

"No, I don't want to." I buried my face in the palms of my hands.

"Why not?" He looked at the emerging image. "You've got it going on, dude. You're smoking." He showed me the photo again while he hooked his other thumb through an empty belt loop of his tan corduroy pants. "You're perfect."

"No, I'm not. I'm just me." I wasn't sure if it was the wine or the heat from the hot tub, but my head was woozy.

"Look at this." He pressed the picture to my face and leaned his torso against the side of my body. "You radiate."

I couldn't focus; the image was a swirl of sepia, tan, black, and white mixed with the embarrassment that a photograph of me naked existed in the world.

As the faceless man turned the Jacuzzi temperature higher, the fog masked the air with thick whiteness. "Come here, my talented boy." His voice echoed throughout the small chamber, and his fingers pulled my hips toward him. He guided my hand to the button of his pants. "I need your help."

I glanced down and lightly rubbed my forefinger along the soft, dark hair cascading down from his navel.

"You got this." He tilted his pelvis forward, accentuating his desire.

I fumbled with the button before successfully freeing it, only to discover that there was no zipper, but more buttons. Impatiently, I tried to unbutton them all with one clean jerk.

"Woo, cowboy. Eager boys sometimes miss dessert." He pulled away from my reach, and I almost slipped further into the Jacuzzi. He quickly grabbed me and guided me to sit on the edge.

Again, I wondered if the wine or the heat from the bubbling water was causing numbness in my feet and hands.

"Here, take this." He handed me the glass of wine. "Sit back, and support yourself with your left hand." He manipulated my body as if I was a Ken doll, placing me in the position he wanted. "Spread your legs a little. There, hold that position."

Flash.

"You're a natural. Can you place your elbow on your thigh and lean forward toward me?" The faceless man maneuvered around to the other side of the Jacuzzi, squatted down, and peered through the camera. "Run your other hand through your hair. Yes, just like that."

Flash.

"Now on this one, I want you to lie on the edge of the hot tub, dangle your hand into the bubbling water, and pretend you are asleep. Bend your top leg. That's it. You're so sexy."

Flash.

By the third pose, my inhibitions melted away. Maybe it was the mixture of the wine's sweetness and the heat from the hot tub, but there was this sense of freedom that relaxed me from being my uptight and 'in control' personality to one of being alive in the moment, with no worries or anxieties.

Flash.

Even with my eyes closed, I saw the momentary brightness shed light on my internal world.

"Pretty boy, I've got something to show you."

I forced my heavy eyelids up and saw the faceless man had lowered his tan corduroy pants, revealing a dense sponge of dark curls surrounding the base of his manhood and exposing fur covered legs. The white fog clouded everything in the room.

"David?" The voice faded into the far recesses of my mind. "David, are you…?"

Like the camera, my mind flashed moments of consciousness:

Water splashing…

Struggling to get free…

Turned and bent over the side of the Jacuzzi…

Face against the tile floor…

Counting the blue tiles. *Sixteen, seventeen, eighteen…*

Someone's nakedness pressed against my back…

Panting in my ear…

Fingers wrapped around mine, squeezing...
My hips pulled up out of the bubbling water and exposed...
Legs forced apart...
Pain and pressure...
Electricity shot up my spine....
The hair on the back of my head grabbed and my face pressed harder against the tiles, bubbles popped in the water surrounding my nostrils. *Twenty-five, twenty-six, twenty-seven...*
Eyes scrunched, mouth tense...
Thrusting...*Eight, nine, ten, eleven, twelve*
Numbness...
No pain...
Blackness...

UNIVERSITY CALIFORNIA IRVINE, MESA VERDE DORM, 1982

I staggered into the dorm, hoping to get to my room without being noticed.

"David?"

I froze.

"I thought that was you. Where've you been?"

I couldn't answer. There was a strange aura in the room, a yellowish tint with the edges blurred like an old photograph. I rested my hand on the wall for support.

Am I dead?

"Did you forget about our pizza date?" The voice became robotic and muffled.

An unknown image appeared before me. It shimmered as if it was a hologram, zig-zagging on different planes and blending into the golden haze like Princess Leia in *Star Wars*. I reached out to see if the form was solid. But as I drew back and opened my hand, it was only filled with air molecules. There were a disconnection between time and comprehension. The delay seemed endless as I tried to convince myself that I was staring at my own hand and I was the one manipulating the movement of each finger.

"David?" The voice warmed and rose in pitch.

I watched the figure solidify as it floated toward me.

"Are you just getting in?"

Every muscle stiffened as I recognized that the voice belonged to Sue.

"You little alley cat," she joked.

Her hand landed on my shoulder, and I flinched and turned away.

"David?" She slowly replaced her hand back on my shoulder and turned me. "Oh, my God." She pulled opened my shirt. "What the hell, David?"

I lost myself in her eyes. "He got me."

"What?"

"He got me."

"Who?"

"I don't know." My eyes blurred, and I started trembling.

"What happened?" Her voice deepened.

I could only gaze at her.

"Are you hurt anywhere else?"

"I don't know."

"Do you remember anything?"

I shook my head. "I'm scared."

I felt the dam break and wanted to collapse. Sue held me up and propped me against the wall.

"Stay here. I'm going to go grab my keys, and we're going to the clinic."

"No." I blindly reached for her hands to stop her.

"It's all right. I'll be with you."

Her curly brown hair framed her thin face. "Sue?"

"Yes, David. It's me, Sue."

"He got me, Sue. He got me." Tears streamed down my face.

"I know. I can see."

"Is it bad?"

"It's not good. But we're going to get it all taken care of. Sit here and I'll be right back." She guided to me to the couch in the common area and she disappeared.

UNIVERSITY OF CALIFORNIA, HEALTH CLINIC, 1982

Just lie still. Just lie still and try to relax.

The coldness of the room snuck under the cotton blanket as I folded myself in the fetal position. My right shoulder ached from the hardness of the metal table and my joints throbbed.

Don't move. The pain will subside. Keep your eyes open. Stay alert! Open your eyes. It's too bright.

I was afraid to move. I was afraid to close my eyes, in fear that I'd see the faceless monster that was waiting on the other side. I jerked my head, trying to keep it from drifting like the fog rolling in from the ocean at midnight and masking the campus in eerie shadows. A faceless monster wanted to lure me into the fog and make me disappear.

Keep focused. It won't be long now. Just hold on.

The constant prattle of clinical jargon and clicking of rushing heels against tiles outside of the floral drapery helped me from entering the fog.

I'm all right. Maybe I should just get up and go back to my dorm to get some sleep.

The man-made eggshell enclosed around me and was too thin to keep the noise and cold outside. The coldness seeped deeply into my bones, and it was no wonder, since all I had on was a paper hospital gown with my backside exposed for the world to see.

How long have I been here? Why did I come here? This is so degrading. How will I explain this?

I drew in a deep breath to quiet my inner thoughts. As the voices subsided, darkness surrounded me, and the commotion outside the shell faded into the distance. Crickets filled my ears with a soft, soothing, and hypnotic sweet aria. Darkness enclosed on me like a mother's caring arms and the music became her voice singing so gently in my ear. As I felt myself cede to the compassion of the music, the disappointment began to build, creating a cacophonous pressure pounding in my head as if it was going to explode.

STOP IT!

With a flash, the music fell silent. Silence. A deafening silence. Another flash. I forced my eyes open, burning my pupils with the brightness from the fluorescent lights before clamping them shut again. I was frozen and not able to move from the terror.

"David?"

Is that a voice from somewhere outside of me, or is it the faceless monster coaxing me further into the depths of the fog? I don't want to go back there.

"David? I'm Sheryl Moss, the RN. Can you hear me?"

It doesn't sound like the voice from the fog.

"David, can you hear me?"

I can hear you, but I can't seem to coordinate the exact muscles to nod. What muscles perform that action?

"David, can you open your eyes for me?"

I'm trying. I really am. Just open your eyes, damn it. Concentrate on lifting the eyelids. That's it. Damn! The lights are bright.

"Well, hello there, David. How are you feeling?"

I only saw a form, a shadow, without any shape.

"That's better. I'm Sheryl Moss, the registered nurse on duty. I'm here to help you. All right?"

A woman's face took shape with straight, mousy brown hair hanging limply around a kind round face dominated by two glowing orbs. I blinked a couple more times, and the orbs revealed that they were glasses. As she leaned in closer, I was able to decipher soft brown eyes.

"How are you feeling?" she asked again.

My lips were dry and seemed glued shut, so I only produce a grunt.

"Would you like some water?"

I nodded, sending pain to shoot through my brain and causing me to clinch my eyes shut.

Keep your eyes open, or else you'll get lost in the fog and find yourself back there. Open your eyes. That's it. What's that object floating in front of me...hold on!

"Here you go, David. Sip it slowly." Her words were kind and encouraging.

Something wedged between my right ear and the metal table. The pressure leveraged my head up as pain attacked my neck and forced me to pull away.

"I know it hurts, but that'll go away. Just a little higher, and you can take a sip of water."

As my head lifted higher, I noticed the light began to descend on me.

It's coming close to me. It's going to get too close and will burn my retinas. But don't close your eyes.

"Just a tad bit higher." Nurse Moss lifted my head.

The light ceased it's advancement at a safe enough distance not to cause damage.

Remember, Mom said never to look directly into the sun, it'll cause blindness. Oh God, is that the sun? Don't look. But keep your eyes open. Where do I look? Relax! It's not the sun. It's okay to close your eyes for a second.

My eyes dilated behind the closed lids, causing my head to spin as if I was performing continuous somersaults.

Take a deep breath. The spins will stop. Peace. The Fog. No, stay away from the fog. Go the other direction. Better. Grayness. Wet grass. Outside. Flash. Oh God, open your eyes!

"David, it's okay. I'm here. You're safe now. Drink some water."

I forced my eyes open, saw the nurse holding the glass of water with a straw pinched between her fingers and guiding it to my lips.

"Take just a little bit at a time." She pried my sealed lips apart with the edge of the straw.

The plastic straw felt like a huge tube being forced between my dried lips, causing them to peel from each other, crack, and bleed. Warm blood lubricated my lips, and the straw slid in easily. I eagerly responded with the suction that freed the liquid into my arid mouth. My tongue soaked up most of the liquid. I challenged myself to draw in more.

"Take it easy, not too much." The nurse pulled the straw away from my mouth, causing water to dribble over the side of my face, down my cheek, and pool on the metal table by my ear. "Is that better?" She dried the table with a paper towel.

I tried to respond, but the water never made it past my tongue to moisten my throat. So, all I could do was a non-verbal grunt.

"Here, have a little more. Just a little."

I accepted the straw without any problems this time. I irrigated the inside of my mouth and channeled it toward the back of the throat. The cool liquid traveled down my throat and dispersed throughout my body like a racing roller coaster.

"So, can you talk with me?" Nurse Moss asked.

"Yes," I hoarsely responded.

"Good." She put the glass on the side table and picked up a clipboard. "I'm here to get some information from you. I only have a few questions. All right?"

"Sure." I cleared my throat.

"They're simple enough, and then you can rest before the doctor sees you. Ready?"

"Shoot."

"You're a freshman at UC Irvine?"

"Yes."

"You reside at Mesa Verde dorms…" her voice faded.

Focus. Look at her. Don't lose contact. Darkness. Silence. Crickets. They're softly singing again. Chest. Blood. Fog. Hot. Wet. There. Over there. The faceless man is standing there. Fog. Flash. Laughter. Flash. Pushed. Legs in hot water. Flash. Laughter.

"David, do you live in the Mesa Verde dorms on campus?"

I forced my eyes open. "Yes."

"What's your sexual orientation?"

I must have looked at her in such a way that she needed to rephrase the question.

"Are you gay, straight, bi?"

The truth was I didn't really know.

What orientation am I? Do I have an orientation? Was my orientation decided for me?

"Have you ever had sex with a male?" Nurse Moss impatiently said.

I nodded.

"It's nothing to be ashamed of." Nurse Moss entered more notes. "How did this happen?"

"I don't know."

Think!

"Do you know how you got here?"

"I don't know."

"Your friend, Sue, brought you in here. Do you remember anything?"

"No."

I'm so ashamed. Just go away, and let's forget all about this.

"Sue said she saw you walk into the dorm early this morning. You told her that he got you. Do you remember?"

Silence.

"Who did this to you?" the nurse asked.

"I don't know."

"I want to help you. But I can only help if you tell me what happened."

"Sheryl, they need to see you at the registration desk." A voice filtered through the floral drape.

"Thanks, Marcia. I'll be right there. David, excuse me." Nurse Moss pushed through the drape, leaving me alone.

Flash.

Laughter.

Bent over the edge of the tub.

Flash.

My arms can't move.

Exposed.

Flash.

Can't yell.

Pressure.

Pain.

Grunt.

Afraid.

Help me!

Wet.

Grass.

Morning.

"David, David, it's me, Sue." Long curls of brown hair slipped from behind her ears and fell in her face as she looked down at me. She pulled the hair back and tied it with a scrunchy that was around her wrist.

The drape pulled open and Nurse Moss was standing next to Sue. "Don't worry, it's just shock."

"But he was more alert when I found him this morning." Sue's voice was worried.

"It's not uncommon. His body senses he's safe now and is trying to heal itself. The body shuts down in order to do that," explained the nurse.

"Is he going to be all right?" Sue asked.

"Are you his girlfriend?"

Without hesitation, she said, "Yes."

"This must be difficult for you as well."

"What do you mean?"

"The cause of this situation," Nurse Moss hesitantly said.

"Whatever the situation, I'm more concerned if he's going to be alright."

Nurse Moss said, "He'll come around. Do you know anything about this?"

"Not really," Sue uttered.

Their voices echoed off each other as I drifted back into the fog. I heard them, but it was like they belonged to another world. A world I no longer was a part. I suddenly felt light. No pain. Calm. Peace. Sweet music filled my ears with a solemn song, gently caressing each tonal note with a sense of love and protection. Loving arms reached for me. I reached for them. I floated toward the outreached arms. But halfway there, I halted. A golden thread tethered my foot to the table. The harder I fought it against to free myself, the more I became entangled. The golden thread tightened and jerked me back down.

Flash.

I slammed hard against the metal table.

Pain.

"Should we call his parents?" Nurse Moss asked.

"No! Don't!" Sue pleaded. "The one thing he kept telling me on the way over here was, 'Please don't let my folks know about this. I won't go if you tell.' So, I promised that I wouldn't."

"Don't you think they should know?" Nurse Moss asked.

"You don't understand. You see, his parents won't understand."

"Don't tell them anything," I demanded.

They both looked at me. Sue caressed my head.

Nurse Moss snickered. "You have a great friend, David."

"I know." I smiled up at Sue.

"We're in this together, kiddo." Sue smiled back. "So, why don't you tell us what happened."

"I'm so embarrassed. Can't we just go back to the dorms?"

"Not until they check you out," Sue said.

"I know you're scared. We're only here to help you. Nothing will leave this area if you don't want it to," Nurse Moss said.

Sue chuckled and coaxed, "Hey kiddo, it's only me and Nurse Moss here. Let it rip."

"I can't remember much." Shame filled me, and I was worried I couldn't remember the details. Maybe it'd be better to make up a story, so I could get out of here. No matter what, it was going to end up being my fault. I must have asked for it. "I was walking home from the library. I stayed too long. I thought I'd take a short cut. The grass was wet; it must have been from the sprinklers. My tennis shoes were soaked. I saw three of them."

"Who?" Nurse Moss asked as she sat on the chair.

"I don't know."

Tell the truth. I can't.

"I don't know the one's name, but I've seen him on campus," I mixed some truth with the yarn I was spinning.

"Three guys, you said?" Nurse Moss took notes.

I was distracted. "Yeah."

"It's all right, I'm here with you." Sue squeezed my hand.

"There were three of them walking toward me. The one, the one that I've seen on campus, he watches diving practice, started to say things to me."

"David's on the diving team at UCI. He's a world champion," Sue said.

I glared at Sue.

"What? You are a world champ."

I continued as if I didn't hear her. "I tried to walk away. That's when I saw a flash of something, maybe a knife. I don't know. The next thing I know, one of them trapped my arms behind my back, and something pressed against my throat. The main guy got real closed to my, face and said, 'I finally got you. You're mine now.' He slapped me across the face. He then whispered in my ear, 'I always get what I want, even if I have to take it.' He unbuttoned my shirt and started…"

Why are you lying? Tell the truth for once.

"Wait a minute, David. You told Sue that there was only one guy. You said, 'He got me,'" stated Nurse Moss.

"What?" I asked.

I don't want to talk about it. I want to forget about it. I'm sure it didn't mean anything.

"David were there really three?" Sue asked.

I was a horrible liar, and I couldn't look at her. I reluctantly nodded my head.

"Okay, okay, David. Just tell us what happened, and we can go home," Sue pleaded.

"I don't remember everything. I feel so ashamed." My throat choked up.

"You're safe here," Nurse Moss said.

"And I'm here with you," Sue said.

I pulled myself up to sit on the edge of the metal table, and my feet dangled, causing numbness deep inside. "They forced me on my knees, while keeping my arms held behind me. Another one pulled my chin up, and the third poured wine in my mouth. They made me drink several mouthfuls. I tried not to swallow, but it was either drink or choke." My eyes burned. I glanced at

Sue for a second and then looked at Nurse Moss. "The next thing I remember is waking up by the lamppost. I'm sorry."

"That's all right. But he forced you to drink wine?" Nurse Moss asked.

"Yes, it was sweet."

"Do you remember his name?" Sue asked.

I shook my head. "I'm not sure if I ever knew his name."

At least you said something that's true.

Nurse Moss jotted some more notes down. "Okay, here's what we're going to do. First, we're going to test for GHB and Rohypnol, also known as the 'Date Rape Drugs.' Have you used the bathroom since this happened?"

"I don't remember." I tried to think. "The last time I remember using the bathroom was at the library."

"David?" Sue demanded my full attention.

"What?"

"Have you used the restroom since the attack?" Sue harshly asked.

"No."

"That's good," said Nurse Moss. "GHB and Rohypnol have short half-lives and rapidly metabolize. Now that we know we're looking for these chemicals, the lab will need a urine and blood sample. The blood sample is important for the investigation if identified within the first twenty-four-hour time period. Positive blood toxicology may be used to build an assault case, whereas the urine sample can only indicate exposure. So, I'm going to order both for you." She wrote on a form attached to the clipboard.

I sighed.

"We have to do this now, David. The window's starting to close," Sue said.

"All right," I muttered.

"Good." Nurse Moss stood. "But first you'll have to answer some more questions. We'll do a full body exam, the urine and blood sample, and check for STDs. We will include the Vitullo Evidence Collection Kit to gather as much DNA information as we can. So, I need you to settle in for a while, this is going to take some time."

I stood up and gathered my discarded clothes.

Nurse Moss stepped in front of me and held out her hands. "We're going to need to keep those for a while. I'm sure the police will need to look at them."

"Police?"

"It's routine. If there's a group of guys attacking students on campus, the police need to know," explained Nurse Moss.

"I don't know. I just want to go home and sleep. I've a test in a few hours and..."

"We have to do this now to make sure you are okay," Sue said.

I shook my head and reluctantly handed Nurse Moss my wadded up clothes.

"I've diving practice this morning too." I tried to find an excuse to get out.

"Have a seat, David." Nurse Moss patted the metal table and I followed the orders. "Good. I'll send in a specialist to do the examination. Sue, may I talk with you outside?"

"Sure," Sue said.

I was alone again. Cold. Scared. There was angst in the pit of my stomach as my intestines twisted and knotted. The fact that I can't seem to remember what happened was bad enough, but the fear of my past coming through was even scarier.

What am I going to do if it's all revealed? What am I going to do when they find out that I lied? How am I going to face my teammates, Jennifer, or even myself? How am I going to explain to Sue that she helped me perpetuate a lie?

Maybe this is the hell that Dad has been trying to warn me about. Maybe hell isn't some random place in the core of the world where the devil resides amid fire and brimstone. Maybe hell is the place in the mind where I torture myself for the rest of my life.

"David Matthew?" a deep voice sounded outside the curtain.

"Yes," I meekly said.

"May I come in?"

"Yes."

The curtain pulled back, and a tall, burly, blond that could grace the cover of GQ Magazine stood there holding a cardboard box.

"I'm Nurse Tate, and I'll be conducting your exam." He placed the box next to me, labeled, "Vitullo Evidence Collection Kit."

"What's that?" I asked, trying to prevent any eye contact.

Nurse Tate said as he filled out a form, "That's the rape kit."

"What?" My cheeks flushed, and my ears rang.

Nurse Tate glanced up under his thick brows, and his ice-cold blue eyes penetrated mine for only a second, and then he glanced at the box. "It's a rape kit. I'm going to take some samples." He placed the clipboard on the side table, turned, took a deep breath, lifted the lid off the box, and inside contained several items. "These tubes and containers are for blood and urine samples. This paper bag is for your clothes and anything else that needs to be examined. This large sheet of paper is for you to stand on when you undress in case any hair or fiber evidence falls from you. Unfortunately, you've already undressed, but just in case, I'll have you stand on it anyway." He lifted a couple of swabs enclosed in plastic. "These will be used to gather biological evidence. This is dental floss. These wooden sticks are for scraping under your fingernails. Some glass slides to put samples on for the microscope. And everything has an envelope or a small box to place the evidence in, and these are the important labels." He hinted at a smile as if he was making a joke, and crossed his arms against his developed pecs, causing his biceps to pop.

Shame flooded me again, and I wanted to evaporate into thin air.

Nurse Tate unfolded the large sheet and laid it on the floor. "Please step on that and remove the gown." He turned his back to me to write something on the clipboard.

At first, I thought he was trying to be polite and give me some sense of privacy. I scooted off the table and stepped on the middle of the sheet.

"I need you to remove the gown." He had maneuvered to the edge of the sheet, maybe a foot from me. A five o'clock shadow pushed through the tanned skin around his full lips, adding to the angular cheeks and jawbones. His long, thick eyelashes made his blue eyes sparkle.

I quickly glanced at the floor and reluctantly untied the string at the back of my neck. The flimsy gown slipped from my shoulders and pooled around my ankles.

"I need you to try and not touch your body. Keep your hands to your side."

A flash of the Faceless Man asking me the same thing rushed my mind and chased my empowerment away. The embarrassment of having to stand in front of this man, any man, was like a tsunami. The weight of the tidal wave crashed over my head and crushed my chest. I couldn't breathe. I was drowning. Everything around me shimmered and shook as the suffocating flood engulfed me. I wasn't able to move. The wave rushed down my body, splashed against the floor at my feet, and cascaded out in all directions. I was naked.

"You need to keep your hands to your side."

I obeyed by uncapping my hands and willing them to my side.

Nurse Tate snapped the rubber glove against his wrist and stared at my nakedness.

What's wrong? What am I supposed to do?

Nurse Tate stooped down and gathered the gown, placing it into the paper bag. As he stood and placed the bag next to the cardboard box, he said, "I'll get you another gown after I gather the samples." He opened a swab from its plastic protection.

I felt small next to him, weak, and inferior.

"Open your mouth."

I closed my eyes and followed the instructions. With my mouth opened and standing completely naked in front of this man, a familiar feeling of compliance and adoration, of submission and obedience, of expectation and needing to be liked for following instructions. I needed Nurse Tate to notice me. I needed his acceptance. Even if it was just for a short moment,

I needed him to like me. I needed him to find me attractive. I wanted him to save me, like the knight in shining armor, and take me way from all this degradation, erase all the past, and make me whole again.

"I'm going to swab the inside of your mouth. Just need to get a sample." The command of his tone sounded demanding, calculating, and clinical.

Suddenly, I couldn't help but imagine him naked. Dark honey colored hair laced the center of his pecs, ran down and over the rippled abs, encircling his navel, before migrating south and growing bushier, and then fanning out to cover his thighs and legs. I wanted to run my hands through the thick forest on his legs and kiss his lips.

"Can you open a little wider?" He sounded almost impatient.

I nodded and immediately want to please. The cotton tip rubbed against the inside of my cheek.

What would it be like to be with someone like this? Would anyone like him like me?

"I need for you to turn and bend over the table. I'm going to take an anal cavity sample."

He doesn't see me. I'm nothing more than an object for him.

I deliberately turned, leaned over, and braced my arms on the table. My fantasy of a knight heaving me up on a stallion and taking me to safety evaporated.

I must go to diving practice. I must go to the library and find an audition piece.

Once again I became numb, obedient, and compliant.

UNIVERSITY OF CALIFORNIA, IRVINE, CAMPUS, 1982

Sue pulled into a parking space behind the Mesa Verde dorms and turned off the engine. "Do you want to just hang out today? I don't mind skipping classes."

I forced a smile. "No, I have to make up that anatomy test and go to practice."

Sue nodded and gathered her purse and books from the backseat. "Maybe we can have dinner?"

I sat there, staring out the windshield.

"Or not. What if we order in some Chinese and eat in my room?"

I didn't respond.

"Davey?"

My eyes welled, overflowed, and tears raced down my cheeks. I was torn between lying and the fear of running into the faceless man again on campus. What was I so afraid of? Adding to the lies and fear was the degradation of going through with the rape kit. What had Nurse Tate thought about me as he gathered swabs and samples from my desecrated and shameful body? Did he find me sinful? Did he think I was a dirty whore? My defensive mind struggled to differentiate between the faceless man, the coaches/doctors/lawyers and Nurse Tate's exploration of my body. All were conducted with measures of discontent, yet I consented. What were the differences? My mind tried to rationalize the events and comprehend why one was okay and the others were not. How was offering myself to one any different from the others? I struggled with the fact that one was morally in the good of exploring my body for any damage, while the others were morally wrong and placed my body in a situation to be damaged. Yet, I permitted both to happen. Did I have a choice? Or was the choice made for me?

The thoughts were overwhelming and unpreventable, and I was unable to stop the unwanted negative self-talk. What about mentally? They all touched, probed, and explored similar areas of my body. What makes one right and the others wrong? Am I ruined for life? Am I a walking heap of discarded trash that no one will ever want? Is this what Dad meant when he quoted, "If a man lies with a male as with a woman, both of them have committed an abomination, Leviticus 20:13?" What's an abomination? Am I an abomination? If I'm an abomination then what about Nurse Moss and her motherly approach, how utterly disgusted was she with me? I uncovered a new level of hate and contempt for myself and saw myself clearly as a hypocrite, a liar, and an abomination.

A sharp rap on the window next to my head caused me to jump, and yelp like a wounded animal. Sue nervously laughed.

Jennifer smiled and waved as she hugged her books to her chest.

I rolled the window down.

Jennifer leaned in the window. "How are you two doing on this beautiful morning? I just love the scent of magnolias in the air. Don't you just love it? Anyway, I thought I saw you pull in, and I wanted to come say hello."

"Hi," Sue said, laced with sarcasm.

"Why Susan, aren't you just thrilled to be alive on a morning like this?" Jennifer's ability to graciously put someone down had been perfected by her upbringing and the sorority system.

"I guess. Sure, it is." Sue knew there was no purpose in engaging in a battle of pleasantries with Jennifer.

Jennifer looked at me. "David, is everything all right? You look like you lost your puppy."

I rubbed my face. "I'm fine."

"Well, did you hear there was an attack on campus last night?" Jennifer said as she pulled the school newspaper from her books.

"What?" I glanced over at Sue.

"What are you talking about, Jen?" Sue dryly asked.

"It's Jennifer, Susan. It's all right here on the front page of the *Anteater Times*." She unfolded the paper and read the headline. "Student attacked by three assailants." She scanned down the article. "It stated that it happened late last night in Aldrich Park." She pointed at the article. "It mentioned the victim was a male freshman."

"Let me see that." Sue reached across my chest for the paper.

"Sure." Jennifer smiled and reluctantly handed the paper to Sue. As the paper passed in front of me, I saw a picture of the lamppost I found myself under and the flattened grass.

Sue snapped the paper against the steering wheel to flatten it so she could read.

"You can get your own, they just put them out," Jennifer said as she leaned in further. "This is really bad, especially with the break-out of the gay disease."

"Jennifer, would you *please* shut up. You don't know what you're talking about," stated Sue.

"I beg your pardon, Susan, I always keep up with the news." Jennifer stomped her foot. "I have never been more insulted in my life."

"You better get used to it," Sue said under her breath.

I cranked my neck, trying to read.

Sue scanned the article. "It doesn't provide a name but states that the victim is an athlete." She roughly refolded the paper and shoved it back to Jennifer. "Thanks."

"You didn't need to wrinkle it." Jennifer placed it on top of her stack of books.

Sue pulled the keys from the ignition, flung open the door, stood abruptly, and leaned over the roof looking at Jennifer. "Anything else, Jen?"

"It's Jennifer...oh, I see what you just did." Jennifer smiled. "Cute. Rude, but cute. So, where are you two coming from?"

I froze, staring out the windshield.

"Breakfast," stated Sue. "Yeah, neither of us could sleep so we went for a bite at Bagels Supreme."

"I love that place," Jennifer cooed. "Next time, make sure to invite me."

"Oh, we will." Sue forced a smile.

"Sounds fab. But I must skedaddle," Jennifer said, with a giggle. "I have to get to the library and research my econ paper."

"Don't let us keep you. Have a great day," Sue said as she tapped the roof of the car.

Jennifer smiled for Sue and then looked at me. "Let's get together later and prepare for the audition..."

Sue interrupted. "Sure, you can prepare, whatever, but now I have to make sure that he gets to practice. And you don't want to be late."

"You're right. I'll catch you later." She leaned in for a kiss.

I didn't move.

"Bye." Jennifer blew a kiss, waved, and scurried toward Aldrich Park.

"Come on, get out of the car," Sue demanded.

"Why? What's going on?" I leaned over the driver's seat.

"Just get out. I'll tell you as we go." Sue rolled up the driver's window and slammed the door.

I rolled up the passenger's window, got out, and closed the door.

"Did you lock it?"

"I think so."

"Check it." She hustled to where I was standing.

I checked the door. "It's locked."

"Good. Let's go." She headed up the stairs to the dorms.

"Wait! Sue, did you say you were my girlfriend at the clinic?"

She took a deep breath. "Yes, I did it so I could stay in the examining room with you. No big deal."

I nodded. "Oh, right, I see."

"Can we go now?" There was urgency in her voice.

"What are we doing?"

She rushed me. "We're going to gather up all the *Anteater Times* so no one else can read that story. Let's go." She took off.

"How could they possibly have had time to print the story?" I asked as I followed her.

"Who knows?"

*****

Sue and I hit every blue and yellow newsstand that we could find throughout campus that contained the free college paper and took them. With arms filled of the newsprint, we ran back to my dorm room and piled them in the corner by my bed.

"That's a lot of papers," I said as we both stared at the piles.

Sue giggled. "That sure is."

"What's so funny?"

"I just had this thought that this is one of those things we'll remember when we are old."

"Yeah, I guess." I walked to the desk to check the voice machine, which was one of the perks that my roommate, Kimo, and I received for being scholarship athletes; a phone line and voice recorder machine. "What are we going to do with them?"

"We'll have to get them out of here. I got it. We'll wait until it starts to get dark and drive across campus and throw them in a dumpster." She quickly stopped, and then her eyes lit up. "We should put them in the trunk of my car until then."

"Will they all fit?" I pressed the play button on the machine. The high-pitched screech of the tape rewinding filled the room, clicked, and grabbled into a deep voice. "I'm trying to reach David Matthew. This is Skitch Hendricks, casting director for *General Hospital.* My assistant was out of the office today, but I wanted to reach you to give you your call time for tomorrow at eight a.m. Please return my call and confirm. My direct line is two-one-three, five-five-five, one-four-four-one." The machine beeped and stopped with a click.

Sue and I stood staring at the silver machine. We looked at each other. Sue leaned back and let out a high-pitched scream and jumped around the room. I could only watch her. She bounced onto my bed and back down, danced around in a circle and stopped. "Why aren't you celebrating?"

"You're celebrating enough for both of us."

"Aren't you excited?" She grabbed both of my hands and tried to get me to jump with her. "Come on. You have to be a little excited."

"I am." I didn't have the heart to tell her that I had already spoken to Skitch over winter break.

"You sure have a strange way of showing it." She shook my hands a couple of more times and dropped them so she could skip in a circle. "You're going to be on *GH* again. You're going to be on *GH.* You're going to be on *GH.* They like you; they love you; they're going to marry you." She stopped abruptly and placed her hands on her hips. "Can you show a little emotion?"

"I don't think I can do it." My voice was strange, like it belonged to someone else.

185

"Why not?"

"With everything that has happened, I'm not sure I'm in the right frame of mind."

Sue's face hardened and her eyes narrowed. "No, no, no. You must do this. You can't let some scumbags keep you from following your dreams."

"I don't know Sue, there's so much going on. I have the conference meet, school…"

"Stop right there. What happened last night does not determine who or what you are. You can't let this stop you. The best thing you can do is push through." Her eyes burned into mine.

I shook my head. "I don't know. I don't have any way of getting to Los Angeles. It's over two hours away or something. I don't even know how far."

"Are you fucking serious right now? What about me? I drove you before, and I'll drive you again."

"You would do that for me?"

"Duh!"

"I couldn't ask you to drop everything and take me to LA. You'd have to skip classes and I can't ask you to do that. And the conference meet…I don't know if it's the right timing." I pulled my hands away from her.

She grabbed my hands again and pulled me to her. "Fuck timing. This is the right timing. If we're going to miss classes, this is the best time—it's the first week back, and we're only going to go over the syllabus. I want to do this. I do."

"It just doesn't feel right."

"That's why you need to do this. You have to take this chance; this is an amazing opportunity, and you need to grab it with both hands. It may never come again."

"I don't know."

"I do. We're going. You're going to call that sketchy Skitch character back and tell him that you'll fucking be there."

"But…"

"No buts. I'll drag you kicking and screaming, but you're going to be back on *General Hospital*."

"You sure?"

"Cross my heart."

The energy started in my toes and quickly moved up to my ankles, knees, and hips. Before I knew it, I was jumping up and down. "I'm going to be on *GH*. I'm going to be on *GH*."

Sue started jumping with me in a circle. We both started chanting, "*GH, GH, GH.*" Sue stopped and became serious. "You call him back right now." She pointed to the phone.

I nodded and replayed the message, and Sue wrote the number down. I dialed. My heart pumped louder than the other end rang. Sue pulled away.

"Where are you going?" I asked.

She grabbed an armful of newspapers and jerked her head toward the door.

"Casting." A deep voice rang through the phone.

"Skitch?" I watched Sue struggle with getting the door open.

"This is Skitch."

"It's David, David Matthew, returning your call."

"Ah, David, I'm so glad to hear from you. You got something to write down this info? I have someone on the other line."

"Sure." I grabbed a pen and nodded to Sue.

Sue winked and disappeared behind the door. "Out of my way, jocks, a lady is coming through," she yelled down the hall.

"Ready," I said into the phone's receiver.

HOLLYWOOD, CALIFORNIA, PROSPECT STUDIOS 1982

The late afternoon sun burned down from the cloudless sky as I leaned against Prospect Studios' cement wall with metal fencing on the corner of Prospect Avenue and Talmadge Street. My shooting for *General Hospital* wrapped about fifteen minutes ago, and I had been waiting at this designated area for Sue to pick me up.

My body tingled from the euphotic experience of having done something that came so easy to me. There was a natural sense of belonging when I entered the studio, going through makeup, costumes, and walking on the set as if I had been a part of this business all my life. It was the same feeling I had when I realized that diving was going to get me out of Aulden. I didn't know how. I just knew the sport came easy and I was good at it. People took notice of me quickly, and before I knew it, I was sitting next to Patti Lakes on a plane going to Tønsberg, Norway, for the 1979 World Games.

The *General Hospital* Studios had this sense of a hard-working community where no one cared about anything else other than making the best possible final product. Diving provided that for me while I was going through high school. I never felt safe or comfortable while at Aulden High. It was more like I was always looking over my shoulder and thinking twice before saying anything. There was always an uneasy anxiety rushing through my intestines, especially before my life changed with the gold medal. I was nobody. I tried to blend into the crowd, but there was nowhere to hide. I felt that I was always on display because I was so different from everyone else. I looked and acted different.

CESAR'S CREEK, 1978

"Hey, you up?" Dewayne whispered in the darkened tent.

"What?" I hesitantly responded.

"I can't sleep."

"I noticed." I looked around the tent we crawled into, which barely had enough room for two sleeping bags, let alone the ability to sit up. We were in a canvas tomb. "I can't sleep either."

"Want to talk?"

"About what?"

"I overheard the Life Scout saying that something was going to go down tonight," Dewayne said.

"It's almost morning." I rolled over within the confines of my sleeping bag, trying to force myself to get some form of sleep, but Dewayne's constant droning, mosquitoes buzzing around my ears, and the campfire's choking smoke seeping into our two-man tent added to a sleepless encounter. Let alone the hard ground and damp air.

"I just love nature. And there's nothing more invigorating than waking up at the crack of dawn, going down to the creek, and washing up in the cold water before a hearty Boy Scout breakfast of scrambled eggs, bacon, and greasy hash browns."

Mother thought this expedition would be good for me, toughen me up by roughing it with other boys in the woods. It didn't help that I had some big shoes to follow, since Caine achieved the top rank of Eagle Scout, before he was seventeen. Everyone expected me to follow in the same path. But what people didn't seem to understand, I wasn't cut out for the Boy Scouts or the great outdoors. The only things I collected on these sleepovers were ticks. I could be with six guys, all sitting in the same area, and within minutes I would have at least ten ticks crawling on me, and the others would still be tick-free. There was just something about the ticks' flat-dark bodies, little legs, and tiny heads that always made me cringe.

"Have you noticed how Sharon Wilson's filled out?"

"What?" I glanced at Dewayne, resting on top of his sleeping bag in his white boxers with his arm crossed behind his head like a pillow. Swatches of dark hair donned his underarms as he gazed at the shadows dancing across the tent's canvas apex roof. "I'm talking about her jugs."

"I know what you're talking about."

"Have you seen them?"

I hesitantly lied. "Yeah."

"Don't they look like swollen watermelons? Damn."

A high-pitched Apache cry pierced outside, and the tent's supports shook. The door flap flipped open as flashlight beams blinded us. Without a word, my sleeping bag, with me in it, was pulled from the tent and dragged past the campfire to the edge of circular clearing, where the trees thickened.

Zziiippp. The sleeping bag opened.

I was pulled out and pushed up against a tree truck. My wrists were slipped through bowline knots and my arms lifted over my head. I was hoisted up into the air with trucker's hitch fastenings until my feet dangled above the ground. A couple of two half-hitch knots secured me to the tree's thick trunk.

"Stop struggling, or the ropes will tighten," advised a harsh voice disguised in low tones.

I couldn't see faces but estimated that there had to be six members of this hoax; two kept flashlight beams aimed at my eyes, three tied me securely to the tree, while one directed. There was a sense of merriment and glee after the final knot was secured and they huddled in front of me.

"Nice job, boys. Proceed," the leader demanded.

"You're not serious?" one asked.

"As a heart attack," the leader said.

"No, come on. This is far enough."

"I'll tell you when it has gone far enough. Proceed."

"No, way." One of the flashlight beams clicked off, and steps stomped away.

"Do I have to do everything myself?" The leader's voice was strained.

"Well, I'm not doing it."

"Neither am I."

"Out of my way."

The flashlight beams jostled, and a shadow approached. For a brief second, I saw the leader; he was wearing a red bandana around his face, like a bank robber. He ripped my shirt from my chest and tugged my sweatpants and underwear down to my ankles.

"Oh my God, is that a baseball bat you've been hiding? That thing is huge." He looked over his shoulder. "Give me the jar."

"This is far enough," someone hesitated.

"The jar. NOW!"

Something was handed to the leader.

"What's going on?" My voice was weak.

"Who asked you to talk?" the leader's voice shot back.

"Why are you doing this?" I bravely asked.

"Because we can. So shut the hell up. Be a good boy and this will all be over before you know it."

The tree's bark pressed into my back, butt, and thighs. I tested the ropes by squirming, but the Boy Scouts have obviously passed their knot-tying merit badges. A bluish glow seeped into the clearing as the sun rose behind the eastern line of trees and backlit the remaining culprits in dark silhouettes.

A sticky gel dripped onto my chest. Hands rubbed the goo over my pecs, abs, along my hips, and groin.

"Look boys, he likes it. Look at that thing harden." The leader batted my penis, causing it to smack and stick momentarily to my thigh before rebounding. "Watch out boys that thing could poke your eye out." He laughed as he continued to bat it back and forth.

Withdrawing my hips from the stinging slaps was impeded by the tree's trunk. My body jerked with each contact. I squeezed my eyes and pretended I was back home in my room, drawing.

More sticky gel was applied down my thighs.

"Dude, you have no hair. Your legs are smoother than my girlfriend's. Do you shave?" The leader returned next to the other contributors. "It has come to our attention that you've broken the bylaws of the Boy Scouts of America, and it is our duty to rectify them in order to keep our troop in good standing and in accordance to these said bylaws."

"What are you saying?" one of the minions asked.

"Shut the fuck up!"

"Not so loud, you're going to wake everyone up."

"So what? It might do them some good to see that we're serious about Troop Seventeen."

Other Scouts crawled out of the semi-circle of mini tents, in various stages of dress, and gathered behind the demonstrators.

"Are you all ready?" the leader asked.

The morning light seeped through the trees and filtered the clearing, providing details. The five held long sticks, with marshmallows pierced on one end.

"It has come to our attention that you tend to play for the other team. And for that, we need to make sure that you're aware that the Boy Scouts of America and Troop Seventeen aren't compliant with these tendencies. So, we've decided to help you redeem yourself through this display of public revealing."

The leader took several steps back and lifted the long stick over his right shoulder next to his ear like a javelin. He ran forward toward me, pulled back his arm, planted his foot, and launched the stick. The javelin wobbled through the air and the marshmallow end pelted against my chest, sticking to the gooey substance.

"Yes, bull's eye!" The leader removed his red bandana, revealing his identity. It was Sonnie Quackenburger, the Life Scout that took charge when the scout leader was called away due to a family emergency. Usually the Eagle Scout would take over, but Caine had a prior commitment and couldn't be here. Sonnie was next in line. "Just like that, boys. It's your turn."

There was a moment of hesitation as the other four looked at each other. The sun revealed that they were the Star Scouts: Randy, Steve, Seth, and Mark.

"What are you waiting for, you pussies?" Sonnie taunted. "Pretty boy needs to be reminded that he's not such a big shot with the Scouts. He's just a lowly peon scout. He's not even a Tenderfoot. He doesn't like to get his dainty fingers dirty, and he's too good to be a part of us. He's only here because his mommy told him he had to be like his big brother. Where's his big brother? Ain't here. So, who's gonna protect this faggot? Fire away, men!"

The other four reared back their makeshift javelins and simultaneously ran toward me, launching the marshmallow-headed spears. Each one landed with a plop and stuck to different areas of my nakedness.

"Now that's what I'm talking about!" Sonnie turned to the gathered crowd. "I want this to be a lesson to all you Tenderfoots and Second Class Scouts. Troop Seventeen is unified, and we work as a team. Now, march to the creek and get washed up for breakfast."

No one moved. They gaped at me.

"What's everyone standing around for?" Sonnie clapped several times and hollered, "That's an order. Or do you want to be next? Move. Move. Move!"

The lower ranked Scouts scampered down the path past the tree to the creek, followed by the four leaders and Sonnie.

I was left behind. The birds chirped their early morning rituals from the tops of the trees and the sun filled in more of the clearing.

The ropes eased and I was gently lowered to the ground.

Zachary Spence, Caine's best friend, came out from behind the tree. A ratty black knitted toboggan covered his long dark hair, and he hinted at a smile causing his eyes to squint and crinkle. He removed the marshmallow spears, while I slipped my wrists from the knotted ropes.

"Pull up your pants," he said. "Caine told me to watch out for you, since he couldn't be here. I'm sorry for all this. I thought I could stop them."

I tied the sweatpants' drawstring. "You helped them tie me up."

"I showed them how to tie the knots." He hung his head which made him look like the Scarecrow from *The Wizard of Oz*.

"Thanks, I guess."

"Don't thank me." Zach's head tilted and he looked curious at my neck. He leaned in. and I thought he was going to kiss me. "What's that?"

"What's what?" I drew back.

"Hold still." He plucked something from just under my jaw line and held it between his fingers to examine it. "Oh, it's just a tick." He tossed it into the woods.

HOLLYWOOD, CALIFORNIA, PROSPECT STUDIOS 1982

I was hoping to get back to Irvine to make diving practice, but even if we left in the next five minutes we would be getting there just as it ended. I guess I could practice visualization, stretches, and lineups.

A slight yet fit young man stood at the corner across the street. He nodded to me with acknowledgement as our eyes connected. He wore a white tank top, skinny jeans, and black high top canvas tennis shoes. He produced a crooked smile, leaned his back against the street sign pole, bent his right leg, and ran his hands through his hair. A sense of confidence and assurance mixed with a vulnerability that was alluring emitted from his presence. He seemed familiar and yet aloof, attractive and yet unattainable, innocent and yet seasoned. He rested his head back against the pole, exposing the length of his bare neck to the receding sun, and hooked his thumbs in his jeans' beltless waistband, causing them to ride down below the length of the tank top and exposing tanned skin. He appeared accessible, like a cat sunning itself.

A car creeped up and stopped.

The young man casually looked at the driver and displayed a dazzlingly smile. He arched his back, shoved off the pole, and slinked over to lean into the open passenger window. Words were exchanged. The young man stood erect and looked both ways until his eyes rested on mine. He nodded. He pulled open the passenger's door, slid into the car, and rode off. The car turned south on Talmadge and disappeared.

I felt a sense of loss as the space he once occupied was empty. Was he ever there, or did I make him up in my mind? I'd never know or ever see him again. He disappeared into thin air.

Devoted fans gathered outside the protected perimeters of the *General Hospital* studio, hoping to get a rare glimpse of Luke and Laura or other regulars from the show leaving for the day. Several pods of fans were straining to see above the cement portion of the wall and in between the metal bars while squawking like chickens.

Two young college girls pushed up next to me as if I wasn't even there.

"Can you see anything?" the thinner of the two asked.

The older girl outweighed her friend by a good thirty pounds and perched as high on her toes as possible to wrap her hands around the metal bars, causing her sundress to expose her cotton panties. "Just that grumpy guard, the one that never smiles." She released the bars and heavily returned flat on her feet, bumping me in the process. "Sorry. We usually stand here." She turned her back to me.

"Are there assigned standing spaces?" I asked, with amusement.

She grabbed a small pad of paper and perched up to glance over the wall again. "No, there are no assigned standing spaces. You must be new here. Everyone knows where their place is."

"I'm sorry." I grabbed my book bag and scooted to the side.

"She didn't mean that." The thinner girl blushed as she spoke.

"Don't apologize for me. I don't need you apologizing for me." The young woman lifted higher on her toes.

"We've been coming here every day and standing at this spot, at this exact time, for the past two months so Mia can get Tony Geary's autograph."

"It's Anthony," Mia said.

"Excuse me, Anthony's autograph. She's obsessed with him."

Mia dropped back down, placed her hands on her hips, and glared at her friend with red cheeks. "Brenda, I'm not obsessed."

"I stand corrected. She's not obsessed." Brenda looked at me and nodded.

Mia exploded. "I can't help it. I don't know what it is, but Anthony is everything to me. He's the ideal boyfriend. And that hair."

"She's obsessed with his hair?" Brenda said.

"Yes, okay, okay, I'm a bit obsessed with his hair." Mia patted her forehead. "I mean who isn't obsessed with Anthony Geary's hair?"

"I'm not," Brenda said.

"So, you two come here every day at this time in hopes of getting Tony's autograph?" I asked.

"Anthony. It's Anthony," Mia emphatically said.

"Sorry. Anthony." I looked at Brenda and widened my eyes. She giggled. "But if you're here every day, when do you get to watch the show? Doesn't it air now?"

"Oh!" Brenda waved her hand in the air. "This one tapes the episodes so that we can be here, and then we go back and watch it over and over again."

"It's not that bad," Mia said.

"Oh, but it is that bad," Brenda said.

"And all this time you have been coming here, you have never gotten Tony's, I mean Anthony's, autograph?"

"We always miss him," Brenda explained.

"He's slipperier than a greased pig," Mia commented as she perched up to look over the wall again. "Someone's coming out."

All three of us looked over the wall, between the metal bars. Tony and Genie Francis came out of the studio door.

Mia collapsed down against the wall. "It's him."

The gathered fans start chanting, "Luke and Laura."

Tony and Genie waved.

"I've got an idea. Come with me." I led the two girls to the gate entrance and shouted, "Anthony Geary and Genie Francis!"

Mia pulled back against the gate's framing, and harshly whispered, "What are you doing?"

Genie smiled and waved. Tony turned to my voice and instantly recognized me. He headed toward me holding Genie's hand. The Guard rushed to put himself between the two stars and the fans.

The autograph seekers all screamed with excitement.

"He's coming this way." Brenda grabbed my arm. "You know him?"

"What?" Mia exclaimed as she peeked around.

"What are you doing over there?" asked Tony as he and Genie signed their names on the pieces of paper being held in the air.

Mia pressed herself against the gate. "I'm literally going to die."

"I'm waiting for my ride," I explained.

"Luke, smile," someone shouted as they held up a camera. Tony obliged.

Genie leaned toward me. "Why don't you wait on this side?"

"Okay," I responded.

"Sam, could you let him in?" Genie asked the guard while signing autographs.

Sam indicated for me to enter through the pedestrian's gate.

Once I made my way through the gate I stopped and turned toward Mia and Brenda. "Tony and Genie, these two are your biggest fans. They have been coming by every day to meet you."

"Every day? Why?" Tony asked with distain.

"To get your autograph," I explained.

"That's so nice," Genie said.

"Where are they?" Tony asked.

When I turned Brenda was standing alone with her face flushed red. I went to her. "Where is Mia?"

Brenda was speechless and stared at Tony. She tilted her head to the side.

Mia was pressed against the cement wall as flat as her body would allow, trying to disappear. I motioned for her to come next to Brenda. "This is Mia and Brenda. Mia and Brenda, this is Anthony Geary and Genie Francis," I introduced them.

Tony reached through the gate and offered a hand to Mia. She just stood there. Brenda quickly accepted the offered hand. "It's a pleasure to meet you. My friend is speechless."

"It's always a pleasure to meet such supportive fans," Tony said.

Genie stepped up next to me and said, "You did a great job today."

"Thank you." I'm sure I blushed.

"Come here for a minute, he'll be there forever." She stepped away from the gate and the fans and I followed. "I heard you're just starting out."

I nodded.

Genie reached into her pocket and pulled out a business card. "This is my agents' card. They're just starting out, too, and I think they'd be interested in meeting with you. They represent Lou Diamond Philips as well. Do you have good headshots?"

I looked at the business card and shook my head.

"You'll need to get some headshots. Give them a call, tell them I gave you the card, and set up a meeting."

"Thank you."

"My pleasure."

"This is kind of crazy." I indicated the crowd, still waiting to get Tony's autograph or a picture with him.

"He'll stay there until he has met everyone. He's so good with the public. I'm more reserved. It makes me nervous." Genie admiringly looked at Tony.

A car honked. Sue was idling in front of the gate.

"There's my ride. Thanks for the card again."

Genie nodded.

I walked past Tony and patted him on the shoulder.

"See you soon," Tony called after me as I weeded through the gathered crowd to get to Sue's car.

BIG WEST CONFERENCE MEET, 1982

I positioned myself on the springboard and waited for the announcement of my fourth dive. I was currently in first, with a comfortable lead and only had to land on my head on this and my next two dives to earn a spot to go to the NCAAs.

A dark shadow casted across the water's surface as enormous and threatening clouds rolled in from the coast. A breeze wafted over the diving well, sending a chilliness to cause goosebumps on my skin.

"David Matthew, U.C.I, will be performing a one-oh-five B, front two-and-a-half somersaults in the pike position," the announcer's voice echoed through the loudspeakers, followed by the crowd's enthusiastic applause.

I double checked that I was standing in the correct position by the numbers that ran along the midsection of the springboard. I brushed my fingertips across the golden stitching of the Anteater mascot on the side panel of my navy Speedo. A flutter of nerves tingled through my body as I prepared to take the first step. My initial goal of extra practices to prepare for this conference meet had been derailed by other issues, events, and engagements. My focus was sporadic at best.

How am I going to get through this?

"You got this, Davey," Sue's familiar voice rang from the bleachers.

It's what I needed. I found that place in my mind where I envisioned the perfect dive. I felt it. I knew I had it.

I stepped down the flimsy metal plank and propelled myself high into the hurdle. I landed on the end of the board, rode the recoil as far up as I could, reached the apex of the dive, and initiated the revolutions. I stretched for the water and allowed it to swallow me. I streamlined to the bottom. The depth's pressure forced my mind to recall the pressure I felt next to the Jacuzzi, as a sharp pain flared down my spine and exploded in a gut-wrenching pain. For a moment, I was paralyzed. I had no control over my muscles, and I floated at the bottom of the seventeen-foot diving well. My lungs burned, and panic crept in. It took all my strength to regain control over my body and push off the bottom.

The sky was darker when I broke the surface, but the crowd was hooting and hollering. I glanced at the score board and saw the scores: 9.5, 9.5, 9.5. 9.0, 9.0, 9.5, 9.0. My name was at the top of the leader board.

I swam to the edge and pulled myself out. My toes were still numb, but I ignored it.

"Nice dive." Jenny Chandler, my coach and the 1976 Olympic Champion said with pride and laced with an Alabama accent. "Only two more, and NCAAs here we come."

I smiled, nodded, and made my way to where I had set up camp with my backpack and towels.

Kimo, my roommate, had a huge grin, grabbed my hand, and bumped my shoulder with his. "You're on fire, man!"

"Thanks," I murmured.

"Keep it up." He slapped my butt.

"Planning on it."

Sue stood in the bleachers, blowing kisses at me.

I waved.

She waved.

I went to my backpack and grabbed a towel. Under the towel was a Ken doll in a blue Speedo and a note tapped to its chest that read:

PARTING IS SUCH SWEET SORROW, UNTIL NEXT TIME!

My world shattered. The Faceless Man was here, somewhere in this stadium, at this very moment. Breath refused to fill my lungs, my hands shook, and my legs weakened. I crumpled to the pool deck and felt powerless and out of control. He won. I no longer was able to defend myself. I felt him pressing down on me, forcing my face into the pool of water next to the Jacuzzi. His hot breath brushed against my ear and neck. The way he manipulated the situation, forcing himself, ripping my insides. I gave over and left my invaded body. I saw the whole thing transpire as an observer from the corner of the ceiling. I watched in horror. I wondered if I was ever going to be able to return to the battered and bruised body.

*****

Sue sat next to my bed and wiped my forehead with a cold compress. "How are you feeling?"

"Like I have been hit by a two-ton truck," I stammered.

"That's good, because most semi-trucks can weigh up to forty-five tons," she joked. "If we can get this one-hundred-and-two degree temperature down, you should recover in no time."

There was a knock, and the door flew open. Jennifer walked in. "How are you doing?" she asked as she placed a brown paper bag on the desk.

"Fine." I struggled to sit up and shimmied my back against the wall.

"Sue," Jennifer dryly said.

"Jennifer," responded Sue, even drier.

Jennifer walked to the bed and looked at me. "Really? You look like shit."

"Thank you. You look fantastic as ever," I responded.

"I know. What can I say?" She sat on the edge of the bed and took my hand. "I can't stay long because I have a sorority meeting, but I had to see how you were. I was shocked to hear what happened. But what's most important is that you are all right and will be well soon, if you get rest and stop all this running around. It's like your body is trying to tell you something and you need to listen to it." She patted my hand, got up, and made her way back to the door. "I brought you some things to make you feel better. There are some crackers and your favorite blueberry Pop-Tarts. I'll come by tomorrow to see how you are doing. Tootles." She exited.

"Was that supposed to be Glinda the Good Witch or the Wicked Witch of the West?" I joked.

"Neither. It was the First Lady of Munchkin Land," Sue said.

I laughed and started coughing. "Are you trying to kill me?"

"No. But they say laughter is the best medicine."

I looked around the room. "Where's Kimo?"

"He's celebrating with the team. We won the conference."

"Wow, that's great." I paused a moment. "Tell me, how bad was it?"

"What part are you asking about?" Sue asked.

"My diving."

"You don't remember?"

"No."

"Let's just say, it wasn't your time to make the NCAAs this year." Sue tried to lighten everything up.

"How bad?"

"You missed it by two places. But in your defense, you didn't do the final two dives." She placed the washcloth in the bowl of cool water, wrung it out, and placed it on my forehead.

"What do you mean?"

"You collapsed on the deck." Sue looked at me for a long time.

"What?" I asked.

"You passed out. They carried you out."

I removed the washcloth and tried to get out of bed, but my body wasn't willing.

"Just relax. What do you need? I'll get it."

"A new body," I jokingly said.

"The one you have is perfect."

I slumped back down on the mattress.

Sue got up and carried the bowl and washcloth to the desk. She turned to face me and crossed her arms. "There's no easy way to say this. So, I'm just going to tell you." She paused. "You're leaving in the morning."

"What are you talking about?"

"Since this was the second time at the health clinic, they contacted your folks. I tried everything I could to prevent it. Your folks contacted a man name Hal, and he has arranged to have you on a plane in the morning."

"No." I found the strength to swing my legs over the edge of the bed and stand. "No, no, no. I can't. I have too much to do." The exhaustion was overwhelming, and everything wavered.

Sue rushed to my side and guided me back on the bed. "Stop it. Now, you listen to me."

The sternness in her voice surprised me. I resigned my dramatic display of independence and sunk back onto the mattress. My head pounded, my intestines twisted, and I fought the tendency to vomit.

"You're really sick. You're going to stay in bed, and I'm going to get your things together," Sue explained.

"What's wrong with me?"

"The doctors aren't sure. They determined that you're anemic, dehydrated, and you're fighting a low-grade infection. It could be exhaustion or stress. But whatever it is, you're going to need every bit of strength you have. And going back to Ohio is probably the best thing you can do. Now, shut your eyes and rest."

DR. ALTHEA WARNER'S OFFICE— DAYTON, OHIO, 2018

Althea gently placed my journal on the table next to her, removed her glasses, and pinched the bridge of her nose. She stood and walked the perimeter of the small office and leaned on the back of her chair. Her lips were tense and eyes closed. She began nodding her head, as if she was taking her time to absorb the words written in the journal. She opened her eyes and look at me. "First of all, I'm so sorry that this happened to you. But I want to thank you for feeling safe enough to share it with me."

My mind tried to remember every word that I had written, but even my short-term memory seemed to be hampered, and I wasn't sure to what part she was alluding.

"I don't want to demean or belittle the experience that you endured, but I want to take a moment and try something. Don't get me wrong, what you shared in this journal is going to take some time for me to comprehend and wrap my mind around. Do you understand?"

"I'm not sure."

Althea rested her elbows on the back of the overstuffed chair and pressed her fingers against her lips. "I'm trying to understand the dynamics of what you have shared and compare it to the man sitting in front of me. From what you shared with me, and the abuse you endured during your diving and at the university, it's a miracle that you're even sitting here with me today."

"I'm not following." I adjusted myself on the couch.

"I was afraid of that." Althea walked around the chair and sat. She stared at me for a moment before picking up the journal and placing it in her lap. She put her right hand on the cover and her left hand on her chest. "How do I say this? You're so brave to share this, and I'm grateful. But I feel there's a major disconnect. I applaud your work on remembering, but there are some things I feel you're negating. And I feel you think, consciously or subconsciously, that distancing these things are protecting you. You have experienced things that no child should ever have to go through, and yet you continue to minimize the seriousness of it."

I had to suppress the rush of anger that ignited in the pit of my stomach. My shoulders tensed up and my face burned red.

"I see you are getting upset. I'm not trying to upset you. You may not be aware of how strong and creative you are. You've had to cope with more than most children, and I feel that you take your coping mechanisms for granted. And as you've matured, I can only imagine that you've started to feel you're incapable of normal problem solving." Althea paused and her forehead wrinkled as if she were dealing with a migraine. "Let me ask you this, have you ever been confronted with something that went wrong or a feeling that started to emerge, and you weren't able to verbalize it?"

I slowly nodded.

"Tell me about a moment when this happened." Althea leaned forward.

"With Jake the other day, I wasn't able to write in my journal. Something was preventing me, like a huge wall or barrier that was standing between me and the words."

"How did you feel?"

"Frustrated. Angry. Lost."

"Good. What did you do?" she asked.

"I tried to pick a fight with Jake."

"About what?"

"I don't remember."

"Why?"

"I don't really know."

Althea nodded with understanding. "Did he do anything wrong?"

"No, not really. He was sitting on the couch and playing a game on his phone with the television blaring."

"How did that make you feel?"

"Like I was not important," I responded, without thinking.

"Tell me about the situation. What happened before you wanted to fight?"

"It was stupid. I don't even remember. All I remember was feeling this complete loneliness feeling. He was going to go hang out with some friends, and I was not going."

"Why not?"

"I didn't want to go." I lied. I wasn't invited. Jake enjoys going out with his friends without me, that way, he doesn't have to worry about me or protect me from triggers that might set off a depression episode. My hands shook, so I slipped them under my thighs. "I don't think his friends like me."

"Why not?"

"I don't know. We just don't connect."

"Okay. So, what happened?"

"I tried to tell Jake about how I was feeling, but I couldn't find the words."

"So, you became frustrated," she said.

"I was more angry than frustrated. And Jake just stared at me. Not saying a word or trying to help me figure it out. When I finally said, 'Say something,' he shrugged and said, 'I don't know what to say.'"

"How did that make you feel?"

I looked at Althea for a moment, trying to figure out what she was trying to do. "It made me even angrier."

"What were you angry about?"

"I don't understand." Frustration filled my voice.

"Were you angry because Jake didn't know what to say or were you angry because you didn't have the words to describe your feelings?"

"A bit of both, I guess."

Althea nodded again.

"I was more frustrated that I wasn't able to find a way to release the anger that was building inside."

"And you wanted Jake to release the pressure."

"I wanted Jake to say something so I could explode. But he didn't. He doesn't ever. He's the most levelheaded person I have ever met, and it makes me so frustrated." I pulled my hands from under my thighs and tightly folded them together on my lap.

"You were trying to pick a fight with him?"

"Yes, I already admitted that." The internal struggle to remain calm and not explode was astounding. I refused the let Althea get me mad. "I needed to fight. I needed to release this pressure that had been building." My knuckles turned white the tighter I squeezed my fingers and I felt that the conversation was going in circles.

"But he wouldn't fight." Althea nodded again. "What happened?"

"The same thing that happens every time this comes up. I shut down. Like right now." Numbness filled me. Although I knew the adrenalin raced through my veins, I couldn't feel anything. My hands opened on my lap with indentations from where my nails dug into my palms. I spoke in a controlled monotone. "I realize that I'm a terrible person looking for something or someone to blame, to help me release all this angst inside me. Then I start thinking that there's something wrong with me, that I'm flawed or broken because I don't know how to release this deep seeded anger and I don't know how to ask someone for help. I just continue to create these moments when I start to feel completely overwhelmed and trapped." My voice shook.

"So, when things become too overwhelming and the pain too intense, you create a moment with Jake to help you release all this built up tension. And when he's not able to assist you, you shut down and distance yourself from this pain. Am I on track?"

"Yeah, I guess so."

"Alright," Althea said as she crossed her arms. "Share with me what you feel when Jake refuses to say anything, you shut down, and then Jake goes out with his friends without you. What goes through your mind?"

"Why are you asking me this?" I defensively said.

"I'm curious."

Anger pulsed behind my eyes. "What do you want me to say?"

"What do you want to say?"

I exhaled a heavy sigh. "Do you want me say that I have thoughts of hurting myself?"

"Do you?"

"Do I want?"

Althea calmly repeated, "Do you have thoughts of hurting yourself?"

"Yes," I said, without thinking and shock replaced the rage. *How did she get me to admit that?* "I mean, I don't sit there and plot how I'm going to hurt myself. It's more like flashes that are taunting me. Not like I'd actually act on them."

"What are some of these taunting flashes?"

"You want me to describe them to you?" I glanced at the time on the church steeple's clock.

"Only if you want. It may help defuse the anger that's building right now."

"I'm not angry." My words were quick.

"I see."

"I'm not." Her calm demeanor infuriated me. "I don't like it when people assume that I'm upset or angry." I grabbed a tissue and dabbed my forehead.

"I'm sorry to assume anything."

I looked at Althea.

Why am I getting angry with her?

Althea drew in a deep and steady breath, which I imitated. She walked to the bookshelf to put space between us.

She spoke slowly at first. "When we feel we're in a safe place and with someone who unconditionally wants to help us or love us, we'll tend to expose little indicators of our emotions as anger or hurt. It's like we've tested this person along the development of the relationship, and when we feel that they aren't going to leave or go away, we have the urge to reveal deeper and more meaningful emotions. I like to think that a person that hasn't been victimized is able to sense this quicker and can maneuver through exposing the emotions with less consequences to their internal psyche. But for an abused person, the stakes are higher, and the exhibition takes more."

Althea methodically walked to the back of her chair. "From what I've been able to gather from you, you've adopted a belief that it isn't okay to rock the boat by sharing your internal anger or disappointment. You've developed this because you've never been taught how to diffuse moments like this and the results have been too costly. So, you'll do everything in your power to keep the boat stable. While focusing on keeping the boat from rocking, you're actually causing small ripples under the boat and you become frustrated when the boat sways from side to side. This swaying predicts that larger waves are on the horizon and can't be stopped, which is fearful to you. So, for you to protect the boat, you try to alleviate the pressure by getting Jake to start an argument or fight with you, that way you can justify the anger that has been building and release the pressure a little bit at a time so the tsunami can be avoided. And when Jake isn't responding the way you need him to, you do the next best thing to avoid the boat from rocking, and that is shutting down. You think that shutting down will keep the waves at bay, and it may for a short amount of time. But what's the cost to you by shutting down? And what are the internal thoughts that are triggered by shutting down?"

I wanted to applaud her monologue but quickly realized that I was deflecting so I didn't have to reveal anything. "Wow, I don't know how to follow that."

"Say whatever is on your mind." Her smile was sincere.

"Okay. After, or when, my attempt to start a fight with Jake fails and he decides to go see his friends in spite of my passive-aggressive plea for him to stay with me, I feel deflated. I feel unimportant, like he would rather be with his friends more than with me. He seems happier when he's away from me. And if I go with him, it becomes uncomfortable and his friends don't know what to say to me. Then I may have thoughts."

"What are these thoughts?" Her voice was kind and encouraging.

"Well, it depends. Usually, the first thought is to binge and eat until I make myself sick. Or it could be I want to look at pornography and force myself to look for certain types. Then I'll berate myself for being so weak." There was a mixture of relief and shame at the same time for revealing these thoughts.

Althea smiled. "This is normal. You're becoming aware of the anger you have buried for so long."

"But why am I directing it toward Jake?"

"Because he's safe, and you know he isn't going to leave you."

"That's not fair to Jake." The words riddled me with shame for unconsciously attacking Jake and trying to force him to fight with me. "So, I'm setting Jake up to fail."

"No, not really. You're trying to get him to save you."

"Save me?"

"If he had the correct words to release the pain that's buried deep within you, you'd be freed from the anger and feel worthy." Althea sat back in the chair. "And when he isn't able or chooses not to say anything, you repeat your feeling of unworthiness, shut down, playing it off that it doesn't matter, and you think that you're distancing yourself from the triggers that caused the problem in the first place." She opened the journal again, scanned a page. "Then you may tend to rewrite your history with pretense and denial in order to make it palpable to you. You chose words that soften the grim details."

"So, you think I'm lying?"

"No. I think you've chosen a way to view the world so that you can deal with it the best you can. I think you've come up with your version of reality that allows you to function despite of the abuse you encountered and haven't yet completely healed from. I feel that you must present yourself in a perfect manner, so others don't suspect something. You've worked on perfecting this appearance for so long that you negate and maybe excuse the perpetrators and justify the experience so that you can function. It's a survival strategy."

I had nothing to say.

Althea looked down at the journal. "Everything you stated in here has a sense that it was your fault. You describe things in an erotic and almost attractive way. The grad student, the nurse, your mother, Tony Geary, and the prostitute you have romanticized in some manner to make it easier for you to accept and share. Even the Boy Scout event, you made yourself look like St. Sabastian, a martyr."

"I didn't intend to," I defended myself.

"I'm aware that wasn't your intention. But listen to how you described the prostitute." She lifted the journal, found the place, and read. "A sense of confidence and assurance mixed with a vulnerability that was alluring emitted from his presence. He seemed familiar and yet aloof, attractive and yet unattainable, innocent and yet seasoned." She lowered the book. "Who were you really describing?"

I stared at her.

"How do you know all this about the young man? Did you talk to him? Or was it an assumption?" Her voice was kind but direct.

I wasn't interested in exploring this layer of diagnosis.

"You don't have to answer. Just think about it. What's important to understand is that forgetting, denying, altering, distancing, and softening the abusive experiences have been valuable tools for you in order to survive. But they're no longer viable tools. We need to find ways to put them away with respect, care, and love." She slowly closed the journal and handed it back to me.

I hesitantly retrieved the book and realized that I didn't want her to have it any longer. I slipped it into my satchel and pulled out my checkbook.

"Can we try something for next week?"

I forced a smile as I filled out the check. "Sure."

"I want you to bring in a picture of yourself when you were a teenager before the time the abuse started happening, and one after you were abused."

"I don't know if I have any."

"Check and see. It can really help us in this journey to find the child within you. Because the boy that you were is an important source of information for the man you have become. And I feel that you've forgotten this boy, and how he formed memories, feelings, reactions, personality, attitude, view of the world, and even physical appearance. This boy has been frozen in time. We've identified that you have splintered from this child to protect him; maybe revisiting him will unfreeze the time you were abused. And comparing the two pictures of before and after may help you to be able to see the differences." She paused." And keep writing in your journal."

The church tower bell rang, indicating the session was finally over. I handed her my check, gathered my things, and headed for the door.

I sat in the driver's seat of the 2004 Toyota Corolla for a good thirty minutes before driving home. As I pulled into the driveway, my mind was swamped with forgotten memories of returning home after the UCI incident.

CHAPTER 6
RECOUPING AT HOME

MATTHEW HOME: AULDEN, OHIO, 1982.

It must have been a couple of weeks since Hal flew me back to Aulden and I proceeded to get extremely sick. I wasn't able keep anything down; even water would come rushing back up as soon as swallowed. Beside the headaches, sore throat, and nausea, I felt as if I had been kicked in the stomach repeatedly and no one seemed to understand. My feverish mind began to make deals with God.

Please God, don't let this be anything serious.

Please God, I will change my ways, if you lead me through this painful experience.

Please God, don't let it be the "gay" disease.

Please God, I don't want to die.

The doctors weren't even sure what could be causing the sickness. The initial diagnosis was food poison, and then it changed to the stomach flu. I was informed I'd have to ride it out.

When the symptoms continued for another week, everyone became concerned. Hal took me to another doctor, and it was discovered I had high levels of lymphocytes or white blood cells and that I was anemic, which led to me being labeled with mononucleosis. This diagnosis explained the extreme tiredness, but not the excruciating abdominal pains. The high levels of lymphocytes were an indicator for the possible exposure to CMV or cytomeg-alovirus, which explained the fever, sore throat, fatigue, swollen glands, and stomach and intestine issues. Although more than half the population experienced exposure to CMV, people with compromised immune systems were known to come down with the Epstein-Barr virus, Infectious Mononucleosis, immune-medi-ated inflammatory disease, and/or other opportunistic infections. I was told to return to bed, drink a lot of liquids, and try to eat saltine crackers. Everyone agreed that stress and anxiety did strange things to the body.

For some reason, one night, something changed. Maybe my body became so exhausted that it just released everything, but for the first time, the cramps in my feet and legs subsided, and the tightness and pain in my stomach eased. The low-grade fever broke and drenched my body with refreshing coolness. It was like my body had won over the infection and permitted itself to the best sleep in a long time. Every position I curled up in was pleasant and relaxing.

Two different voices carried up the staircase and filled my space with unrecognizable babble.

I hesitantly rolled over and confronted the familiarities of my childhood room with fresh eyes. Everything was vibrating with brilliant colors and details. The intimacy of this landing/bedroom occupied a twin bed, a chest of drawers, shelves and everything exactly how I left it. The posters of Bruce Jenner and Mark Bradley were still pinned to the wall, exploding with red, white, blue, and exhibiting the strength and agility of top-level athletes. A diving trophy's intense golden hue bathed three horse figurines posturing on the top of the chest of drawers. Everything seemed familiar, but it was as if they belonged to someone else.

On the shelves above were Charlie McCarthy, Danny O'Day, Mortimer Snerd, and Mickey Mouse ventriloquist dolls staring blindly down at me. They always disturbed me, but not as much as the various clowns of different shapes and sizes occupying the rest of the shelving. Clowns! There was Bozo the Clown that had seen better days. Also, many Harlequin clowns with ceramic white faces, tear drops painted under their eyes, and donning satin ruffle collars and matching triangle hats with bells. The scariest of all, Pennywise, the clown from Stephen King's *It* menacingly stared down at me with judgmental eyes and a mocking smile, as if it knew every dark secret I have tried to hide. Normally, I placed Pennywise facing the corner so I wouldn't have to encounter its terrifying gaze—but every morning, it somehow turned itself around.

I never understood how this collection started or why people thought I liked clowns or "dummy" dolls, but every Christmas or birthday I knew someone would give me another one. I figured they'd become collector's items in the future, so there they sat, collecting dust.

A pine box resting in the space between the chest-of-drawers and the window caught my attention. I mustered enough strength to swing my thin legs over the edge of the bed and reached for it. It felt heavier than I remembered, but I managed to retrieve it and pulled it onto the bed. I unfastened the hook and eye and lifted the half-inch wood cover, revealing a shadow box with a pane of glass protecting my World Game's gold medal. The warmth of distant memories flooded my mind and filled me with the ideology that anything was possible, like an unknown kid from the hick town of Aulden, Ohio, traveled to Norway, dove against the best divers in the world, won the gold medal by the narrowest of margins, and stood on top of the victory stand with the national anthem playing. It was surreal that I had pushed these memories to the furthest part of my mind like hiding the medal in a wooden box.

Am I always hiding myself?

As I closed and returned the box to its isolation between the chest-of-drawers and the window, another thought entered my mind. Without hesitation, I pulled out the bottom drawer and there were my pencils, ink pens, watercolors, charcoals, sketch-pads, and drawings. I rummaged through the piles of horse sketches in various positions and came to my secret sketchpad. I was amazed that it was still here. I quickly pulled it out and flipped it open. The first pages were more drawings of horses as decoys, and then appeared the nude drawings that I hid from Dad. I was struck with awe at the drawings' details. For the first time in my life, I was filled the sense that I could've been an artist. I was impressed by the attention to the hands, the contour of the body, and the realism of the hair.

MATTHEW HOME: AULDEN, OHIO, 1978.

Dad turned the sketch and pointed to the figure's thigh. "You need to be aware that the hairs on the legs extend out from the patch of pubic hairs surrounding the private area. As the hairs extend over the thighs, just like the forearm, they grow in a wrapping formation." He exemplified this by placing his hand on his thigh and motioning at how the growth patterns moved across the upper and under side of the thigh until they met. "You did a good job with the hair pattern here. You see how you allowed the hairs to help keep the circular evolution of the human body? Nice work."

He stopped, laid out several sketches, and examined them. Without looking at me, he asked, "Why are you drawing Zach naked? Why are all these of Zach?" He looked at me. "Did he pose for you?

The words burned through me like a heated saber. I shook my head.

He slowly stood, letting the drawings fall to the floor.

"They aren't of Zach," I managed to say. "I promise."

His eyes were stern. "They look like Zach."

"But they aren't. I was just practicing the figures from your art books." I gathered the drawings from the floor.

Dad's head cocked, and he stepped closer. "Why do they have the same hairstyle, lips, eyes, and hairy legs?"

"I don't know. I just drew them without thinking." I looked down at the sketches in my hands. "I had no idea."

"Is that how you see him, naked and all out of proportion?" He took the sketches from my hands. "It's unnatural to draw images of the flesh in such provocative ways."

"But what about the woman you drew, the one I tried to copy?" I asked.

"That's different. That was an assignment." His neck started to turn red as the veins on each side pulsed.

"But…"

"No buts." He held up the sketches. "These types of drawings will cause you to burn in hell and are against the Bible, which states, 'He who sins sexually against his own body…'" He stopped in mid-sentence. He looked at the sketches and then back to me, and calmly asked, "Do you think Zach is attractive?"

I quickly shook my head.

"Then why do you draw him?"

"I just drew those pictures. I'm not sure why they look like Zach." My face flushed from lying.

Dad slowly nodded and sucked air through his lower teeth. "Leviticus Twenty says, 'If a man lies with a man as with a woman, both have committed an abomination, they shall surely be put to death, their blood upon them.' An abomination," he stressed. He took a moment to look out the window. "Maybe we should refrain from drawing any more nudes of Zach, or any man. You don't want to bring disappointment and shame to the family, do you?"

I didn't say anything.

He calmly stood there and said, "I asked you a question. Don't you see the temptation that these drawings have?"

I flinched. "They're just drawings."

"Smut. You're drawing smut. I can't have such smut in my house. You'll obey my request, or I'll forbid you from drawing anything. Do you understand?"

"But it wasn't…"

"Do you understand?"

"Yes." I hung my head in shame.

"Yes, what?"

"Yes, sir."

He gathered the remaining sketches from the bed. "Why don't you pray for forgiveness?"

I wasn't sure if he was suggesting or demanding me to pray. I didn't want to take a chance. I prepared for the wrath of anger to spew from him, not this calm and controlled demeanor. My muscles trembled with the anticipation of some type of physical encounter. None came.

I knelt on the floor and rested my folded hands on the bed. "Dear God, forgive me for my misguided ways. Please accept my apologies if I offended you with my drawings. I was in no way wanting to offend anyone. Please help me to see the temptations of the flesh, and help protect me from its sinful ways in the future."

Dad placed his large hand on my head. "You aren't alone, my son." He leaned down and kissed the top of my head before removing his hand.

I remained on my knees next to the bed, afraid that he could still be there, watching me. I imagined myself tearing up the sketches and gathering all the pieces of evidence and rushing to the silo. I struck a match against the side of the box, and the paper accepted the red and orange flame. I watched the paper crinkle with the heat. I witnessed my illustrations breathe with the life of the flames as it caused the paper to blister before charring to ash. When I felt it was safe to open my eyes and stand, all the sketches were gone. Dad took them with him.

MATTHEW HOME: AULDEN, OHIO, 1982.

Something inside me would not refrain from sinning and drawing naked men. I never knew why, but these drawings seemed, as a way, to help me figure things out in my mind. By sketching these secret images, I came closer to answering the questions that filled me every day, like trying to understand why the older men wanted to be with me and the younger people had nothing to do with me. They helped me question why I found Zach and Mark interesting and maybe attractive. They displayed everything that was opposite me, the dark hair, hirsute, and confidence in their appearance. They helped me understand and justify why I allowed myself to be with men. So, I secretly continued drawing and hiding them.

I looked down at the secret sketchpad in my hands. The more I examined the images, the more they did resemble Zachary Spence in all his Gothic glory. I often fantasized about Zach, especially how he saved me from the Boy Scout incident and the way he pressed his lips against mine on that New Year's Eve before his life was accidentally cut short. I remembered the way his dark hair escaped from under the knitted toboggan and draped over his brown eyes. How he stood in the doorway with his crooked smile and dressed in his long, dark coat and ripped, skinny black jeans exposing his hairy thighs. He stood there, wanting to be invited in like a vampire. By drawing Zach, I felt that I was near him.

"Would you like some more coffee?" Mom's voice clearly traveled up the stairs and pulled me back to reality.

"No, I need to be going. I have a meeting," a male's voice followed, which sounded like Hal's.

"It seems like I'm always saying thank you. But thank you for getting him home. I don't how we could've managed it."

"My pleasure. I was hoping to see him." Hal's voice was filled with concern.

"I can wake him," Mom said, setting down her coffee cup.

"No, the doctor said he needs all the rest he can get. How's he doing?"

"Better. He's been sleeping a lot. He was a pretty sick kid."

"I thought I was going to have to carry him out of the airport." Hal forced a laugh. "He was so thin."

"Yep." Mom's voice cracked. "I thought we were going to lose him. The first couple of days, he couldn't keep anything down and now he looks like a skeleton."

There was a moment of silence.

"Well, he's home, in safe hands, and on the mend. Let him know I stopped by to see how he's doing."

I cowered to the corner of the bed next to the window as they walked past the staircase.

218

"Are you sure you don't want me to wake him? I know he'd love to see you."

"No, let him sleep. Maybe when he's feeling better, he'll join me for dinner." There was hope in his voice.

The door opened.

"He'd enjoy that." Mom's voice was muffled as she stepped out on the front porch with Hal.

"Thank you for the coffee."

I peeked out the window and watched Hal walk to his car. I noticed that he had a balding spot on the crown of his head and he walked with his shoulders stooped, as if gravity pulled him forward. He struggled to get the door opened, and winched when he shimmied onto the driver's seat. He waved back to Mom and shut the door.

Mom shouted. "See you soon."

The Black Lincoln Town Car backed all the way down the driveway before shifting into drive and disappearing behind the woods.

I sat there on the twin bed with my sketchpad and drawings. *How did I end up back in this room? Did I fail? Was I not good enough? Everything seems to be slipping away from me. Will I ever amount to anything?*

"David? You up?" Mom's voice flew up the staircase.

"Yes," I mumbled.

"You just missed Hal. He stopped by to see you."

"Oh, that's nice. It's a shame I missed him."

"I'm going to the grocery store. Need anything?" Her voice seemed impatient.

"Maybe. May I go with you?" My voice felt weak.

"You feel strong enough?"

"I do. I think I need to get out of the house for a little bit."

"Sure."

"I just need to change." I gathered the sketches.

"Take your time." Her voice faded off.

I replaced the "Zachary" drawings back into the secret protection of the bottom of the drawer, replaced the decoy horse images on top, and securely closed it. I shrugged off my sweatshirt and sweatpants, pulled on a pair of shorts which were too big for me and I had to use the aid of my belt, which was now at its last notch. I slipped on a T-shirt that engulfed me like an oversized tent. As I stepped into my tennis shoes, I ran my hands through my dirty blond hair and threw on a baseball hat and adjusted it down to hide my tired eyes.

The first four steps down to the small landing were unsteady, and I needed the aid of the banister. When I turned to face the main staircase, I wondered if I could make it all the way down. My vision wavered with vertigo and my temples pulsed. I ignored the warning signs, took a deep breath, and stepped down. It was slow moving at first, and my legs felt unstable and feeble. I was quickly out of breath as each step was a combination of mental and physical strategy of how to accomplish the simple task. Even though exhaustion took over when I reached the main floor, the desire to get outside was stronger, and I pushed through the pain.

As I entered the kitchen, Mom was at the sink, popping two oblong green diet pills through the cellophane packaging and downing them with the last of her coffee. After discarding the coffee cup in the sink, she waited for the controversial ingredient, phenylpropanolamine, to burst through her blood stream. She was dressed to impress the good people at the only grocery store in Aulden. Her hair was pulled up and sprayed, blue eye shadow, liner, and mascara; cheeks highlighted with rouge, and lips painted red. The way the morning light streamed through the window made her appear ethereal, untouchable, and beautiful. I admired her and loved her deeply.

As she turned from the sink and saw me, her hand rushed to her chest, and she gasped for air. "You scared me." She quickly hid her concern. "There's my baby boy. How are you feeling?"

I leaned against the refrigerator and tried my best acting. "Good. I feel so much better."

She reached out her arms and made her way around the counter, never wavered her eyes off me. She placed her hands on my cheeks. "You're still pale. Are you sure you want to go to the grocery store? I can pick up anything you need."

"I really have to get out of the house for a little bit. Maybe see how the people of Aulden are getting on," I joked.

"Nothing ever changes in Auden I can tell you that right now." She kissed my forehead. "The fever's gone. That's a good sign." She kissed both cheeks.

I pulled back and defensively crossed my arms in front of my face. "Enough already."

"All right, all right. You can't blame a mother for loving her baby son."

"I'm not a baby."

"You'll always be my baby boy, even when you're a hundred and ten years old."

"That's depressing."

She laughed. "That's just the way it is." Her face became serious again, and she took hold of my head. "I don't want you to push yourself too soon or too hard."

"I can't stay in my room all the time." I pulled away from her.

"I know."

The phone screamed, and I jumped.

Mom nonchalantly went to answer it, with her sweet and pleasing voice. "Hello."

The sun was shining brightly on the silo, and I had to stand next to it.

"Yes. Oh, that's great." Mom sounded more like a customer service operator than the recipient of the call.

"I'll be outside," I whispered.

She held up a hand to stop me, but I smiled and moved to the back door.

I walked through the porch and saw Bear chained in the back yard. The sun felt marvelous on my face as I headed out the screen door. The day's warmth engulfed me and sent a cold chill down my spine. I stretched my arms out and wanted to feel the warmth all over my emaciated body. I walked past the parked car and along the curve of the gravel driveway to the hill that led to the silo. The solid cement structure stood majestically alone at the foundation of where a barn used to stand before we moved here.

As I gazed in awe at the silo reaching up into the clear sky, I remember fantasizing that it was the only visible part of a castle and I was truly a prince. For some reason I was projected to another realm of existence by an evil stepmother who wanted me to be sent far away. As she cast the spell on me, the silo was caught as well, sending us both through time and space to this dimension. Like Superman's pod-spaceship, the silo became my anchor to my real world and a reminder that I'd eventually figure out the spell and return to my rightful life. Until then, I could only stand next to it and absorb all the energy it bestowed on me. As I reached my arms out as wide as they could stretch, as if I was going to embrace the circumference of the silo, warmth wrapped itself around me like a pair of loving arms. I remained there, soaking in the love that this relic emitted onto me.

The magic was broken by Mom's voice, "You ready?" She stood by the car.

"I'll be right there." I looked back at the silo and whispered, "Soon."

QUACKENBURGER'S GROCERY STORE: AULDEN, OHIO, 1982.

The five-mile drive to Aulden's only grocery store, Quackenburger's was uneventful. I relished the warm wind whipping through the opened window and forcing my hair off my forehead.

Mom seemed to be talking, but it must've been another language, because I didn't understand her. I was entranced by the crisp shooting colors of the farmland, alternating from fields freshly plowed to tobacco in neat rows, knee high corn stocks, green wheat, and soybean sprouts whizzing past. I longed to connect to the hues of this farm community.

Before I knew it, Mom turned right onto State Route 73 and then another immediate right to Aulden's quaint Main Street aligned with antique shops and the Humbler Inn. The locals were greeting each other and milling on the sidewalks like a Norman Rockwell painting or a Hallmark film. Mom pulled into a parking space in front of Quackenburger's. The familiar smell of the store wafted out every time the glass doors opened. It was busy for a Thursday morning.

"Do you want to come in?" Mom asked as she turned the ignition off, withdrew the keys, and dropped them into her purse.

I nodded and pushed the trepidation of running into someone I may know to the back of my mind.

"It won't be long. I'm just picking up a couple of things. I called in earlier to have the order put together." She looked at herself in the rearview mirror, checking to see if any lipstick smudged on her teeth and replacing any flyaway hairs.

I nodded again.

"Let's do it." She pushed open the driver's door.

I got out of the car and followed her to the entrance. Before we even got to the door, Mom had said hello to five people, and many more stared at me. Mom ignored the stares and confidently walked into the store.

"Lydia, how's things?" a familiar voice bellowed from the depths of the first aisle.

"Howdy, Sonnie." She waved like Miss America. "Look who I got back home," Mom proudly announced.

Sonnie Quackenburger, the store's owner and former Life Scout leader, heavily dropped a box and lumbered to the front. "Well, well. Can it be the prodigal son and world traveling diver?"

"And he was recently on *General Hospital*," Mom added.

"Wow, that's impressive. I hardly recognized you. What brings you back home?"

I forced a smile.

"He came back to recoup and recharge," Mom said with authority.

"It's good to see you." An awkward pause invaded as Sonnie looked me up and down. "Oh Lydia, we have top notch ground beef on sale and a two-for-one special on marshmallows."

I wasn't sure if Sonnie was smirking on my behalf and remembered that camp excursion where he and several others tied me to a tree and shot twigs with marshmallows at me, or if he didn't remember and was being the perfect salesman for Mom.

"I'll have to check them out." She kindly placed her hand on Sonnie's large shoulder and scaled the store to see if there was anyone else she needed to impress.

"I can always hold one of the ground beefs back for you if you want, because those are going to go fast."

"You're always so good to me." Mom's voice turned sugary.

"Excuse me," I said and moved down the aisle.

"He looks really thin." Sonnie's voice carried.

"We thought we were going to lose him," Mom replied for sympathy.

"What made him sick? If I may be so bold to ask."

"We're not sure, but they think it could be Epstein-Barr," Mom stated.

My whole body cringed.

"What's that?" Sonnie asked.

"It's a severe form of mononucleosis." Mom's voice grew louder for everyone in the store to overhear.

"You mean the kissing disease? See what happens when you kiss outside of the family?" Sonnie's laugh rumbled deep from within his forty-six inch waistline.

I meandered forward to get away.

"That's unfortunate," said Sonnie.

"Lydia, I've your groceries here," the cashier said.

"Liz, that's so kind of you. What do I owe you?" Mom's voice faded in the distance.

Sonnie's voice bellowed, "Dewayne, could you empty that box in aisle one and get rid of it?"

I rushed to the next aisle, not wanting to converse with Dewayne, if he somehow recognized me. As I turned the corner, I ran into the young man that was my tent mate in the Boy Scouts.

"Sorry," he said and kept moving. He looked older than his age with thinning hair, dark circles under his eyes, and a potbelly.

I tried to get lost among the Mikesells and Pringles. I wanted to blend in with the Little Debbies. But no matter how thin I was, I could not disappear. Dizziness took over and I grabbed the shelving to remain stable.

"There you are." Mom stood behind a cart, with three stuffed brown bags. Her smile was huge for her audience, or else her diet pills were taking effect. "Do you want anything?"

"No, I'm good."

"Are you feeling alright? You look pale."

"I'm fine." I pulled myself erect.

"Alrighty. Let's blow this popsicle stand." She turned the cart and headed for the exit.

I slowly followed.

"Next time, Lydia," Sonnie shouted from the back.

"Thank you, Sonnie," Mom called back.

"David? Is that you?"

I paused and looked at the person who appeared eight months pregnant.

"It's me, Liz. Liz Wilde. I mean it was Fields when we went to school together. Jake Wilde's girlfriend?"

"Jake, the captain of the swim team, Wilde?"

"The one and only." She smiled.

"Wow. You look great," I immediately said.

"That's kind of you to say." She rubbed her belly. "You haven't aged a bit. You look exactly the same."

"Are you...?" I was afraid to ask but looked at her stomach.

"Yes. Two more weeks, and I'll be getting this critter out." Liz leaned in. "I can't wait. This one's always kicking and punching me. Nothing like Rebecca; she was so easy."

"Is this your second?"

"Third. Two girls, and now this little bundle of joy." She rubbed her swollen belly again.

"With Jake?"

Liz nodded. "We got married right after high school."

I looked at her differently and wondered if she was happy. She always seemed happy being Jake's girlfriend in high school, and now his wife.

Could true love really exist? Was this what true love looked like, married and living in the same small town?

"What's Jake up to?" I asked.

"Are you ready for this? He's a teacher now at Aulden High. And he's the swim team coach."

"That's great. That's, that's really great."

"Jake wants a boy, and guess what names he's thinking about choosing?"

I shook my head. "I have no idea."

Her face brightened with excitement. "Darius or Alexander."

"Cool." I made no connection with either name.

"Remember Ms. Winthrop's history class when she was telling us about Alexander the Great?" She said, like I'd never forget.

"Of course." I saw Mom talking to someone by the car, and I wondered what embellishments she was sharing. "And what if it's another girl?" I asked.

"Jake said I'd have to send it back." Her laughter was contagious. She saw me looking out at Mom. "Your mom's so proud of you. She talks about you all the time."

"That's what worries me," I accidentally said.

"No, seriously. All she does is brag about what you're doing. All about the diving, Movie of the Week, and *General Hospital,* and who you're meeting. She was so worried about you, and I think she's relieved you are home. How are you doing?"

"Much better. Thank you, Liz. I better go help Mom put the groceries in the car. It was great to see you, and say hi to Jake for me." I started for the exit.

"He's going to be so bummed that he didn't see you first."

"Maybe we can all get together."

"That'd be great."

"Later." I left the air-conditioned store and made my way to the cart to retrieve a bag.

"David, you remember Kathy, Jake's mother?"

"Oh, of course. Hello, Mrs. Wilde." I juggled the bag to offer my hand. "It seems like everyone's here at Quakenburger's. I just saw Liz inside."

"What else are we to do?" Mrs. Wilde shook my hand. "It's great to have you back home. Your mom has been sharing all your adventures with me."

I could only smile as I pulled my hand away. "Do you have ice cream in here Mom? We should be going, or it's going to melt." I popped open the back door and set the bag on the seat.

"Yes. And we should, I guess," Mom said with regret.

"I have to hurry as well. Liz and I had to get out for a while, and we left Dale with the two *grand-girls*. I don't want to leave them too long together. You can never know what shenanigans he'll teach them," Mrs. Wilde joked.

"If he's anything like Caleb or Caine, you better hurry. But if he's like David, you don't have anything to worry about." Mom smiled at me.

I grabbed another bag from the cart and transferred it to the car.

"You take care, Lydia, and please tell me what your secret is. You look fantastic," Mrs. Wilde said.

"Kathy, you're so kind. Thank you." Mom giggled and touched up her hair.

I grabbed the last bag from the cart.

"Lydia, do you mind if I take your cart?" asked Mrs. Wilde.

"By all means." Mom posed in front of the grocery store.

"I'll tell Jake you said hi, David."

"Please do." I shut the back door.

"He's going to be so jealous that I saw you first," Mrs. Wilde said as she pushed the cart toward the entrance.

I smiled and opened the passenger door and leaned on it.

"Have a great day, Kathy." Mom waved and stood there, as if she was waiting to speak to someone else. It dawned on me that this was more a social event for her.

"Mom, the ice cream."

"Oh, yes." She remained there as she dug in her purse for the keys, just in case someone else came by to say hello. When she realized there was a lull in the comings and goings of the locals, she made her way to the driver's side. Once she was situated with the key in the ignition, she once more checked her reflection in the rearview mirror. She turned the ignition and pulled out of the parking space, continuously looking to see if there was anyone else to talk to or be seen by. She abruptly hit the brakes, sending me forward and having to use both hands to keep from crashing into the glove compartment and dashboard.

"Sandy, look who I finally got back home," Mom called out.

Ms. Winthrop, my history teacher strolled to the window and looked over Mom. "David, you're back. Lydia, you must be so excited."

"I am. Now if I can just keep him here long enough to get some meat back on his bones."

"Mom."

"How long are you planning to stay?" Ms. Winthrop asked.

"Just till he gets well, and then he'll be heading back to Hollywood or some other faraway place. He just can't stay still. He's busier than a one armed paper hanger," Mom's joke fell flat. "He was on *General Hospital*."

"I heard about that," Ms. Winthrop forced a smile.

"Are you still teaching?" I asked.

"Oh, no. I retired."

"You're too young to retire." I tried to emulate Mom's sweetness.

"That's so kind." Ms. Winthrop's face blushed as she pushed her turquoise-colored bifocals up the bridge of her thin nose. "I lasted until your class graduated. Now, I want to travel and see the states and all the historical landmarks I taught about."

"That sounds exciting." Mom plunged back into the conversation.

"As a matter of a fact, I'm leaving this afternoon to go see the Rocky Mountains. I've always wanted to see them."

"Are you going by yourself?" Mom pried.

"There's a group of us, mostly retired teachers from different areas. We chartered a bus," Ms. Winthrop proudly said.

"That sounds so fun. We have to get the ice cream home before it melts, and this one needs to take a nap." Mom's words rushed together to end the conversation.

"Feel better, David." Ms. Winthrop waved and moved toward the grocery store.

"Thank you and enjoy…"

Mom pulled away.

I reclined against the back of the seat, realizing that the conversation was not centered on Mom, which made me giggle.

"What?" She turned left onto Main Street.

"Nothing."

"Something made you laugh." She migrated into the left turning lane and hit the brakes as the light turned yellow.

"You can make a left on yellow," I instructed.

"This light turns so fast that I don't want to chance it."

The car behind us honked as we sat there waiting for the yellow light to turn red. Mom looked in the rearview mirror and threw her hands up in the air. "Patience is a virtue."

The driver of the car threw up his hands and honked again.

Finally, the light turned red, and Mom let out a sigh. "People are always rushing and in a hurry. They need to learn to relax and enjoy the moment."

The light turned green, and Mom turn left, heading south on State Route 73 and immediately got in the left hand lane to turn onto State Route 42.

The man behind us passed us on the right and yelled, "Learn to drive, bitch."

"Go to hell, bastard," Mom yelled back.

"Mom!" I was in shock.

"What?"

"I'm at a loss for words."

She turned onto State Route 42. "What? He's an asshole."

"Where's all this inappropriate language coming from?" I stifled my amusement.

"I'm tired of men thinking they're better drivers. I did nothing wrong. I was following the laws of making a left-hand turn."

"Okay." I didn't know what to do. So, I decided to let it go and enjoy the freedom she was feeling.

"Anyway, that's no way to speak to a lady."

"You're correct," I said.

She picked up speed for the five miles back home. I rested my head on the back of the seat, allowing the late morning's warm air to rush in the open window and blow against my closed eyes. The sound of the wind and the humming of the engine relaxed me.

"Pig!" Mom shouted as the car swerved to the left and then immediately to the right.

I sat up to witness the spinning of the landscape as the car performed two 360° turns, skidded across two lanes, and came to rest on the lip of the ditch.

"Pig." Tears streamed down Mom's face as her hair stood in all different directions. "Pig. There was a giant pig in the middle of the road."

I quickly looked behind us. There was nothing there.

"I swear, there was a pig in the road. Right there. Standing right in the middle. I thought I was going to hit it."

I looked out the window and couldn't see a pig or any animal anywhere.

"It was right there. You believe me, don't you?"

"Sure." My heart raced as I wasn't sure what to believe.

DR. ALTHEA WARNER'S OFFICE— DAYTON, OHIO, 2018

I handed my journal to Althea and got comfortable on the couch.

She sat there, looking at the leather-bound journal on her lap. She held her hands above the book with her fingertips pressing together and forming a triangle. She said nothing for the longest time. She lifted her head and looked at me with soft eyes. Again, she said nothing. I wasn't sure how long we sat there, but the silence was deafening and unsettling.

Finally, she took a deep breath. "During our last session, I asked you to bring some pictures of yourself. You were to bring one photo that was taken before your abuse started and at least one after the abuse. Did you do that?"

"I did." I reached for my satchel and pulled out a plastic bag. "I had a hard time finding pictures that were distinctly from before and after." I handed the pictures to her.

She took the plastic bag but didn't open it. "This bag holds so many answers for you. When you look at these pictures, the answers may not appear right away." She handed the bag back to me. "I want you to open this bag and put the pictures in some type of order. It doesn't matter if they are placed perfectly in sequence, but some type of a semblance of an order for you."

"Sure." I took the bag, opened it, and empty the contents on the couch beside me. There was a detachment from the images splayed out on the cushion. They were mostly black and white and seemed to be a stranger's captured moments. I shuffled through the images, trying to place them in some kind of order.

"Don't think too hard about this. I just want you to arrange them. There's no right or wrong way to do this."

I randomly picked up a photo, and then another, and piled them together.

"Good. Okay, you're going to look at the one that's on top."

I stared at Althea, trying to figure out the reasoning for this exercise.

"As you look at a photograph, tell me what you see and if you feel any connection to it." Althea picked up her clipboard to take notes. "Describe the picture to me, so that I can see it in my mind through your words."

I decided to play along even though it felt like a big waste of time. I looked at the top image of the pile in my hand. I studied it for a moment and nonchalantly described it. "It's a black and white picture of a group of kids, they're cheerleaders. I see Vicki, Becky, myself, and part of someone's head. It's a football game because we are outside and I'm yelling through a megaphone."

Althea nodded. "I'm impressed you remembered the names."

"Me, too. I haven't thought about those two in years."

"Tell me more about the picture. What feelings are being evoked?" She leaned back in the chair.

I examined the picture again. "I can't really tell. The photo isn't that great."

"Do you remember when it was taken?" she encouragingly asked.

"I don't. It had to have been my eighth grade year. I was probably thirteen years old, since it was the fall."

"So, this was before the abuse with the coach and the professionals?" asked Althea.

"I think so."

"How does it make you feel?"

I looked at the picture again. "Proud."

"Why?" She took notes.

"Because I did something that I wanted. I broke the rules and wanted to try out for cheerleading so I could do my gymnastics. Before that, only girls were cheerleaders. I remember asking Caine to talk to Mrs. Watson to see if it I could try out when I was in the seventh grade. She let me and I made it." My chest expanded, and I took a deep breath. "I was nervous about what everyone would say, but I knew once they saw me do a round-off, back handspring, back somersault that they would accept me."

"And did they?" Althea asked.

"For the most part."

"What can you see in the boy's eyes?"

"I can't really see his eyes, but there's an intensity, a motivation to connect with the crowd. You know, to get the spirit moving."

"Is there another picture from around the same time?"

I rummaged through the pile of pictures and found one. I held it up. "This must have been taken at the same time. It's a closeup of me screaming through a megaphone."

"What do you see?"

"I see a boy with blond hair, long eyelashes, and intense eyes. He's on the verge of being too pretty."

"What makes you say that?"

"Because he looks almost like a girl. His face has not matured, and he could pass as a girl."

"What else do you see in his eyes?"

"I can see the same determination, as if he was going to do the best possible job."

"What about his spirit?"

"What do you mean?"

"You've used the words 'motivation' and 'determination' to describe the boy in the pictures. Can you get a sense of his spirit?"

"Untouchable is the first thing that comes to mind."

"How so?"

"There's a questioning in his eyes, as if he's on the verge of discovering something, like his sexuality and desires. Even though there's this questioning quality, he appears strong and focused."

"Okay." Althea wrote down more notes. "See if you have another picture from that time."

I shifted through the pile of photographs.

So much for putting these photos in some type of order.

I pulled up another one. "It's a photo of the junior high football team and cheerleaders. I'm in the front and off to the side. There's a distance between me and Becky. The other cheerleaders are all shoulder to shoulder, but Becky and I aren't. The football players are behind us, and they are shoulder to shoulder as well."

"How does that make you feel?" Althea's voice was warm.

"Sad."

"Why?"

"Because the boy in this picture looks like he doesn't really belong. There's a pensive look in his eyes, like he's trying to get through this moment. Even his body is pivoted away from the others, as if he'd rather be somewhere else. It's like he's thinking or dreaming about something different."

"Do you remember what his dreams were at that time?"

"No," I immediately responded.

"What else do you see?"

"A boy that wants to belong but really doesn't. Desperately wants to belong but is too different."

"Different, how?"

"I don't know." I impatiently discarded the picture.

Althea explained, "Don't get upset. We're just exploring."

"I don't see the point of all this."

"Trust me. You do trust me, don't you?" Althea's voice was calmer than usual.

"Yes."

"Okay. Remember this isn't easy. This is stirring up memories. But remember that you're in a safe place, and I'm not going to judge you."

I nodded.

"May we look at some more?"

"Fine."

"Do you have any other pictures from the eighth grade?"

"I think I have my class picture." I looked at the pile and found it. I looked at the kid with blond bangs and dimples. "He appears happy, but there's a growing distance in his eyes."

"How can you tell?"

"It's more of a feeling. I can see that he knows that he's different from everyone else. But that doesn't concern him. He knows there's a reason for his differentness, but he isn't sure what that is. He simply knows he's special."

"How do you mean?"

"Just look at him." I turned the picture for Althea to see it. "Look how brave he is to be wearing a multi-colored turtle-neck sweater for his school picture. There seems to be a sense of abandonment about him, a c'est-la-vie quality. His eyes are wide open. He's clearly aware of the choices he's making. They're bold choices but remain in the acceptable confines of the situation. He's pushing the boundaries. He's an individual, independent, and a mover and shaker, but careful not to upset the cart."

"Good, very good." Althea wrote more notes down. "What's another picture you brought?"

I blindly pulled one from the stack. "It's a picture of the freshmen class officers. I was elected secretary. This is the last picture I know of before the abuse started. It was taken right at the beginning of fall. I had gotten back from the Junior Olympics in Lincoln, Nebraska, where I took eighth place. It was right before Hal started introducing me to the professionals." As I looked at the picture, a smile crossed my face. "I'm squeezed between Mary and Robert. I'm not sure who I was more excited to sit next to, but Robert is looking at me and smirking."

"What does the boy's face in the picture tell you?"

"His eyes are dark and hidden by his glasses. Again, there's a sense of wonderment, possibilities. He was selected by his class-mates." A sad reality landed. "This was the last time he ever held a class office. This was the verge of getting ready for Norway and when the abuse began, and he started pulling away from everyone."

"Can you see the effects of him pulling away in this picture?"

"Not in this one." I retrieved the freshmen class picture. I looked at the teenager's eyes. "This one, I can see changes. There's a brave front, but his eyes are filled with pain."

"How so?"

"Look." I handed the picture to Althea. "The boy's eyes are dead. Disconnected. They have an older quality to them than the picture with the class officers. His eyes are hiding shame." I pulled another picture, and my breath escaped my lungs.

"What is it?"

My eyes filled with tears, and my bottom lip trembled.

"David. Can you talk about it?"

I looked at her, and tears streamed down my face.

"Can you describe the picture?"

I looked at the boy in the picture. "It's the first time I can see his beauty. Or the beauty that others must have seen. He's wearing a flannel shirt, suspenders, jeans, and a cowboy hat. I remember it was during a pep assembly, when he was a varsity cheerleader. This was his last year of cheering. He never tried out again. He made the excuse that diving was taking up too much time." I looked at the boy in the picture. "God, he's pretty. It's his eyes and mouth that are stunning. Despite his beauty, I see the pain he's trying to hide behind his eyes, they look dark and opaque. He's so alone and confused." My whole body convulsed, and I lost it. I fought to regain control and wiped away the snot on my sleeve's cuff. "I miss him. I want to hold him. I want to protect him. I want to tell him he's okay."

"You just did." Althea tenderly smiled.

"What?" The connection shut down, and I was no longer whole with the boy in the pictures.

"You're doing great work, David. Let's take a moment and check in. How are you feeling?" Althea encouragingly asked.

"Numb."

"How so?"

I adjusted myself on the couch and embraced a throw pillow to my chest. "There was a moment, a very brief moment, I felt I was going to break through this barrier. I'm not sure what the barrier was or is, but it felt real. My whole body was tingling with a sort of electrical current. But it dissipated. Maybe I switched it off? And this emptiness rushed in."

"What do you mean by emptiness?" Althea's voice was low and soft.

I looked at her for a moment. "I can't find the words to describe it."

"Is it a sense of loss?"

"Not really. It's more like a sense of detachment. Avoidance. It's more of a familiar feeling of ignoring this thing, object, or mass. Like, I know there's this object in the closet. I know that I hid it in there, way in the back corner, but I don't want to look at it or acknowledge it. I'm saving it. I don't want to throw it away, because I know how important it is and someday I'll want to take it out and look at it. But the more I ignore it, the less impact it has. And somewhere in my head, I keep telling myself that someday it'll lose all its effects on me."

"What does this object look like?"

"I can't tell you. It's constantly morphing into different shapes and forms, trying to confuse me. It tries to get my attention when I am tired, worn out, or sick."

"Does it have color?"

Was she trying to get me to look at it? "I don't know."

"If this object had a color, what would it be?"

"I don't know."

"Just think about it for a moment."

I quickly responded. "I don't want to."

"Why not?

"Because it scares me." My face was on fire. "Don't make me do this. I don't want to look at it or acknowledge it. Not right now."

Althea leaned back in her chair and inhaled deeply. "Okay. Let's move away from thinking about the object. Do you have any pictures from college?"

My hands shook as they clutched the pillow's corners crushed against my chest. I gently placed the pillow on my lap and rummaged through the pile of pictures next to me. My mind flashed with fleeting images, slow at first and then sped up into a strobe effect.

Dr. Schultz standing at the sink at the motel bathroom.

Coach Trevor saying, "It's like a lollipop."

A blinding flash of light.

Washcloth.

A glass of wine.

Naked torso.

Flash of light.

Water.

Pain.

Fear.

Flash.

Ejaculation.

A blade of grass.

Flash.

"David, is everything all right?" Althea's voice rescued me from a downward spiral.

"Yes." I glanced at the picture I held in my hand. "Here's one." I held it out to her.

"Can you describe it for me?" Althea's eyes were filled with encouragement.

The colored images burnt on the photo paper were aged with time. I reluctantly spoke. "This picture appears to have been taken on the day the students moved in the dorms, a couple of days before classes started. The boy, me, is struggling with a huge taped box resting on his thighs, while Kimo and Sue are watching and laughing."

"Who are Kimo and Sue?"

"They were my dorm-mates. Kimo was my roommate and Sue was my best friend." I saw the dorm in the background and the path leading to Aldrich Park.

"Tell me about the boy in the picture."

"He seems in good spirits. He managed to survive high school, and this is a new beginning. He appears hopeful and filled with possibilities. He's fit, wearing a tight black T-shirt, jeans, and a bandana tied around his head with blond bangs draped over it. He's enjoying Kimo and Sue's company as they laugh at him struggling with this box."

"So, you get a sense that this boy has a new outlook on life?"

"I'd say that. Yes."

"What do you think enabled this change from the pictures that were taken during high school?"

I studied the picture more. Kimo towered over me and placed his huge hand on my head and his other one on Sue's head. She was leaning into Kimo's chest, with her head against his shoulder. They were paired, and I'm a bit off to the side. I was the third wheel, so to speak. But that didn't bother me. I had such a joyful smile from laughing and my eyes were dancing.

"I'm not totally sure what the reason or reasons are that the boy in the picture has a sense of change. He seems happy. Maybe it's the fact that he's in a new place, with new friends, and he can pretend the past isn't a factor. He can create a new identity. He's happy and I miss his joyfulness."

"I want you to hold on to that feeling and remember it. When you're ready, I want you to look at a picture that was taken after the incident with the grad student."

I froze. I didn't want to move. I wanted to remain in the picture with the happy boy and relish in his desire to recreate himself. I reluctantly laid the picture on the pillow resting on my lap and shuffled through the pile of pictures on the cushion beside me. I discovered one that was facing down. I instinctively knew this was the one I needed to see. As I lifted the picture and turned it to view, my breath rushed out of my lungs, and my chest collapsed.

"What do you see?" asked Althea.

"The boy with his shirt unbuttoned and exposing the claw marks on his chest. There are dark circles weighing heavily under each eye. There's a darkness looming around the boy." My voice cracked. "He's broken."

"What do you mean by 'he's broken?'"

"His eyes have a distant expression, like everything was taken away from him."

Althea nodded. "Do you remember when this picture was taken?"

I nodded.

"Is it painful to remember?"

I shook my head.

"Why is that?"

"I can't feel anything about it."

"How so?"

"It's like it's not me. It's someone else."

"But it is you, isn't it?"

I slowly nodded.

"What is it about this picture that stands out?"

The picture was a bit grainy, and not very well thought out. "I took this picture myself, before Sue took me to the medical center."

U.C.I. MESA VERDE DORM, 1982

Sue went to get her keys, and I decided to go back to my room to get something. But when I got to the room, I couldn't remember what it was that I wanted.

As I stopped and looked in the mirror, a stranger stared back at me. I noticed his eyes and the blank expression. The spark for life was gone, and all that was left was a shell of a young man I thought I knew. But I didn't know this reflection. He was as foreign to me as passing someone at the airport—he looked like someone I knew from afar, maybe because of his hair color, or the way he walked, or how he smiled; but as we neared, the realization revealed him as a complete stranger. The closer we got, the more I saw cracks in this perfect veneer, broken chips in his porcelain façade, and damaged darkness behind his zombie-like eyes. He appeared floating through space and time, existing without rhyme or reason and stuck in a past that wrapped heavy tentacles around his shoulder, weighing him down and not allowing him to live. I'd never want to know this person.

Maybe I chose not to recognize the image locking eyes with me, because that would mean that I would have to accept his baggage. I wasn't ready for that. I wasn't ready for the fragmented parts that collectively made up this stranger's persona, like a jigsaw puzzle where the pieces were forced to fit, and the completed image didn't exactly match the picture on the box cover. And yet, with all the intuition not to connect with the stranger, a stronger truth forced me to recognize the truth.

Somewhere and somehow, we were one and the same.

The stranger in the mirror tried reaching out to me, pleading for me to acknowledge our connection. He guided my vision down to the open shirt and the claw marks transcending down his chest and stomach. The wounds were irregular, jagged, purple with yellowing edges, and caked with dried blood. I reached out and ran my fingertips along the image's wounds. All at once, the deep abrasions stung and burned, reminding me that the reflection and I were one.

I grabbed the camera sitting on the dresser next to the mirror and the flash blinded me as it refracted off the mirror's reflective glass and filled the entire room. I kept snapping photos, causing a strobe light effect with the evenly spaced flashes.

"David?" someone said as they entered the room.

My eyes were filled with black spots from the flashes and I couldn't make out who was talking. I kept snapping pictures.

"What are you doing?" the voice calmly asked.

I pressed to take another picture, and nothing happened. I tried again. Nothing.

The camera was removed from my hand. "You're out of film."

"Sue?"

"Yes, David, it's me."

"When's the next full moon?" I randomly asked.

"What are you talking about?" Sue stepped into the mirror's reflection with me.

"Look. It looks like a werewolf attack." I forced a chuckle. "The beast clearly marked its prey. So, when's the next full moon?"

"Not for another two weeks." Sue tried to lighten the moment.

"I wonder if it'll be painful to shapeshift into a lycanthrope."

"You won't be alone." Sue's brown eyes were filled with care.

"You might have to chain me up in the utility closet."

"If that is what I have to do."

The thought was so ludicrous that I started to laugh. Sue joined in.

"Now no one will ever want me." My laughter turned to tears.

"I'll always want you." She guided my head to her shoulder. "Let's go, before it gets too late." She led me out of the room.

DR. ALTHEA WARNER'S OFFICE— DAYTON, OHIO, 2018

"What's the picture of?" Althea slowly asked.

My jaws clinched, and my eyes burned. My upper lip twitched. I turned the picture for Althea to see. "It's a picture of a boy with claw marks down his chest." I forced the lump from my throat.

"You can't really see, but his right cheek is bruised from where his face was forced against the tile flooring. And there's the hidden damage from the internal intrusion."

Althea took the picture and gasped as she looked at it.

"I forgot that I took the picture until I got the roll of film printed. When I picked up the prints, the salesman said he thought it was the best Halloween costume and the claw marks were realistic." I forced a smile. "But there's something else in the picture that seems invisible. I mean there is evidence of the physical abuse with the claw marks and bruises, but there's something else that can't be seen."

Althea placed the photo in her lap and looked at me. "What do you mean?"

"That boy in the picture is broken." I said, with as much detachment as I could muster.

"Broken? How so?" Althea asked.

"Inside. Where it's invisible." I scooted to the edge of the couch and pointed to the picture. "That boy is broken inside." I sounded clinical and unattached. "For some reason, that boy survived the constant stream of professional men and his coach taking pieces from him. Because every time one of those moments occurred, that boy lost a piece of himself. But for some reason, this grad student did something more damaging. So much so that it was like the straw that broke the camel's back and it broke that boy. That boy in that picture was never going to be the same again. Look at his eyes; they're completely black and blank."

Althea held out her hand. "Pass me all the pictures and the plastic bag."

Without thinking, I followed the instructions.

She carefully placed the pictures back into the bag and positioned it on her clipboard. She grabbed a box of Kleenex and handed them to me. She spoke with such care and kindness. "You did incredible today. What you did takes so much courage and guts. Thank you. I want to thank you for trusting me and this process." She paused for a moment. "I want you to do something for me for next week. I want you to write a letter to the boy in the last picture. I want you to tell him how brave and strong he is, because if it wasn't for his bravery and strength, the adult you wouldn't be sitting here with me today. Tell him how resourceful he was to be able to handle the unconceivable, unwarranted, and unnecessary abuse he endured. Tell him to forgive himself and that it's not his fault what happened." Althea's eyed filled and her voice shook. "But most of all, tell him that you love him, miss him, and need him with you. Reach out to this scared and shameful boy, and fill him with the love you have been hiding from him. Tell him how beautiful he is, then look into a mirror and tell yourself."

"I'll try."

"Can you do more than try?" She challenged me.

I smirked and nodded. I extended my hand to retrieve the plastic bag of pictures.

"I'm going to hold on to these for a little bit, if you don't mind."

"Why?" I was shocked that I asked.

"I don't want you to look at them while you write your letter. I think it's best that we keep these out of sight for a time."

I nodded and sunk back into the couch.

"We have some more time. Tell me about a time when you were happy."

KINGS ISLAND AMUSEMENT PARK, 1982

"Where do you want to go first?" I asked Magdalyn as we pushed through the turnstile gates to gain entrance into the amusement park.

As the crowds dispersed in different directions along International Street, the Royal Fountain majestically greeted us. The animated waterworks with dancing geysers timed to the music spewed water high into the air, expanded longer than a football field, and ended at the base of an Eiffel Tower replica.

"I want to see all the shows," Magdalyn excitedly said.

"Don't you want to ride any rides?"

"Of course, but we have all day. Gee, we have all summer. I really love to see the shows, and since it's going to be hot, it'll be nice to get out of the sun." Her excitement emitted from her as her eyes darted from side to side.

"Lead the way."

She grabbed my hand and started off down the brick walkway along the side of the fountain. We sped past colorfully decorated shops and restaurants with German, French, Italian, Swiss, and American accents. Sugary confection filled the air as we passed the sweet shop. The gift shops peddled every type of tchotchkes, from plastic rings, snow globes of the Eiffel Tower, stuffed animals of every size and shape, and more.

We took a moment to stop in front of Festhaus with "Ein Prosit, Ein Prosit, der Gemütlichkeit" posted under the huge clock. A trumpet tooted, and glockenspiel characters emerged from swinging doors to the German music.

We were off again, almost colliding with a little girl eating a large pink cotton candy on a stick.

"Let's eat first," Magdalyn said as she pulled me through the maze of people and outside tables. "By that time, the Country Show should be ready to start."

I abruptly stopped. "Why do you want to see the Country Show?"

"You'll see. Come on." She tugged on my arm.

"I thought you wanted to go on *The Racer* or *The Beast*?"

Magdalyn's eyes grew, and she stomped her foot. "I do, but we've all summer to ride rides. Are you coming or not? I've an agenda today, and I've it all planned out."

I was amused by my nine-year-old sister's intentions. "By all means, lead the way."

She skirted around the elaborate bronze statue of Don Quixote and Sancho Panza that stood in front of the Spanish Shop to bypass people moving at a slower pace. We migrated around tables, benches, trash cans, and people gawking at the fountain. Finally, she came to a halt in front of a yellow façade and an arched entrance under the famous red and green sign for LaRosa's Pizzeria.

"Tada!" she announced and lifted her hands into the air.

"This is what you want for lunch?"

"Duh. It's the best pizza, and besides the Country Show is right over there." She pointed to an outdoor theatre that was to the right of the Eiffel Tower. "We can eat here and then get in line to get my favorite seats for the show."

"You've already seen the show?" I asked, not understanding.

"Of course. How else would I know it's a show I want to see again?"

The aroma of pizzas' herbs, tomato sauce, and yeast filled my head.

"And look, there's not a huge line yet. This is perfect." She guided me under the archway and zig-zagged through the marked maze to the counter. Huge pizza pies of pepperoni and cheese sizzled behind the glass with the worker dressed up in old fashioned Italian garb of a red and white shirt with a red kerchief tied around her neck.

"Alright, alright. How many slices do you want?" I asked.

Magdalyn held up two fingers for. "Two slices of pepperoni, please."

The worker with the nametag of "Sissy" smiled. "With pleasure." She looked at me.

"I'll take two cheese slices, please. And could we get a small box?"

"Of course," Sissy cheerfully responded. "There are sodas at the end of the counter, right before the register." She handed over the paper plates, with the huge slices and cheese dripping off the ends.

Magdalyn took both plates and called over her shoulder. "Why don't you get two Diet Cokes and pay, and I'll grab a table."

"Sounds like a plan."

By the time I got to the selected table, Magdalyn had consumed one slice and was pulling the pepperoni off the second while staring off at the growing crowd flowing past the restaurant.

"A penny for your thoughts." I sat down next to her and wondered if my stomach would accept the pizza.

"What?" Her huge green eyes looked worried.

"What are you thinking about?"

"Not much." She pulled the last pepperoni from the pizza and placed it with the other discarded ones. She took a napkin and pressed it on the top of the pizza to soak up the grease.

"If you didn't want the pepperoni, you can have my cheese slices."

"Oh, no. I wanted them. But I have a ritual," she said as she removed the soaked, filled napkin and pressed a new one against the pizza, which didn't change colors as dramatically.

"A ritual?" I sipped the Diet Coke.

"First, I remove the pepperoni and then soak up as much grease as I can. Once that's completed, I then eat the pizza, saving the pepperoni for last."

"Sounds like a plan." I suddenly wasn't hungry.

"You should do this." She handed me some napkins. "It'll be better for your stomach."

I took the napkins and placed one on my pizza slice; it immediately almost disappeared from soaking up the grease.

"You'll thank me later that you didn't consume all that grease." Her attention was pulled outside the restaurant.

I transferred the paper plate with pizza slices into the box and closed the lid. The Diet Coke would have to do for now. I didn't want to chance upsetting my stomach.

Magdalyn reached for the pepperoni and continued to stare off.

"Maggie, is everything all right?"

"What?"

"There seems to be something on your mind."

"Oh, I'm sorry. I was wondering if everything's going to work out how I planned it." She took a long swig of Diet Coke. "How long are you planning on staying home?"

Sometimes talking with my nine-year-old sister was like talking to a forty-five-year-old woman. "I'm not sure. Why?"

She placed the drink back on the table, took a deep breath, and contemplated. "I don't want you to go back."

"Go back where?"

"Back there. You know where I'm talking about. Don't make me say it." Her voice became defiant, and her face flushed red. "Look at you. It makes me so crazy that no one is allowed to talk about it." She curled her hands into a fist and banged the table. "I'm so angry."

I gently placed my hand on top of her fists to keep her from banging the table again.

She looked at me with hurt in her eyes. "They almost killed you. It's not healthy for you out there. They don't care about you, and they only want to use you."

"Who are you talking about?"

"Those people." Her hands escaped from under mine, and she flitted them near her piggy tails. "Those monsters out there." She covered her face in frustration as if she identified the people then everything would come true.

I gently pulled her hands from her face. "Why do you say that?"

"Look at you. You're a walking skeleton."

I could only nod in agreement.

"You're too sensitive. And you take everything to heart. You want everyone to be happy, and you'll go out of your way to make that happen." She sat back and crossed her arms.

"I didn't realize I was such a wimp."

"I didn't say that. I said that you're too sensitive. There's a difference."

"Well, what's the difference?"

She leaned into the table and pointed at me. "First of all, being too sensitive isn't a negative thing. It means you feel everything everyone else feels. And you want to make sure they're okay. But sometimes you forget to take care of yourself. Taking care of others takes a toll on you. You make yourself sick. Your body's trying to get your attention to tell you to slow down and take time for you."

A couple of teenage girls came into the restaurant and looked at us and started whispering.

Maggie turned to see where I was looking and then turned back in her seat. "Don't mind them."

"Do you know them?"

The two continued staring, whispering, and laughing.

"They're groupies and go to all the shows," she explained as she popped another pepperoni into her mouth.

"Like what we're going to be today?" I asked.

"But we're different."

"How so?"

"I'm actually friends with some of the performers."

When I looked back, the two teenage girls stood near our table.

"Excuse me. We've a bet going on. Are you in shows?" asked the redhead with freckles dancing across the bridge of her nose and cheeks.

"Are you asking me?" I was confused.

"You're Calvin from the Country Show, aren't you?" stuttered the blonde girl with braces.

"No, he's not Calvin. But he's on *General Hospital*," Magdalyn dryly said and forced a condescending smile.

"The soap opera?" asked the blonde.

"The one and only." Magdalyn turned away from them.

"You look just like Calvin," responded the redhead.

"But he's not. I know, he's my brother." Magdalyn expressed limited patience.

"Calvin's your brother. You're so lucky." Both girls squealed and rushed to the counter to place their order.

"What was that all about?" I asked.

"You'll see."

"Okay, what's really going on? Why all the mystery?"

"All right. I'll tell you when we get our seats for the show. It's starting soon and we have to go." She stood up and threw her empty plate into the trashcan and waited for me by the door.

For some reason, I was slower at getting up. I had to gather the pizza box and my soda. As I got to the exit, Magdalyn nervously hopped from foot to foot. She grabbed my elbow and led me across the pavement to the outdoor theatre's entrance.

Country music blared from the speakers as we walked up the ramp that leveled off before a decline led to aluminum benches for the audience. Magdalyn rushed to the fourth row in the middle aisle and triumphantly sat down.

She took the pizza box and soda from my hands and placed them under the bench and instructed, "You'll need your hands to clap."

A voice announced, "Ladies and gentlemen, on behalf of King's Island, Taft Productions, and the International Showplace, it's with great pleasure to welcome you to our show. Clap along with the heartwarming, down-home sounds of country music at its finest. Join our cast of talented entertainers as they present country music's greatest hits from the past and present. Please keep the aisles clear, and enjoy *Sweet Country Music*."

The music swelled, and one by one, cast members entered from different parts of the theatre and made their way to the stage. The females wore white blouses with fringe and brightly colored spandex pants that matched the color of their male partners, which wore monochromatic matching jeans and cowboy shirts with white fringe. All the performers had cowboy boots and white cowboy hats and sang their rendition of *Thank God I'm a Country Boy*.

As soon as I saw the male singer in all yellow, I was amazed. I thought I was looking into a mirror. And when he saw me, he stopped singing for a moment. It seemed like the world halted and we were frozen in time, looking at each other. The only thing I could hear was my breath. The moment was broken when his partner slipped her arm in his and Do-Si-Do-ed him in a circle to hit their final pose.

The audience clapped, whistled, and hollered.

The male in orange stepped forward as the others gathered in a huddle behind him. "Howdy, folks, and welcome home. This is *Sweet Country Music*. I'm Steve and these are my friends. We're so tickled that you decided to join us and celebrate the best that country music has to offer. Throughout the show, you'll meet my friends and get to know them a little better. But let's start with that famous brother/sister duo, Lucy and Calvin."

The music transitioned into a Donnie and Marie Osmond hit.

Lucy stepped out from the other performers and walked downstage. "I'm a little bit country."

"And I'm a little bit rock-n-roll," sang the male performer dressed in yellow, waved to Magdalyn, and joined Lucy.

"That's Calvin," Magdalyn gleefully shouted.

"I'm a little bit of Memphis and Nashville." Lucy hit a pose.

"With a little bit of Motown in my soul." Calvin hit the same pose.

The music turned into a two-step, Lucy and Calvin performed a dance break.

The rest of the show was a blur, and before I knew it, the cast struck their final pose. The audience was on their feet, clapping and cheering. The cast lined up, bowed, and waved to the audience.

Calvin looked at Madgalyn and said into his microphone, "Maddie, meet me." He pointed to the cast entrance.

Madgalyn shouted back, "Will do."

I looked at her.

"I told you I was friends with some of the cast members. Come on, let's go before everyone rushes over there."

As I grabbed the pizza box and drink, she took my elbow and led me back the way we came, dodging people to get to the exit first. We arched around and came to a wooden fence with a sign that said "Cast Members Only" in blue lettering, just as the performers were coming out. Magdalyn greeted everyone by their first names and introduced me as her brother. Finally, Calvin came out and gave Magdalyn a hug and swung her around in a circle.

"I'm so glad you came today." Calvin put Magdalyn back on her feet. "I needed to see your smiling face."

Magdalyn laughed. "Calvin, this is my brother I told you about."

Calvin looked at me, and his hypnotic blue eyes filled me with a calm that I had forgotten. We looked at other for a long time without saying a word.

"He's home for the summer. He's the one on *General Hospital*," Magdalyn said, with pride.

Calvin offered his hand.

His palm kissed mine and sent a rush of warmth up my arm and caused my heart to swell.

Calvin looked at our clasped hands, back into my eyes, and smiled. He must have felt the warmth, too. "It's a pleasure. Maddy has told me all about you. At first, I thought she was making you up. But now, I see she was downplaying you."

His charm captivated me.

"See, I told you that you two are look-a-likes," Magdalyn said.

"He's definitely my doppelganger," joked Calvin.

"A what?" I finally found the words to say.

Calvin smiled. "A doppelganger is German for 'double walker,' which is someone that resembles another person not only in looks but in how they walk, talk, act, and so on."

"But I don't speak German," I embarrassingly said.

"Neither do I. I just pick things up here and there," Calvin said.

"Are you two twins?" said the redheaded girl with freckles from the restaurant.

"Seriously?" asked Magdalyn.

Without taking his eyes off me, Calvin said, "No, we're not twins, but brothers."

"I told you," said the blonde girl with braces.

The redheaded girl stared in awe and said to Magdalyn, "You're so lucky."

"Sophia and Agnes, let's go," a mother pushing a stroller called. The two girls ran off to meet her. Obviously, they told the mother about Calvin and me because she soon nodded and waved.

Calvin waved back. "So, what are you two planning on doing today?" he asked.

"You'll have to ask my tour guide. She has everything planned out for us today," I said, with some sarcasm.

"I do have it all planned out," Magdalyn proudly reported. "We're going to ride some rides, maybe see some other shows. Do you want to come with us?"

Calvin quickly answered, "Yes. I'm the swing today, and that means all I must do is report back here ten minutes before each show to make sure no one has gotten sick or broke a foot or whatever, but the rest of the time is mine. Have you eaten? I'm starving."

I was filled with excitement and confusion. Did Magdalyn orchestrate this as well?

"We just had La Rosa's," Magdalyn shared.

"I love La Rosia's," Calvin responded.

"We have leftovers. Are you interested?" The words flew out of my mouth as I held up the box.

"Are you sure? I don't want to take your food," Calvin said.

I watched as his lips formed the words, and the sound that came out of his mouth was music and placed me in a mesmerized trance. I uttered, "Please be our guest."

"Thank you." He flipped the lid up, grabbed a slice, and took a bite. "This is perfect." He glanced at his watch. "We've an hour before I have to report. What do you want to ride first?"

Magdalyn jumped with excitement. "*The Beast,* of course."

"Will we have enough time?" I asked with trepidation.

"Of course," Calvin said between bites. "One of the perks of doing shows, I get to go to the front of the line with my guest. Let's go." He licked his fingers and handed me the box back with the remaining slice. "Thanks again." He took a hold of Magdaglyn's hand. "Let's show your brother how to have a good time."

"He needs a good time," Magdalyn said.

And they were off. I had to hurry to keep up.

The day was filled with rushing to different rides and shows, but always returning to the outdoor theatre so Calvin could check in.

Calvin pushed through the gate, and stated, "I'm a free man. That's the last show. Where to now?"

The Eiffel Tower's lights lit up the ashen sky.

Magdalyn quickly responded, "*The Enchanted Voyage.*"

Calvin smiled. "So be it."

The three of us climbed into the little boat via a turntable outside a large building that looked like a television set. Magdalyn sat in the middle. As we voyaged through the colorful world of Hanna-Barbera characters and six vignettes, *It's a Small World* piped through the speakers.

We floated through a colorful cave, celebrated a wedding in the Land of Little People, hoedowned with hillbillies, took a trip under the sea, ventured through a haunted house, and ended up at a big top circus. During the entire ride, Calvin rested his arm behind Madgalyn and ran his fingers through my hair. His touch was gentle but filled with electricity. The simple touch belonged to something that I had never felt before, tenderness. I didn't want the five-minute ride to end.

When the ride was over, we exited the boat and walked toward the Royal Fountain and the front gates.

Calvin stopped and said with disappointment, "Hey, I have to go through the employee entrance and that's all the way in the other direction."

Magdalyn exclaimed, "Today was the best, especially when we got wet on the log ride."

"I got most of it," Calvin said, with a laugh.

Magdalyn joined the laughter. "That's true, you were soaked."

"Okay, give me a hug so I can send you home." Calvin opened his arms for Magdalyn to walk into. He tightly enveloped her.

Magdalyn perched up on her toes and kissed Calvin's cheek.

"What was that for?" Calvin asked as his face blushed.

"For you spending the day with us and showing my brother how to have a good time."

"It was my pleasure." He released Magdalyn from his embrace. "When will I see you again?"

"Maybe tomorrow?" Magdalyn shrugged. "We have season tickets."

I watched as this beautiful man interacted with Magdalyn and treated her with such respect and politeness. He didn't treat her like a child, but an equal.

The sky behind the Eiffel Tower lit up with bright explosions of red, white and blue fireworks. We ooed and ahhed as sky twinkled and sparkled. The short display indicated that the park was closed for the day.

Calvin turned me and held out his arms. "Your turn, get in here."

I hesitated. Not sure how to react.

"Come on," encouraged Calvin. "I'm a hugger."

"He won't bite," Magdalyn joked. "And he gives good hugs, too."

I laughed nervously.

"What are you waiting for?" Calvin shook his hands. "Don't leave me looking like a fool here."

I stepped into his embrace. His arms seemed to wrap around me with ease and eagerness. The way he enclosed the back of my neck with his hands and held me in place was intoxicating. The warmth of our chests pressing against each other was comforting. His scent ignited all my senses. His lips caressed my earlobe as he whispered, "I want to see you again. Soon."

DR. ALTHEA WARNER'S OFFICE— DAYTON, OHIO, 2018

"I brought you a gift." I rummaged through my satchel and retrieved a clear green bag with a dark green tree imprinted on the front. I handed the bag to Althea.

"What's this?"

"It's something that I thought you might like. It's hand lotion. It's all natural." My nerves overtook my speech, and everything that I practice saying in the car was no longer viable.

"Where's it from?"

"Arbonne," I stammered.

"I've heard of them. It's expensive products if I remember." She opened the bag and took out the white box with green labeling.

"Well, if you look at the retail price, I can see that you think that way. But there are ways to get discounts, and the products last longer than over-the-counter items, because they are natural and concentrated. The hand cream doesn't have any petroleum oils most hand creams have and is paraben-free. You only need a little and it goes a long way," I explained as my palms became clammy.

"Are you selling this?"

"It's an online company, and yes, I'm thinking about becoming an independent consultant."

"What made you want to do this?"

"I don't know how long I can teach, and I wanted something that I could do on my own and possibly make money doing it." The room's temperature rose.

She unscrewed the lid and removed the protective seal and sniffed it. "I like the smell. It's not so perfumey." She squeezed a small dab on the back of her hand, replaced the lid, and set the tube on the side table with the discarded box. She rubbed the cream in. "It's really smooth, and not oily. I like this. I really like it." She smelled her hands again. "Thank you, but you know you don't have to bring me gifts."

"I know, but I thought you might like it, and if you know anyone who may be interested."

"I'll be sure to share. Do you have a catalogue?"

"Yes." I pulled one out of my satchel and gave it to her.

"Good. I'll look at it and then put it on the waiting room table. Maybe we can get you some sales."

She placed the catalogue on the floor and lifted my journal. "I really love the smell of this hand cream."

I smiled. "I thought you would."

Althea's eyes narrowed as she looked over the edge of her bifocals. "Last time you were here, we looked at pictures. How have you been feeling since?"

"It's been strange. I feel a sense of loss, as if a part of me is still missing." I crossed my legs and collapsed my torso.

She handed the journal back to me. "I want you to hold this today. You can refer to it if you need to. But I want you to have it during our session."

I nodded, even though I wasn't following where she was taking this.

She leaned back in the chair and placed her hands on her lap. "I want you to do all the talking today. Think of it as a stream of consciousness or free-flow writing. But I want you to use your words. Don't try to edit your ideas or judge yourself. Try not to think too much, and just allow the words to flow out. Can you do that for me today?"

The journal weighed a ton and I placed it on the cushion beside me.

"I want you to put the journal on your lap and keep at least one hand on it during this exercise," Althea instructed.

"Okay." I reluctantly positioned the leather journal on my lap and placed both hands on it.

Althea smiled. "Good. Are you ready?"

I nodded.

She took a deep breath. "What are you so afraid of?"

The words slapped me across the face.

"Don't think. Just start speaking." She reminded me.

"What am I afraid of?" My mind raced through my jumbled thoughts to try and find the perfect answer.

"Stop thinking." Althea's voice was stern.

"I'm afraid of being average." I was shocked with the words that emerged. "Of not being special. Being mediocre." I stopped the flow and looked at Althea for a reaction. None came. Her expression was neutral and unaffected.

I continued, with reserve. "I never finish things the way I want before I get this strong urge to run away. I feel like I never complete or accomplish the goal." I forced myself to breathe. "By not finishing, I don't have to experience failure or success. I just am. I exist. I'm someone always dreaming." The words started to flow without hesitation. "I carry this burden—this suffering artist ideology character of doom. I feel that I must suffer like Montgomery Clift. And I feared that I was going to have to die young like James Dean, if I wanted to matter or be remembered.

"I have specks or clear moments of happiness or what I think are moments of pure joy—like when I walk the puppies or when I'm writing with no pressure of deadlines. But these are rare moments, and they slip in and surprise me and then slip away as fast as they come. Sometimes I discover that I'm smiling, and my body has released all the tension that I constantly place on it. Sometimes, in these short-lived moments, I can see that I have everything that I ever needed surrounding me. But these freeing moments are fleeting and far apart." I pushed my hands through my hair and rested my head on the back of the couch. "What's more frustrating is I can't seem to stop placing this added pressure on myself. I mean, I know I shouldn't stress or become anxious, but sometimes I can't stop the flow of depression from taking hold, no matter what I try."

"Keep a hand on the journal," Althea reminded me with a soft and kind voice.

I looked at her. Her smile encouraged me, and I replaced my right hand on the journal.

"I always wanted to be someone else, different, special. I never wanted to be someone who was sexually exposed or exploited at such an early age. But that's what I am. I thought I could handle it and it wasn't a big thing. Looking back, no matter how much I thought I was able to handle everything, I couldn't. I kept pushing all the confusing feelings to the back of my mind and tried to make everything not a big deal. I managed the feelings the best I could. I managed poorly. By hiding the feelings, I started hiding parts of my true self. I lost myself little by little in order to protect what little innocence I had left. So, I started to constantly run, never staying too long in one place—never getting to know others or let them know me. And losing touch with people who cared about me."

I paused to allow the reality of the moment and the words to sink into my brain.

"If I allowed anyone to see the cracked surface, I would have to recognize it myself, and I wasn't strong enough to do that. Although I fooled myself that I was spending quality time rather than quantity time, I was constantly on the run. If I ran fast enough, I appeared confident and people saw me how I wanted them to see me or how I thought they wanted to see me. I was afraid that if they really saw me, really got to know the true me, they would think I was meek, weak, phony, an imposter, and a wimpy kid."

I paused again.

"But what I desired more than anything was to be seen, really seen and the flaws wouldn't matter. I wanted to be loved for who I was, not for what I was pretending to be. I thought I could achieve that with Calvin."

"Achieve what?" Althea quietly asked.

"I really don't know. I became obsessed with constantly reinventing myself. I thought I could distance myself from the past or push it far enough away it would appear as if it never happened. And if it never happened, then I could present myself with a clean slate. On the one hand, I wanted to matter so much to someone and the past would be obsolete. I could push this debilitating fear away far enough to have the space to love someone and to be loved, without the shadows of the doctors, lawyers, coaches, and grad student. Somehow, I could know what it was like for a knight in shining armor to love, respect, and honor me as I loved, respected and honored him. Calvin didn't really know me or my past. All he saw was that I worked professionally as an actor in Los Angeles." I stopped and adjusted my position on the couch, making sure that I kept one hand on the journal. "All I ever wanted was to feel something inside."

"Keep going. Don't stop." Althea looked intensely at me.

"I feel like I'm all over the place," I confessed.

"That's completely acceptable. Please continue, and don't judge yourself," Althea encouraged.

I sighed heavily.

"Stop judging."

I nodded. "As I went through my diving career and the experiences with the professionals, I felt myself being torn apart little by little. Every time I gave myself over to one of them, I gave away a piece of my soul as well. In return, I received numbness.

"Looking back today, I can see evidence of my soul dying, hardening, and becoming cold. When we looked at the pictures the last time I was here, pictures of me before and after the professional men, I noticed the glimmer leaving my eyes. I saw that I was becoming a stranger to myself and someone that I no longer identified with or recognized. Of course, I didn't notice that then I was too busy trying to appear normal and cope with the secrets that were growing inside. The self-hatred and shame became a secret and ugly demon that was overtaking me. But there was still this hope, or optimism that one day I could shed this past if I could get physically far enough away.

"But what I quickly learned was that the choices were no longer mine. Choices were made for me. I wasn't allowed to make any choices. If I wanted to be the best diver that I could be, there was a price to be paid. The cost was much larger than I could imagine at that age. Every time a doctor, lawyer, dentist, accountant, or whoever touched me and expected me to do they wanted, it separated me further from my true self. The transaction of money or gifts or whatever you want to call them became meaningless—but expected.

"What came along with this was the belief that God created me for this and that this was the only means for me to make a living. This was all that I was good for. Even when I made the money from the soap opera and movie of the week—they were mere moments or mistakes. I believed that I won in Norway by a mere accident. It was never supposed to happen. Something in the scheme of the universe messed up, and I somehow managed to break through the fate I was given, for that fleeting moment. I was never able to understand why I could never recreate a victory like that ever again. But maybe, just maybe I exhausted myself enough to allow something good like winning the gold medal to happen.

"Somehow, the good fairy appeared again when I discovered acting—but there was another price to pay. To become effective at the craft, I had to learn how to feel, all over again, something that I tried to avoid, and it scared me. I had to find a way to place the past in a specific place deep inside, so that I could bypass it in order to appear that I was able to feel, like reconfiguring a computer's circuit board so I could display emotions without tapping into the emotions of the past. Somehow, I managed to figure it out just enough in order to taste success again with the movie of the week, the play, *General Hospital,* and Calvin. But as easy as these things came to me, bad things always seemed to follow." I grabbed my water bottle and took a long swing. I wasn't sure if I truly needed the liquid or if I was running away from this moment.

"You are doing great. Please continue," Althea said.

I looked at Althea as if she had lost her mind. "I'm done."

"No, you aren't." She was steadfast.

"I don't want to do this anymore."

"Why?" she challenged.

"Because.." I paused. "I'm scared."

"Of what?"

"I'm not sure."

"Okay. Try this. Let's just sit here and see if anything else comes up."

"What if nothing does?"

"Then nothing does. But you must be honest about it. I don't want you to shut down and edit yourself. So, just sit there quietly, and see if anything else comes up."

My eyes darted around the room as the sound of the clock's ticking loudly echoed. I tried to force all thoughts away, but they kept coming.

"Say what's on your mind."

As I sat there, the thoughts became more intense, and the words wanted to come out. Before I knew it, I couldn't stop them. "What the grad student did was something that I've not been able to voice. Words always failed me. By that time, I knew I was disengaging from my physical body. I believed that I was only good enough to be a vessel for other people to use, abuse, and get off on." I shook my head. "Please believe me, I never saw myself as beautiful or handsome or attractive. I saw myself as average looking at best. I never understood what people saw when they looked at my outer appearance. I convinced myself they only recognized that I was an easy mark, as if there was some invisible indicator or symbol that informed them that they could do whatever they wanted with me. I was not beautiful, because I didn't feel that way inside.

"I knew I had an okay body, but nothing more than average. I was too skinny. There were others with far better bodies than mine. So, I'd get confused when men said that I was beautiful. I never got that. All I could comprehend was they only thought I was an easy target and had a big dick. I hated my body.

"But what the grad student did accomplish was to completely break me. I was broken after that night. That's the only way I can describe it. It's the first time I felt nothing, and I wanted to die. I no longer cared about anything or anybody. The numbness took over me, and I no longer could feel anything. As he thrusted harder and harder against my backside and forced my face against the tiles pooled with water, I could only think about counting the bubbles. I no longer felt the pain of him tearing my insides—I felt nothing. I thought I'd rather die right then and there than live the rest of my life as his victim. He broke me. And I knew from that moment forward he'd always be lurking in my mind and dictating the way I'd respond to sex, intimacy, and relationships. He physically and mentally marked me as his prey. He not only broke me, but owned me." I paused. "I became confused that this single person broke me, even after all the professional men passed me around. It was like when I was younger, I was more resilient, but as I got older, I became more rigid and inflexible."

I wiped my eyes with the back of my hand. "When I didn't qualify for the NCAA and Hal flew me home, I no longer felt like I had the right to be in my body. It was a curse. My body was a shell that somehow I had taken residency in for a while until I could find a better one. I was a stranger in my own body. I no longer connected with it. I hated it. I was ashamed of it. I couldn't look at it. I hid it every chance I got. It was a constant reminder that I was broken and it was a vessel for others to use." My body shook. "When I was home in Aulden, recovering, I couldn't look at my body. I weighed about one hundred and twenty-five pounds. I was a bag of bones, and I looked ghostly. As I recovered, I hid my body every chance I got. This body betrayed me, and I blamed it for all the things that transpired. And then I met Calvin. That summer, I wanted to feel again. I wanted to be in my body again. I wanted to feel what it was like to choose to share my body with someone, with someone I wanted and wanted me. But I didn't know how to do that."

CALVIN'S APARTMENT, CINCINNATI, OHIO, 1982

I trembled as tears ran down my cheeks.

Calvin placed his head on the pillow next to mine. "Are you okay?"

"Yes," I lied. I sensed the grad student watching from the shadows in the corner. I knew he wasn't physically there, but I was afraid to look. Ever since that night, he was always lurking and watching me.

"Why are you crying?"

"I don't know." Calvin's thick eyelashes accentuated his blue eyes. I felt the stubble on his jaw and chin and lightly touched his full lips. "I'm happy."

His smile formed dimples in both cheeks. "I'm glad I make you happy."

I brushed his dark blond hair from his forehead. "I'm sorry, I'm not that adventurous with sex."

"Do you hear me complaining? I'm not either. This is all new for me, too. We don't have to do anything you don't want to do."

"It's not that I don't want to do it. It's just, I don't...I don't know." I watched the early morning sneak in through the window and illuminate the darkened corner with bluish light, proving that the grad student was not there.

Calvin's face filled with concern. "You'd tell me if anything was wrong, wouldn't you?"

"Yes, of course." I lied again. "This is nice, being here like this."

"I dig it." He chuckled.

My fingers trailed down his neck, collarbone, and came to rest on the soft patch of brown curls between his tanned pecs. I was in awe that this attractive person liked me. *Could he be my knight in shining armor?*

I imagined myself standing by the silo, as fog surrounded me, making it difficult to see. A horse's whinny and sounds of hoofs against the cold solid ground broke the silence. From the dense white mist emerged a magnificent white stallion and a knight. He smiled and said, "I've come to take you home." He offered his hand and pulled me up behind him. I wrapped my arms around his waist and rest my chin on his shoulder. He clicked his tongue twice and said, "Getty up." The horse sprung to a gallop and the fog engulfed us.

Calvin leaned up on his elbow and pulled me back to reality. He stared down at me.

"What?" I nervously laughed.

"God, you're so beautiful." He leaned in to kiss me, but I stopped him.

"Don't say that."

His brows furrowed. "Why not?"

"Because I'm not beautiful," I defensively said.

"But you are."

"No, I'm not."

Calvin sat up with his back against the headboard. "I don't know who hurt you or how they hurt you. But there's this sense that I get that it was bad. But I'm not that person."

I sat up next to him. "I know. I know that."

"So, what happened?"

263

"Nothing, really." I scrambled to find an excuse. "It's just that my agents told me that I couldn't be gay. It'd ruin my career if it ever got out. But I have all these feelings inside for you, and I'm not sure what to do with them."

"We're not doing anything wrong."

"I know."

"What we're feeling is natural. We can't deny it. At least I can't. I've never felt this way for someone, especially a man. This is all new to me as well. That's why we're being so discreet. I don't want everyone knowing our business."

"But your castmates suspect something. They must." I crossed my arms.

"Lucy knows. I confided in her. I was confused and I told her about you, and she said I had to follow my heart and see where this could go."

"Yeah, she threatened me, if I ever broke your heart, she'd make sure I was castrated."

Calvin laughed. "That's Lucy."

"I'd never do that. Break your heart."

"I hope not." He smiled and flashed his perfect white teeth. "But you seem to be holding something back."

"It's just fear."

"Let's be scared together."

"Okay."

"Good." Calvin got on his knees and straddled my legs and embraced me.

I felt safe and protected with him.

"When are you going back to L.A.?" He sat on my legs, and I caressed the soft golden fur on his thighs.

"I'm not sure. I may not go back."

"What do you mean?"

"I don't know if there's a reason for me to go back right now."

"What about *General Hospital?*"

"I only have to call Skitch when I'm ready."

Calvin's fingertips traced my chest and down my stomach, the same path that the claw marks once inhabited. I prayed that he couldn't notice any remnants of them or pick up any essence of the grad student. "Your skin's so smooth."

"Like a girl's, I know." I couldn't hide the embarrassment.

"No, I like it. It's like porcelain."

"I always wanted to have hair on my legs and chest, like you," I said.

He smiled. "You like that?"

I grinned sheepishly.

Calvin leaned back and ran his hands over the light brown hair on his chest, the trail of hair below his navel, through the public hair and the soft curls on his thighs. "Let me tell you, it gets so hot in the summer. And I have to shave my face every day." He caressed my chin. "Do you ever have to shave?"

I pushed his hand away and defiantly stated, "I shave."

"Yeah?" He cupped my jawbone with both hands. "When, once a year?"

"No!" I tried to squirm out from under him.

He pinned my shoulders down and inched closer to my face. "I like it. It's what makes you so irresistible."

"And I like you with your scruffy chin."

"Does it scratch?" He ran his chin against my cheek.

"Yes." I giggled. "In a good way."

Calvin's eyes grew serious, and he pressed his mouth against mine, long and hard. He pulled back and stared into my eyes. "I don't want this to end."

"Me either."

Sadness clouded his blue eyes. "Well, the show will be ending soon, and I'll have to go back to Chicago for school."

"Maybe I can stay and go to school myself?" I suggested.

"Why would you want to do that when you have L.A. to go back to?"

"Maybe there's something more important here than L.A."

"Like what?"

"Oh, I don't know." I placed my hand over his heart.

"You don't mean?"

I smiled, hoping he got my meaning.

"You'd do that for me?"

Again, I smirked. "I've scheduled an audition for Wright State University's Theatre Department in a couple of days."

"I couldn't ask you to give up your career."

"You're not. I'm choosing."

Calvin covered his open mouth. "Are you serious?"

I nodded.

"No one has ever done something like this for me. Oh, my God." Calvin rolled off my lap and flopped on the mattress, with his head sharing my pillow. "How would we get it to work?"

"Mom has been pushing Wright State, saying I should take a year and get stronger before going back to L.A. I could take acting there."

"And we could meet up over the weekends. I could come down here to see you perform, and you could come up to Chicago. It's only six hours away. We could have a secret rendezvous."

"I guess; if that's what you want."

"But what about L.A.?" His voice filled with concern.

I wondered if he was more concerned with my career or himself. "It'll still be there," I said, with confidence.

"And then I could move out there with you after I graduate. And we could live happily ever after."

"That would be fantastic."

He rolled on his side and looked straight into my eyes. "Let's do it. We can build a life together. We could adopt a couple of children and take them to Disney Land."

I never thought about children or trying to raise them. I never wanted to pass any residual residue on to them.

He wiped the corner of my eye with the tip of his finger and sweetly added, "Just like we have with you, me, and Maggie."

I looked at him.

"What?" he asked.

"Who are you?"

"I'm just a man, who really likes a beautiful man, and wants to spend the rest of his life with him."

"How do you know? We've only known each other for such a short time."

"I know a good thing when I see it," he confidently stated. He placed his hand on my chest. "Do you believe in soulmates?"

I placed my hand over his. "What do you mean?"

"You know, soulmates, when another person makes you whole. The person you've always been searching for."

"Yea, I guess."

"And when you find that soulmate, your life feels complete, and anything is possible." He rested his chin on my hand.

"Do you feel whole?" Nerves flooded my body.

Calvin's face became pensive. Then he nodded. "I do. You make me whole."

Fear replaced the nerves, and I fought not to push him off my chest and run away. I tried to keep my heart from racing. I contemplated how long I could keep my secret from him and how he would react to it.

"Are you all right with that?" he asked.

"Yes."

"Then why's you heart racing? I can feel it."

"It's excited."

"Why?" He smirked slyly.

"Why are you smiling?"

"Don't change the subject."

I looked at his blue eyes for a long time, mesmerized by the length of his eyelashes. "I'm not changing the subject."

"Then say it," he challenged me.

"Say what?"

"What you wanted to say."

"I don't know what you're talking about."

His smile grew. "You know you want to say it."

"Say what?" I giggled.

"You know."

"What?" I didn't want this moment to end, to disappear like everything else in my life. I took a long and deep inhale and slowly exhaled.

"Say it. You can do it." He encouraged me.

"I…I…" I froze. The words wouldn't emerge. I took another deep breath and held it. "You…"

"I what?"

"You complete me." I released my held breath.

DR. ALTHEA WARNER'S OFFICE— DAYTON, OHIO, 2018

"Tell me more about Calvin."

"He was everything I ever wanted, or thought I wanted. Maybe he was just what I needed at the time. He was gentle, caring, and never pressuring. He let me go at my own pace. But I guess in the end I was not enough, or I couldn't give enough."

"What makes you say that?"

"Well, that summer we spent all our free time alone together. I fell hard and fast. I felt things that I never felt before. There was such power in choosing to share myself with someone that I wanted to be with. And there was power in it being secretive and no one really knowing. Maybe it was the lie that everyone thought we were actually brothers, and we played that card every time we could. Once we were in Calvin's car at a graveyard when a police cruiser with the lights on stopped behind us. When the cop came to the driver's side, Calvin told him we were brothers and we were here to visit our mother's grave. When the cop asked why we were in the car with the windows steamed up, Calvin told him that were talking and that we were overcome with grief. Maybe it was because we appeared as two privileged white males with blond hair and looked like each other, but there was no hassle. As the cop shined his flashlight at us and the interior of the car, he asked if we had any drugs or alcohol. Calvin calmly said, 'No, sir. We're just talking.' The cop nodded and said, 'Sorry for your loss. Don't stay too long, it's getting late.' And Calvin agreed."

"Calvin lied to the police?" asked Althea.

"Yeah, I guess he did."

"Did you two lie all the time?"

I slowly nodded. "Not directly, but we never told anyone that we weren't really brothers and that we were secretly together."

"You kept it a secret that you two were seeing each other?"

"It seemed easier that way. I was amazed at how many people were willing to believe and were relieved to hear that we were brothers, and not two attractive males spending time together."

"Did that bother you?" There was concern in Althea's voice.

"What do you mean?"

Althea pinched the bridge of her nose. "Did it bother you that you two lied about being brothers, when actually you were secretly seeing each other, especially when the AIDS epidemic was rampantly killing men?"

"Wow! That's pretty blunt." A rush of shame and guilt spouted in the pit of my stomach.

"I don't mean to come across as insensitive. But why else do you think people were so eager to believe that you two attractive young men were brothers?"

I slowly nodded. "Oh, I see, because if we were brothers, we couldn't be lovers."

"So, did it matter that you two were lying?"

"Not really. Sometimes it seemed easier to lie than to try and explain that we were together. It was like we had this special secret. And besides, I felt like I had lied all my life."

"But this was more blatant than hiding your secret. Telling the cop that you two were brothers and crying over your mother's death is not the same as hiding the shame of being sexually exploited." There was a sense of disappointment in Althea's tone.

"I guess."

"What else made you attracted to Calvin?"

"I'm not sure I'm following."

"Why were you attracted to someone that looked like you? Or who could pass as your brother?"

I could not stop my words. "Because it was easier?"

"Easier?"

269

"Since we were brothers, there wasn't any pressure of expectations from others or myself, and I could explore my feelings and not worry about what others thought."

"Do you really think that other people thought you two were only brothers?"

I hesitantly replied, "Yes."

"Or was that what you wanted to believe?"

"There was this veil of protection in my mind. A sense of exploring myself…yet, there was a sense of…oh, my God. It was like I was trying to love myself, or at least the parts that I lost." My eyes grew wide. "I was trying to love myself, and by opening up to Calvin and everyone thinking we were brothers, it allowed me to fall in love with someone who looked like me, like Narcissus."

"Now wait a minute. I'm not convinced or saying that you were experiencing Narcissistic Personality Disorder. I agree that maybe you were trying to subconsciously identify and reconnect with the image that you dissociated in your mind about yourself by allowing yourself the permission to try and bring those splintered parts back together. By loving someone like Calvin, during this time, you were on a crash course in figuring out the feelings of love for yourself and for another. He was like a mirror for you. But what was Calvin's agenda? Why was he perpetuating the 'brother' lie? What was he hiding from?"

I sat there for a long time. "I don't know. Maybe I was so narcissistic and so focused on becoming a whole person that I became blind to the reality of the situation and what other people thought."

"Did Calvin ever ask you about you or your past?"

I took a long moment to think. "We never openly discussed it. I mean, we talked about winning the gold medal and the acting gigs."

"But he never asked about any past relationships?"

"Not really. But in his defense, he did try. I didn't want to share."

"So, he thought this was your first time?" Althea sounded judgmental.

I squirmed in my seat. "I guess so. It was the first time I opened up to someone and let someone in."

"It was all under the protection of a lie. How open were you, if you had to keep remembering the lie and who you told?" Althea removed her glasses and tapped them against her chin. "What about Mark and Erik or Jennifer and Sue?" she asked.

I had to take a moment. "Well, Mark was like a crush that never happened. Erik was an extension of an extremely bad situation, and we came together for moral support. Sue and Jennifer were completely off limits because I was afraid that I was gay. Calvin was the first person closest to my own age."

"So, those were fleeting moments of connecting with someone?"

Her words were punching me in the stomach. "They were impossible situations," I defensively stated.

"And yet, with Calvin, you two created an incredible lie and thought you would live happily ever after like in the fairy tales based on this lie?"

Each word landed squarely on my abdomen and forced out more air. I could only shrug my shoulders.

"Did you talk about Calvin's past relationships?" Althea asked.

"He was with a girl for a long time, and it didn't work out."

"Wait a minute, he was straight?"

"I don't know how straight he was, because he kissed me." My joke fell short.

"Was he just experimenting?" She wasn't letting up.

"Maybe, I really don't know," I responded with finality. I fought against my urge to flee from the room.

"How long did he have a girlfriend?" Althea appeared more concerned than ever.

"He said they were high school sweethearts. But he messed around with a guy earlier in the year."

"I see. So, you spent the summer together?"

"Yes, he came to the house, and on his days off and we would take Magdalyn to King's Island, go to the movies, or just spend the day together. We were like a little family. And he took me to some parties."

"How was the sex?"

"What do you mean?"

"Was the sex good?"

"I feel uncomfortable talking about this."

"I'm just trying to see if it was a healthy relationship."

"Why would it be an unhealthy relationship?" I asked.

Althea sighed. "You're different. You're not like everyone else."

"So, you think people were able to take advantage of me?"

"I'm afraid so. You wouldn't see it coming. Since your abuse, you're wired differently than other people." She looked at me and raised her hands. "So how was the sex?"

"It was good. We didn't do a lot."

"What do you mean?"

"We kissed and mutually masturbated, but that was most if it."

"You never had intercourse?"

I felt like she had started kicking me in the stomach. "No."

"Why not?"

"We decided that we didn't need it. We were happy with how things were. And I wasn't ready for it."

"Oh, I see."

"What do you mean by that?"

"Nothing."

"It doesn't always have to be about fucking."

Althea's eyes widened.

"I'm sorry, I didn't mean to use that word." I felt such shame.

"It's all right. And you are right. It doesn't have to always be about fucking. But it does have to be about satisfying each other's needs."

"We talked about that, and we were both good."

"Did you ever want more?"

WRIGHT STATE UNIVERSITY AUDITION FOR THE THEATRE PROGRAM, 1982

"Good morning, I am Gerald Monroe, and this is Wendy LeBaron, and we are seniors in the BFA program here at Wright State University's Theatre and Dance Programs, and we're here to help you go through this audition process."

Gerald was tall and thin and towered over Wendy.

"Has everyone received the audition packet and questionnaire? If you have not, make sure you come to me to get one. You'll not be seen if you haven't completed the questionnaire," Wendy said.

Gerald made a goofy face and nodded his head. "I'm excited to say that you'll be auditioning for the faculty of the Theatre and Dance Departments, and the Chair of the Music Department."

Wendy added, "It may seem intimidating at first to see all those people when you walk in, but believe me, they all want you to do your best."

At the moment, the door swung open and this bubbly, beautiful, light-skinned Black girl came bursting through the door. "I'm not too late, am I?" she said with such exuberance and immediacy.

"What a way to make an entrance," Gerald stated.

The young woman realized that she was the center of attention and laughed nervously while looking at all the people that had managed to arrive on time. "The car wouldn't start, and then I called a friend…"

"We're not interested in your plight of getting here. Take this packet, fill out the questionnaire, and find a place to prepare. Quietly," Wendy stated, with authority."

The young woman nodded and accepted the packet and questionnaire.

"What's your name, sweetie?" asked Gerald.

"My name?" she responded as if she hadn't heard the question correctly or forgot her name. Her cheeks blushed, and she scanned the room, as if she was trying to bide time to figure out her name.

"Yes, your name." Gerald dryly said.

"Oh, yes. My name is Valerie. Valerie Battle."

Gerald marked her name on his list. "Thank you, Miss Battle. Please take a seat."

Valerie nearly bowed before Gerald and Wendy. She quickly looked around the room to find a space to unload her arms. She rushed next to me.

"Hello." Valerie plopped her things loudly on the floor and quickly turned to Gerald and Wendy. She whispered loudly, "I'm so sorry." She sat on the floor, giving her full attention to Gerald and Wendy.

"Are there any questions?" asked Gerald, but he didn't wait for any responses. "Good. We'll be starting soon."

Gerald and Wendy walked out of the room.

The silence dissipated quickly as each person prepared in their own way.

I filled out the questionnaire.

"Excuse me." Valerie's large light brown eyes were accented with flecks of aqua and filled with concern. "Do you have an extra pen? I'd forget my head if it wasn't attached." She laughed nervously.

"Sure." I reached into the front pocket of my backpack, retrieved a pen, and offered it to her.

"Thank you so much. I'm Valerie."

"I know." I smirked.

"I suppose you do by now." She buried her face in her hands. "How embarrassing."

I chuckled. "You were great."

She quickly lifted her head and smiled. "You're sweet, even if you haven't told me your name yet."

"I'm David Matthew." I offered my hand.

"Well, David Matthew, we are destined to be best friends."

"We are?"

"Yes, it's fate. I know these things."

"Oh, okay."

"You just wait and see, David Matthew. I better complete my questionnaire." She turned away.

"Sure thing, Valerie Battle."

She quickly looked at me. "See, we're already on a first and last name basis." She went back to filling out the questionnaire.

The dance studio was the holding room for the many hopefuls that dreamed to validate their desire to become performers on the stage by being accepted into this prestigious program. Nervous energy bounced off the two white walls, the mirrored wall, and the fourth wall comprised of windows looking out on the campus. Each auditionee had his or her own way of preparing. Some sat in seclusion and ran their monologues and songs silently through their heads. The more overt and attention craved applicants were pacing or walking in circles, audibly repeating vocal exercises and scales. Others utilized the ballet bars mounted on the walls, to stretch and limber their bodies.

I was in awe at the performance that was taking place in this space and wondered if I was missing something. Was I supposed to be nervously moving around and annoying others who wanted quiet time to prepare?

Was I an outcast in this room of potential Tony, Emmy, and possible Oscar winners?

My limited audition experience consisted of three times. The third audition resulted in me getting a part in the UCI fall play and a lead in a movie of the week. The second was when I audition to get into Norma Sharkey's Modeling and Acting classes. But the very first? I can't remember.

I filled in the blank spaces for the general questions, like name, address, and past theatrical experience. My hand shook when I tried to respond to the question, "Why do you want to be a part of Wright State University's Theatre Program?" *How do I answer this? Do I even have an acceptable answer?* I thought for a moment. *Can I state that I want to go to WSU so I can be as close as I can to my boyfriend? Was Calvin my boyfriend? What is a boyfriend? If he's my boyfriend, that must mean I'm gay. But I'm not allowed to be gay. I don't feel gay. I feel like I'm someone who likes someone who happens to be the same sex as me. So, am I damned for the rest of my life because...*

"David Matthew."

My attention was pulled back into the room.

"David Matthew?" A husky young woman stood at the entrance looking down at a clipboard.

"Here." I raised my hand and got up.

"Gather your things, and come with me. You're next."

I followed the instructions.

"Break a leg, David." Valerie's bright smile filled her face.

"Thanks."

I slowly walked to the exit, making as little eye contact as possible with the others in the room. I followed the stranger to the next dance studio.

"Do you have your questionnaire, picture and resume?" she asked in a monotonous tone, as if she had asked this question a thousand and two times already today. She impatiently held out her hand.

I presented to her the requested items.

She checked off my name and indicated for me to be quiet and wait as she listened at the door.

As I stood there waiting, I recalled the first time I had auditioned. I was in elementary school and I auditioned for the high school's talent show.

MATTHEW HOME, AULDEN, OHIO, 1973

"Do it just like you saw Flip Wilson do." Grandma Fisher directed me to the center of the room. She and Pops moved in with us after Dad's accident.

As I positioned myself and asked, "Why do I want to do this?"

"Because it's funny." She lit a cigarette and sat on a dining room chair, with her legs twisted around each other. "Make sure you have the attitude; it's not funny without the attitude."

"Why do I have to wear this dress?" I tried to pull the mini-skirt's hem down a bit. "It's so short."

"Because that is what the character wears." She inhaled deeply on the cigarette, and the smoke streamed out of her nose like a dragon. She fanned herself to clear the grey plume. "Let's go for it."

"This wig itches." I scratched my head, which was covered with a black bouffant flip hairdo wig topped by a big hat made from the same material as the dress.

"Leave it be." She rushed to my side and readjusted the hat and wig. She pulled a couple of bobby pins from her hair and stuck them through the wig.

"Ouch."

"Stop squirming." Grandma patted down flyaway hairs, grabbed a can of hair spray from the table and dowsed me in a cloud. She stood back and admired her work. "Okay, from the top, as they say in show biz." She backed up to the chair and sat down. "Now, you'll walk out when you hear the jazzy music. Go over there so you can walk in. That's it. Ready?"

I nodded.

"Don't forget the attitude."

"I won't. Wait a minute. Isn't this character Black?" I asked.

"It doesn't matter. It's the essence we want to go for. Are you ready?"

I nodded.

"Okay, here we go." She started. "Da-da-da-da. Da-da-da-da."

I strutted to her beat, a hand on my hip and the other swinging a purse that matched my mini dress and hat. I took two quick steps back and followed with quick steps in a semi-circle, arms out to the side, and rolled my head back and to the sides while alternating my shoulders up and down. I shimmied and popped my hips to both sides, then regained my focus and strutted to the center of the room with one hand back on my hip and other swinging the purse. I stop, clapped my hands, and cooed. I spoke in a high-pitched voice. "I know what you're thinking, but you're wrong. When you're hot, you're hot, and when you're not, you're not. Ohhhhhhh, and I'm hot." I clapped again. "I can see you're jealous of my fabulous dress. Well, let me tell you, the Devil made me buy this dress! That's the truth, well, it helps that my boyfriend, Killer, wanted me to wear it." I turned serious, and I pointed out into the audience. "Don't you look at me like that, honey, you don't know me that well!" I smirked. "But we will soon enough." I clapped again and swiveled my hips. "Ohhhhhh. Don't you know who I am? Why, I am Geraldine Jones, and that's Miss Jones to you. Killer is the only one that gets to call me Geraldine."

Grandma laughed out loud, causing me to stop. "This is so funny," she said.

"But the panty hose keeps bunching up."

"Leave it be." She batted my hands away.

"Are you sure this is going to work?" I felt a strange ache in my stomach.

"They're going to love it."

I can't remember the actual audition. I can only recall brief moments of the spotlight hitting my face and the audience laughing when they realized that I was imitating Flip Wilson's famous character. The only thing I remembered was going to the bathroom to get out of my costume. I took out my jeans and sweatshirt from a brown grocery bag and placed them on the window's ledge. I was in the process of taking off the panty hose when two high school kids wearing football jerseys came in and made their way to the urinals.

I froze.

The taller of the two stopped midway unzipping his pants and staring at me.

"What are you doing in here?"

The other, shorter and heavier, came up next to him. "What the freak?"

The taller guy explained, "You're in the wrong bathroom, little girl."

I pulled the wig and hat off.

"No shit," said the stocky one.

"Are you serious?" said the taller one.

I shoved the wig and hat into the brown paper bag. I started to take the dress off.

The shorter guy blushed and said, "That's fucking fucked up, I'm not pissing while that freak's in here."

"What are you afraid of, that he'll see your tiny weenie?"

The short, stocky guy punched the taller one on the shoulder. And the taller one reciprocated.

"Ouch, that hurt." The shorter one rubbed his arm.

"You are such a puss." Then the taller guy looked at me. "Are you some pansy boy or something? Why are you wearing a dress and makeup?"

I was nervous and scared. The exit was too far away and I'd have to make it past the two of them. I was trapped. "I auditioned for the talent show."

"That was you doing the Flip Wilson thing?" The taller one seemed interested.

I could only nod.

"That was funny. Really funny."

"Thanks, I guess."

"It's still kind of freaky, because you're a dude, but funny."

"I'm outta here, man," the stout guy said and started to leave but stopped at the door. "You coming, dude?"

"Yeah, we can come back after he/she's finished changing."

They both left me alone.

WRIGHT STATE UNIVERSITY AUDITION FOR THE THEATRE PROGRAM, 1982

"David, they're ready." The young woman held the door open for me.

"Thank you."

A voice bellowed out from within the room. "It was a pleasure meeting you Nancy and we'll be in touch."

An attractive and statuesque young woman smiled and excitedly said, "Thank you for this opportunity."

I waited by the door for her to exit.

She smiled as she walked out.

As I walked in, I found a baker's dozen sitting behind a long table discussing the last auditionee. I overheard them talking as I placed my things in the corner by the door, pulled out my sheet music, and walked to the pianist.

"I find her fascinating," said a female.

"I'm not sure she's a fit," responded a baritone voice.

"Why not?"

"She needs to lose weight."

I placed the sheet music on the piano and pointed to the sixteen bars that I had marked. "Would you please start here and end here?" I asked in a whisper.

"What tempo?" the pianist asked.

I sang a little bit to indicate the desired speed.

"Good to go."

"Thank you." I walked to the center of the room where there was an "X" in the floor, and waited patiently for their discussion to end.

"But what an interesting choice of song."

"We don't have anyone like her."

"But will she be able to get work professionally?"

"She has good comedic ability."

"But can she do dramatic roles?"

"No matter what, she has to lose the weight."

"All right, everyone." The man in the middle hushed the conversation and indicated for the panel to focus on me.

Thirteen sets of eyes burned through my skin.

"Hello, and welcome to Wright State University Theatre Department's open auditions. Can you please state your name?"

"Sure, I'm David Matthew." I felt the nerves in my stomach.

"Welcome David. I'm Abe Bassett, the chair of the department. Let me quickly introduce our panel this morning. On the far end to your right, representing the dance department are Gayle Smith, Pat White, Mary Giannone, Sandra Tanner, and Suzanne Walker." Each woman waved in acknowledgement. "On your far left, we have Charles Darry of the motion pictures department and Joseph Tilford for design and technology. The acting department is being represented by Bob Hetherington, Jessica Beltz, Deborah Bartlett-Bair, and Richard Meyer. Next to me is the chair of the music department Sarah Johnson."

"Wow, hello everyone."

"What song and monologue are you going to perform for us this morning?" Abe asked.

"I'm going to sing sixteen bars of 'They Say It's Wonderful,' from *Annie Get Your Gun,* and I'll play Tom Wingfield from Tennessee William's *The Glass Menagerie.*

"You have the stage," Abe said.

MATTHEW HOME, AULDEN, OHIO, 1982

I extended my arms as wide as they'd go to recharge my psyche with natural energy surrounding the silo. But no matter how much I tried to infuse the essence of this sacred place, nothing seemed to be easing the anxiety building inside. Although my insides were a nervous wreck, my health seemed to have found its way for the better. I gained my strength back, and ten pounds. This time in Aulden had been beneficial to me.

Three days had passed since I experienced that incredible rush from auditioning for the Wright State panel, by exposing as much of my inner self as I could possibly permit at that given moment before strangers. The intoxication that engulfed me flew away by the time the audition was over. As I was walking out the door to let in the next person, I received the same comment that was given to Nancy, "We'll be in touch."

A loud, descending screech earned my attention as a red-tailed hawk majestically circled above the silo, searching for prey. The buteo's broad wings expanded to its feather tips and its short, fan-shaped tail pivoted to navigate the wind currents. The large bird gracefully circled around again, with its focus on the ground. With another screech, it tilted its wings, dove toward the field, skimmed the top of the grass, extended its talons, and nabbed a field mouse. With its victim securely clutched in its claws, the bird swooped back up into the sky and disappeared into the woods.

I envied the hawk's freedom to soar through the vastness of the sky and navigate where it desired. I envied the hawk's instinct to be the creature it was naturally meant to be, with no outside factors invading its psyche and deterring the flight of its destiny.

I felt trapped within my prison of a body, not sure how to return to my instincts. I allowed outside factors to dictate the course of my destiny and shove my true self further and further somewhere I no longer recognized.

It had also been three days since I last heard from Calvin. Three days of wondering what I could've possibly done wrong. Three days of waiting for the phone to ring and longing to hear his voice.

As I stood by the silo, absorbing all the energy I could, a breeze brought the scent of fall. I imagined the all trees dressed in glorious shades of reds and oranges and then covered in snow. Everything seemed to have a natural progression, just like how the seasons go from one to the other. But which season is the beginning and which is the end of the cycle?

I tried to chase the worry from my head about Calvin. I created explanations and ran them through my mind and practiced my nonchalant responses. But my confidence was waning. I left messages for him at the theatre and on his apartment's answering machine. Today was the Country Show's last performance at King's Island, and Calvin would be heading back to Chicago. I worried that I'd never see him again.

"David," Mom called from the back porch. "David, you have a call."

"Coming." Another chilly breeze snuck under my collar and sent a shiver through my body as I hustled to the house.

As I came through the backdoor, Mom was talking to the caller. "Here he is. Now, you don't be a stranger." She handed the receiver to me and whispered, "It's Calvin."

My heart lightened as I anticipated hearing his voice. "Hello."

"David, it's Calvin." His words were short and clipped.

"How are you?" I tried to cover up my longing.

"Not so good."

"What's wrong?"

"I heard something, and I wanted to ask you about it."

"Okay."

"Did you know Dr. Chuck Miller?"

The walls caved in, and the floor disappeared from under me.

"Well, did you? Answer me." Venom filled his voice.

"I...I..." I couldn't think of anything fast enough.

"It's rather an easy answer, yes or no." His words shot through the phone line like a machine gun.

"What about a guy named Erik? Or Dr. Schultz? Or Harold Hall?"

Punches pummeled my stomach with each name. "What're you saying?" I couldn't breathe.

"That's what I thought."

Silence filled the phone's receiver and I only heard white noise, fearing that he was regrouping for another attack, or worse, he already hung up.

"Were you a Miller Boy?"

There it was. His words stabbed me deep in the gut causing me to double over. I braced myself against the wall to remain standing. "No, not really."

"You were, or you weren't!" There was finality in his voice.

"It's not that easy," I meekly confessed.

"You lied to me all summer. So, don't lie to me now."

I couldn't speak.

"I was at a party, and I met this guy who looked like Clark Kent, and he said he knew the diving champion who went to L.A. to be a star. He also said that the only way you got to do all those things was because of the benefits that Dr. Miller and the other professionals, that's what he called them, professionals, gave you." Another round of silence filled the airwaves. "And did you hook up with Todd from the Celebration Show?"

"No. I introduced him to Hal. Hal offered to help Todd with the legal actions because he injured his foot during a performance," I defended myself.

"Did you sleep with him, too?"

"No."

"Did you want to?" His voice raged with anger.

I felt ambushed.

"Was I your sloppy seconds, or thirds, or hundreds? Was everything you said a lie? How many people have paid to sleep with you?"

Each accusation wounded me deeper than anything I had previously experienced and equaled the physical and emotional scars the grad student bestowed on me.

"Can I explain?"

"I trusted you. How am I supposed to believe anything you say? Don't come to the park today. I don't want to ever see you again." He ended the call.

I listened to the buzzing sound until it completely went silent. I don't remember hanging up the receiver. I shook uncontrollably, and my stomach twisted in knots. I managed, somehow, to walk to the staircase.

Mom sat on the pulled-out couch. "How's Calvin?" she asked.

I kept walking.

"Davey, is everything alright?"

I stopped and looked at her through watering eyes.

"Come here." She reached out her arms to me.

I hesitated before making my way to her.

"What is it?" She guided me to sit next to her.

Everything was piling up and ready to burst forward. I tried to take a moment to get my emotions under control.

"What did Calvin say to you?"

"Mom, I have to tell you something." I tried to stop the words from emerging.

"You can tell me anything."

I stared at my interlaced fingers. "I made a mistake. I can't help it. I like someone. I mean, I really like someone. And I don't know what to do."

"It's okay to like someone."

"I more than like this person."

"Okay."

I looked up at her. "I think I may even love this person."

"Who? Who do you think you love?"

"I'm so sorry. I didn't want to, but I couldn't stop it."

"Tell me who it is."

"Calvin." My throat knotted up.

"Of course you love Calvin. You two are like brothers."

"No, it's more than that," I confessed.

"I don't understand. There's nothing wrong with having feelings for a best friend."

"He was more than a best friend."

I saw her eyes fill with fear. "He stayed overnight here, and you stayed with him. But he said you had a crush on Lucy."

"He lied to you."

"Why'd he do that?"

"Because I was in love with him." I lost it. I verbalized the one thing I tried to keep near and dear to my heart and not let anyone know.

"I see." She pulled her hands away from me. "And why are you so sad?"

"He never wants to see me again." I fought to hold the pain off.

Mom stood, walked to the hall, and stopped. She couldn't look at me. "Did you tell him that you loved him?"

"Yes."

Her spine lengthened and she remained with her back to me. "Maybe he loved you like a brother and this was too much for him." She forced her voice into the higher pitched phony tone she used on the phone when talking to creditors. "Everything's going to be all right, you'll see. Don't let this bother you." She turned, forced a smile, but couldn't look me in the face. "And let's not mention this to anyone. People wouldn't understand." She nervously patted her forehead with the back of her hand. "Things have a way of working themselves out. Do you need anything from the store? I have to pick a few things up."

"Everything's falling apart." My words choked in my throat.

"You're not going to do anything rash?"

"No," I lied. I wanted to die.

"Good. We've had enough nonsense to last a lifetime." She made her way to the kitchen and grabbed her keys. "There's a letter for you on the side table." She called back before closing the door.

I stood in the same place, unable to move and feeling abandoned. I listened as the car started up and backed down the driveway. I listened to the ringing of silence. The pain I felt was more than anything I had ever experienced, as if the hawk ripped open my stomach with its sharp talons and began pecking at my innards. *Was this death? Being all alone and not knowing what to do?* I wanted to scream and share my pain with someone. Who would listen?

I screamed as loud as I could, "I'm sorry I'm an abomination!" But I knew my words fell on deaf ears.

I started for my room, when I saw a letter on the side table. It was addressed to me, but it had already been opened. I pulled out the trifold letter and opened it.

Dear David Matthew,

Congratulations. You have been selected as a candidate for the BFA Acting Program for the Wright State University Theatre Department's Freshmen Class of 1982...

I dropped the letter and envelope back on the side table, made my way up the stairs to my room, dropped onto my bed, and passed out.

DR. ALTHEA WARNER'S OFFICE— DAYTON, OHIO, 2018

"No, I didn't tell anyone about Calvin, our relationship, or the breakup. I wanted to forget about it."

"So, you buried that with everything else?" The corners of Althea's mouth curled down.

I shrugged my shoulders. "I told myself heartbreaks were a part of life, life happens, and not everything was going to work out like in fairy tales."

"Just like that?" Althea imitated me, shrugging my shoulders.

"Everything happens for a reason and you just have to look at it from a different angle and find the silver lining."

"Thank you, Tony Robbins, for that mumbo-jumbo-positive-thinking-bullcrap." She leaned into me. "Do you really believe that?"

"I did. Or I convinced myself that I did. What else could I have done?"

"You could've gotten angry, shouted, cried, broke a plate or something. You could've marched yourself down to King's Island and stood up for yourself and told Calvin the truth."

"Why? What good would that have done by making a scene?" I felt defensive.

"It would have allowed you to put the anger outside of yourself. You could've directed it toward the person who contributed to the lie that you two were brothers. You could've confronted that coward for ghosting you for three days and breaking up with you over the phone." Althea's face flared red. "Where does that son-of-a-bitch get off by listening to gossip and not letting you have your chance to explain?"

"He did try to let me explain, but I couldn't find the words."

"No! Calvin attacked you. He didn't let you explain. He was more worried about his image and reputation. He blasted you and told you that he never wanted to see you again. He never took the time to find out if the accusations were true, and if they were, why were they true. He never took the time to see if you were okay. It was easier for him to push you aside and pretend it never happened."

My eyes widened, and my jaw hung loose.

She noticed my reaction. "Well, I'm sorry. This gets me so riled up that I want to shake something." She stood, paced the room, and grabbed a pillow from the couch. She violently shook it. "Why are you not upset?"

"Because it happened so long ago," I said in awe as I watched her display of emotions.

"Wrong," she shouted and shook the pillow harder.

"Because it was my fault?" I started guessing.

"Wrong again." She shook the pillow even harder so that her head started jerking back and forth, causing her hair to whip around.

"I don't know."

"What?" She stopped and looked at me with bewilderment.

I slowly said, "I don't know how."

"That's right. You never allowed yourself the permission or were taught how. You held it in."

"I can see that," I mumbled.

She held out the pillow. "Take this."

"What?"

"Take the pillow."

"Why?"

"Just take the damn pillow, will you?"

"Okay." I reluctantly took the pillow from her.

"Now shake it."

I looked at her like she was crazy.

"Shake it."

"Like this?" I wiggled the pillow back and forth.

"No, really shake it."

I froze. I couldn't demand my body to follow through. I realized that I didn't know how to tap into that emotion, or I was scared of that emotion.

"Shake it," she demanded.

"I can't," I whispered.

"What?"

"I can't."

"I can't hear you."

"I can't!"

Althea paused. "Why not?"

"I don't know."

"You do know. Why can't you shake the pillow?"

Anger was brewing deep within me, but I was trying to hold it at bay. "I don't want to."

"Why?"

"Don't make me do this," I pleaded.

"Why?"

"Because I'm scared." Tears streamed down my face.

Althea's face softened, and she returned to her seat. She released a deep breath, which caused me to do the same. Her voice was soothing. "Now there's still hope yet."

I was confused. "I've cried in here before. And I've gotten angry in here before."

She nodded. "You're correct, but you controlled those displays of emotion. It's a form of delimitation. In research, it's the choices made to describe the boundaries set for the study. In survivors, delimitation is the boundaries the victim sets to try and keep anger at a distance." Althea smiled. "I came up with a theory on my own and I'm not even sure if there's any scientific support." She pointed toward me. "As you were surviving every day and keeping the secrets deeply buried, you remapped the way your brain works, like a person who has had a stroke. As you rewired the synapses to avoid the area that stored the painful memories, you were able to distance yourself from these experiences. And depending on your truth, there are some things that you'd never allow yourself to do. I believe that you're unable to act aggressively because it's not in your nature."

I stopped her. "I can get extremely angry and sometimes it's a short fuse."

She nodded. "There are different types of anger. And yes, if we're pushed to a certain degree, everyone can become capable of almost anything. But those are circumstantial, and probably you would've demonstrated some warning signs by now. Have you ever let yourself feel or tap into this emotional side?"

WRIGHT STATE UNIVERSITY, DR. MEYER'S ACTING CLASS, 1983

"Miss Battle you're late," Dr. Meyer said, standing in the center of the studio and taking attendance.

I wasn't aware that class had even started, because I was looking at my notes in my journal. The notes I bulleted to fulfill the acting exercise due this morning.

"I had to use the bathroom," Valerie defended.

Dr. Meyer motioned for her to get settled.

Valerie rushed to sit next to me. "He's sure in a mood today." She busied herself by pulling out her journal and some props from her floral tote bag. She whispered, "Where were you at breakfast? I waited, and you never showed."

I whispered, "I was working on my exercise for this class."

Valerie's eyes widened. "That's due today?"

I nodded.

"All right class, settle down," Dr. Meyer's voice bellowed throughout the room. "As you know, this morning you'll be performing for a grade. Let's review the criteria for this assignment. You were to make bullet points about a situation you encountered, focusing on the time, place, prior circumstances, intentions, transitions, changes of intentions, and desired outcome. Keep in mind any obstacles that may occur and how those obstacles may change the circumstances without telegraphing these moments. I'm looking for an organic and authentic presentation of this selected moment. Allow each moment to move into the next naturally, without telegraphing or indicating. Oh, and yes, this will be done without any dialogue. In your journals, you'll evaluate the performance and identify if the actor achieved the objective. As an observer, you'll provide five positive attributes about the presentation and five negatives. You'll turn in the journals at the end of class and be graded on your performance and observations. Any questions?"

Valerie's hand shot into the air.

"Yes, Miss Battle?" Dr. Meyer nodded to her.

"How long do you want the presentation?" Valerie asked.

"Good question. The scene should be as long as it needs to take. However, I may stop it at any time if I feel the need. Otherwise, keep working until I do stop you."

"What will cause you to stop it?" Valerie challenged.

Dr. Meyer grinned. "I'll stop you if I feel you're telegraphing and not emotionally anchored in your core. I may stop you if I feel you're probing in an unhealthy area. And I'll stop you when I feel you've achieved the objective of the exercise." Dr. Meyer walked to his chair and sat. "Any volunteers?"

I wanted to get this over as quickly as possible, but I also wanted to see someone else go first.

"No volunteers?" asked Dr. Meyer, with disappointment. He looked at his roster.

I stood. "Dr. Meyer, I'll go."

Dr. Meyer nodded and notated in his gradebook.

Everyone pulled out their journals.

I walked to the center of the stage, looked at my notes one last time, and then slid the journal across the floor to the back wall. I anticipated the potential of sharing something that I was holding within me and scared to reveal. I've been disconnected from myself since the day Calvin called and said he never wanted to see me again. Mom shut me out when I tried to get comfort from her. So, I decided I wasn't ready to return to Los Angeles and proceeded to take a year and focus on acting.

What I didn't realize was that I shut down and became numb. I no longer felt anything about Calvin, the grad student, the professionals. I decided I didn't need or deserve any type of romantic relationships and swore off ever getting involved with someone again. I silently proclaimed I was going to become the best actor I was capable of, return to Los Angeles, and have a career on my terms. I fumbled through the first quarter at Wright State University, emotionally unavailable, and unable to connect with anyone or to my wounded soul. I created a brooding James Dean persona, and Valerie became my Natalie Wood.

What I didn't count on was enrolling in a class where the acting instructor was a product of the Actors' Studio's Method. A process composed of training and rehearsal techniques that required the performer to react in a sincere and emotionally expressiveness way based on real-life authenticity and truth. The Method was derived from the Stanislavski System with contributions provided by Lee Strasberg, Stella Adler, and Stanford Meisner and enhanced many great performances given by Marlon Brando, Montgomery Clift, James Dean, Marilyn Monroe, Julie Harris, Kim Hunter, Paul Newman, Dustin Hoffman, and Al Pacino, to name a few.

I had a simple goal for this graded exercise. I wanted to get out of my way and connect to my inner self. I didn't care about the grade or what my classmates thought. I only cared about me and breaking through this concrete wall I created.

My palms sweated as I knocked on the imaginary door. I envisioned the door opening, and I was back in the grad student's apartment. I reenacted the ordeal as honestly as I could. Something took over me, my body, and my emotions; it guided me. Without words, I told my story without judgment or editing. Before I knew it, I was standing before the class with my shirt wide open and baring my soul.

There was not a sound in the room. The eyes of my peers were glued on me. Their faces told a story of being mesmerized and in shock.

I felt vulnerable, exposed, and naked. *Had I failed?* Adrenalin raced through my veins, causing my fingertips and toes to tingle. My head pulsed from the pumping blood, and my vision was blurred.

Finally, a staccato clap emitted from Dr. Meyer as he slowly stood. He continued to clap as he walked to my side. He removed his tweed sport jacket and draped it around my shoulders. He wrapped his arms around me, pulled me into a tight bear hug, and whispered in my ear, "That was a breakthrough, and very brave. Meet me in my office after class." He pulled back to arm's length and said loud enough for everyone to hear, "Thank you for sharing that." He turned to the class, with his hand cupping the nape of my neck. "That's how it's done, folks. Are there any comments or questions? Remember, the actor must not directly comment on the choices he or she demonstrated or give any details about the situation. It's up to you, the audience, to interpret the performance."

No one moved. They just sat there, staring.

Valerie slowly lifted her hand and glanced at all the motionless classmates.

"Yes, Miss Battle?" Dr. Meyer broke the silence.

Valerie took a deep breath. "Wow. I'm at a loss for words." She forced a laugh. "I know, I know, it's a miracle, I'm never at a loss for words." She paused and grew serious. "That, whatever you want to call it, was, I don't know how to describe it verbally. It was a glimpse into your internal world. It was outstanding and raw." She looked down at her notes. "Let me start with my constructive criticisms first. There were moments that seemed not as clear as others, as if you may not have been able to remember things precisely. But they were fleeting. The rest of the performance was concise and filled. I was scared for you and felt I was taking this journey right alongside you. And at the same time, it was beautifully performed."

"Good. Anyone else? All right." He turned to me and released my neck. "Good job. You may sit."

I gave back Mr. Meyer his jacket and scampered back to my seat next to Valerie. She grabbed my hand and placed her head on my shoulder.

"So, who is next?" asked Dr. Meyer.

*****

"Why does Meyer want to see you?" Valerie asked we held hands and winded through the underground tunnels to the theatre department offices.

"I don't know. He said he wanted to talk to me," I replied as we made our way up the stairs.

"Do you want me to wait for you?" Her bubbly enthusiasm brightened her face.

"I'm not sure how long it'll take."

We turned the corner and entered the hall that housed the staff's offices. Sitting outside of Dr. Bassett's office was Nancy, the woman that auditioned before me. She seemed tense and anxious.

"Hello, Nancy," Valerie enthusiastically said.

Nancy forced a smile and nodded.

"What are you sitting out here for?" Valerie asked.

Nancy hesitantly responded, "I had a meeting with Mr. Basset."

"Is everything all right?"

"I think so." Nancy forced another smile.

"Is there anything we can do for you?"

Nancy shook her head.

"Mr. Matthew and Miss Battle," announced Dr. Meyer, who came up behind us, walked to his office door, and entered without hesitation.

Valerie turned to me and kissed my cheek. "I'll meet you in ballet." And she disappeared down the hall.

I felt this bravado that Nancy may have thought that Valerie was my girlfriend. I settled in the seat next to Nancy. "Are you sure everything's okay?"

"No." Nancy's eyes filled with liquid. "I don't know if I'm more hurt or angry. You're David, right?" She dabbed her eyes with a Kleenex.

I nodded. "You auditioned right before me."

"I'm a transfer, or was."

"What do you mean?"

"Bassett gave me an ultimatum. Either I lose weight, or I'll be dropped from the program. I feel so discriminated against." Pain colored her words. "What a bastard, right?"

"Can they do that?" I asked.

"They can do anything they damn well want," Nancy said.

"I don't understand."

"Me either. If they didn't want me in the first place, then why accept me as a transfer?"

"Mr. Matthew, could you please come in?" Dr. Meyer called from within his office.

"I'm sorry." I nodded to Nancy and marched into Dr. Meyer's office.

He sat behind his desk and motioned for me to sit.

"This won't take very long." He placed his elbows on the desk and rested his chin on his interlaced hands. The thick lenses in black frames reflected small images of me as a slight smile appeared on his face. "That was some nice work today."

"Thank you."

"In fact, you've been doing good work all quarter. What's changed?"

"I feel like I'm starting to understand the approach to the work better."

"You seem to be opening up to it."

"Yes."

He leaned back in the chair and tapped his fingers on the desktop. "First quarter, you had me worried. You were unreachable, distant. You didn't display the qualities you shared during your audition. I started to think we made a mistake. You were unmotivated and not putting yourself out there. It was like you didn't want to be here. What changed?" He quickly held up his hand. "Don't answer that. Whatever it is, I hope you keep doing it. Also, you're excelling in class participation, and your overall work attitude is high. Your efforts in the group exercises and class discussions have improved. Your energy and concentration in performances are of a different person. You're getting attention from all the departments, especially the acting and dance departments. I want you to seriously start focusing on auditioning, because there are some shows coming up that I really think you're being strongly considered for, if you continue to progress."

I wasn't sure I was supposed to respond.

"What you did in this morning's class was a major step forward in the right direction. You tapped into something raw, real, and truthful. I'm not sure of the full story or if the story is completely real, but your vulnerability was powerful. If you ever want to talk about it, my door is always open. What you did was brave, and if there's anything I can do to help, please let me know."

"I will. Thank you."

"Good. I don't want to hold you up any longer. What class are you heading to?"

"Ballet."

"How do you like it?"

"I really enjoy it."

"I'm glad. You better get over there, I don't want Suzanne Walker mad at me." He rose and offered his hand.

I stood and accepted the offering.

"Keep up the good work."

"Yes, sir."

When I left his office, Nancy was no longer sitting in front of Dr. Bassett's office, and I wondered if I'd ever get the chance to talk with her again.

I had a resurgence of energy, vibrating from every cell in my body. I skipped down the hall and couldn't wait to get into ballet. I was looking forward, more than ever, to pushing my body to its limits and drenching myself with sweat. Dance became the physical activity, replacing diving, with the freedom of movement and sailing through the air.

When I arrived at the dance studio, the warmup music was in full swing.

"You're late, Mr. Matthew," Suzanne yelled over the music.

"Sorry, Dr. Meyers…"

"I'm not interested," she interrupted me. "Come on people, feel the music, and reach."

I threw my things in the corner and pulled off my sweatshirt and jeans. I adjusted my belt around my tights and pulled on my ballet shoes.

"Loosen up the hips, you're dancers; not robots. If you're feeling stiff, make sure you arrive early and stretch out. Valerie, nice use of the music."

I rushed to a space in the back behind Valerie and joined in with the rest of the class.

"Relevé, and hold," Suzanne demanded. "Hold the relevé as the music fades. Keep holding. Lift from your core and send the energy out the top of your head and through your fingertips and toes."

Suzanne Walker was the epitome of a professional dancer, five-feet tall and full of fire. Her resume ranged from dance companies, Broadway, and films. Her no-nonsense presence had many people fearful of her, but as time proved, she was brimming with passion for dance and didn't want anyone to waste the opportunity to perform.

Suzanne walked around the students still holding relevé. "Engage the core, and don't let me see you're working. A great dancer makes it look easy. Hold the position. Breathe. Dance is a living expression of the arts. It isn't static. You're not statues. You're humans. And you need your breath. Don't hold your breath. Breathe!" She tapped me on my stomach. "Lift."

I extended my spine and pulled my core inward, making me taller and stronger.

"That's better." Suzanne addressed the class. "Imagine the source of the energy emitting from your core and reaching up and out of the ceiling and down through the floor to the tunnels under the building. Don't lower; keeping expanding. Inhale and extend an inch further. Hold that position and continue to expand. And down."

Most of the students nearly collapsed and uttered various disgruntled mutterings.

"To the corner," Suzanne said and pointed to the far side. "Complaining isn't going to make it any easier."

I took the opportunity to elongate the momentary suspension of the relevé.

"Enough you show-off," Valerie said as he playfully punched my stomach. "How did it go with Meyer?"

I lowered and smiled. "Good."

"Less talking and more dancing." Suzanne waited in the corner looking directly at Valerie and me.

As we rushed to join the rest of the class, I paused as a cramp seized the lower right side of my back.

"Mr. Matthew, you alright?" Suzanne asked.

A flood of heat rushed through my body. "Yes." I pushed the pain away and jogged to the corner.

Suzanne clapped her hands twice to get everyone's attention. "All right, we're halfway through the year, and we've been doing this next combination across the floor for some time. I want to remind you all you're auditioning every day and every moment. When we were rehearsing *Oh, Brother!* on Broadway, the director, Don Driver, was constantly watching us because he had not finalized casting all the roles. And it was from my work ethics, I got to understudy and go on for Alyson Reed in the role of Fatatatatime. You're only as good as how people remember you. So, for another reminder, you all will be auditioning for *Guys and Dolls,* but the audition process has already been going on every day you have come in here to take class. Some of you are taking this seriously, and some are just doing it for a grade. But let me advise you, your reputation will precede you. In this business, it's not only who you know and how well you know them, but how they see you. Yes, having talent is a must, but when it comes down to you and four others, the director will usually always go with the person they know they can count on, and not necessarily talent all the time."

"That sucks," said a tall kid in the back.

Suzanne quickly faced him and said, "Welcome to show biz, kid. It's not always your abilities; it's more about your working relationships and reputation. So, I advise you to start practicing now. Today. With that said, I want to see what you can add to this floor combo. I want to see musicality, interpretation of the movement, and I want to see the steps done perfectly. I want to see you perform." She turned to the diagonal and talked through the combination. "Tombé, pas de bourrée, glissade, jete, step, step, prepare, double turn, step out, arabesque, and hold, swing the leg through, grande battement, and pose. Got it?"

The response was muttering.

"Got it?" Suzanne asked, louder, and looked around.

The class enthusiastically responded, "Yes."

"Good. Play the music."

The class as a group went through the steps, with Suzanne in the front.

"Alright, hurry back, and let's do it in groups of three," Suzanne directed.

As I hustled to the corner, the pain grew in my side. I shook it off and prepared for the combination across the floor. Sweat dripped into my eyes, and before I knew it, I was performing the steps. I felt great demonstrating the control I had gained from the classes all year. As I hit and held the arabesque, my body tingled. When my leg swung through to go to the battement, the amount of pain that shot through me sent me sailing to the floor.

DR. ALTHEA WARNER'S OFFICE— DAYTON, OHIO, 2018

Althea leaned forward. "But what's also interesting is an abused person has the ability to negate or ignore that they've recreated the situation or experience and is able to justify it as a belief that the 'world is against me' or 'this always happens to me' mantra and become blind to the opportunity to learn from the situation."

"So, are you saying that people 'like me' subconsciously created the abuse to happen in the first place?"

"No. You're not hearing me. What I'm saying is after the initial abuse, or the series of reoccurring abuse, the mind of the abused person remaps itself in such a way that it functions to avoid reliving the pain and trauma. But as the person grows older, they tend to put themselves in situations that can safely recreate a similar scenario in order to try and comprehend why it happened in the first place." She paused a moment. "For example, a happily married man who was sexually abused as a child or teen may go to a public bathroom. While at the urinal, someone comes up next to him, and exposes himself. Now, the abused man can either chalk it up as something that always happens to him, or he can try to understand why he entered a bathroom in the first place, where he may have had an inkling that this could possibly happen. Is he wrong for this? No. He's most likely subconsciously trying to understand why the event happened to him when he was younger. Is this man aware that he may have created this situation?" Althea shook her head. "Is the man completely aware that some type of abuse ever took place? Not necessarily. He could've buried the memories, just like you tried, but eventually the human mind will provide indicators that something took place at an earlier time. Have you ever found yourself creating certain scenarios or situations and found you were repeating an event without even being aware of it?"

I sat there in silence. If she was correct, when my mind felt it was a safe distance away from the actual events, it started giving me clues or indications that something had happened, and I must have ignored it. Because after I came home from the U.C.I., I made a conscious decision to stay as far away as possible from Hal and anything that was connected to the professionals. I promised God that if He made me well, I would change my life. I was determined to make my own life through my own choices.

Although some of the things Althea said made sense. It seemed there were always two worlds going on at the same time. One world where I was trying to survive in an environment that seemed untrustworthy, and another where I was constantly trying to navigate around the painful memories in order to try and forget about the past events. My mind wasn't able to comprehend why I'd subconsciously recreate or repeat certain situations in order to reveal some hidden secret.

Althea asked a question in such a caring manner. "Have you ever found yourself in a situation that was questionable or could trigger old memories?"

I held my tongue to try to formulate a response and resist fleeing from the room. "Acting became my safe place, where I was able to safely explore those dark areas. I seemed to be able to tap into something, when I needed, and it allowed me to ease some of the pressure constantly building up inside. Wright State was important for me to experiment with different methods, and for the first time, to consciously compartmentalize certain feelings and start reconnecting to myself. It seemed that everything was going in the right direction for me, and was confirmed by Dr. Meyer during my meeting with him."

"Like what?" Althea asked.

"I was finding my way, a voice, and a purpose. Maybe I was discovering how to navigate around the painful memories and utilize them in a positive way when it benefited me. I started getting called backs for roles. Dance became my new sport, and I thrived. I found a way to emote my passion through words and movement. I was creating independence. I had distanced myself from Hal and the professionals. I convinced myself I was living my life on my terms and making my own choices."

"Did you cut communication off completely from Hal and the professionals?" asked Althea.

I nodded. "For the most part. But not completely, I guess."

"What does that mean?"

"Well, I started trying to think things through on my own, without asking what Hal or Mom thought. I allowed time to pass to before returning Hal or Mom's calls. I stopped meeting the professionals. I tried to blend in and be a college student. I reinvented myself and pushed all those memories to the furthest part of my mind. I was in the process of forgetting they ever happened. I wanted to have a clean slate. I became the freshman who had been to Hollywood, did a movie of the week, and was on *General Hospital.* I was the guy that decided to return to Ohio and attend Wright State University to improve my talent before returning to Tinsel Town. I was the poster child for the theatre department, and I enjoyed it."

"Did Hal and the professionals disappear that easily?" asked Althea.

The reality of her statement hit me like a two-by-four. My voice was shaky and forced. "I pushed them as far away as I could. I told them that I didn't have time to meet up with them. I threw myself into classes. I truly convinced myself that none of it ever happened. Even the grad student was simply a nightmare. I was no longer going to dwell on the past."

"Did these memories play by the new rules you created?"

"Not all the time."

"How do you mean?"

"Memories are tricky, and they never really disappear. They lurked. They hovered in the corners of my mind, just waiting to remind me of my past. Certain things would trigger the memories to rush to the foreground, like you said, through a smell, image, or sound. And I'd go into immediate ninja defense mode to confront the memories and push them back. I was always on standby, because these memories were getting stronger and stronger. When I was tired, stressed, or emotionally weak they'd relentlessly attack. It was as if I knew they'd find a way to get my attention."

"Can you give me an example?"

"I remember after Dr. Meyer's meeting, I went in dance class. In the middle of a high kick, I fell to the floor and my side started cramping. I was embarrassed but laughed it off with the rest of the students. But I knew something was wrong. I couldn't stand completely erect. My lower back throbbed with a dull ache and I became nauseous. I thought I was relapsing with the unknown sickness that brought me home from California. And I worried that the memories caused the sickness and wanted my attention again. But I wasn't going to allow that to happen, so I pushed and continued taking class.

"My stomach throbbed, and I had to use the bathroom. I excused myself. I sat on the toilet for the longest time with the worst constipation, until sharp stabbing pains attacked my lower right abdomen. I gathered my things and staggered to the health center to discover that I was experiencing a ruptured appendix and needed an immediate surgery. At first I feared that the memories created this, my past was never going to go away no matter how hard I pretended they were not real. The next thing I remember was waking up in a hospital room."

MIAMI VALLEY HOSPITAL, 1983

"How are you feeling?"

I forced open my heavy lids to find Hal standing next to my bed and holding my hand.

"You scared a lot of people," he said.

"Hal?" I asked, through blurry eyes.

"Yes, Davey, it's me."

"What happened?'

"You decided to do a high kick and busted your appendix."
He chuckled.

I tried to skooch up in the bed, but to no avail. "How did
you find out?"

"I'm your emergency contact," Hal said, with pride. "You
don't have to be admitted into the hospital to see me. I've hardly
seen you since I flew you home from California. All you have to
do is call me." He chuckled.

I tried to laugh, but it hurt my side too much. "Stop, it hurts."

"You sure are popular. You've had a stream of people stopping
by to check in on you. Especially someone named, Valerie. She's
been here several times. She's quite the spitfire and I think she
really likes you." Hal winked his eye. "A tall guy by the name
of Gerry or Gerald, said for you to get well soon. And some of
the faculty poked their heads in. Miss Walker said you needed
to heal quickly because you're going to be in the spring musical
and dance concert."

"What?"

Was I going to be dancing on stage?

"If I remember correctly, the title of the musical is *Guys and
Dolls.*"

"How long have I been here?" I looked around the room;
there were balloons and flowers with cards everywhere.

"Almost two days. But don't worry, everything's taken care
of. You just need to rest and get back on your feet. "

I looked at Hal. "What about Mom and Dad?"

"They should be here later today. I made sure they knew I
was here, and everything was under control." I must have looked
at him strangely because he quickly added, "I told them it was
a case of food poisoning and not to worry."

"Thanks."

"I didn't think it was necessary to inform your mother how serious this was. She would've had you die twice and resurrected as a modern Jesus miracle."

"Probably." I giggled and held my side. "Ouch."

"Are you in pain?" He looked at his wristwatch. "It's almost time for your medicine."

"Looks like someone's up." A male nurse came in and stopped at the end of the bed to check the chart.

"David, this is Mike, he's your nurse. Dr. Miller helped him through school too."

"That was some time ago," Nurse Mike uttered as he wrote something on the chart. "How's the pain on a scale of one to ten?"

I thought for a moment before responding, "Maybe a six. I'm not sure, I feel kind of loopy."

"That makes sense." He came to the right side of the bed. "I'm just going to look at the sutures." He lifted the blanket and the flimsy gown exposing my side dressed in white bandages.

"Where's my underwear?" Panic rushed in as I was exposed.

Nurse Mike explained, "You'll be going commando for a while until this heals."

I glanced down again. "Was I shaved?" Not only did I feel exposed, but I felt a sense of violation. The one area that had hair, beside my arm pits, was naked like a child. I wanted to hide.

Nurse Mike remained professional. "The hair had to be removed for the operation."

Hal joked, "It'll grow back. Maybe even thicker."

I tilted my head back on the pillow and squeezed my eyes. The sense of violation turned onto embarrassment, not only was I exposed for the handsome Nurse Mike to see my nakedness, but Hal was privy to the view as well.

Nurse Mike lightly pressed on the bandage and I automatically grabbed his wrist.

I quickly realized that I was touching the soft brown hairs on his forearm. I was mesmerized by the thickness and how the hairs spread out on the top of his hand. I slide my fingertips down his arm, over his wrist, and to his fingers. "So soft." I repeated the action.

Hal rushed to the side of the bed. "Let Nurse Mike do his job."

"It's alright," said Nurse Mike. "They have him on some good pain meds." He lifted my hand off his. "Let me change the dressing, alright? I can't very well do that with you petting my arm."

I covered my face. "I'm so sorry."

"No worries." Nurse Mike replied.

When I peered through my fingers, I saw the three-inch incision laced with midnight blue stitches.

"How does it look?" asked Hal.

"Good. It's healing nicely," said Nurse Mike.

When Nurse Mike turned to get the sterile dressing from the side table, I removed my hands and looked at the area. The battle wound was a mixture of purple with specks of red, surrounded by a pale yellow and puffy where the threads ducked under the skin. Otherwise, the seam was fusing nicely, and it was evident that I'd have a thin scar for the rest of my life.

Nurse Mike dressed the area with new gauze and replaced the gown and blanket over me. He then retrieved a small paper cup with two pills and a glass of water. He held it out for me and produced a dazzlingly perfect smile.

I opened my palm and envisioned Nurse Mike as the Knight giving me the antidote to the spell and taking my back to my real life where we'd get married and live happily ever after.

"That should help in a few minutes. When I come back, we're going to get you up and take a short walk down the hall and back," Nurse Mike instructed.

I took the pills and handed the glass back to him. As he took hold of the glass, I petted his forearm again and caused him to laugh. "I can't help it," I confessed.

"I can see that." He broke free. "I'll see you in a few minutes. Rest up."

"I will." I watched him leave.

"What do you think about going back to Los Angeles?" Hal asked.

"What are you talking about?"

Hal was back lit from the morning sun pouring through the window. He was a mere silhouette as he shifted a chair next to the bed. When he sat, the character lines on his face slipped into view. He pulled out a small note pad from the inside pocket of his jacket and dramatically flipped it open. He gave a knowing grin and announced, "I've become your secretary it seems." He laughed. "When we last spoke on the phone, you said you were ready to go back to Los Angeles. So, I did some research and I'm excited to announce, although I must finalize some details, I've found a place for you to stay in Beverly Hills with a person who owes me a favor. He's house sitting and said that you could stay in the quest room until we find you a more permanent residence. It's really funny, because his name is, Matthew David, and you're David Matthew."

"That's interesting."

"Anyway, he said there are some strict guidelines to follow, since this house is on the market and he's responsible for showing it to realtors. He said you'd only be permitted to reside in one area and use the back entrance. But you can use the pool whenever. The owner wanted to have someone there, so it doesn't look empty and to collect mail and stuff."

"Who is this Matthew David?"

"Well, he goes by Mac. I don't know why, because his real name is Matthew, but he wants to be called Mac. So, Mac it is. I helped him through paralegal school." He paused. "Are you sure you're feeling alright?"

"It's a lot to take in."

Hal nodded and closed the note pad. "You're right. Let's take one step at a time. Let's get you back on your feet. And then we can tackle Hollywood."

DR. ALTHEA WARNER'S OFFICE—
DAYTON, OHIO, 2018

"So, you see. No matter how hard I tried to get away from Hal and the professionals, I was still in their clutches. I was still trapped by the memories and the expectations. I was never going to be rid of them." My shoulders tensed and my breath was shallow. "The only solution I could think of was to try and find the positive in the moment and open myself to what the people could provide me."

"Let me get this straight. Hal and the professionals paid for your schooling at Wright State and covered the hospital bills?"

"Everything, even at U.C.I, as if it was all free," I said with distain.

"If it was their choice…"

I cut her off. "No. Don't you see? I didn't see it back then either, I thought they were just being nice and generous, but what I failed to recognize was that I was getting deeper and deeper entangled with them. I was perpetuating and strengthening the hold Hal and the professionals had over me. I realized at that moment in the hospital, I was never going to rid myself of the belief I was only good enough to be someone's toy. I was unable to take care of myself, I didn't know how, and I was going to rely on others for the rest of my life. I needed to be told what to do and when to do it."

"What makes you say that?" Althea's eyes were pensive.

"Dad was right. I was pampered and taken care of all my life. I was never going to be able to take care of myself. People always wanted to help me. And without realizing it, I let them."

"What a minute. Let's take a step back for a second." Althea stood up and walked behind the chair to lean on it. "You had distanced yourself from Hal and the professionals while you were going to Wright State."

"Yes, at least I thought I did. I tried, but they were footing the bills. Even the apartment I rented."

"What happened after you got out of the hospital?" Althea asked.

I took a deep breath and ran my hands through my hair. "I got well and went back to classes. I was cast in *Guys and Dolls* and Hal invited all the professionals to come to the show. I did a good job and was informed that L.A. was all set up. The professionals and Hal had everything organized. What I didn't realize, at the time, I was auditioning all over for the professionals' support. They seemed to like what they saw and noticed my potential. So, I moved to L.A. when classes were done. No one asked if I was ready to return to L.A. It was all decided for me. Hal was excited because this replaced the diving."

"I see." Althea looked at her wristwatch. "We only have a few minutes left. I want to continue with what took place in L.A., but I really want to hear the letter you wrote to your younger self."

"Now?" I felt like I was being forced to shift gears and go into a completely different direction.

"If you wouldn't mind."

"Ok." I shoved the emotions and feelings of Hal and the professionals to the side as I reached into my satchel and opened the tri-fold letter. My voice was thin and uncertain. I felt detached from the words on the page.

Dear Younger David,

I'm so sorry that you went through the things you endured. I'm sorry that I wasn't there to help you through, to hold you when you were scared, or to help you understand what was happening. I'm so sorry your innocence was taken away by older men. I'm sad that you never had the chance to discover your sexuality for yourself on your own terms. Would it make any difference? I don't know, but you were never given the opportunity to find out.

You are so brave and strong. You found a way to deal with your fears. When I look at you in pictures, I see a beautiful person on the inside as well as the outside. You have energy, magnetism and you light up a room when you enter. You aren't even aware of it, but you are very special. Everyone sees it. But unfortunately, you never got to discover that for yourself. That was taken away by the selfishness of others.

I'm so proud of you and how you've been able to become successful in spite of all the things you went through. You always seem to be able to recognize the silver lining in every situation. I miss you terribly. One day we will reunite. I love you.

Love, David.

TO BE CONTINUED...

SHATTERED SURFACE
SNEAK PREVIEW

701 N. MAPLE DRIVE, BEVERLY HILLS, CA, 1983

"This is it. It used to be the maid's quarters." Mac held the door open for me. "You'll need to always use the garage entrance. Never go through the front door."

I walked in to an area that separated a kitchen from a family/den room.

"Here, put your things here." He helped unload my arms, descended two steps, and positioned my duffle bag and backpack next to a couch. "This pulls out into a bed. Here's where you'll be staying." He opened the curtains, revealing a swimming pool aglow with underwater lights and surrounded by palm trees and ferns.

I was amazed by how big the backyard and pool were. From outside, one would never know.

Mac stopped in front of television with a fifty-inch screen.

"Wow. That's huge," I said.

Mac smirked, lifted his hands to the side, and popped his hip. "Thank you for noticing." Then he looked over his shoulder. "Oh, you're talking about the TV." He indicated the drawers under the screen. "You can put your things in here. That's the kitchen we can use. So, like I said, this is the area that you're to stay in. Don't go into the rest of the house unless I'm with you. Whatever you do, do not answer the door. The house is being shown frequently, and a buyer may appear anytime. I've permission for you to stay here; I told the realtors that you're my cousin coming in to shoot *General Hospital.* But I must stress that this is merely temporarily. My reputation and my position at the Loeb and Loeb law firm are at stake here. You must follow the list of liabilities I mailed you and Hal. Do we need to go over them again?"

I shook my head. I took in the simplicity of the area: white walls, cream couch, TV, side chair, and eggshell curtains. The kitchen had an island with a granite marble surface and surrounded by white cabinetry which hid the appliances.

"If it wasn't for Hal helping me through paralegal school, this wouldn't have been an option. Hal helped you with your diving, right?" Mac didn't wait for a response, but went to the refrigerator, took out a beer, twisted off the lid, and gulped. "Thirsty?"

I shook my head.

"You must be hungry?"

I shrugged.

"Do you ever talk? You've hardly said anything."

"I'm in awe and speechless," I said.

Mac forced a laughed. "Yea, you'll get used to it." He took another swig and put the bottle on the marble countertop. "And there are always looky-loos that walk right up, ring the doorbell, and hope to get a peek inside. So, don't talk to anyone. Since the house has been on the market, people think they have a right to stop by anytime they want. A potential buyer will always be with Kevin or Marta, the realtors. You'll meet them. I'm pretty much assured of at least a month after the closing before I must evacuate. But this place can sell any day. As a matter of a fact an offer was made yesterday. But who knows if it'll go through? Five previous offers have failed." Mac adjusted his belt. "It may come to pass that we grow so close that we get our own apartment. Don't worry, Tom's open about this whole arrangement. We've been seeing each other for the past five years. You two will meet tomorrow." He grabbed the bottle and downed the rest of the beer.

Mac's cheeks flushed red under his golden tan as he wiped his mouth with the back of this hand. His dark hair receded on both side of this forehead and thinned around his crown. His thick moustache seemed to be a compromise for his premature balding, and spread across his face when he smiled. Tuffs of hair splayed from the opened collar of his tight polo shirt which was tucked into his khaki pants accentuating his thirty-two-inch waist. The ensemble was completed with a pair of brown penny loafers with tassels. He wasn't my idea of a knight in shining armor, but he did help get me away from Aulden.

"Are you excited about *General Hospital*? He asked as he got another beer.

"Yes."

"I think you're going to find success, happiness, and hopefully a brother." He produced a toothy smile. "With the way you look, I've no doubts. I must say, you're even better looking in person than the picture you sent."

"Thanks. I guess." I was still frozen in the same spot.

"I love singing, but have no aspirations in that regard. This place has the most fantastic acoustics. I guess Diana wouldn't have had it any other way."

"Diana?" I asked.

"Yea." He finished off half of the second bottle of beer. "Diana Ross. This is her house."

"The Diana Ross?"

ACKNOWLEDGEMENTS

I want to take a moment and thank everyone that helped and supported the Kickstarter Campaign that enabled this project to become a reality. I am touched and humbled by the 200 people that made this dream possible. Below are the some of the individuals:

Leland (Buddy) Goldston, Jr., Leith and Char Adams, Bill Alverson, Irene Bosma-Smallwood and Marty Smallwood, Mark Brewer, Chuck Campbell and Chad McCoy, Stacy Emoff, Sophia Fifner, Marian Glancy, Leslie Hasselbach, Randy Hodge, Rev. Debbie Holder, Steve Koenig, Pam Ku-Snyder, Jason Lee, Eric Marlin, Billi Mayfield, Gerald McCullouch, Kevin Moore, David Moyer, Neil and Cameesa Pikas, Elizabeth Karns Poole, Deirdre Root, Raymonde Rougier, Brian Sharp, Jackie Siebelist, Emily Slaght, John B. Smith, Kirt Stager, Dan Stone, Matthew Tolson, Mike and Judy Webber, Karen Westerbeck, Michael Wheeler, Scott Winters, David White, and many more.

ABOUT THE AUTHOR

 John-Michael Lander is creating a voice for sexually abused men everywhere. Through writing, speaking, and consulting, he helps individuals and organizations identify the signs of grooming, manipulating, and stigmatizing of sexual abuse and how to help survivors (of any type of abuse) face the past and find their true self.

John-Michael battled with finding his true self and authentic voice. As an elite athlete, he endured sexual abuse from coaches, benefactors, and medical teams which resulted in years of PTDS, depression, anxiety, and even suicide attempts.

Today, John-Michael is passionate about helping people face the past and find their true self. He educates parents, guardians, coaches, teachers, and officials how to spot and recognize the signs of abuse.

John-Michael competed in international Springboard and Platform diving competitions. His entertainment experiences include *General Hospital, All My Children,* and national commercials; the lead in the independent films *All the Rage* and *Pilgrim;*

and originating many roles on New York stages. He taught high school English for seven years at the nationally recognized Stivers High School of the Arts in Dayton, Ohio.

John-Michael presented the speech "An Athlete's Silence" at the TEDxDayton 2018 Convention and was a Keynote Speaker at the 2019 Coalition to End Sexual Exploitation Global Summit in Washington D.C. In 2020, He spoke at Wabash College and Sinclair College on "The Effects of Sexual Abuse on Male Athletes." He has recorded several TV and radio interviews about abuse, spiritual journey, and finding his true self.

RESOURCES

Break the Silence Against Domestic Violence and the National Speakers' Bureau

Mary Bawden: DA:NCE stands for "Dance Awareness: No Child Exploited". www.danceawareness.com

David Lisak, Ph.D., Forensic Consulting, Board Chair 1in6.org

1in6.org

THE BRISTLECONE PROJECT

Men Overcoming Sexual Abuse

The Bristlecone Project
https://1in6.org/get-information/bristlecone/

PAVE

PAVE's updated mission statement is: "PAVE is a movement creating a world free from sexual violence and building communities to support survivors." Please let me know if you need anything else!

https://www.shatteringthesilence.org

pave

PROMOTING AWARENESS | VICTIM EMPOWERMENT

PFLAG:

Parents, Families & Friends of Lesbians and Gays - Dayton
Chapter

http://pflagdayton.org

Merle James Yost, LMFT
https://merleyost.com

Psychotherapy Intensives, Workshops, Public Speaking
The website has many videos, and articles that are about sexually abused males

Julia Cameron, *The Artist Way*

Eckhart Tolle, *The Power of Now: A Guide to Spiritual Enlightenment*

John-Michael is available for Speaking Engagements about Sex Abuse Surviving, Sex Abuse in Sports, and Grooming.

Join An Athlete's Silence Facebook Page: https://www.facebook.com/johnmichaellander1214/?modal=admin_todo_tour

John-Michael Lander
An Athlete's Silence

John-Michael Lander is creating a voice. Through writing, speaking, and consulting, he helps individuals and organizations identify the signs of grooming, manipulating, and stigmatizing of sexual abuse and how auto help survivors (of any type of abuse) face the past and find their true self.

John-Michael battled with finding his true self and authentic voice. As an elite athlete, he endured sexual abuse from coaches, benefactors, and medical team which resulted in years of PTSD, depression, anxiety, and even suicide attempts.

Today, John-Michael is passionate about helping people face the past and find their true self; educate parents, guardians, coaches, teachers, and officials how to spot and recognize the signs of abuse.

John-Michael represented the USA in international Springboard and Platform diving competitions. His entertainment experiences include performing on television on *General Hospital, All My Children,* and national commercials; the lead in the independent films *All the Rage* and *Pilgrim; and* originating many roles on New York stages. He taught high school English for seven years at the nationally recognized Stivers High School of the Arts in Dayton, Ohio.

John-Michael presented the speech "An Athlete's Silence" at the Coalition To End Sexual Exploitation in Washington D.C. and TEDxDayton Convention. He has recorded several TV and radio interviews about abuse, spiritual journey, and finding his true self.

IT'S NOT YOUR FAULT.

Contact Information for booking:
937-241-7136
lucas27land@gmail.com
@johnmichaellander1214

* Coalition To End Sexual Exploitation Global Summit, Key Note Speaker, Washington, DC. https://vimeo.com/351839227

* TedxDayton Talk: https://www.youtube.com/watch?v=1-4YH82PqiA

Made in the USA
Monee, IL
18 August 2020

37909099R00198